Dragons at the Schoolhouse Door

*A Novel
of Schooling*

Clyde Woolman

 FriesenPress

Suite 300 - 990 Fort St
Victoria, BC, V8V 3K2
Canada

www.friesenpress.com

ISBN
978-1-5255-6475-8 (Hardcover)
978-1-5255-6476-5 (Paperback)
978-1-5255-6477-2 (eBook)

1. *Fiction, Humorous*

Distributed to the trade by The Ingram Book Company

DEDICATION

To public school teachers who, day in and day out, work in a sometimes efficient and sometimes crazy system, attempting all the while to make lives better for young people.

ACKNOWLEDGMENTS

Thanks to the many educators who have provided advice after reading complete early drafts of this novel. Reading roughly hewn manuscripts is never an easy thing to do: Leslie Berends, Judy Berkeley, Dave Brooker, John Bucher, Marilyn Bucher, Gerald Fussell, Judy Hutchinson, Mary Ann McRae, Geoff Manning, Janet Maund, Phil Maund, Marlene Neil, Todd Phillips, Mike Sutcliffe, Pat Sutcliffe, Dave White and Andrew Young.

As always, love and appreciation to my loving wife, Ileana, partner-in-life.

ABOUT THE AUTHOR

Clyde Woolman has been a teacher, counselor, and principal of three high schools, as well as a middle and an elementary school. For six years he was a Superintendent of Schools (CEO) in a school district on Vancouver Island, British Columbia.

Having doled out his fair share of edubabble, and after experiencing the governing bureaucracy first hand, he voluntarily returned to a school, finishing his career as a principal.

He has authored countless reports on school and district programs and chaired numerous committees tasked with reporting on school effectiveness.

He has always felt that those who worked directly in the classroom were subjected to too much pontificating from those who either had never done the job or were far removed from it. This list of people included politicians, bureaucrats, school board members, and education professors and theorists.

Now retired, Clyde lives on Vancouver Island and divides his time between there, metropolitan Vancouver, and Maui.

BOOKS BY CLYDE WOOLMAN

EDUCATION NOVELS

Dragons at the Schoolhouse Door: A Novel of Schooling
– *FriesenPress 2020*

Hepting's Road: A Novel of Teaching – *FriesenPress 2018*

EDUCATION SATIRE SERIES

High School Edubabble: A Teacher-Talk Glossary – *FriesenPress 2020*

Edubabble: A Glossary of Teacher Talk – *FriesenPress 2018*

YOUNG-ADULT NOVELS – THE BEN TAVERS SERIES

Smugglers at the Lighthouse – *Moosehide Books 2010*

Yurek: Edge of Extinction – *Moosehide Books 2013*

For more information visit the author's website at
www.clydewoolman.com

1

In fiction, an enigma ends with definitive explanation. Motive is exposed and truth laid bare. The satisfied reader knows all and returns the novel to the shelf. In real-life, closure is not so easy. Answers may be vague — explanations inadequate.

Why had Steve Hepting, of all people, been appointed the leader of Greenside Community School? One year later, the reasoning behind then-Superintendent Bill Danchuk's surprise job offer remained a mystery. Danchuk had announced his retirement the following day. Steve asked about the man's rationale over lunch, expecting praise about an African aid project he had developed. Instead, Danchuk gestured nonchalantly. In contrast with his normal verbosity, he simply said, "You're a good guy. The system needs more good guys." He seemed supremely satisfied with the response.

And why had Steve Hepting, happy fifth-grade teacher at Meadowvale Elementary, accepted the proposal? He loved the classroom. When he was teaching, the incessant babbling of the bureaucrats was easily ignored. As a principal, he would be close to that mindless chatter, perhaps even a part of it. Had he fallen for the implied flattery? Maybe his ego was too easily stroked and Danchuk knew the right buttons to push?

Danchuk's move may have been nothing more than a parting shot at his nemesis, the Assistant Superintendent, Jennifer Capelli. The man had a reputation for being crafty, clever, and occasionally vindictive, and she was the likely candidate to assume his position. The scattered, system-fighting Hepting was the polar opposite to uber-organized, data-nut Capelli. She had clashed with him before when he was a teacher on her staff, describing Hepting as, "A royal pain in the ass." Maybe Danchuk hoped Principal Hepting could survive a few rounds with Capelli before being knocked out of the ring?

It had not taken long for Capelli to dig her claws into the rookie leader. She was nothing if not a determined scrapper.

Greenside was the only K-8 school in the district. Cooking instruction and an introduction to Woodwork was a requirement for eighth-grade students. Facilities were available since the building had been a middle school. Finding qualified teachers was more difficult since each position was part-time.

When treating the recently retired superintendent to a lunch, Steve had asked about filling the part-time openings at the school. Tucking into his cheeseburger, between bites Danchuk suggested combining the positions and giving them to a teacher from his principal days —Summer Martin.

Steve did not know the procedural intricacies of filling teacher vacancies. "Can I do that?" he asked Danchuk warily.

"You're the principal. It's your school." He hiked thick shoulders into an indifferent shrug. "Go ahead."

Five days later Steve received a call from the newly appointed Superintendent, Jennifer Capelli. "Mr. Hepting, where's the posting for those part-time positions? The union president tells me you placed Summer Martin in a combined role and that you're posting a different job." Capelli struggled to remain calm. Nothing grated her more than union leaders having the upper hand regarding district information.

"I switched the assignment," Steve admitted. He took nervous swallow. "I'm the principal," he added, more bravely than he felt.

"Exactly, principals can't do what you just did. Only Human Resources can do that," snapped Capelli, breathing fire. Why the hell did that idiot Danchuk put Hepting in that Greenside job? "Fortunately," she said, managing only a mildly terse tone, "nobody in the bargaining unit wants those piddly-ass part-time assignments way out in Greenside. But that's not the point—proper process was not followed." There was momentary silence on the other end. "I suppose I could sell it that there's now a full time second-grade position vacated by Summer Martin. The union might buy that."

Steve stayed silent before gulping and finding his voice. "Um, I switched a current Greenside teacher into that job. The third-grade class is the new opening." Silence. Steve was sure he could hear the superintendent's teeth grinding. This was a hell of a way to start his administrative career.

"I'll get back to you," Capelli said abruptly, though she never did. She had other ideas for Greenside Community School, ones that far exceeded an easy claw-gouging of Steve Hepting, that sorry excuse for a principal. She would bide her time and leave that mushy incompetent man alone for the time being.

September 2011 marked the start of Hepting's second year as principal of Greenside. He had spent the first year filling out forms, attending meetings, and attempting to veer clear of Capelli. He knew from experience how cunning she could be. He had been a teacher at Lakeview High when Capelli had been the principal. He grated her. She transferred him out. Expecting a deluge of Capelli venom, rookie-principal Steve had anticipated another forced transfer. But Capelli had paid scant attention to his performance, or the small K-8 school he led. Greenside served an outlying community, physically removed from Taylerston, the central hub of the district. Time was too valuable to waste on a minor fish like Steve Hepting. Capelli's first year as superintendent had been occupied with a series of ongoing battles with the teachers' association in a string of labor grievances. She never backed away from a dogfight with those she referred to as, "The loony left."

Hepting learned the job on the fly, helped by earth-mother Summer Martin and various members of the Greenside Parent Council. The parents would have ripped the yarn off the suit of a slick city principal. The parental rumor mill regarding Hepting's past was in his favor. The new principal had been a stock broker and walked away from that money-grubbing industry. He was a hard-working guy with a self-deprecating sense of humor. He dressed in polo shirts and casual pants. He was not afraid to take on the Taylerston big shots who were always messing around with Greenside schools. The central office "suits" had closed the elementary school and combined it with the middle school. Who knew what the hell they'd do next?

Looking back, Hepting's first year as principal had not been a disaster. It had not been much of a triumph either. He had survived, built relationships, and developed confidence. He felt more at ease as the new year beckoned. He had experience. He had plans. This school year the Greenside community was going to see a more polished principal. He would meet the inevitable challenges with a mix of new skills and old-fashioned tenacity.

The first test of the new school year was a meeting with a member of the school district's Human Resources (HR) Department. Steve worked hard to avoid the central office. It was rare that anything good came from a visit there. Today, Steve's first day returning to work, had the potential to be an exception. There were two unfilled teaching positions at the school and he anticipated having significant input on who would be placed at Greenside. New teachers meant fresh ideas and new skills.

With a banana-blueberry muffin wallowing in a gurgling belly, and another parked inside a paper bag on the front seat, Steve took a slurp of coffee and started his royal-blue SUV. The *Best of Wham* blared from the speakers as Steve hummed a George Michael favorite from his teen years, "I'm Your Man." A red light signaled the corner of Tayler Drive and Roder Boulevard, the main intersection in Taylerston, a small city that clung to a wide bay in the northern reaches of Puget Sound. Logging, fishing, and agriculture remained important to the local economy. Recreational tourism had been a relatively recent boost—boating and golfing in summer, skiing and snowboarding on nearby Mt. Baker in winter. Though the service industries were relatively low-paying, employment was plentiful. There was a vibrant aura as a new artistic vibe took hold, bolstered by recent retirees cashing in their single-family dwellings in Seattle. As the city grew, outlying areas felt the effect. Once a relatively separate community based on agriculture and a small sawmill, Greenside was losing its distinctiveness and becoming a bedroom community of Taylerston.

Steve parked in the visitor's lot behind the shiny school district edifice. The building had picture windows, skylights, an auditorium for presentations, a boardroom with up-to-date electronic wizardry, and spacious offices with hardwood flooring and motorized curtain blinds. The stagnant student population across the district had not yet been reflected in the number of high-level bureaucrats. Only school-level staffing allocations reflected enrolment. A first-class operation required a first-class central command.

Winding his way along a corridor, smiling and chatting with the many clerical personnel he knew, Steve made his way to Perry Watkins' office, knocked softly, and entered.

Born a decade before Steve, Perry's parents had been fans of the fading yet still popular singer, Perry Como. Musical themselves, they hoped their son would succeed in the entertainment business by crooning a path to fame and fortune. As it happened, Perry's dancing skills far surpassed his vocal ability. His late 1970s band, Fever Pitch, attained a level of regional notoriety by pumping out disco numbers under swirling mirror balls in Taylerston, Everett, and surrounding area clubs.

As Steve gazed at the HR man, he recalled a photo of lead singer "Prancing Perry" shuffling high thick-heeled shoes and shaking his booty in tight-bummed, flare-legged polyester pants. Gaudy gold chains of zodiac signs hung on a moderately hairy chest, visible to the world by a shirt open to the navel. Steve had seen that photo late one night when he and Perry had an up-close evening with Jack Daniels. Steve's guffaws made him gasp for air to a point when a worried Perry had a phone cradled in hand, ready to call 911.

Now a round face and pudgy form sagged on Perry's hunched frame. Wrinkle lines creased the sides of widely-spaced eyes, their pupils sheathed with blue-hued contact lenses. While his eyes could still sparkle and charm women, the body now short-circuited any electrical mating energy the brain could muster. The frequently unfaithful, divorced Perry pined for his ex-wife who had tired of his philandering and hitched her wagon to a millionaire ski bum.

Perry's attire was more Como than disco. A black cotton cardigan fell over a white oxford shirt, one button undone at the neck. He had more hair on his feet than on his head. The high-heeled shoes had been replaced by loafers. The once tight-bummed polyester slacks were loose-fitting Dockers. "Are you signed up for the administrators' golf tournament tomorrow afternoon?" he asked with a smirk. Tales of Steve's errant golf shots smacking into various portions of Capelli's body were legendary.

Suspicious of Perry's exaggerated smile and perky countenance, Steve countered. "I never aimed at Capelli, that's just a bunch of bullshit stories."

"You've hit her twice, the first when she was your principal at Lakeview." Perry grinned stupidly. "You should never smack your boss in the ass with a golf shot." The HR man's face beamed with perfect recall. "And then last year, a perfect shot! Smack in the ass again!"

"It was the upper thigh." He stared at the chuckling Perry. "I thought I was speaking to an adult, not a teenager with a warped, juvenile sense of humor." Though Perry slowly stopped smirking, Steve continued to protest too much. "No one could make that shot on purpose," he grumbled, forever defending his wayward shots that seemed to zero in on Capelli's derriere. "It ricocheted off a tree."

"I don't know Steve. You are a good golfer." Another smirk flashed across Perry's face.

"Let's get to it Perry. What have you got for me?"

A slight grimace at the end of frivolity, a downward glance, a shuffle of loafers— bad news was on the horizon. Perry's hand grasped two Personnel Summary forms. "Okay," he sighed, "Let's do the fourth-grade position first." He scanned the sheet, preferring a verbal outline before passing the paper to Steve. "You get Emma Martinez. She's been with us for six years in five different schools due to enrolment decline combined with her low seniority." Perry shook his head for a moment before pulling his blue contacts back to the paper. "She was downsized from Beech Park Elementary. She's got experience and training. It's a no-brainer."

"What's she like?" asked Steve.

"What do you mean?"

"Beech Park is filled with rich kids, and we've got . . . well you know what we've got. Can this Martinez woman relate to Greenside kids?"

"How the hell do I know? The forms don't provide information like that." Perry passed the single-page form to an awaiting hand. Steve accepted it, yet laid it gently on the desk.

"Am I in the right office?" Steve swirled around in mock exasperation. "This is Human Resources?"

"Hey, I'm just like Sergeant Schultz on that old TV show, *Hogan's Heroes*. I know nothing."

Steve grimaced. "Bullshit, and that's the worst Schultz imitation I've ever heard. What have you got?"

Perry's eyes flicked as if checking for hidden cameras or microphones. He may well have been passing nuclear secrets to a terrorist group. He enjoyed the notoriety of holding critical information. He may have been passed his "Prancing Perry" days but he still craved center stage. Apparently convinced he was free of electronic surveillance, Perry cleared his throat and motioned for Steve to close the door. "Okay, this is what I've heard." Perry described Emma Maritinez at length as Hepting alternated between nods of understanding and frowns of doubt.

Steve finally interjected, tired of Perry listing Emma's impressive list of professional development activities attending conferences and workshops. When Steve heard, "This is where education has to go in the future," he often thought of the futurists in the late 1970s predicting a world filled with leisure time. Now all Steve saw were stressed-out teachers scratching for any minute they could get. "So, Martinez is really into professional currency. What the hell does that mean?"

"Shit, Steve. I don't know. You're the educator. Don't you guys invent new terms every few years to resurrect methodology you once threw out? Then they rise again, like the albatross."

"Phoenix."

"Whatever. Martinez knows the current lingo, which is a hell of a lot more than what can be said about you." Perry smiled, pleased at the verbal punch that should have landed with some force. The expected counter-thrust never came. It was as if Hepting enjoyed the blow. Perry waited in the silence for a moment before continuing. "Martinez is an eco-nut and a little aggressive from what I hear." Worried, he glanced out the window to the hallway. "Remember, not a word of this, we're in the cone of silence."

"Yeah, I got it Perry, the cone of silence." Steve gesticulated with a swing of a fleshy arm. "So, she's an eco-nut, big deal. That's got nothing to do with her teaching ability which I take it you've heard is good?" Perry's nod led Steve to lean forward. "She's current and she's aggressive, which I take it means feisty." He watched Perry nod, this time less comfortably. "Okay," concluded Steve suddenly, "Hand me the approval form. I can handle feisty. She'll need it at Greenside."

Steve ignored the Capelli-generated gibberish covering two-thirds of the page and scrawled his name. He was more interested in the sixth-grade position. For Steve, this was a critical vacancy with a unique situation. Any class or student labeled "special" was not usually high on the agenda for HR people. They dealt with process. A laid-off teacher placed in a job was a success. How the person would fit specifically into a school or class situation was not their issue. It was critical from Steve's perspective though; the sixth-grade class had a boy with significant special needs.

Perry bit his lower lip and mindlessly shuffled a sheath of papers. The paperless office had not yet reached the HR department. Hepting was not going to like this and there was no way to soften the blow. Perry looked up, the face a blend of regret and empathy, the voice no more than a murmur. "This next placement is a bit tricky." He sensed Steve tensing tight muscles and grinding already clenched teeth. Avoiding eye contact, Perry reached into a file and pulled out a second form.

Steve groaned inwardly as he caught sight of the definitive initials of Jennifer Capelli. They were scrawled at the top right of the transfer page underneath the word, "approved."

2

Deciding to dive in head first into the shallow end of the swimming pool, Perry handed Steve the transfer form while blurting, "Colin Redford is a Calculus and Computer Science guy."

He never made it to the second sentence.

"A what?" Steve interjected. He scanned the form and flashed a hand in the air as if a child with a question. "We don't teach Calculus and we have twelve broken-down computers in the library held together with bailing wire."

"I know that," Perry said curtly, "There's been a drop in enrolment in Redford's programs at the high school level."

"He's never taught in a middle or elementary school. Why am I the one who has to take this guy?"

Perry shrugged. "Capelli and Chow want to make sure he has a job. You've got an opening." He held out his hands, "Another no-brainer."

Steve glared at the JC initials adorning the top right corner. "What the hell is her highness Capelli doing getting involved in assigning a sixth-grade teaching position? That's pretty small potatoes for her."

Perry shrugged, waiting for Hepting to make another connection. It came soon.

"How do you know Chow also wants Redford at Greenside? Since when does the business manager get involved in placing teachers?" Steve rolled frustrated eyes. "What the hell did this guy do to piss off the big shots?"

Perry shrugged. "I don't know but it sure as hell must have been something."

"You really are as clueless on the info front as that Sergeant Schultz character." Steve stood quickly, his large frame crowding the small office. "I'm not signing the damn form."

Leaning forward, Perry's hand gesticulated wildly, matching the pleading in his voice. "C'mon, Capelli will burn me to a crisp. The frigging form is not worth the paper it's printed on. It's just a formality, you know that." Hurtful puppy-dog looks were followed by, "I don't make the rules, I just work here. Everybody signs the form." Perry glanced worriedly down the corridor toward Capelli's office. "Redford will be placed at Greenside no matter what you do." He played his trump card. "You came from high school or have you forgotten that little bit of history? Look how well you did. A good teacher is a good teacher, that's what you've always said." Satisfied with the logic, Perry leaned back in his chair.

"I never thought you were listening!" Raising his hands in the air in mock surrender Steve plunked his tired carcass in the chair. "Can this guy teach younger kids?" He stopped the thought. "Never mind. That's just silly of me to ask. If Capelli and Chow want to exile this poor bugger to Greenside, there's not much I can do. Hand over the damn form."

"I love it when you take a district perspective," chuckled Perry as Steve's pen scribbled on the paper.

"Yeah, then why does it always feel like I'm being screwed when I do?" He rose. "I'm going home. I'm going to grab my school keys from the drawer and put them back on my key ring." He jabbed a fleshy finger at Perry. "Then I'm going to the school to see if I can do something to help this poor Redford guy get started."

If the statement was intended to make prancing Perry feel guilty, it was unsuccessful. He grinned. "Good luck Steve. Let me know how it works out!"

The late-August sunshine put Steve in a better frame of mind as he drove home. His modest bungalow sat on a quiet street near central Taylerston. He had acquired the house with a sizable down payment eleven years ago. He was hauling in money by the truckload as a financial analyst. Though he could have afforded more lavish accommodation at the time, he had chosen well. After being terminated from his stock broker position, Steve had to spend a year without a paycheck while he completed the required teacher certification. A teacher salary never made anyone rich. Last year's principal compensation, about thirty percent more than what he would make as a teacher, helped him pay off the mortgage.

The house and property had served him well. There was a large yard in which to putter, a patio off the small kitchen, a single attached garage, and a comfortable living room. One expansive blank wall had been perfect for the monster TV he used to watch sports. A second wall formed the backing for a wide bookcase. Steve was an avid reader, his once-academic tastes shifting from Dickens and D.H. Lawrence to the more plebeian Lee Child and John Grisham.

Steve checked the sports highlights on TV before grabbing his school keys. He headed out on the thirty-minute drive to Greenside, school issues dominating his thoughts. He knew Perry did the best he could. The hapless HR man was routinely pummelled by the principals who rarely used the same tone when addressing those higher up the district food chain. Starting the second year, Steve felt more like a real principal than the carboard cut-out he had been previously. He had read a few books on effective leadership over the summer. He had experience. He had plans. When he was at the school the central office seemed a distant, almost irrelevant thorn. It promised to be a good school year.

Success started soon. Steve had brought his keys, a feat in itself, and opened the front door. He remembered the code for shutting off the alarm, another good omen, though the system was already shuttered by the custodian. Wax fumes permeated the still air. The normally dull linoleum on the floor glared under the droning lights. The sheen would remain for the first three days before returning to the usual dirty hue. The fluorescent's hum would remain for the year, soon unnoticed. He entered the office reception area. The carpet, formerly shrouded in dust, grime, dried fruit juice, and assorted toxins had been cleaned. The wet fibers and darkened detergent sat in buckets oozing a rancid stench. Particles of grime wafted through the air, free to enter and disturb unwary nostrils.

Steve held his breath and entered the inner sanctum. His small office reeked. He quickly pulled the curtain and opened a window drawing in the warm morning air. A menacing hiss responded to the sunlight.

"What the hell is that?" Steve stayed still and stood away from his desk, the source of the snarling. He lowered his large frame and peered downward. Bending was difficult. His rotund, forty-one-year-old body indicated displeasure as bones creaked and joints ached. He caught a glimpse of the felines from hell, staring at him with demonic, unblinking eyes. He backed away and headed for the public address mike to call for help. The janitor, Frank "Tiny" Little, had to be somewhere in the building.

"Hey Mr. H." came a familiar voice no more than thirty seconds later. "What's up?"

Turning around, Steve came face-to-face with Tiny. He had once been labeled the "King of the Alphabet Kids" by several Lakeview teachers owing to his record-setting ten special needs and vulnerability designations. Tiny had been a student in Steve's Basic English and Investment classes. He may have been slow-witted in core school subjects, but astute investing in the stock market had made him a rich young man. He had been a big boy with a thick neck when he attended Lakeview High. Now he was a hulking twenty-three-year-old man with no discernible space between head and shoulders.

"Tiny, there are feral cats under my desk."

Tiny did not know what feral meant. If it was another word for mean then the principal was right. "That's Thor and Xena," he said leaning down, ensuring his torso kept a safe distance from the hissing felines. "They bully the other cats."

Steve stared blankly. Thor, Xena? He managed to give voice to a query, "Other cats, what other cats?"

"There's lots of 'em. At least they catch the mice. Thor and Xena don't, though. They bully the other cats into giving them all the mice the two of them can eat."

"Mice, what mice? I thought they were gone."

Tiny went solemn. The fate of last year's mice was a sore point. "That was last year when the cats ate them all," he muttered. Perking up, he added, "We have new ones now."

Steve groaned silently, hoping this year's rodents met a similar fate. "Can you get," he paused, "Thor and Xena out of my office?"

"Oh sure," said Tiny. "I'll give 'em some catnip. They love that stuff. It's like they get all drunk and I can grab 'em. School's startin' pretty soon and these two are gonna scare the kids." Tiny scrunched his face, a sure sign he was thinking. "I'll give them to a friend who lives on a farm near Mount Vernon. There are lots of mice on the farm, rats too. Thor and Xena will have to do their own hunting for a change."

Leaving the tough task to cat-hunter Tiny, Steve searched for alternate work, ultimately deciding on making coffee. He sauntered to the staff-room. Like all such locales, the staffroom at Greenside was rectangular and too small. The architects designing 1950s and 1960s-era schools thought in terms of one teacher for thirty to thirty-five students. Now the pupil-teacher ratio was much different. There were no para-professionals in the ancient era either. Now every school had a number of them on the payroll, meaning more adult bodies to be stuffed into the inadequate staffroom space.

Three circular tables were covered in orange laminate. The chairs were lime-green vinyl with silver metal frames and tubular legs. The flooring was the same as the office, grimy gray carpet. A battered couch occupied the least popular corner. Nobody sat on the stained and soiled cushions. Nobody wanted to clean the couch either. The custodians refused since the sofa did not adhere to Taylerston School District Policy 5023 (Purchasing Furniture). A school could only buy vinyl or leather-covered couches for ease of cleaning and handling.

Unused as a place of rest, yet marginally useful as a paper and book collection, the couch remained, untouched and unloved. Steve well-remembered his initiation to school district procedures. He had approached Lou Tayler, almost a year ago to the day, asking that eyesore be removed.

A definitive refusal bounced back. "That sofa has upholstered fabric."

Steve scrunched a puzzled face. Perhaps he was asking the wrong guy? Lou was the district curriculum supervisor and had a reputation as a stickler for protocol and the ability to duck responsibility. It was a valuable skill that kept him employed in the lower echelons of the bureaucracy. "So what?" he ventured.

"Cloth picks up mites and lice. It's a health risk to the guys that have to pick it up."

"What about the people who have to sit on it?"

"Nobody is stupid enough to sit on that thing."

"Okay," Steve admitted, "Point well taken. What about the mites and lice affecting the teachers who eat here?"

Lou shrugged. "School furniture has to be vinyl or leather and purchased commercially." It's district policy. That sofa came from somebody's basement."

"That must have been a more than a decade ago. I'm asking to get rid of it now." It was the rookie principal's initiation into the structured world of district protocol.

"Maintenance doesn't move furniture that wasn't purchased properly."

'Okay," muttered Steve. "I'll get Tiny and we'll haul it out ourselves."

Lou shook a disapproving head. "I'd have to report that to the union. Only maintenance personnel can haul large furniture. It's a health and safety issue."

Steve sighed. "You're not in the union."

"These are modern times Mr. Hepting, 2011. There would eventually be a grievance. I would not advise making Ms. Capelli angry." He knew the new superintendent did not need much of an excuse to dig her claws into the rookie principal. He patted the man on a fleshy shoulder, "If there's anything else you need, just let me know."

"Now I know why this sorry excuse for a carpet has been here for an eon," Steve grumbled. "With the process you explained, it will never be replaced."

Heading for the door, Lou stopped and turned. "Mr. Hepting—as a beginning principal the most important aspect you need to learn is about district procedures. Carpet removal regulations are being discussed at the liaison committee meetings between union and management as we speak. In a couple of years that carpet could be gone."

A year later, Steve glanced around the room. The carpet had been cleaned, with little positive result. The couch remained in the corner of the room. An enterprising individual had stacked the paper and binders into several neat piles. A toaster and a microwave sat on a long counter a deeper orange hue than the table tops. A three-year-old dishwasher sat under the counter, a prized acquisition until the inevitable conflict erupted over who should empty the clean dishes. The once-a-year cleaning had left the staffroom almost unrecognizably pristine.

The thump of Tiny's boots scuffing waxed linoleum broke the silence. "Thor and Xena are chowing down on catnip. They should be gonzoed in ten minutes and I'll haul them out in this cage I brought."

"Thanks," Steve said, eyeing the young man, proudly holding up a wire-fronted box that might or might not be able to hold the demonic felines. His hefty frame was covered by half-clean overalls. It was not that Tiny was surviving solely on janitorial pay. He owned a small bungalow in Greenside and had eyes for Chelsea Mains. She was the receptionist at the Maintenance department and a former classmate who had taunted the boy mercilessly when they were students. Not blessed with an abundance of school smarts and lacking any semblance of a verbal filter, Tiny had been a behavioral and academic challenge. Yet he and Steve had formed a special bond. It had carried over to Tiny's half year as a supervision aide at Meadowvale Elementary during Steve's first year as a teacher at that school. Even now as an adult, Tiny could not call his friend, "Steve," opting for the "Mr. H." moniker he had used during his teen years.

"You hit that stupid little white ball around the golf course this summer?" Tiny asked.

"Yeah, the handicap is better," replied the ardent and proficient golfer.

Tiny nodded vacantly. He never understood what a golf handicap was and why Mr. H. talked about it all the time. Most people did not talk about their handicaps. Tiny was too polite to ask about other people's disabilities. He had enough of his own.

"Lady Macbeth was touring a bunch of dorky-looking guys in suits and ties around the first-floor last week." The Shakespearean femme fatale was Tiny's nickname for Jennifer Capelli, his former principal at Lakeview High. The Lady Macbeth character was one of the few tidbits Tiny remembered from Steve's Basic English class. To Tiny, Shakespeare must have been a time traveler who had met Principal Capelli. How else could he have written about Lady Macbeth, a character so similar to the power-mad principal-turned-superintendent?

"Who were they?" asked Steve.

Tiny shrugged thick shoulders.

"What were they doing?"

"I dunno, but Mr. Chow was with them too." He was referring to the business manager of the Taylerston School District, Phil Chow. "He was the biggest guy there and he's mega-skinny. All the other guys looked like computer geeks."

Choosing to avoid a discussion about Tiny's propensity to stereotype, Steve wondered why district big shots Jennifer Capelli and Phil Chow were escorting a group of suit-and-tie types around the school in the summer. They could be anybody—architects, engineers, or HVAC people trying to obtain a contract on a new heating and ventilation system.

Mr. H. looked interested so Tiny warmed to the story. "They weren't talking teacher stuff, it was more about rooms for computers, wiring, knocking walls out to make bigger classrooms, stuff like that." He paused, watching Steve carefully. The principal's interest was clear. "I followed them around secret-like. I wanted to make sure they didn't see the mice."

"What mice?" Steve immediately regretted the question. "Never mind," he said, holding up a hand to block Tiny's response. "I know. They're the mice that cats like Thor and Xena devour."

Tiny did not know what devour meant but he had to defend the more placid felines who were bullied into giving up their food to Thor and Xena. "The nice cats aren't doing nothing wrong." Tiny paused, "They have to eat too."

"Yes," agreed Steve, "I suppose they do." He flashed a look at Tiny's face. The young man always scrunched his face when he had more to say or when he was thinking. The visage remained normal. "You don't know anything more about all this, do you?"

Tiny shrugged. "No, but if I see those guys around again do you want me to haul 'em down to the office?" Tiny scrunched his face. "Not Mr. Chow though, I don't want to grab him; not Capelli either, she'd get pretty mad."

Steve let out an audible sigh, his mind running through a series of possible explanations behind the summer tour. "Don't grab anyone Tiny, just let me know if you see that group around the school again."

After Tiny left, Steve to continued to ponder the strange story. Who the hell were those guys and what were they doing in his school?

3

It was not long before Steve's spirits were lifted. Fluid-teaching advocate Summer Martin glided in. Her flowered peasant skirt billowed softly in the self-generated breeze. Her light brown hair was braided with a daisy clinging precariously to a few strands. "Steve," she squealed, zipping into the office and hugging the principal, her arms failing to reach around his girth. She sized up his six-foot plus frame with the protruding paunch.

"I've lost a few pounds," Steve declared defensively.

"Weight is not the issue Steve, it's your health," Summer said, stepping back and shooting a stern eye. "You must eat more salads. And digest more fruit and fiber. It will help with your bowel movements you know."

Steve winced. "Thanks for the insight into my bodily functions," he said. It's always nice to get your input." Red-faced, he scanned the office, happy no other ears were present.

An infectious laugh followed from the gregarious Summer. The thin face sparkled when she smiled. The blue eyes danced. The light-brown hair shone. Though she was over forty, the skin was smooth, almost translucent. Summer was the poster child for the alternate food brigade. Whatever she was eating, or smoking, it was working. "Oh Steve, you're as red as a tomato! You know I love to tease you. One day you'll throw off the shackles of the foodie dark side that consumes you—cheeseburgers, donuts, and white bread. You'll be part of a culinary rebirth. You've been reborn before when you left that horrible stock-trading job." In Summer's mind, Steve leaving the investment industry was akin to turning his back on Mephistopheles.

A former high-flyer at Darrington Investments, Steve was a casualty of the tech bust of 2001-2002, almost exactly a decade earlier. Steve nodded agreement with Summer, building a visible bond while harboring inner doubt. For him, the escape from what Summer described as the clutches of rapacious corporatism was an easier task than abandoning the sustenance he enjoyed from calorie-laden processed food. "The world of stocks and corporate profit is well behind me," he affirmed. "The only financial wheeling and dealing I do is to put money in my savings account at the local bank." He smiled. "I'm an educator now, in mind and spirit."

"Good," chirped Summer, sending off a coquettish vibe. She slipped away, heading to the woodwork shop.

In his first decision, Steve had reassigned Summer from a second-grade position to teach the cooking and woodwork classes. He had known Summer from their days at Meadowvale Elementary. It was his first year there, her last. When he had been appointed as the Greenside principal, she invited him for dinner. The meal had been delicious. Summer could clearly cook and bake. Steve had noticed the tribal masks she had carved. She could work with wood as well. Since she had no official certification, the students could not use the power equipment. They had whittled and carved instead. Even Summer drew the line at etching the outline of pot plants onto wood plaques that could be hung on basement or bedroom walls. She had been equally adept teaching Foods and Nutrition. The students made salads with a range of vegetables and herbs they had never known. They concocted fruit smoothies and made heaps of quinoa, kale, and bok choy.

Summer was also assigned to the library for an hour a day and that was where Steve found her later in the morning, performing yoga stretches on a mat. Remaining prone on the floor, she looked up, zeroing in on the logo on Steve's coffee mug. "Isn't that the football team that never wins?"

"Baseball. The team is the Chicago Cubs."

Summer propped her head with an elbow. "And are they doing any better this year?" She thought for a moment. "It is baseball season isn't it?"

Steve sighed. "They're near the bottom of the division as usual." The lovable-loser Cubs had not won a World Series since the Model T went into production. "One of the best players in Cubs history, Ron Santo, went to my high school in Seattle. That's one reason why I like the team." Steve's face turned sad. "Mr. Santo passed away last year."

Steve wondered if he ever would be rewarded for the decades-long blind faith. Growing up poor and disadvantaged, he always supported the underdog. There was no better example than the Cubs. The Seattle teams, baseball's Mariners and football's Seahawks, were far from perennial powerhouses, but their mediocrity far surpassed the Cubs' futility. The Seahawks recently had a few decent seasons and seemed to be ready to improve from the 7-9 record in last year's 2010 season.

"Perhaps this Cubs team of yours will win a championship one year. Being an underdog builds character."

"Maybe. If losing builds character, the Cubs have a warehouse full of it."

"You like that other team too, the local one, Seahawks I think they're called. Are they better than these Cubs?"

"They're a football team. They do a little better but not much."

"Well they will win a championship at some point in time too. You just have to be patient Mr. Hepting. It will happen."

Steve smiled. Though Summer Martin didn't know a strikeout from a touchdown, the comments reflected her perfectly—always positive, ever optimistic. "The books you ordered are in the office," he explained. "I'll get Tiny to move them to the library this afternoon. I'll swing by later and maybe we can catch a quick lunch downtown?" Downtown Greenside consisted of one main street boasting a post office, a gas station, three retail outlets, two cafes, and the same number of old-style taverns.

Happy with Summer's positive response, Steve departed. He had avoided checking on a matter that had not been resolved in the previous year. It had subsequently climbed its way up a number of rungs on the important-issue ladder. Action should have been taken over the summer break, though a skeptical Steve doubted that anything had been done. He finally decided to abandon procrastination and undertake an eyes-on probe. He unlocked the door to the stairwell and slowly climbed the stairs.

With expectation building, Steve checked the stairs for telltale signs of work boot treads—there were none. At the second floor landing he opened the door to a janitorial closet, anxious to find empty, unused boxes—none were there. Perturbed, he entered the dark hallway and flicked a light switch, hoping the bleak illumination would reveal piles of neatly stacked crates, waiting to be hauled away. The hallway was dirty, dusty, and empty. Now annoyed, Steve opened the first classroom door and peered inside. Enough sunlight broke through the window grime for him to see what he had hoped he wouldn't. The piles of dirt-encrusted boxes were still scattered about the room. He had a strange feeling that someone in the shadows was staring at him. "Tiny?" he said breaking the silence. "Tiny?" he whispered, before abandoning the silliness. There was no reason for the janitor to be here. He closed the door and quickly checked three other former classrooms—all filled with the flotsam and jetsam of a school district.

Mumbling a blend of threats, cusses, and curses, Steve tromped down the stairs, kicking up dust as he went. He needed a positive task to divert the negative energy. He pumped air into storage-room basketballs. He shot a few hoops in the empty gymnasium, easily dunking the ball on the side-wall baskets that were elementary school height. Sufficiently calm, he spent time visiting with the recently arrived Joan Mackenzie. She was a veteran teacher who worked harder and with more passion than colleague's half her sixty years. By the time he returned to the library the piles of junk on the second floor was temporarily forgotten. He and Summer went for a long, leisurely lunch during which she handed over her house keys. She was attending the "Friends of the Planet" folk festival in a farmer's field on Whidbey Island. Steve had agreed to water her plants, most of which he hoped were legal. He agreed to feed Moonbeam, her placid cat. Summer believed in reincarnation and thought Moonbeam was the soul of Mohandas Gandhi.

Steve had a cat of his own, Charles. Though the animal was named after Charles Dickens, Steve did not believe the cat was the reincarnation of the famous Victorian novelist. To this point in a long life, Charles had not displayed a shred of talent for writing.

Returning to the school in the afternoon, sitting at the standard-issue wood veneer desk and sipping coffee, Steve prepared to tackle the emails.

He did not plan on actually reading any of them; that would be a waste of time. Like a machine Steve worked the keyboard. "So long suckers," he murmured with pleasure as each screen full of messages was wiped away. And people said he was useless with technology. He sent a few missives of his own—to Perry Watkins, HR Coordinator, confirming an upcoming meeting scheduled for the next day and another to Jennifer Capelli, complaining about the second-floor junkyard.

The floor contained discarded desks and broken magazine racks. Crumpled chairs with snapped welding and gouged plastic were stacked precariously. Old janitorial cleaners filled decrepit buckets. Science materials stood on rickety shelves. Barely used readers were relegated to grime-coated boxes. The next great reading series that had followed was piled in slightly less grotty boxes in another corner. In the previous year, the accumulating dust had drifted down the vents to the classrooms and hallways below. Steve had sent several complaining emails to the Maintenance department. He thought the material would be removed during the summer break. Clearly, he was wrong.

Tiny walked in, the glum face initially missed by Steve. When the principal noticed the sad demeanor, he made a wrong assumption and broached the issue in a roundabout manner. "How was your summer my young friend?" He paused, searching for the appropriate tone. Former-student Chelsea had teased the boy mercilessly, but as young adults, they were taking embryonic steps up the romance staircase. "How are you and Chelsea?"

Tiny blushed pink and nodded. "I was working out of the Taylerston maintenance shed so I saw her tons of times. Sometimes I don't know what to say and I get messed up in my head and then I say the wrong thing and she gets mad at me and then ..." He shot out a heavy sigh. "I don't get girls sometimes Mr. H. They're not like guys."

Tiny waited for a response that was not offered. Maybe Mr. H. didn't understand women either. He shifted to a topic the principal might be more interested in. "We don't have to take a tour to go over the maintenance list."

Steve frowned. "Okay," he said, fumbling through the early summer file for the start-up reminders. He finally extracted the torn ragged-edged piece of paper. Peering at the list, Steve started, "Did they paint the girl's restroom in the primary wing?"

"No," replied Tiny quickly.

"How about the counselor's office?" asked Steve.

"Nope."

Glancing upward, Steve decided to save time. "There was no painting done?" Tiny's silence spoke volumes. 'Shit,' whined Steve inside his head. "What about fixing the floor in Room 12?" He saw Tiny flashing a morose look followed by a sad shake of the head.

"It's not your fault Tiny. You were on grounds crew in Taylerston."

"I know Mr. H., but I coulda snuck in here at night and done some work."

"That would have been breaking the rules Tiny," said Steve curtly, missing the irony of him telling another employee to follow procedure. "You'd get in big trouble."

The youth shrugged with a who-the-hell-cares attitude.

Rifling through the papers the principal pulled out the top priority, "Tell me they repaired the fence along the primary playground?"

"Sorry Mr. H." It was not like the principal to appear so confused. In an attempt to cheer him up, Tiny blurted, "Thor and Xena are in the back of my truck. They won't be around to bully the other cats. You don't have to worry about them no more."

Steve had forgotten about the two felines from hell. The remaining placid cats and wayward mice were not foremost on his mind. More concerning was that no maintenance requests had been completed. "Thanks Tiny, you can go now."

Steve flipped the file to the side of the desk. He had submitted the requests as per district protocols. He had not whined and sniveled. He had not fabricated stories about parent council agitation. He had not had a spat with any of the maintenance crew. If anything, the working relationship was friendly. He had even used the proper forms. Like a good boy he had followed proper procedure and nothing had been accomplished. What the hell had gone wrong?

There were more meetings scheduled at the central office the next morning. Though all school-based administrators were expected to attend, Steve had worked up a reasonable excuse for an absence, a semi-official Greenside Parent Council meeting, courtesy of chairperson, Donna Medford. Now he was going to have to fire off a few more emails, this time at Capelli, and try to arrange some face-to-face time with Lady Macbeth. He leaned back in his chair and scrunched an anxious face. Two visits to the central office in successive days was two too many. But where else could he get answers to the many questions stacking up in his addled head?

With meetings at the district office, Principal Hepting would not be in the school until later in the morning. It was a very early 7:30 am and Tiny Little was sitting in Joan Mackenzie's room, getting ready to clear the emails from her inbox. Joan had little time for such tasks. For Tiny, it was an opportunity to practice his reading with Mrs. Mackenzie present to help when needed. Tiny's reading ability had never been close to average.

"Hey Mrs. Mack," said Tiny, using his verbal shorthand for the teacher. "Are you related to Mrs. McKenzie who works in the office?"

Relatively formal when at work, Joan permitted Tiny to use a shortened version of her name. It helped him distinguish her from office secretary Bridget McKenzie. This was not the first time the janitor had asked the question. She looked up from a picture book she was perusing. "That is a very good question Frank." Joan always used Tiny's proper name. "Our last name looks and sounds the same but the spelling is slightly different." Rising, she walked to the whiteboard and wrote the two surnames. "Do you see the difference?"

Tiny took a moment. The task was similar to the puzzles where a person had to list the differences between one drawing and another. He was good at those. Suddenly brightening, he said, "Yeah, I see it. That's really weird."

"We probably came from the same clan in the Scottish Highlands. Maybe someone was a bad speller a long time ago." She noted a frowning face and realized she would need to explain the term clan. "Never mind right now Frank. Can you start taking those messages off my computer?"

The room was quiet except for Tiny pecking at computer keys and Joan organizing big books on a stand. A soft dragging noise from above was easily discerned. Tiny looked up. "Did you hear that Mrs. Mack?"

Joan stopped placing a book on the stand and cocked her head toward the ceiling tiles, catching the slow scraping sound. "That must be one of those cats that were wandering around the school last year."

"Yeah, but they're usually upstairs in the storage rooms in the morning. They wander at night." Tiny froze, aghast at what he had said. Mr. H. was the only other adult who knew about the cats. He said that the animals would eventually have to be taken away but did not seem to be in a big hurry to do it as long as the cats didn't bother the students or teachers. Tiny wasn't sure what Mr. H. would say this year.

"I know about the cats and the boxes upstairs Tiny. I've been at Greenside a great deal longer than you so there's not much that gets past me." Joan stared at the young man. "I even know about the mice. For now, I would like you to shoo that cat back to the upstairs storage rooms where it belongs. That scraping noise is irritating." Tiny nodded, eager to help the elderly teacher who could keep a secret.

The sound seeped through the ceiling tiles, moving slowly. The cat was in no hurry, making its way along the main duct that led to a T-junction above the newly named Learning Commons. Tiny lumbered to the store-room. He grabbed a ladder and headed to the room he still called the library, arriving well before the vent-crawling cat. Climbing the ladder, he snatched a screwdriver from a pocket and unscrewed the cover located high on the wall. Sticking his large head into the vent, he peered right, then left. Nothing. A grab for a flashlight in another pocket was followed by a click and a beam of light splitting the darkness to the right—nothing.

Tiny swung the beam to the left. Shocked eyes, wide as saucers, stared back. They blinked; an action Tiny knew was impossible for cats. "What the hell . . ." he yelped.

"Shit!" came a grunted reply. A little man backed up to the vent's T-junction and bashed his forehead on the metal. "Shit," he groused again. Instinctively, a hand raised to check his injured head.

"Come back here you little asshole." Tiny tried to clamber into the duct but his bulk was far too large to navigate the space. He barely got his shoulders through the opening and lost valuable seconds extricating himself. The scrawny figure scurried away, heading along one of the two vent paths. Tiny could not tell which one.

Clambering down the ladder, Tiny hustled to the office. He listened for any sounds from the ducts above the ceiling tiles, a task particularly challenging given his panting and wheezing. There was no sound from the vents. There was no sound at all, until he heard a car engine. Running to the entrance Tiny caught sight of a black suv careening out of the parking lot. A scrawny man sat in the passenger seat, hand held to head. It was impossible to see who was driving.

Muttering profane promises of retribution should he ever meet the intruder again, Tiny hauled out his cellphone and tapped the number for the school district office. A recorded message indicated that the reception-ist was not on duty until 8:30 am. He punched in Mr. H.'s number at home. There was no answer. Mr. H. was one of the few adults in North America without a cellphone, so contact using that device was impossible. With no choice but to wait until the district office opened, Tiny trundled back to Mrs. Mackenzie's room and continued to clear off her emails, grumbling and muttering the entire time. He vowed to wring the scrawny worm's neck if he ever caught the little bugger crawling through the vents again.

4

Steve Hepting was enjoying a leisurely shower when he heard the phone ring. Toweling down he strode to the receiver only to find whoever had been on the line had hung up. He checked caller ID, concerned that it had been a message from his brother about their mother. It was rare to get a phone call before 8:00 am. Not recognizing the number, Steve shuffled to the kitchen, poured a mug of coffee and sat on a chair on the back patio, enjoying the sunshine and the splash of color from the flower beds. Steve had developed his love of gardening from former live-in partner Monique Lambert. He enjoyed digging, planting, and pruning. Puttering in the yard was far less punishing on the emotions than his other pastime, playing golf.

Gardening and golfing formed the perfect yin and yang. One soothed the soul, the other tortured the psyche. The usually calm Steve could launch a baleful broadside over a missed putt, a stubbed chip, or an errant drive. The only other occasion of histrionic overload was when watching the Cubs blow another late-inning lead, or the Seahawk offense failing to execute at a level approaching that of a community-college squad.

Monique had eventually moved out in 2003, her teacher values conflicting with Steve's then love affair with stocks and money. Eight years later, he and Monique were cautiously re-connecting and Steve was paying more attention to domestic chores. Now as a fervent educator, he understood Monique's passion for the public-school system—better yet, he shared it. The mutual interest acted as an initial springboard in an albeit tentative reconciliation.

Monique's lengthy absence had been filled by soulmate Charles; a British Shorthair feline picked from the cages of the SPCA. Chunky, with a broad face and a big head, Charles was neither an active gardener nor interested in sports. In his advancing years he was not much interested in anything except sleeping, eating, and snuggling. He performed those tasks with aplomb. Like many of his breed, he was big-bodied, bordering on obese.

Having finished his coffee Steve provided Charles with a big breakfast; then he exited and steered the new royal-blue Honda CR-V onto Tayler Drive, the main street. He passed purveyors of fast food. gas stations, and strip malls on his way to the meetings. Though adept at avoiding the district office, Steve had little choice but to attend today.

The meeting with Perry concluded with information about the training sessions for the new teachers. Since Colin Redford was moving from a high-level high school Math position to a sixth-grade class, he qualified for a half day of orientation and two days of training prior to the school year, with pay. As Perry explained, Steve only had to provide the two-hour orientation. "None of your veteran teachers offered the training. I thought Summer Martin might but she's at an earth-mother festival, probably sampling the herbal produce." He shot a quick glance at Steve.

"It's just a folk-music festival," said Steve. "Not everybody liked your Fever Pitch disco tunes in the seventies or fantasize over Celine Dion like you do now. Not everyone who attends a folk music festival is smoking pot all day."

"We're talking about Summer Martin. Don't defend her just because you and her have a thing."

"We are not having a 'thing' as you so eloquently state. We're good friends and that's the way it will stay, not that it's any of your damn business. I'm hoping to reconnect with Monique." He paused, thinking of his former partner. It was difficult moving her off his thoughts. "Who's going to do Redford's training?"

It was Emma Martinez.

"The teacher who just got transferred in? What does she know about Greenside?" Sighing in defeated resignation, Steve asked his friend to arrange the program, surprised that Perry had already done so, starting the following day. Perry passed a set of keys to Steve. "These are for Emma Martinez. Redford got his set earlier this week. I guess he's a keener. He'll be in to see you at 9:00 am tomorrow for orientation. He'll meet with Martinez next Monday and Tuesday for training."

Steve pocketed the keys and stood up, readying to leave. "Thanks Perry. I'm glad my approval signature was so important to the HR department."

"Don't get cynical on me yet Mr. Hepting. There's more district attention coming your way. The boss wants to see you."

"Good," responded Steve with more confidence than he felt. "I sent her a few emails yesterday. I need to have some questions answered."

Perry's eyes narrowed. He had wondered what could concern Jennifer Capelli to such an extent that she was involved with a specific teacher transfer to Greenside. Now she was willing to meet her prickly antagonist Steve Hepting almost immediately after he had sent her an email or two. He watched his friend rise and exit his office. What the hell was in those emails Hepting had sent? He eyed Steve lumbering along the corridor. What the hell is Capelli going to do to him if she didn't like what he wrote?

Steve slowly made his way to Capelli's lair. He was drained already. He had been at the central office fifteen minutes and already had his fill of bureaucratic mumble. He needed to meet with Capelli and then get the hell out of the building. Shuffling toward the coffee room, egged on by a desperate need for caffeine, he felt a squeeze on his elbow. It was Capelli.

"Forget the coffee Steve. I want to see you about yesterday's emails. I've only got a few minutes."

Tall and thin with auburn-colored hair tumbling loosely over elegant shoulders, Jennifer Capelli reminded Steve of Angelina Jolie minus the sultry lips. The woman reveled in her physicality, tall enough in ever-present three-inch heels to fall only a few inches short of Steve's six-feet, two-inch height. She was slim enough to shop for clothes at young women's boutiques. She was as dangerous as an ebony-eyed femme fatale in a 1940s film noir. The summer tan removed the need for heavy make-up, the Roman nose showing slightly red from sun exposure.

She was wearing a white three-quarter sleeve blouse with a flowered-print skirt. Capelli almost never wore pants, a hold-over from the days when she thought they made her derriere appear heavy. She glanced at Steve, his polo shirt a victim of too much pounding in a washing machine. The khaki trousers and faux-leather shoes were Hepting specialties. The tan made the man appear more healthy than usual, though he could stand to lose the flesh rolls. She grimaced slightly. Hepting was a square peg that would never fit into the round holes that made an efficient modern organization operate smoothly.

Dropping softly into her jet-black, high-backed executive chair covered in supple leather, a suddenly nervous Capelli quickly used a remote to kill an image on a flat screen monitor that hung on the wall. "Just finished a conference call about a project I'm working on," she said by way of explana-tion. Questioning eyes probed Steve's face. Had he seen the company logo and the project's title on the screen before it went black? She bore into him again but Hepting showed no sign that he had made note of what had been displayed. Satisfied, she placed forearms on the massive cherry wood desktop devoid of paper and asked about Steve's summer vacation. She scaled back increasing impatience and forced herself to appear interested when he replied with snippets of golf, gardening, and checking on his elderly, ailing mother in Tacoma. The robot-like questions sounded as if Capelli was reading scripted lines for the first time. The words were voiced, yet there was no emotional connection that made them come alive. They hung limp and ineffective.

The divorced Capelli told Steve she had spent the summer visiting her two grown children in San Francisco. She had attended a summer computer conference in Las Vegas where, she noted sprightly, her annual battle with the one-armed bandits had resulted in yet another windfall. Though she did not mention any male contacts, she was rumored to have a number of testosterone-charged friends who lived in San Francisco, Los Angeles, and Vancouver BC with whom she traveled during holidays or met clandestinely at conferences.

In contrast Steve had never had much romantic success. He was witty, even charming in a dorky kind of way. He could engage with women in superficial banter, especially someone like Donna Medford. Steve had courted her briefly when she and her husband had a trial separation. Though fond of each other, they had little in common. While the romantic aspect of the relationship fizzled, they remained friends. Donna had mended her marital fences and lived in Greenside, their two girls attending Steve's school. She worked at the school district maintenance department and was the Chair of the Greenside Parent Council.

An infatuation with a vivacious teacher named Charlotte Wilson had ended in disaster. She had left teaching and was married to a Seattle businessman. The sole serious relationship had been with live-in partner Monique Lambert when he had been a high-flying stock broker. She grew disenchanted with his love affair with money. She never understood what it was like to be without it. Money was a narcotic to a man deprived of any growing up—a man who was raised by a single mother barely scraping by; a man his father had abandoned when he was six and his brother two. The two women Steve had loved had issues with money, his mother for never having any and his live-in partner for bemoaning its ill effects.

"Are you golfing in the tournament this year?" Capelli asked warily. The first of Hepting's errant golf shots had struck when she was his principal at Lakeview High. Capelli's sore right buttock made her limp for a week. Last summer, first-year principal Hepting hit an approach shot. It took what he claimed to be a bad bounce off a tree beside the green and smacked Capelli on the same body part, this time on the left. The new superintendent had endured another week of hobbling. Hepting was as much a literal as a figurative pain in the ass.

"I have other plans," Steve replied. He couldn't risk a third strike.

Masking profound relief, Capelli queried Steve's choice for the upcoming administrators' workshops. The presenters were representatives of A-1 Education Software Incorporated, providers of the new office and administrative computer system. "What they can do is truly exciting," gushed Capelli. Steve nodded numbly. Attendance was compulsory for administrators who had a choice of three workshops. Steve had chosen "Data and the Dynamic Growth Plan" option as the least painful of a truly horrific lot. He assured Capelli he was looking forward to a scintillating session.

The superintendent issued a mirthless smile. Hepting didn't give a shit about data, growth plans, forms, and district-level direction. His was the old world of gut-instinct, intuitive leaps, and independent thinking. Consistency and conformity were the valued attributes in the modern era. The leaders of the teachers' association were only too willing to join her in clipping the wings of school-level decision-making. Though Capelli inevitably locked horns with the union leaders, they understood the systematic, impersonal thrust she emphasized. They were the lead representatives of their own oligarchic bureaucracies. Capelli understood them far better than the likes of Steve Hepting.

Steve had spent much of the previous afternoon trying to reach Capelli by phone, an instrument far too low-tech for the modern-day CEO. He finally fired off a long email requesting a brief meeting. Capelli loved email correspondence and then half-complained, half-bragged about how many she received in a day. In her tech-laden world, the number of emails you were sent was directly correlated to importance, just as some believed the number of friends on a Facebook page was indicative of popularity. Steve tolerated emails and had only a vague idea of Facebook. Twitters and blogging may as well exist in an alternate universe.

"Let's get to your email," stated Capelli, glancing at the digital clock on the wall before scrolling down her inbox. "Here it is," she noted with satisfaction, perusing the information. The confident expression eroded as Capelli read the missive. By the time she had finished, a frown shrouded her face. She looked anything but happy.

Should I dive in or wait until she says something? Steve decided to take the lead. "I wanted to talk about the cats and mice too."

"What cats?" responded Capelli; "What mice?" She looked at the screen. "What the hell are you talking about?"

A little hyperbole never hurt anyone. "The animals are holed up in the storage boxes on the second floor. There are feral cats chasing wild mice all over the school. It must be in violation of about eleven regulations."

The last line grabbed Capelli's attention. She looked up from the screen. "Get the custodian to get rid of the boxes."

"I tried," explained Steve. "The second story is regarded as district jurisdiction, not site footage. Tiny is not allowed to touch it."

Capelli's eyes narrowed at the sound of the name. Tiny had been a student at Lakeview when she had extended her authority and expelled the football-playing lunkhead. Then that asshole Danchuk had given the kid a job with the school district to prevent the media from grabbing the story of a disadvantaged, slow-witted, hard-working football hero being unfairly punished by an uncaring principal. "Have you talked to Lou?" Capelli asked, referring to Lou Tayler, Supervisor of Elementary Curriculum.

"Yeah, he says it isn't his issue since the books are in storage, not in the classroom."

Capelli nodded understanding, pleased at the inaction and the bureaucratic excuses causing it. The system was working. "Well, try Lou again to make sure we don't throw out anything useful. I'll tell Phil Chow to make sure the Maintenance Department moves all that crap after Lou has checked it out. We can't have mice using the school as a hotel. They carry diseases. Kids could get sick."

"Don't forget the cats." Steve said, caught off guard by Capelli's willingness to intervene. He caught the questioning look. "They chase the mice," he added.

"We get rid of the mice; the cats will bugger off too."

Steve was satisfied with the response. Phil Chow was the Taylerston district's business manager, second in command to alpha-dog Capelli. "I'm glad you brought up the maintenance department Jen. It seems like there was a no-work order on Greenside for the summer."

Raising a palm to indicate the conversation was closing, Capelli said, "I'll talk to Phil about that too. I'm sure he'll get someone to take a look at what happened, okay?"

Steve was less confident about this response but decided to shift gears. "Who were those guys you were showing around the school this summer?"

Capelli's eyes transformed from orbs to slits. Hepting was such a nosy pain in the ass. Maybe the guy did get a look at the computer projection on the screen before I closed it down? "Those discussions had nothing to do with mice, cats, or storage junk" she snapped, revealing a scorched nerve.

"Why the sudden snarl?" Steve asked silently.

Capelli chose her words carefully. "Those visits have nothing to do with your role as principal this year. Just don't believe all the nutty stories you'll hear from your paranoid maintenance pals."

"Maintenance didn't respond to a single request this summer," Steve shot back.

"I know," said Capelli with a humorless smile. She rose from the executive chair, covered in supple leather. "Now if you'll excuse me, I have a meeting to attend."

One more prick at the Capelli balloon was too enticing to pass up. "Do you know a teacher named Colin Redford?"

Capelli stopped in her tracks and leaned across her desk, staring at Steve. "What about him?"

"He was transferred to Greenside. I heard you and Phil wanted him there. That seemed a bit strange . . ."

"Like I said, don't believe everything you hear from your so-called pals." Capelli straightened. "Now, excuse me but I've been called to a meeting. If you've got any problems with Redford coming to your school, talk to HR."

5

Wanting a quick exit from his version of hell, Steve made a bee line for the front door, only to be stopped by the receptionist who said Tiny Little had been trying to reach him. The young man had not been able to get through on the phone for some time. Calls had been heavy since school was starting in a little more than a week. When Tiny had finally managed to connect, Steve had been in Capelli's office. There was no way in hell that the receptionist was going to interrupt the CEO unless Greenside school had been blown up by terrorists. Tiny had assured her that was not the case.

"Has someone been hurt?" Steve asked.

The receptionist shrugged. "I don't know."

Searching for a phone with greater privacy than the one in the reception area, Steve was forced to wait while Perry finished a meeting with the principal of Oak Grove High. Body language indicated that not all was going well. The principal was shaking her head. On one occasion she slammed her hand on Perry's desk. Why anyone would want to do HR work was beyond Steve.

Finally, the meeting ended with the disgruntled principal grumbling as she left Perry's enclave. She managed a curt, "Hi Steve," and tromped down the hallway. Steve watched the confident swagger as the principal headed off in search of Jennifer Capelli. High school principals always thought they could lean on the superintendent to get what they wanted, more so than those leading elementary or middle schools.

Perry did not look the worse for wear as Steve entered his office.

"Having fun today?" jibed Steve.

"Coincidence is a strange bedfellow," remarked Perry. "Now the principal wants Colin Redford back at Oak Grove. There's not enough teachers for the Math and Computer Science classes."

"Is he going back?"

"I don't know. Oak Grove admin is saying they never wanted him to leave in the first place. He wasn't on their protected list last spring but they claim that was preliminary. I don't think there's much of a chance Redford will be moved back. You know what Capelli's like for procedure. She'll never go against her own protocol." Perry stared at his friend. "Why are you back visiting me? You don't even look like Capelli clawed you too badly."

"Ah hell, she's just a big pussy cat," claimed Steve with a smirk. He sat down and explained the need for privacy for his phone call. Reaching Tiny, he listened intently, his jaw dropping with each phrase the janitor spoke. Tiny did not lie, but he was prone to exaggeration. The described event seemed more than ludicrous, even for a Tiny-generated tale. The duct would have been dark. The interloper could have been a large cat. However, Tiny was adamant that he shone a flashlight at the creature and it was human. At first, the janitor had thought it was a kid causing trouble before realizing it was a scrawny little man.

Steve's doubts intensified. If it was a man, he must have been small, almost jockey-sized. It was unfortunate that Tiny had not been able to apprehend the phantom or that Joan Mackenzie had not been present for corroboration. If the event occurred as Tiny had described, what could possibly cause a man be crawling around in the ventilation ducts between the two levels of Greenside school?

Since he was already at the central office, Steve decided to report the incident to either Capelli or Business Manager Phil Chow. Would they believe the tale? Would they want Steve to phone the police? Sure as hell, if they believed him, Steve was going to be in for a load of paperwork. He had time to ruminate on upcoming form-filling since Capelli was in a meeting in Phil Chow's office. The Oak Grove principal was occupying the only available seat near the closed door. She vented at Steve, vehemently claiming that Redford had been on Oak Grove's protected teacher list.

Steve listened patiently, hoping the high school principal could convince Capelli to repatriate Redford.

Chow's door opened quickly. Capelli stormed out. The Oak Grove principal leaped to her feet, ready to follow the superintendent. Steve was at least several yards away. His view of Chow's doorway was partially obstructed by a cubicle wall and the now-standing Oak Grove principal. Despite this, he caught a glimpse of what he believed was a small man slip quickly out of Chow's office and scurry in the opposite direction along the hallway. Turning around, he saw the Oak Grove principal follow Capelli into the inner sanctum. The door slammed shut. Capelli was furious, presumably about what had occurred in Chow's office. Steve waited for a moment and thought better about adding fuel to Capelli's fire. Tiny's story was too bizarre to share. Even through the closed door Steve heard muffled, yet distinct, Capelli venom, directed toward the Oak Grove principal. He headed for the exit. There was no chance that Capelli was going to reverse a decision in her current frame of mind. Colin Redford was coming to Greenside.

A face-to-face discussion with Tiny later in the day provided no additional information. The young man's story stayed remarkably consistent. Steve decided against phoning the police. What was he going to say, that there was a jockey-sized man crawling around in the ducts? The police had more important issues to deal with. So did Steve. He needed to ensure the next day's orientation with Colin Redford went as well as possible.

At exactly 9:00 am the next day there was a soft knock on Steve's office door. Facing inward was a man with an elfin face, ropy arms, thin legs and a gangly physique. "Are you Steve Hepting?" asked the man.

"Yeah," replied Steve, "Site supervisor at your service." Irritated eyes remained glued to the monitor. He angrily tapped the keyboard, snapping the buttons with quick stabs. "C'mon, c'mon," he muttered, willing the recalcitrant machine to do his bidding. "Good riddance," he grumbled just as the district motto pulsed at the bottom of the screen, "Taylerston Schools: The Future is Now!" Then the screen went blank.

Pulling away from the image, Steve said, "You must be Colin Redford." He rose and extended a meaty hand.

The young man nodded. "Mr. Watkins at HR told me to be here for my orientation."

Deciding to have informal chat, Steve led the way to the staffroom where he had already made a pot of coffee. He and Colin poured the liquid in their mugs and plunked down on wobbly chairs at a table with a scratched surface. Catching the young man glancing about with question marks in roving eyes, Steve said softly, "I'm afraid this isn't Oak Grove High."

Oak Grove was the newest school in the Taylerston District. Predictably, the school name reflected a landscape that once existed and had almost been totally destroyed—a Garry Oak forest. The remnants were the crux of a conflict between local environmentalists and developers. The high school was bright, big, and brimming with resources, everything that Greenside was not.

Fixing cautiously on the principal, Colin nodded. He scanned the dilapidated staffroom. "It seems quite different."

Steve watched the young man take a nervous pull on his coffee before deciding to bring the unspoken matter to a head. "I realize this is going to be a challenge for you. Your career has been teaching senior level students academic Math and Computer Science. Here you'll have to teach all kids, not just the smart ones. And the sixth-grade teacher has all the subject areas. Since there's only one class there is no one else to take over some subjects while you teach other classes Math and Science."

"I was told there would be others who could take the subjects I cannot teach."

Steve shook his head. Why was this poor fellow assigned to his school when Oak Grove wanted him for an assignment much more suited to his background? Steve glanced at the placid young man who did not seem to be a person who would ruffle the feathers of Jennifer Capelli or Phil Chow. But he must have done. Why else would he be here? "I checked about job sharing. The other teachers are happy with the way things are scheduled. I'm sorry but I won't force them to change."

Redford nodded slowly. "They might hold any disruption against me?"

Steve chose not to respond and decided to move on quickly. "The building is old. Many kids have difficult home lives. We don't have the fancy computers and resources that you're used to."

Colin chuckled, stopping Steve's monologue and eliciting a perplexed gaze from the principal.

"What?" Steve asked, baffled.

"Well, Mr. Hepting, I don't . . ."

"Call me Steve."

"Okay Steve, I don't mean to be rude but you're not selling the school very well."

Nodding at the young man's honesty, Steve responded, "Good point. I'm just giving you the straight goods. We've got a gung-ho staff here, you'll like them. This place is a challenge. I love it." Steve stared at the young man before adding, "But not everybody does."

The first stop on the tour was Colin's room. Greenside rooms were huge, built in an era when there were thirty-five or more students in a class. The blackboards were, as usual, green, and placed so low that Colin's head reached the top edge. He had never used a blackboard or chalk before. Wandering eyes launched an unsuccessful scan of the room before spying a probable location, "Is the computer projection unit stored in there?" he asked, pointing to a closed closet door in the corner.

"Uh, I don't think so," muttered Steve.

"I used a new Math software program from A-1 Education in my Calculus class last year. A few instructional computer programs would help reach the range of student ability that you say is in each class." He brightened. "Is Greenside piloting any of the new software?"

"Uh, no, not as yet," murmured Steve, searching for something positive to say. "We have lots of overhead projectors in the library storage room. Feel free to sign one out."

Steve opened the closet door and found two cassette tape recorders, covered with dust. A teacher copy of *Math Moves* sat on a shelf, a series that supervisor Lou Tayler had energetically promoted just five years previously. Piles of the student textbooks were filling dust-caked boxes on the second floor. The program had been discarded in favor of the new problem-solving, process-oriented *Math for the Future*, another of Lou's fanfare projects. A few cardboard clocks, various plastic shapes, a train timetable, five old stopwatches and an abacus were piled into plastic totes that sat on lower shelves. Catching Colin's baffled look, Steve explained, "Part of our math manipulative collection. It's like a really old-fashioned software program."

"Oh," replied Colin, trying to sound as if he understood. He turned his attention to the novel sets lined up neatly along the top shelving. "Are there class sets of these?"

"Those are the sets," explained Steve, "Eight of each novel." He noticed Redford's confusion. "Never mind, we'll deal with that later."

Steve explained that Colin would receive a teacher kit at the beginning of the year, a box of pencils, pencil crayons, pens, a few rulers, some erasers, a box of chalk, scotch tape, masking tape, a box of paper clips, two sheaths of white paper for the photocopier, a box of baggies, three highlighters, each a different fluorescent color, and ten specialty pens, six felt and four for an overhead. At the end of each term, secretary Bridget would have another pack prepared.

"What happens if I don't need the chalk?" asked Colin.

Steve shrugged. "Don't ask Bridget to keep it out, she doesn't respond to personal requests. It takes too much time," he continued as way of explanation. "Make sure you treat her well and she can pull some favors for you, get you more stuff mid-year."

Steve led Colin back to the office. smiling and patting the young man on the shoulder. "The small number of teachers means more playground duty, once before school, once at recess, and once after school every week. Each teacher has three prep periods a week, a half-hour each."

Colin stared, hoping to detect a hint of humor from this strange man who seemed proud of the sorry state of his school and the workload faced by the teachers. Three supervision times a week? There was no supervision at Oak Grove. Three half-hour preps? That was half the time Colin had for prep in his high school assignment. Inadvertently the young man scrunched his face. Surely there was no future for schools like this? Certainly there was no viable future for teachers like him in schools like this?

Ignoring the frazzled look on the young man's face, Steve told Colin to get his photocopy code from Bridget. "For now, you can use mine," he offered, fumbling through a pant pocket. "Damn," he muttered, failing to locate the four-digit code, "Bridget will be in Monday, you can get it from her." He turned to Colin, hope dancing in his eyes. "You know how to use the alarm system?" he asked cautiously. Steve held the single year record for alarm code violations, never quite being able to grasp the technical aspects of the procedure. When Colin nodded, Steve sighed with barely hidden relief. He concluded with, "Good, anything else?"

Shrugging, Colin could not choose one or two issues from a list containing dozens. "My trainer will be here Monday?" he asked. After Steve's nod he added, "Do you know who it is?"

"Another new teacher to Greenside, Emma Martinez."

Color drained from Redford's face as if a thirsty vampire was sucking blood from a straw inserted in his ear.

"Colin, are you okay?"

Recovering slightly, the young man asked softly, "Can another person be assigned?"

"I don't think so," commented Steve, "Not at this late date."

Redford nodded with understanding, the slow movement drawing more blood to his face. "Emma and I know each other," he explained. "We went out together, but it didn't work out."

Warning bells bonged inside Steve's head. "Just how long were you a couple?" he asked cautiously.

"Two years. We lived together last year. The break-up was pretty ugly."

After watching the sullen Colin depart, Steve immediately grabbed the phone and punched in Perry's number, ready to lambaste his so-called friend for failing to mention the personal animosity between the two new teachers. Perry was not in his office or, knowing Redford's orientation would be over, more likely too afraid to pick up and listen to Steve's grousing. "He can run but he can't hide," muttered Steve maliciously. He would corner Perry at the afternoon admin sessions.

The professional development meeting for administrators was prefaced by a lunch at the school board office. The culinary-correct fare provided a change from the burger and fries Steve had wolfed down at noon over the last two days. Jumping on the latest gastronomical bandwagon, the district provided sandwiches with gluten free multi-grain buns, or wraps in thin pita bread. The chicken, cheese, or falafel fillings were complemented by alfalfa sprouts. The salad dressing was strawberry vinaigrette. It was poured delicately over a combination of butter and romaine lettuce with walnuts and dates dotting the greenery. Juice filled the glass containers. The dessert was fresh fruit. Steve and others secretly pined for a hit of sugar but the days of cream donuts had disappeared forever.

The administrators were expected to peruse the recently released 2010-2011 Taylerston School District Annual Report as they took delicate bites of their lunch. They gestured approvingly with nods and smiles. They traded positive comments in groups of two or three. Steve sat alone, scanning Capelli's first annual report, finding little that was relevant or interesting. Capelli was circulating the room, soliciting opinions and smiling and nodding as the positive comments flowed about the wealth of valuable statistical information.

Only the front page of the annual report was devoid of data. Capelli's brainchild motto, "Taylerston Schools: The Future is Now" filled the top quarter of the page. Steve had no idea what the motto meant. He was not even sure it made any sense. The rest of the page comprised of a picture of the photogenic Capelli and the professorial Phil Chow, flanked by six school board members. The seventh trustee, from small outlying Greenside, was absent. Most of the general public did not know who the board members were. Neither did the teachers.

Three inside pages were filled with charts and graphs regarding student demographics and achievement according to various standardized assessments. The reams of numbers were mind-numbing and no sane person would read the maze of data. This was fortuitous. According to the statistics, most Taylerston students displayed average achievement at best. In every category their performance could best be described as mediocre. It was Capelli's stated goal to transform district achievement results to, "Lighthouse levels using vanguard teaching and evaluative techniques." Fortunately, individual school scores were not included. Early in the week,

Steve had glanced at his school's results, pitiably poor in virtually every category. Though small in number, the abysmal Greenside achievement was a drag on the district results. By how much Steve was not sure, though he would bet that Capelli had dived into that data and be convinced that Greenside students were spectacular dullards.

The annual report concluded with a few short articles on "Highlighted Programs," buried on the back page, including a short note featuring the five-year anniversary of the Namibian College project Steve had started while teaching at Meadowvale Elementary. A photo was included, showing Steve and the inaugural class smiling proudly for the camera. Steve stared at the photo, glowing over the teaching memories it generated. Was that project really five years ago? It seemed like yesterday. Life in the classroom, so far removed from job postings, data manipulation, and purposeless meetings, seemed so positive. Almost trancelike, Steve recalled the teenage Tiny struggling through his Basic English course. He scanned the photo, successfully putting names to the smiling faces of those fifth-grade Meadowvale kids.

Had teaching in the classroom really been that good? And if it had, why did Steve abandon it for life in the principal's chair?

6

While colleagues teased Steve abut his apparent fascination with his photo on the back page, the sheepish principal cradled recently poured java and made his way to the data session. The rectangular assembly room was no larger than a classroom with track lighting and auditorium-style seating. A projector hummed. The guest speaker studiously checked switches, dials, and screens. Finding a seat in the back row, Steve watched six young vice-principals enter and sit in the two front rows, jabbering excitedly.

The A-1 Education representative began. There was no introduction, explanation, or even a lame attempt at humor. The man's monotone voice read every line from a laser-point slide as if the audience lacked basic reading skills. A second screen was marked into quadrants with a smattering of black dots, an array resembling mosquitoes plastered on a car windshield after two hours of summer driving in Cascade wilderness.

In a slow sonorous voice, the A-1 Education rep stated, "These are the results from the district's word recognition assessment last year. Notice the preponderance of hits in the high-recognition, low-usage quadrant. Eventually the new administrative software from A-1 Education will be operational and you will be able to conceptualize the alternative instructional strategies that will maximize impact on the data."

Huh? Steve shifted in his seat. What the hell did this guy say?

A vice-principal asked in a serious tone, "What would account for the current marked result in the distinctiveness of range differential of the various quadrants?"

Huh? Steve stared at her. What the hell did you ask?

Data-man praised the excellent question and launched into a tedious analysis that lost Steve after the first three words. Five minutes later the man concluded, "Thus A-1 Education will give you the tools to ensure your teachers will develop more robust instructional and evaluative techniques to ascertain with greater levels of certainty what these numbers may be indicating." The man grinned, clearly pleased with himself. "Are there more questions?"

"Please dear God no!" Steve screamed silently. But one query was voiced, uncomfortably nearby.

"How's it going?" It was Capelli. She had slipped in the back door and quietly moved to a seat beside Steve. "I've seen some fantastic software from A-1 Education," she gushed in a stage-whispered voice.

"Oh yeah, this guy's top drawer," echoed Steve, wondering how long Capelli would remain. He would miss an opportunity for a quick afternoon snooze, courtesy of data-man.

Mercifully Capelli rose, gave a quick nod to the speaker and slipped out via a rear doorway.

Her departure had no impact on the young administrators who lobbed inane questions trying to be the stag with the biggest set of antlers. Steve was easily gored. The lingo may as well have been Greek blended with Chaucer's old English. He dozed with his eyes open, a skill he had perfected while an undergraduate in university lecture halls. An outlandish, though pleasant, dream of the Cubs winning the World Series was interrupted by polite applause and ensuing silence. There was a need to re-enter the real world.

"Great stuff, eh Steve?" one of the Young Turks gushed as she headed toward the exit.

"Yeah, no kidding," Steve responded, his tone exuding thoughtful contemplation. "It's great." He grinned and rose quickly, fearful that she may engage him in a robust conversation about school growth plans. Steve couldn't leave fast enough. He hurried to the exit, planning a robust conversation of his own—with HR man Perry about Colin Redford and Emma Martinez, the pair of estranged lovers assigned to his school. He quickly strode to Perry's office, catching his friend on the phone. Steve's laser-like eyes and stone-cold face prompted the HR man to end the call quickly.

"How was Redford this morning?" asked Perry nonchalantly.

"He seems like a nice guy, but he knows nothing about sixth-grade instruction. He's going to drown for a while." He tapped a finger on the desk during a short span of silence, pondering how to approach the next question. Finally, he decided on the direct approach. "Did you know he and Emma Martinez were engaged, were being the operative word?"

"You're kidding," said Perry, wide-eyed. "How would a Schultz-like guy like me know that?"

"You're in HR for chrissakes."

"We don't track people. We don't follow teachers around and snoop into their personal lives."

"You knew Summer was at a folk festival!" blurted Steve, unsuccessfully covering a timbre of emotion.

Perry offered a thin smile before proceeding. "You were the one who told me she was going. You were whining that you had to look after her plants and that Moonshadow cat she thinks is Gandhi in feline fur."

"Moonbeam," Steve corrected.

"Whatever."

Rebuffed, Steve reconsidered chastising Perry for his lack of insider knowledge. Instead he went on offense. "According to Colin, the emotions between he and Emma are still raw. You're saying they have to work side-by-side in a small school?"

"There's no policy against it," Perry stated lamely.

"What about common sense?" snapped Steve before realizing what he had just said, "Forget that, there'll be none of that from HR. Who's going to referee between the two of them?" He stopped and held up a palm. "I know, don't tell me, this is my problem, I'm the principal, it's my school."

"Exactly right," claimed a satisfied Perry, "You're finally catching on." He leaned forward in conspiratorial fashion. "Quit whining, I've got more important info, a scoop for you about Capelli and Chow." The voice was whispery soft.

The angst about Redford and Martinez forgotten, Steve replicated the tone. "What about them?"

Like two kids sharing a secret, Perry issued a furtive scan and leaned closer. "I don't know any details," he said. "Capelli and Chow have been meeting with some business guys and no one seems to know who they are."

"We're huddling like spies passing on state secrets and you give me that! Your sleuthing has improved from utterly useless to basic incompetence." Steve rolled frustrated eyes upward. "The end result is still dross."

Perry huffed at the English major's use of weird words. His riposte was abandoned when several principals slid by the large picture window dividing his workspace from the hallway. A few passers-by displayed a mock golf swing, motioning for Steve to join them. They clucked and chuckled with child-like anticipation. Betting was heavy on what portion of Capelli's anatomy Hepting would aim for this year.

Steve waved the colleagues on, hearing their muffled titter as they headed along the hallway. He turned attention back to Perry. "Okay, I'm listening."

"That's all I know."

"That's it? Nothing about Greenside?"

It was Perry's turn to roll exasperated eyes. "Not everything is about your school." He laid out the information, reiterating Steve's complaints. Not a single maintenance request had been completed at the school over the summer—other principals voiced similar concerns. There were still piles of junk upstairs—alternate spaces or the labor to move it may not have been available. Capelli and Chow had supposedly intervened to assign Colin Redford to Greenside when he was clearly better suited for Oak Grove High—he may have simply pissed them off about something. Perry concluded his points. "And don't forget it was Tiny who claimed there was a geek squad touring the school during the summer." He sat back, satisfied with the summary.

"Why would a man would break into a school and crawl around in the duct work?"

"That alleged episode was also according to Tiny. Face facts Steve, the young man is prone to a bit of exaggeration." The HR man waved a hand, symbolically brushing the issues aside. "Forget about it, buddy. You always think Capelli is plotting to screw you." He leaned closer and stage-whispered. "I'm sorry to say this but I don't think Greenside or you are on her radar screen. She wants to be a renowned educational innovator. Little Greenside school is hardly the place to accomplish what she's after." He shrugged thin shoulders. "It's just a bunch of unconnected issues. Have a good weekend. Play golf, dig in the backyard dirt, forget about Capelli."

Steve nodded. "You're right. Sometimes that woman just gets in my head, usually when I'm here at the district office. When I'm home, she never enters my mind."

Saturday mornings usually began with quality time between cat and human. Charles knew when it was the weekend. The cat's big human servant moved more slowly and there was time for curling up and snuggling on the expansive lap.

Steve played Saturday golf with his usual foursome, none of whom were educators. As golfing buddies, the men rarely talked about their work lives. Normally a low-handicap player, Steve occasionally toyed with par and was in demand as a partner. It was not the beer and burger lunch prize that was important. It was bragging rights and the opportunity to trash-talk your hapless opponents.

"My man is on fire!" yelped Terrel Lewis gleefully as Steve's birdie putt on the third green made the distinctive mild thunk of ball meeting the bottom of the cup. Terrel was a former mining engineer, and like Steve, an ex-stock broker. He was the first instructor at the Namibian Mining College project that Steve's Meadowvale class had started five years previously. His wife's illness had forced the couple to return to Washington state and she had recently passed away. Terrel's book, *Confessions of a Corporate Citizen* had made the business best seller list. He was a free-lance journalist, focussing on corporate and investment issues. Though his attire frequently leaned toward bohemian, none of it was the consignment store variety. His was a cultivated look, casually and expensively avant-garde. He was competitive. On this Saturday he was enjoying a ride on Steve's four-over-par coattails and the free beer and burger that was the reward.

Steve spent Sunday watching baseball, brushing a reluctant Charles and puttering in the yard. Charles lolled on the backyard patio in the warm sunshine and peered vacantly at the big man dead-heading the potted geraniums and weeding the garden beds. It was one more week before the school year started and soon Steve would have little time for much else except school-related tasks.

Summer Martin returned from the folk festival mid-week, on the last day of August. She dropped into the school and poked her slender frame into Steve's office, catching him swearing at the computer. "Thanks for looking after my plants. You fattened Moonbeam up too. That better not have been the result of the Friday night pepperoni pizza you force down poor Charles' mouth. I don't want a cat addicted to junk food lolling around on my couch."

"Charles doesn't need much forcing to chomp a slice or two of pizza," countered Steve. "Don't worry, Gandhi was not a big junk food guy so pizza wouldn't be Moonbeam's food of choice." Summer seemed satisfied with the logic so Steve continued. "And Charles does not loll around. He is appropriately active for his age." Charles loved pepperoni pizza. Moonbeam did too, though Steve was not about to divulge that to Summer. He glanced up from the screen wearing a goofy grin. "Moonbeam and I bonded, both spiritually and gastronomically. That's all I'm going to say about that."

Summer eyed him suspiciously. "I heard you fell asleep at the administrators' Pro-D session."

"How do you know that? And I didn't fall asleep, I was in deep contemplation."

"You were snoring! Perry told me. He ducked into the room and you were having a snooze-fest. I don't blame you though. Sessions for teachers are just as boring, maybe worse. At the last conference I went to in Seattle some suit read from the slides as if we in the audience were illiterate. He had his jokes lined up at exact spots. Nothing was spontaneous. All the workshops were by companies like Majestic Publishing or A-1 Education. They weren't really workshops, they were sales presentations."

Rarely did Summer's passion blend into annoyance, though on this occasion she was straddling the edge.

Steve admitted that data-man had sent him into lullaby land.

"You didn't even golf in the admin tournament." She caught the questioning look. "Perry told me that too. He thought you were afraid of hitting Capelli in the ass again."

Narrowing eyes indicated a hint of principal displeasure. For a supposedly tight-lipped HR guy, Perry sure did a lot of yapping, especially with Summer.

The teacher gave no hint that she had noticed Steve's non-verbal signal. She resumed picking at the muffin crumbs dotting her white cotton skirt. "You could have aimed for Phil Chow this year," she said casually.

I never aim for anyone and . . ." he caught the broad grin. "Never mind, here are your house keys. Say hi to Moonbeam."

"Capelli was at the folk festival for a day," she blurted after slipping the keys into a batik-covered purse.

As with many conversations with Summer, topics flew hither and yon without any particular order. The rambling dialogue matched her fluid teaching style. Steve had significant doubts that Jennifer Capelli would attend a folk festival. Summer's thought processes were likely affected by consistent inhalation of herbal hallucinogens. When Summer explained that Capelli only seemed interested in a music session sponsored by a software company called A-1 Education, Steve altered his view. It would be just like Jennifer Capelli to attend a folk festival to enjoy the only computerized music demonstration. To her, the future of music would reside in the hard drives and monitors of a soon-to-be-developed machine.

Sensing Steve's lack of interest in the superintendent's choice of weekend entertainment, Summer smiled sweetly and skipped off to the library, almost bumping into a mother and her son entering the office. The boy watched, seemingly enraptured with Tiny repairing a display case in the nearby hallway. The glass shelves held a snarling model alligator, in honor of the school's "Greenside Gators" nickname. The short woman pulled the boy along, edged past Summer, and ignored secretary Bridget

McKenzie before standing in Steve's office doorway. A muffled snort and a roll of the eyes provided clear hints of what Bridget thought of the woman.

The words, "I'm Ms. Coolwater," was followed by extending a hand. She turned and waved the boy into the room. "This is my son River," she said proudly. A small lad shuffled nervously into the office. The boy's darting eyes caught quick glimpses of the office before deciding there was nothing of interest. He settled on gawking at the principal.

Steve introduced himself and offered seats. "Hello River," he said, flashing a smile. The boy nodded shyly and wiggled his rear end on the seat. "What grade are you going into?" asked Steve, guessing the third. The boy shrugged and began fidgeting. He shot an irritated glance at his mother before craning his neck around the open door to watch Tiny finish the task with the display case.

"River's been home-schooled," claimed Ms. Coolwater, "Haven't you?" she added, tweaking the boy's cheek as he awkwardly leaned away. "Don't be shy my little man."

The boy's countenance remained impassive. His feet continued to fidget.

"He's very bright, but he's learning disabled. He loves animals, don't you River?"

The boy stayed wooden-faced and silent.

Steve directed his question squarely at the child, hoping to elicit a response. "How old are you River?"

"He's nine years old," replied the mother. She opened a battered green purse, the vinyl scratched and marked. "I've got a birth certificate in here somewhere."

As Ms. Coolwater fumbled in her bag, Steve had an opportunity to gauge her son. He was short for his reported age, slightly pudgy with a pasty face. His legs were too long for his jeans and he had dark socks and worn runners. His T-shirt was white, though marked with food stains, likely gravy. The boy was studying Steve carefully as if trying to decide the level of trust he should grant.

Hauling the birth certificate from the purse, Ms. Coolwater handed the card to Steve. River had just had his ninth birthday and Steve suggested an age-appropriate placement of the fourth grade.

"Yes, that's fine," came the immediate response from the mother. Anticipating the next question, she stated, "We don't have a set address right now." She smiled thinly. Her lips were steady though her eyes flitted about. "I'm still looking around."

"Where are you staying?" asked Steve.

"With friends," she replied quickly. "I'm afraid I don't know their address and they just moved in so they don't have a phone."

Smiling with understanding, Steve responded, "Well, as soon as you have a permanent address, please let us know so we have an emergency contact. I'm not supposed to register you without one." He raised hands in mock surrender. "Our superintendent expects us to follow insurance company policies. Those guys rule the world, don't they?"

Rising in sync with mother and son, Steve whispered, "Could we have a quick private chat Ms. Coolwater?" He caught the elevated anxiety in her eyes. "Don't worry, River can sit behind the counter in the main office and Bridget will take good care of him." The mother nodded warily as Steve led River out and gave instructions to Bridget. The boy glanced nervously to his mother. She blew him a kiss as Steve closed his office door.

"Thank you. I think what I am about to say is a bit delicate so please do not take offense. I think there is another issue here that we should get on the table." He could sense the muscles tensing in the thin woman's body. Her eyes narrowed as she waited. "I think there is much more to River's background that the school needs to know." He stared at the mother. "That's true, isn't it?"

7

Ms. Coolwater's mouth dropped slightly before recovering. "How did you know?"

Sussing the truth had not been difficult. Most nine-year-old boys who had been home-schooled all their lives would gaze around the office in wonderment. Everything would be new. Yet River gave only a cursory look before realizing it was like all the other school offices he had seen. Ms. Coolwater had not challenged or questioned the grade placement, a common occurrence with home-schooling parents. Nor had she asked any questions about the school, having heard the same general introduction from several principals. She had anticipated that Steve would ask for an address, likely because she had faced the same question on numerous occasions. Even her fake answer seemed rote.

Ms. Coolwater rose and opened the office door. For a moment Steve thought she was going to take River and leave. Instead she smiled at her son, checking that he was fine. Satisfied, she closed the door and sat down again. Digging into her purse, she pulled a folded sheet of paper, a copy of River's record card. The boy had attended six schools in the last three years. The lowest absence year had been in first grade, with twenty-three days missing—the highest next year at forty-one days.

'You're wondering if I'm trying to stay one step ahead of social services so they don't apprehend River?'

Calmly, Steve's eyes looked up from the paper, "Are you?"

An edgy tone crept into Ms. Coolwater's voice, "If I was, what would you do?"

It was a strange question coming from a woman in her position. Steve did not hesitate. "I'd assume there would be a safety or care issue for River so I'd be on the phone to the authorities faster than you could blink." He gazed at the woman, wondering how she would respond. A moment passed, then several, before the mother's demeanor altered.

"My ex, Tom Golbeck, abused River physically, not sexually," she added quickly. "The guy is a jerk, especially when he's drunk, which is most of the time. He's been trying to grab River for a few years so we stay on the move."

"You have a restraining order?"

Another search in the purse revealed a crumpled document which she passed to the principal. Steve opened the door and asked Bridget to make three copies of the order—one for the office file, one for counselor Anne Shaw, and one for the classroom teacher, before returning to his chair.

Ms. Coolwater gave Steve a description of the father. It would be typed and pinned on the so- called "Rogue's List" posted, with an accompany photo, in the staffroom. "I don't have a case worker. This is a straightforward police and court matter." She paused. "The Women's Resource Center has a temporary contact number for me. If my ex finds out where we are and comes to the school I need to be informed. More importantly, phone the police and protect my son."

Promising he would do all he could for River, Steve watched mother and son depart before instructing Bridget to place the boy in Emma Martinez's fourth-grade class. Bridget was quick off the mark when registering new students. Keeping the rolls clean was a source of clerical pride. "I think you have an issue with the two new teachers, Redford and Martinez," she said. "They've been banging a table and yelling at each other since they arrived. There are some bad vibes there. I hope you brought some stronger happy-dust today. The stuff you sprinkled on them yesterday didn't last very long." She began pecking at her keyboard.

Colin and Emma had not met on Monday, hoping Steve could switch personnel for the training session. Finding no one else willing or available, the former lovers had started on Tuesday. Steve had been called in as a peacemaker. An hour later the two argued again, stomped off, and missed the rest of the day. They were scheduled for another attempt today, Wednesday. The start had not been smooth.

"Is there anything else before I go referee?" Steve remarked hopefully, looking at Bridget. With peppered hair, slightly wrinkled olive-toned skin and horn-rimmed glasses, Bridget McKenzie was of an indeterminate age, somewhere between forty and sixty. Short and stubby, she dressed in a professional if outdated manner. She favored skirts over slacks, blouses rather than T-shirts, pumps instead of sneakers. A stern yet fair emperor, she organized supplies, ordered material, provided first aid, and alternately welcomed and fended off parents. With her adult children living far from Greenside, she mothered Tiny, bringing the custodian baked goods and providing unsolicited fashion advice. Happy for the office freedom and responsibility, she was loyal to Steve, almost to a fault.

Bridget announced that the teacher supply packages would be ready for the afternoon, as would the package for the opening day staff meeting. The class lists were completed. Rarely using critical language, she referred to the new student records software program as, "Garbage." The software company, A-1 Education, was providing a two-hour workshop for the district's clerical staff on Thursday afternoon. "I don't know why we need such a massive program when we're just inputting and transferring student marks and records. Other parts of the software program are blocked. I'm sure this program can do a lot more than simply store student demographic and achievement records."

Steve tried to think of an appropriate response. Computerizing student records was not high on his interest scale. "That's what you get when you're an employee of the Taylerston School District," was the chosen retort, "The future is now."

"That's Capelli for you," snorted Bridget. Steve was the only person she allowed to hear her grousing about the superintendent. "That woman makes passionate love to computers."

Steve shook the unpleasant visual from his head before lumbering out the office doorway. He made his way to Colin's room, entering quietly. The two young teachers were glaring at each from across a scarred laminate table. "How's everything going?" he asked cheerfully.

"This is impossible," Emma stated flatly, scrunching her round face in a petulant scowl. Frustration seeped through her frumpy frame. "Colin's not listening to a thing I say."

"I am," spat Colin, "But you're the big show off, firing too much stuff at me. How'd you like it if I crammed differential calculus at you in two days? You'd feel pretty inept."

"You should feel inept, because you are."

"Whoa," said Steve, pulling up a chair. "This is getting a little too personal. Let's keep the insults on a professional level." He glanced at the two adversaries, the hostile edginess draining slowly from their faces. "Colin needs to learn a lot in a short time Emma. He needs you."

"He didn't need me when he started seeing that tramp, Marilyn," groused Emma.

"What about that gray-haired professor-guy, Doug?"

'What about him?"

It was a rare event when Steve displayed temper and even then, the theatrics were an act. Given the rare display, the desired outcome could occasionally be achieved. Suddenly rising, he tromped to the corner closet door. The sudden movement quieted the two teachers as they turned to stare at the principal. Steve opened the door and rifled through the stored junk. He fiddled with a gadget. Seemingly relieved, he hauled it out and carried it to the table. "Do you know what this is?" he snapped, clunking the black contraption on the table.

"I dunno," replied Colin glumly, gazing at the apparatus. "It looks like a speaker with some dials." He glanced at Emma for support, but she returned a baffled look and lifted heavy shoulders.

"This is a cassette tape recorder from the Cro-Magnon era. There's even a blank cassette in it and a built-in microphone on the side." He stared at the young teachers. "If you two don't stop whining and sniveling at each other like spoiled thirteen-year-old kids I'm going to begin taping the dialogue. Then I'm going to play it at the staff party."

"You wouldn't do that!" whined Colin. "That's illegal!"

"We'd go to the union, we'd grieve." echoed Emma.

Smiling with eerie intent, Steve pushed a button and watched as Emma and Colin leaned forward and peered through a narrow window. They spied two tiny circular disks turning in harmony. A soft whirr emanated from the machine. They looked up in unison at Steve's hard scowl. The man looked like he was used to grievances, probably lawsuits too. They turned and gazed at each other before Emma smiled and Colin nodded in agreement with the unspoken communication.

Emma said, "You can turn it off, we're okay."

Steve clicked the button.

Colin peered in the window to check that the whirling wheels had stopped.

"The biggest issue is probably Language Arts, am I right?" asked Steve quietly, returning to his normal persona.

Colin nodded miserably. "Emma knows how to teach kids to read. I don't have a clue. Even the English teachers at Oak Grove don't know." His look at Emma was a mixture of pity and desperation. "There's so much to learn," he moaned.

With the earlier tension dissipating, Steve asked Colin if he felt comfortable with putting Science and Social Studies in the hopper to be taught in October. "For now, you could do a map of the United States, states, cities and such, coloring, shading, like you did in the sixth-grade." He looked at the map rolled up and hooked onto the top edge of the blackboard. "Make sure the wall map has Hawaii as an insert, not all of them do."

"Is it okay to leave Science and Socials for that long?" he asked.

"It is for now," claimed Steve, quieting Emma with his eyes. "A few old-fashioned lessons never hurt anyone, eh Emma?" Not waiting for a reply, he added, "With some experience you'll learn to integrate some Science and Socials with Language Arts. That's for later, right Emma?" he asked, turning to her, working to keep her part of the support process.

Nodding with enthusiasm, she added, "I can show you some strategies for integrating subjects after you get your feet wet Colin."

"Thanks," the young man replied, relief flooding his countenance.

"Is Physical Education (PE) a problem?" asked Steve.

Colin shook his head, explaining he played basketball while in middle school.

The quick look of warning from Steve to Emma stopped her from a critical comment. "You might find teaching all children a full PE program quite different and a lot tougher than playing basketball," said Steve softly, "Isn't that right Emma?" again gradually drawing her in.

"Yeah, no kidding," agreed Emma with a smile, before adding, "You played soccer too, Colin. Start with that outside while the weather's good. I've got a list of games that encourage all kids to participate."

Steve asked Emma to concentrate on helping with Language Arts for the first week, assuming Colin would most easily adapt to teaching Math. She nodded and threw out a few suggestions for group novel study. Steve agreed that they were great choices—high interest-low vocab works that would slowly ease the students back into schoolwork. Emma said she had some activity sheets for all three novels.

"Don't all the kids read the same book?"

"There will be a wide range of reading ability. That's why I use three different books, each with separate activities. These groups are called Lit Circles and here's some quick ideas to get you started," explained Emma softly. First you…"

Rising from the chair Steve looked at the two, Emma patiently explaining with Colin alternating between listening and staring at his former lover-turned-colleague. Their anger was gone, replaced by a silent connection that was difficult to place. "Are we good here now?" he asked.

"Yeah," replied Colin, pulling his eyes away from Emma. "We're good." He turned back to face her and smiled softly. "I knew coming to Greenside was the right thing to do."

A departing Steve needed to shift mental gears. Admin work could be a roller coaster ride with a successful conclusion to one episode quickly followed by a new and frustrating challenge.

Supervisor Lou Tayler, master bureaucrat, arrived mid-morning. It was his first and likely last visit to Greenside for the year. He was a member of the pioneering Tayler clan. His short, slender frame carried a thin head topped by a comb-over hairstyle of wispy dark hair. August heat caused no respite from the white polyester dress shirts and navy bowties that were his sartorial trademark. Joan Mackenzie claimed the man bore a resemblance to the Dilton Doily character from the Archie comic book series. She once brought an old, crumpled issue to show Steve. He had to agree.

Lou had been mercilessly teased and taunted as a child. Bullying behavior, as negative as it was, was hardly an activity born in the new millennium. Desperate to please everyone, Lou learned to articulate opinions and then alter them as the wind blew. The ideal bureaucrat, he avoided responsibility for anything. The perfect education official, he had surfed on dozens of instructional waves, flipping like a fish floundering on a boat deck. Each new innovation shot to center stage with Lou blowing the fanfare trumpet so many times his lips were blue.

Steve had complained to Lou on several occasions last year about the piles of discarded material crammed in boxes and stored on the upstairs floor. The information had been deftly handled by the supervisor. Nothing had been done and no promises made. Renewing the assault, Steve informed Lou of the recent conversation with Jennifer Capelli which drew the reluctant Lou to Greenside.

"Hey, the hallway has been swept," Lou declared after using his key to open the door at the top of the stairs that led to the second story. He removed his fogged glasses, revealing squinting eyes that resembled coin slots on a vending machine. He wiped perspiration from an oily forehead. The stairs had been a physical challenge. Even Steve managed the ascent better.

"Maybe Tiny has a key," Steve offered. "He knew you were coming. He probably wanted to clear a path through the dust."

"I am allergic to the stuff," muttered Lou, still wheezing, still squinting.

A concerned Steve stared at the struggling Lou before leading him to the first classroom door and slowly pushing it ajar.

'I don't see any cats," Lou stated. The glasses were back in place and the wheezing had slowed. Lou's interest in what lay before him in the room apparently trumped his physical suffering. The timorous head peeked into the room and thin eyes peered into the shadows. "I don't hear any mice scurrying around either."

Steve had not seen any mice since he had returned to work. He had not seen any felines either, except the snarling Thor and Xena that Tiny had whisked away. The damn cats had vacated the space just when he needed them most. "There's still a lot of junk in these rooms Lou. It's got to be moved. Believe me, there are feral cats and marauding mice around here. They think the place is the Ritz. Four old classrooms are crammed with junk. At the very least this has to be a fire hazard."

"Yeah," said Lou thoughtfully. "You've got a problem." He grabbed one of the books from a discarded reading series. "Hey Steve, remember these?" he asked wistfully, flipping the pages. Dust wafted airborne, sending Lou into a sneezing fit, his eyes watering. "I always thought they were good. I wonder why we trashed them."

Steve was not to be sidetracked, a particular skill of Lou's. "What do you mean, I've got a problem?"

Plunking the book onto the pile and closing the cardboard box, Lou shrugged bony shoulders. "You're the site supervisor. It's your school, handle it."

"C'mon Lou, don't give me that crap. I was told the upper floor was a district site and responsibility." He poked a finger in Lou's scrawny chest. "Jennifer said you're the guy to talk to. I'm tired of chasing crazy cats and raucous rodents."

Lou flashed his trademark understanding and sympathetic smile that usually accompanied a blunt refusal.

Steve hated that look. He knew what was coming.

"No can do, Mr. Hepting. I'm the instructional supervisor. Jen only told you that I was to make sure that the district did not throw out any books of value. I can't do that unless they're cleaned. That's a job for the maintenance department. If there are any cats and mice up here and maintenance won't help you, then you might want to check with the health and safety people." He paused. "Hmm, health and safety personnel are part of the maintenance department. Yes, I can see you have quite a conundrum here Steve."

"Bugger that," responded Steve. Pinning Lou Tayler down was like trying to nail Jell-O to a wall. "Jennifer said she didn't know this stuff was here. Now that she does, something will be done. She'd go nuts if the media got a hold of this. I might just let those jackals know. It would get the issue on the table and out into the open."

Unlike in his teen years, Lou was not easily cowered, especially by those with less authority on the adult totem pole. "There's more going on than you realize, Steve." He jabbed a bony finger at the principal. "I would not make an issue out of this," he said ominously. "I know Jennifer well and she would not be happy if you went to the media. It would put a big dent in her pet project."

Steve stared. Project? what pet project? He let an awkward silence fall, intended to wheedle additional information. Lou was not easily fooled. The damn supervisor appeared unfazed, apparently comfortable with the quiet standoff. Steve realized he needed to take his case to the phantom-like Phil Chow, the Business Manager; a mysterious form lurking in the shadows of the Capelli beacon. He exhaled audibly. "Let's go back downstairs Lou. You've made your point. You're not the guy I need to see."

Happy with another deft dodge of responsibility, a smiling Lou followed Steve down the stairs, the descent much easier on his lungs and legs. At the bottom, he said, "I should welcome that new teacher to your school, then be on my way. His name is Colin Redford, isn't it?"

Steve nodded. "Yeah, and there's another new one, Emma Martinez.

"Hmm, yes, but I only need to talk to Mr. Redford," Lou said with odd overtone.

One last attempt to suss something important from Lou was worth a try. "Is there a connection between Colin Redford and Jennifer or Phil Chow?" probed Steve.

"I don't engage in gossip or discussions about personal relationships," stated Lou, the tone strangely sharp.

"Does that mean there is a relationship?"

"Must I repeat myself? I don't engage in discussions of that kind," Lou sniped before turning abruptly and striding along the hallway. After a few moments he realized he did not know where Redford's classroom was located.

"Room 12," yelled Steve since Lou still seemed lost. "Tiny will take you there. He's just around the corner." It was a long shot but Steve hoped that Tiny would be able to gather some information about why the supervisor needed to talk to Colin Redford but not Emma Martinez.

8

It took a few moments for Steve to decompress from the discussion with Lou Tayler. He grumbled his way through an hour worth of paperwork before a late morning tussle with another central office official. "I know the budget is tight. I can read the emails from Phil Chow as well as anyone else. But I sure as hell can't have one paraprofessional working with Jay Woznicki and three other students. Another special needs kid walked in the door yesterday, a fourth-grade boy, River Coolwater. His mom says he's learning disabled." Steve waited patiently for the anticipated response. "I know he's not been tested yet," he groused. Squeezing the phone to release tension, he rolled his eyes skyward as he listened to the woes of the district's Special Education department, swamped as they were with so many more special needs children per capita in 2011 than previous decades. Steve had witnessed children displaying standard mischief who were labeled as suffering from "Maladjusted Behavior." Dark, hidden motives supposedly were at the root of such misconduct. Lobbying ensued for increased support. Additional staffing was clearly required to cope with the alarming tsunami that threatened the safety of other children.

Steve had difficulty keeping up-to-date with the list of special designations from which he could choose. A churlish, insolent student could have "Authority Sensitivity Syndrome," or ASS. Two six-year-old boys comparing penises could be suffering from SOT, "Sex Organ Transference." Horny thirteen-year-olds needed help to combat their HI, "Hormone Intoxication."

"When am I going to hear back from you?" Steve grimaced at the glacial decision-making. "Really, you don't know? Okay, who does know? You don't know that either. The budget is so tight Capelli or Chow may have to be involved in any decisions regarding increases in paraprofessional allocations." Weary of repeating the lines, Steve huffed an ornery conclusion and slammed the receiver into its cradle. He turned and blushed as Anne Shaw stood in the doorway.

"Problems?" asked the counselor quietly.

"You are very perceptive Ms. Shaw," grumbled Steve. "You must be a mental health professional."

"No, I'm just a run-of-the-mill counselor. One who has a boss with apparent issues with nasty phone receivers." She nodded toward the innocuous gadget perched on Steve's desk surrounded by a jumble of papers. "Are you having a bad day? Has that mean phone been bullying you again?"

Steve quickly warmed to the banter. He waved off the sarcasm with a thin smile and a chuckle. "Everybody's picking on me Ms. Shaw," he joked. "I need help."

"You're likely far beyond any help I can give Mr. Hepting, but I'll do the best I can."

Smiling broadly, the principal and counselor exchanged a hug and summer-event pleasantries. A thick torso and average height could have made Anne appear hefty, but heeled shoes, a thin face, and spiked dark-brown hair made her appear taller than she really was. She had a ski-bum male friend in Taylerston. His love of 1990s Nirvana and everything Kurt Cobain led to Anne adopting the music. The couple performed in a local band, Wild Strut, the music merging contemporary ski and surf frolic with old-style Seattle grunge. The group only played gigs in the summer, and as far away from Taylerston as possible. Steve had seen snippets of a video and could not believe it was his thirty-something counselor cradling the mike.

"We were going to go through the class lists?" Anne said expectantly.

"Right, yeah, this is a good time."

Class placements were the single most important decision at the school. Just as the right mix could help promote a positive year, the wrong one could spell disaster. There were formulas for the total number of children as well as the type of child assigned. The few normal students—not special learners, not gifted, not behaviorally challenged, not economically disadvantaged, not hyperactive, not uber-lethargic, not a slow learner, and not a fast one either, were awarded one point. All other children counted for more points, depending on the severity of the disadvantage. Any allocated paraprofessional time affected the total, at times dropping the individual student score back to one.

Steve and Anne worked through the scoring system for each class. The principal was required to prove that all had been done to achieve a balanced score for every teacher. As with most systems based solely on numbers, the end result always seemed unfair. Some teachers wore their class point totals like badges of honor, making staffroom proclamations of high totals just under the limit provided in the collective agreement. A few grumbled privately that their point total made for a far more challenging class than that of a colleague with a higher accumulation.

"Is there a normal kid in this school?" muttered Steve, staring at the piles of paper.

Anne had an unusually high level of common sense, especially for a counselor. She replied with gusto as she rifled through a class list. "Of course," she stated. "There are eighteen unlabeled kids in the Kindergarten group alone and there are only twenty in the entire class."

"We haven't got around to poking and prodding the little gomers yet. After the K screening with the Speech and Language, Hearing Impaired, Visually Impaired, K-Readiness, Aboriginal Heritage, and Behavior Therapy people, we'll have ten kids labeled before the new calendar year."

"You exaggerate," Anne soothed, tugging at her black T-shirt. "There will be labels on only three or four of the Kindergarten kids by Christmas." She held out a hand to shake, as if concluding a deal. Warily, Steve stared at her strikingly thin face and intoxicating dark hair. Her black eyes, wide as saucers, danced with the challenge. "A bottle of wine on it," she said firmly.

"You're on," spouted the principal, oozing confidence. He pointed a finger at the valued staff member and with mock derision said, "I don't want any of that sweet syrupy plonk all you young people drink. I want a real bottle of wine!"

Grinning with glee, Anne revealed that the Special Education department had three specialists on stress leave. The Kindergarten screenings were going to take much longer than normal. The final totals would not be ready until well into the new calendar year.

"After Christmas? You're kidding!" Steve's eyes narrowed in mock accusation. "You withheld vital information. That's unfair!" He stared at Anne, barely suppressing a smile. "Counselors shouldn't cheat."

"And principals shouldn't snivel! You're the big boss. You're supposed to know what's going on. If not, too bad. A deal's a deal!"

It was one wager Steve would be pleased to lose despite his continued fake grousing for a time. His office door now open, he spotted the janitor walking by and called him back. "Tiny, have you been going upstairs?"

Big feet shuffled. The wide neck sent a round head to face Anne Shaw as if the clever counselor could think up a quick and believable reply. But she was sending a surprised look at Mr. H instead. There was no point in scrunching his face to drum up a good answer. Thinking was not going to help him out of this mess. He had broken the rules and now he was caught. "I'm sorry Mr. H., I was bad," he said as he lowered his head.

"What did you do?"

The feet stopped moving. "The cats go up there at night. I check on them to make sure they're okay." The work boots renewed their little slide across the floor.

Familiar with Tiny's non-verbal signals, Steve probed, "There's more to this story, isn't there?"

"Well, I did bring some books down for Ms. Mackenzie. They're real old and I had to wipe the dust off them first, and . . ."

"Those are just some of those old phonics books Steve, what's the big deal?" It was Anne, reacting to Tiny's distress as a counselor would, coming to the young man's defense. "Who cares if Tiny checks on the cats. They should not be there in the first place. If the district isn't going to do anything about it, and the cats are not bothering the kids when school starts, who cares?"

Tiny jumped in, eager to help. "They'll stay upstairs during the day like they did last year. They only come out at night to hunt the mice."

Steve groaned, tiring of Tiny's tales of felines and rodents. He agreed with Capelli—the cats and mice would depart when the maintenance department moved the junk from the second-story rooms. After a moment of staring at Tiny's perturbation, Steve's resolve softened. "Okay, let's make a deal. I don't want to hear anything more about cats and mice unless they're bothering the kids or teachers when school starts. How does that sound?"

Tiny beamed and gushed, "Cool, thanks Mr. H." Suddenly he turned serious as another thought slid into his brain. "Are you going to tell the police about the little man in the vents?"

Anne fired a perplexed look at Steve. What the hell was Tiny talking about?

"I don't think so," said Steve, ignoring Anne's unspoken question. "I might let Mr. Chow know about it." He focused on the young man's face to ensure Tiny understood the next statement. "If you see that man again around the school make sure you come and see me right away."

"Okay, Mr. H." agreed Tiny. "Can I go now and tell one of the kids the good news about the animals? He's been mega-worried." The contorted face meant that once again Tiny's mouth had opened before his brain was engaged.

"What kid?" Steve asked. Watching Tiny withhold information was painful. The feet shuffled, legs shuddered, the face scrunched. Not wanting to cause the young man any more distress, Steve said, "Never mind, just tell that one kid who's really worried and then keep it a secret, okay?"

"Okay, Mr. H." He caught Steve's nod and hustled out, heading down the hallway eager to spread the good news.

"Who's the kid?" asked Anne.

"I don't know, could be anyone I suppose."

"Who's the little man in the vents?"

"I don't know. Tiny might have been mistaken. It's a crazy story that I'm not sure really happened."

"You're right on top of things around here aren't you?" Anne's remark came with a chuckle and a broad grin.

"Ooh, that's a real hit to my self esteem, and coming from a counselor no less. I'm gonna show you who's boss and exercise some decisive leadership. I've got an important task to complete right now so let's meet after lunch."

"Eating out with Summer again?" Anne jabbed.

"An appointment awaits," he said mysteriously and left with a grin, leaving Anne to wonder what the hell he was talking about.

The Baker View golf course was located just off the main road about half-way between Greenside and Taylerston. Steve was a member and had spied potential first-day garb on sale in the pro shop after the Saturday round. He could not browse this apparel with his golfing mates. He was aiming for childish and tacky. Being non-educators, they just would not understand.

Since he started teaching, Steve always wore one, two, or even three new articles of clothing on the first day of school. Students were challenged to guess what they were. At Greenside the winning name was pulled from a giant jar. The student received a poster provided by a local bargain store. Kindergarten students had gradual entry and would not be in school for the first few days so they were not involved in the contest. The new Kindergarten students really did not know much about school at all. For the next few months, they were clueless as to why they were being dropped off at this strange building every day. Returning children would be the ones anticipating the silly contest. Even the middle-school students were eager participants. For some reason it had become kitschy-hip to be guessing the new duds adorning Mr. H.'s large frame. It promised to be old-man fashion that was decidedly uncool.

"Is that clothing you had on sale on Saturday still here?" asked Steve as he surveyed the pro-shop filled with more golf attire than equipment. The golf pro pointed to a rack at the rear. "It's been on sale for months." She flashed a hopeful smile. "We've got a bunch of shirts in your size Steve, and a few Tiger Woods belts too. You'd get a further markdown on those." She pointed to a nearby display. "I can give you a real deal on one of those ties. I brought them in for Christmas presents last year."

"Not a big seller then?"

She shrugged. "They're still here."

Steve looked at the scarlet neck accessory. The design comprised a white tee holding up a black golf club resting on a golf green. It was signed by Tiger Woods, the embattled athlete, recently more famous for carnal escapades than golfing prowess. His current unpopular status and the hideous design helped explain the minimal sales.

"Buy one and I'll throw in a second of a different color."

"You've got more?"

"Oh yeah. I've got more," the pro said glumly.

Steve flipped through the ties, debating between them and the purchase of a more standard polo shirt. "They're pretty ugly."

Watching with bemused interest, the pro offered a suggestion, pointing to a second sale rack of black and navy long sleeve cotton mock-necks with a white 'V' down the middle. A black bowtie was printed at the neck. "Those are on an end-of-summer sale. They have a loose fit."

"You mean they'll cover my gut?"

The pro shrugged, watching the principal's heavy walk to the rack.

"No wonder you haven't sold any of these," commented Steve, pulling one of the shirts. "This looks like a T-shirt version of a tux, and the little bow tie design is stupid. I'll look like a penguin."

The pro shrugged again before deciding to speak. "It's in a slimming dark color. You'll be a thinner penguin."

Ten minutes later Steve carried out two double extra-large cotton mock-necks with bow-tie designs, one black and one navy. He snagged a cream-colored Tiger Woods belt and laid down his Visa card. During the return drive to the school he contemplated changing into one of the new shirts to surprise Bridget and counselor Anne. He chose to refrain. A new parent could register a child. An initial meeting with a principal seemingly determined to win an ugly shirt contest may not project a proper initial image. He was, after all, the principal. If the parents regarded him as the guy in charge of his school, who was he to upset that fantasy?

Settling in for the afternoon meeting, Anne watched as Steve was unable to keep a goofy grin off his face. "You bought your first day garb, didn't you?" she said. "That was your mysterious appointment."

"Maybe."

"It's more goofy than last year isn't it?"

"It's more formal than usual," admitted Steve, "My lips are sealed. You will have to wait and see me on the first day, like everyone else."

Anne launched into a mock frenzy of pleading for a preview for five seconds before shifting the conversation to the topic at hand. Steve grumbled and groused as he and the counselor began working the numbers linked to the class lists. It was not long before Anne gathered up the papers. "I'll take these class lists to my office. I know this type of work is not your favorite task."

"Thanks Annie. I owe you one."

"If that's an offer for another bottle of wine, then I accept."

"You are very perceptive Ms. Shaw," Steve replied, before shifting to a serious tone and Greenside's most disabled student, Jay Woznicki. The boy's age put him in the sixth grade, but there was no educational significance to the placement since it was not likely he would ever come close to approaching grade-level. Compounding Jay's challenges was a muscular disorder that impeded his coordination. With a slightly misaligned face, extremely slow speech, and off-kilter gait, Jay was a poster child for special needs.

"Are you going call his mom about paraprofessional time being stretched?" asked Anne, glad she was the counselor and not the head honcho.

"Yeah, I'll tell her we're working on it. I'm more concerned about the new teacher for that class, Colin Redford, and how he's going to handle Jay." He caught Anne's puzzled look that requested more information. "He's a high school Math guy who has probably never seen a student like Jay." Steve smiled. "I guess I can work with Jay sometimes."

"You guys were cute last year," Anne said, grinning. "I think the boy's got you wrapped around his little finger." Anne flashed a hundred-watt smile. She waved the stack of papers, clutched in her right hand. "Remember about that bottle of wine," she said and headed off.

Steve sat alone in his office. With Anne looking over the class lists there was little for him to do except ponder the fond memories of last year's rituals with Jay Woznicki.

9

While Steve was not supposed to be providing sugary treats, the jelly-jar game had improved Jay Woznicki's counting and fine motor skills. While jelly beans were nutritionally suspect, they were a mighty motivator to a ten-year-old boy. The meetings had a distinct pattern. After a happy verbal greeting the duo would move to physical gestures, starting with a finger-flick, followed by a knuckle-knock, and finishing with an elbow-edge. Then Steve and Jay would work the jelly jar.

Jay would choose either numbers or colors to commence the ritual. If numbers, Steve would hold fingers upward and Jay had to remove that number of jelly beans while counting out loud. It was remarkable how such a simple game had improved the boy's numeracy and finger dexterity.

If Jay chose colors, Steve grabbed a jelly bean and Jay had to name the color. A correct answer entitled him to two similarly colored beans. After a time, Steve taught Jay synonyms for popular colors and Jay was required to use scarlet instead of red, or ebony rather than black. Steve had spent several Saturday's hunting for more esoterically colored treats. After two weeks of success, Jay received a poster for his bedroom wall. A local bargain store had supplied Steve with dozens of posters and he used them as prizes for all manner of competitions and games.

Bridget popped her head into the office. "Jay's mom is on the line. Do you want to take it?"

"Yeah," replied Steve, his mind coming back to the present, "I was just going to call her."

Explaining the situation about stretching the available paraprofessional time, Steve emphasized that he had requested additional support and that no decision from the district office had been reached. Mrs. Woznicki asked if it would help if she called the Special Education department. Tempted by the thought of the tenacious Mrs. Woznicki tackling the bureaucrats, Steve decided to calm the waters. "I'll let you know if I need any help but I think we can manage for the first bit."

Trust resembled deposits in the bank and Steve had an impressive account with Mrs. Woznicki. "Okay, Mr. Hepting," she said. She always referred to him as Mr. Hepting rather than Steve. "I'm available if you need any help."

The remainder of the week was smooth. Bridget whined about the new A-1 software. The volatile lovebirds Emma and Colin fought, kissed, and made up, then renewed their conflict. Summer changed the jungle-theme in the library to a marine-inspired space as a favor to Steve who was to act as the teacher-librarian when the school year started.

Tiny made yet another suggestion regarding a supposedly hot stock called Amazon. According to him, the electronic retailer had a slow start since its inception in 1997 but was starting to make buckets of money. Occasionally Steve missed the investment world, especially when listening to Tiny's latest trading triumph. The young supposedly dim-witted janitor was a natural at picking winner stocks. He rode Research-in-Motion stock to the summit and sold it before it crashed. He had hopped on the Apple Computer train early and never disembarked.

Despite the advice, Steve chose not to put any money into Amazon, a company that sold merchandise but didn't have a storefront.

Tiny repaired the fence surrounding the primary playground one evening. He also overhauled the toilet's automatic flush system in the primary wing restrooms, work that had not been completed via the official summer maintenance requests. Tiny was particularly enamored with the system, spending several after-work hours ensuring it was operating properly. The automatic flush system seemed magical to the average primary-aged child which, according to Steve, explained Tiny's seeming obsession. From predicting the vagaries of high-tech stocks to child-like fascination with automatically flushing toilets, Tiny's behavior frequently displayed surprising twists and turns that confounded "normal" adults.

The Friday before school started was often frenetic and frenzied. This was likely why the state government chose that day to make its annual education pronouncement, the tone of which had altered over the years. The current trend was to target specific topics, ranging from exceedingly dull to controversial. If dull, the press would at least provide some air time on the first day of school on Tuesday. If controversial, the media would often use the material over the Labor Day weekend, a notoriously slow period for news except for reports of car pileups and traffic jams.

This year the topic-at-hand was animals in schools.

In the previous school year there had been three incidents that had garnered a prodigious level of publicity. Firstly, a guard dog had been brought into a class by a ninth-grade student as part of an animals-who-work unit of study. Unmuzzled, the dog had chomped on the teacher's hand, causing a worker's compensation claim from the teachers' union. In considerable pain, the teacher had yelped an instinctive, "Aw fuck," in front of his students, prompting a public debate about whether the use of such language was justified under the circumstances. Whether the teacher lacked judgment, brains, or both in allowing a guard dog in the class unmuzzled provided fodder for those old-fashioned citizens who wrote letters to a newspaper editor. The more tech-savvy people used the relatively new opinion cauldron called twitter.

Later in the year, a large iguana escaped from a cage in a counselor's office. Searching for water, it located the mother-lode in the boy's restroom. Holed up in a toilet, it was an unwelcome surprise for a child using the facility. Unhurt though shaken, the boy used the flush mechanism. The clever lizard clung to the toilet edge as the water swept away and the bowl re-filled. The boy snatched the slippery reptile and proudly displayed it as he ran down the hallway, enjoying the shrieks from fleeing girls. That he boasted of snatching the reptile from inside a toilet bowl added to the mayhem. Questions surfaced as to why a counselor would keep a large iguana in her office and then allow it to escape without reporting the disappearance. More citizens wrote letters to various editors. More tweets hit social media.

Near the end of the school year, a previously pleasant tabby cat had been brought into a classroom by a first-grade student for a show-and-tell session. It escaped from the arms of the owner and launched its claws toward the class pet, Herman the Hamster. Not used to anything beyond the cuddling and cooing of the soft hands and hearts of little humans, Herman was unprepared for the hissing, clawing, and snarling from a ferocious feline. Not gifted with a big brain, Herman failed to realize the cage would protect him. Not endowed with a strong constitution, the hamster's heart halted in mid-beat. Herman swayed for a moment before rolling over, dead. The mortified children required a troupe of grief counselors. Why a school would allow so many innocent children to be traumatized by witnessing the tragic passing of a beloved pet was a serious question that begged for an answer. A flood of citizen-penned letters flowed into the inboxes of newspaper editors and angry tweets dominated the social media grapevine.

Calling to Bridget, Steve asked, "How do I forward this government announcement to the teachers?"

Stifling a chuckle at the ineptitude, Bridget entered, leaned over the computer and tapped a few keys. Standing back, she said, "There, now everyone's got a copy, including me."

Steve leaned back and clicked the open button for the email. Being a missive from the government, there was a distinct possibility it would be on the goofy side. Steve wanted to read it carefully and make sure that he understood what it said.

Today the Governor announced that school districts will be required to develop policies restricting animals from the following list, including, but not limited to, school classrooms, hallways, offices, libraries, gymnasiums, storage rooms, boiler rooms, closets, cupboards, electrical rooms, parking lots, playgrounds, and any school activities, wherever and whenever held. Given recent serious incidents compromising student safety, the government has determined that timely comprehensive action is required.

Animals are defined as any non-plant-like entity that is not a human being. The only exception to any policy shall be licensed visual assistance dogs formally linked to certified visually impaired students with permit papers filed in the school office.

The announcement continued. Waivers would be required for any field trips to locales that housed animals, including zoos, aquariums, and even fish hatcheries. Steve groaned. Was there really a need for children to be protected from spawning salmon taking a break from laying eggs to turn into man-eating marine monsters? Demonstrating what they defined as reasonable, government officials were giving school districts until January 31 of the following calendar year to submit comprehensive policies to the Education Department in Olympia for review.

"They must have heard about our mice and cats," Bridget remarked after reading the release.

"Yeah, vicious creatures that they are. At least we don't have skunks."

"Yech, I hate those things," muttered Bridget. "I'd take our yearly encounters with bears before I had to deal with skunks."

A chuckling Steve responded as he scrawled a note to add the animal ban to the opening day staff meeting agenda. "Nothing is worse than ornery guinea pigs," he said. "Joan brought one in last year and the carnage was horrible." The new restrictions were not likely to be well received. They promised to be the highlight controversy for the year. "C'mon Bridget, everything is done. Let's knock off a bit early and enjoy the long weekend before the hordes arrive on Tuesday."

Sweeping a hand across an immaculate desk top, Bridget grabbed her purse and followed her boss out the door, happy to join him and leave the school behind.

Steve always played a round of golf on the Saturday of the Labor Day weekend. Enjoying another victory beer with Terrel Lewis, he spied Jennifer Capelli and Phil Chow having lunch with two impressively coiffed men. They were dressed in classic golf attire, down to the little alligators on the breast of their polo shirts. Steve smiled and raised his glass in acknowledgment. Chow issued a nod in return. Capelli did too, hers quick and stern.

On Sunday Steve always watched football. On Labor Day Monday, he left early and took the two-hour journey south on Interstate 5 to Tacoma. His mother lived in a senior's home in a low-rent district a mile from the freeway. Monique's planned visit to the Aquarium in Vancouver BC had quashed any ideas of spontaneous Labor Day romance. She was investigating the logistics of taking her class on a "Sleeping with the Whales" field trip early in the school year before the idiocy of the government's animal announcement took hold.

Steve left the multi-tasking Charles, who was busy sleeping and shedding hair at the same time. He quietly filled the food dish and made sure the litter box was clean. The big furball was fastidious about personal hygiene. In early Monday sunshine Steve started the engine of his SUV, a box with wheels. The vintage red Camaro, the last physical remnant of the stock broker days, had finally succumbed to the automobile equivalent of a heart attack. Steve's large-framed, forty-year plus body made exiting and entering the car challenging. Now principal-practical and teacher-frugal, Steve chose a Sports Utility Vehicle. The roomy interior could handle his bulk in the front and golf clubs in the back. He had not spent much time searching for the vehicle, since all the bulbous SUV's looked similar. He chose the royal-blue color so the vehicle would stand out from the sea of silver in a mall parking lot. The dealer asked if he wanted Bluetooth or USB interface and had received a numbed wooden-faced stare in return. A DVD player was as tech-laden as the vehicle was going to be.

Steve gorged on George Michael and ABBA music as the SUV ate up the miles. There was nothing like sugary pop to enhance the blood flow on an early morning drive. He arrived at his brother's 1960s split-level house well before noon. Steve and his brother, Peter, were close. Ribald, testosterone-fueled back-slapping sports talk was punctuated with serious communication. Their father had abandoned the family when Steve was six and Peter, two. Raised by a single parent, there had been very little money. The brothers played sports in a public school, borrowed books from the public library, and played in a nearby public park. They received government scholarships and bursaries to enter and continue at university. Public enterprise had been kind to the Hepting brothers and they had reciprocated. Steve was a public-school principal and Peter a mid-level manager in a Tacoma probation office.

Probation officers shared many of the same character traits as teachers—caring, passionate, and involved with people. Like teachers they were relatively disinterested in finances, both on a macro and individual level. Conversation at parties never turned to the stock market or personal wealth. Like most of his colleagues, Peter's major investment decision was beefing up the savings account before devoting a small amount to a conservative mutual fund comprising corporate behemoths such as Microsoft, Chevron, and Bank of America.

For years the brothers had contributed evenly to their mother's rent and paid half the monthly cost of the government-subsidized, assisted-living residence. The ailing mother was ecstatic when Peter delivered the news that Belinda, six years younger at thirty-one, was expecting their first child. A celebration was held at a local restaurant and Steve's mother drained two glasses of Shiraz which sent her to sleep on the short return trip to her residence.

Returning to Peter's house, the siblings had time for a brief catch-up chat. Steve had never mentioned Summer Martin and kept the relationship conversation linked to a possible re-connect with Monique. Peter had liked her and believed that Steve's money-grubbing stock market addiction to have been the catalyst for the break-up. "Don't screw-up this time," he said bluntly. "And now that you're a big shot principal don't become one of those pencil-pushing, control-freak bureaucrats. If you do, I'm gonna have to kick your ass." Taller and leaner, Peter was in much better physical condition than his flabby brother. "You don't have to act like a tough-ass shithead to impress Monique or to be a good supervisor."

"Do I look like a tough-ass shithead?"

"You look like Yogi Bear, but I think you get my point. Don't try to emulate that power-mad boss of yours, Capelli." Peter gulped his beer while Steve, having enjoyed a glass of wine at lunch, had a long drive ahead and was alcohol free. "Is power-woman still the same?"

"Oh yeah," muttered Steve, "Maybe worse. She's working on some pet project that is being kept top secret. She's a superintendent of a public-school district who sometimes thinks she's running the CIA. The intrigue is almost comical. It's probably nothing more than a shiny coat of paint on a well-worn hobby horse. Repackaging old ideas to make them look new happens all the time in education. Not even Capelli can budge a massive public enterprise more than a fraction of an inch. There's an inertia thing happening that corresponds to some physics law I can't remember."

"Well bro, the only advice I've got is to stay away from Capelli and get closer to Monique."

"No argument there," Steve declared as he said his goodbye. "I'll be back in October, my treat on the Thanksgiving lunch. Thanks for dropping by to see mom every week." He held out a hand. "Congratulations on the news about the baby. My little brother's gonna be a dad. That's pretty cool."

With late summer sunshine wrapping the vehicle, Steve returned to Taylerston listening to his favorite Andrew Lloyd Webber musical, *Phantom of the Opera*. Peter's impending fatherhood and the musical's homage to romance combined to focus Steve's thoughts on Monique. The steps they had taken to rekindle the relationship were tentative at best. He was unsure how she felt. She had been cautious, almost wary, preferring a glacial approach at *rapprochement*. She needed to see that Steve was no longer the overgrown adolescent that he had once been. She needed to know he was a mature professional ready to commit to a relationship.

The arrival home in the evening moved thoughts of Monique to the sidelines and transferred focus to the opening of school the next morning. The trip to Tacoma had helped clear a cluttered mind of the detritus of school affairs. Were the class lists completed with as evenly distributed point scores as possible? What could be done to stretch the paraprofessional time to ensure River Coolwater and Jay Woznicki received the assistance they deserved? Where had the damn cats gone when he had showed Lou Tayler the junk-filled rooms? What happened to the mice that were scurrying about the school last year? The questions went further, from the minor issue of wayward animals to more problematic ones of unpredictable humans. How often would he have to intervene to calm the volatile relationship between the sparkplug Emma Martinez and the soft-spoken Colin Redford? What was Capelli's pet project and who were the two guys playing golf with her and Chow on Saturday afternoon?

The questions swirled in Steve's head as he struggled for solid slumber, not unusual for the night before the start of school. With almost no sleep, Steve should have been tired and grumpy in the morning. Yet his demeanor was the opposite, cheery and vibrant. Stepping sprightly out the front door and squinting from the glare of another sunny day, he made his way to his SUV. He fired the ignition. Though not a fan, he slipped in a Beatles CD. The Liverpool group was ancient history to him, breaking up the year he was born. But the "Get Back" McCartney rocker was always apropos for the first day of school. Steve joined in, warbling, "Get back, get back, get back to where you once belonged." He glanced at the plastic bag on the front seat holding his first-day goofy garb. The kids would love it!

Steve wore his standard golf shirt and khakis into the school and planned to change into the special outfit during the day. Though there was no teacher dress code, attire mimicking a giant penguin would be noticed. Steve wondered what action he would take if a teacher wore a T-Shirt with a picture of a pot plant on the front. What could he do if one wore a tank top with a "Beer – It's Not Just For Breakfast Anymore" slogan? What was the appropriate response if a female paraprofessional arrived with a ripped sweatshirt revealing swaths of shoulder and chest flesh? He knew what Capelli would expect. Did he have the guts to take such action?

Fortunately, the Greenside teachers were conservative, practical, and sensible dressers. This was due to a combination of low finances, lack of sartorial interest, and workplace activity. Wearing the latest expensive fashion was not a wise choice when you were sitting on a horribly stained carpet during story time, or supervising a children's outdoor play area, or playing basketball with middle-school kids in a gym.

Principals, at least those in elementary and middle schools, had a distinct sartorial code. While the attire was not a formalized uniform, there was little variance form one leader to another. Steve adhered to the contemporary fashion look for men with a polo shirt, the presence of a collar distinguishing it from a T-shirt. Like his male colleagues, Dockers and casual shoes, though not runners, completed the ensemble. Steve thought female colleagues dressed more professionally than the men but the reasons eluded him. It may reflect the perceived need to establish an image. It may be simply an innate ability to match clothing style and color at a level greater than that of a fourteen-year-old boy, a bar many men rarely exceeded.

Arriving at school early, Steve posted the class lists on the front window. Not a full-time principal, Steve had a .2 teaching component which meant an hour to the library each day. This would help him provide an instructional link with all the teachers and a chance to meet and work with the entire student body. It was just like Summer to spend hours on the library's marine theme so Steve would not be burdened with designing a stimulating learning environment. He remained woefully inadequate in that regard due to his years at Lakeview High. Many teachers there did not rate visually appealing classrooms as a high priority.

First day classes began an hour later at 9:45 am. Steve picked up muffins for the morning staff meeting. He had placed the order the night before. There would be a morning rush as fellow administrators crammed into Taylerston's premier donut shop, ordering first-day goodies for their teachers. Skipping the line ahead of a few young colleagues, he tapped his noggin as he passed by. "Wise leaders order the night before," he boasted with a broad smile, leaving them grumbling in his wake. He always over-ordered. Some Greenside students went without breakfast and the lunch program did not start until the second week.

While Steve was busy gathering sugar-laden treats, Tiny was at work, well before his official 7:30 am start time. The first task was to de-arm the school. The next half hour was spent shooing wayward cats through the vents and into the ducting that led upstairs. Next, he trudged with purpose. A gunny sack was draped over a thick shoulder as he checked the mousetraps he had laid in the janitorial closets. He felt sorry about trapping the mice. He needed a system that would display more respect for the deceased rodents and another plan to keep the feline presence secret. Mr. H. had said that the best way to do that was to ensure that any of what he called cat "waste" was removed before the kids arrived at school and that the cats stayed upstairs during school hours. Groaning from the mental energy required, Tiny decided to focus on the mice issue since he had not yet had to clean any cat urine or feces. "Maybe they'll piss and shit outside until the weather gets colder," he muttered to himself.

Tiny's face was scrunched in thought as he lugged the bundle away from the school. He met Jay Woznicki standing by the soccer goalpost in the back field. A worried Tiny explained his dilemma and the two talked over possible solutions. Finally, Tiny smiled and happily clipped Jay on the shoulder, almost sending the boy tumbling to the turf. Tiny had a plan— and he knew it was a good one.

10

Bridget was in the office when Steve entered at 8:00 am. "Yum, smells good," she said, pulling open the donut box Steve had plunked on the counter. "Yes, you remembered to get banana cream."

"When have I ever let you down?" asked Steve with a smile. He gazed at the matching ensemble of yellow T-shirt with three-quarter sleeves and beige slacks. "New outfit?" he ventured, eyeing the unusually striking blouse and pants rather than a skirt.

Beaming, Bridget blushed before answering. "I got it at Sears last week. My sister picked it out."

"She has good taste," remarked Steve before pausing and adding uneasily, "Uh, not that you don't, Bridget. I just meant . . ."

"Oh, I know," Bridget replied, her hand waving the air. "My sister's a clothes horse and I'm going to learn to wear more modern outfits. Office attire is changing." She paused, a look of consternation in her eyes. "You don't mind, do you?"

"You always look great," Steve said, "Modern or traditional."

"You too," Bridget fibbed while gazing at Steve's black and white mock-neck shirt with embroidered bow tie draped over the back of an office chair. "Is that supposed to be a fake tux?" She launched a more detailed examination. "You'll look like a giant penguin."

"Perfect, just the look I was aiming for."

Bridget was left to guard the donuts while Steve tromped to the staff restroom near the gym. Returning in five minutes, he was ready for the staff meeting. He carried the agendas and the precious treats proudly.

"Wow, donuts!" remarked a surprised Colin Redford, snatching a calorie-laden indulgence as he entered the library. He scarfed the treat down, the icing sugar sticking to the side of grinning lips. Following close behind, Emma Martinez passed on Steve's offer. "She won't eat donuts unless they're made with organic flour," Colin whispered to Steve while licking jelly off thin fingers.

Steve nodded with grim understanding. Emma was destined to be a culinary soul mate for Summer Martin. Steadfast, he guarded the donuts, checking for Tiny's marauding paws. The janitor had already snatched two. While the man-mountain was not attending the meeting, that did not eradicate the potential for another sugar sortie. Tiny was quicker and wilier than he appeared.

Emma sat with Joan, clearly signaling a message to Colin who shrugged and sat on the opposite side of the room. The new teachers were staring at Steve's garb with a, "Who the hell is this guy?" look.

Everyone except Summer and Emma was munching on not-so-healthy muffins or deadly donuts. Too busy chatting excitedly, the teachers ignored the one-page agenda. The elderly veteran Joan Mackenzie picked out a second muffin and brought a bran one with raisins for Emma. The young woman slowly peeled the paper bottom away. Carefully taking a bite-sized chunk, she examined it before cautiously slipping it into her mouth.

Crushing some of the excitement of opening day, Steve called the meeting to order. After welcoming Emma and Colin, he said, "If we move quickly enough, we will not have the second staff meeting at the end of the day." This roughly translated to, "Don't ask a bunch of questions or get on a soap box about your favorite bug-bear. You will be scorned by me and your colleagues." Everyone nodded and stared at Emma who had abandoned her interest in the muffin and appeared to be readying a question. Steve groused silently prior to issuing a look that barely concealed a signal for Emma's silence.

With theatrical flourish, Steve announced, "Okay, now for the big moment; in accordance with Policy 1012 of the Taylerston School District I am required to read out the following at the first staff meeting of the year before posting the notice on the staffroom bulletin board." Pausing for effect, he read, "There is an expectation that our workplaces are harassment-free, bully-free, toxic-chemical free, violence free, both in physical and verbal forms, pesticide-free, drug-free, (except prescribed medication), tobacco-free, alcohol-free (except at retirement functions), and scent-free when so requested by an employee at the site and supported by medical evidence." He looked up. "It really is a free country isn't it?"

No one laughed, so Steve plowed on. "Given the recent announcement by the government, it is required that the Taylerston District will also be animal-free by Christmas of this school year, an animal being tentatively defined as a living organism that is non-plant and non-human." Expecting questions, Steve stopped, peered over the top of his paper and scanned the room. Already the teacher faces were vacant and numbed.

"Okay," he said satisfied. "I'm glad that's clear." He took a sip of coffee to give him strength to carry on. "There's just a little more." He recanted the district expectation to institute a recycling program, an energy reduction strategy, and to purchase organic meats, vegetables, and fair-trade products. Health and safety minutes had to be posted. The student medical list was distributed. Fees for the social and coffee funds were announced.

"Here's the last point," said Steve to a perceptible sigh of relief from the anesthetized teachers. "The Taylerston School District also cautions against employees consuming unhealthy sugar-laden foods and drinks." Steve stared at the two almost-empty donut boxes and watched the shameful glances as teachers brushed crumbs off clothing. Some instinctively wiped the remnants of sugar and cream from their mouths. Others chose to whisk the evidence away with the back of their hands. Summer Martin smiled. Emma stared at colleagues with barely-masked superiority and suddenly asked a question. Soft groans filled the room. The prisoners were about to be freed. What the hell needed to be asked now?

"What's the school policy on cellphones in class?" Though the issue had been on five staff meeting agendas the previous year, no agreement had been reached.

"Teacher discretion," Steve responded rapidly. "I'm sure we'll be discussing it again." He stared at the group. The vibrant humans who had been so evident at the start of the meeting had vaporized. A mindless troupe of zombies remained. Fortunately, they would revive. What they were here for, what energized them, was the crowd of screeching banshees that were clamoring at the front door.

Only Emma and Colin had been taking notes during the meeting, the latter on his iPad. He was clearly swamped by the numbing quantity of information flow he received. When he taught Math at high school, he paid no attention to library news or gym storage issues. The Special Education staff looked after the calculations for classroom scores. Reading tests to establish beginning-year benchmarks, if they even existed, were for other teachers. If Colin felt particularly motivated, he might place a poster or two on a classroom bulletin board that would never be touched again until stolen or vandalized. At Greenside, the rooms were a blast of visual stimulation. Colin had to borrow several posters from Emma just so he could quickly stick something on the bulletin boards. He had printed a lame "Welcome" in colored chalk on the front blackboard.

With ten minutes remaining until the scheduled opening, there was an eerie calm around the office. The teachers had scattered to their class-rooms. With no kids or parents yet in the building, only Steve and Bridget occupied the office area. She was on the phone, leaving Steve with nothing productive to do but lean on the counter and wait. Checking with her every half-minute he finally saw her nod. He forced himself to walk calmly to the front entrance.

When the students saw him, they screeched and jostled for position.

Like a volcano spewing molten lava, shrieks, yelps, and cheers greeted Steve as he opened the front doors. A mass of pint-sized humanity flooded in. The middle-school students stood behind the younger ones, working hard to look cool and unfazed. Dozens of knuckle-knocks, hi-fives, and happy greetings later, the mob slowly dispersed. Parents nodded and smiled, most using his first name in greeting. So thick was the eagerness in the air, Steve thought he could wring it out with twisting hands and drop the resulting liquid in a pail. It would be an elixir as sweet and golden as anyone had ever tasted. Smiling and cantering along the hallway, Steve asked children about their summer holidays and helped remove backpacks as big as the bodies that carried them.

Making his way to Colin's room Steve peeked in the doorway and was happy to find Jay Woznicki smiling. "Hey, hey Jay, what d'ya say?"

"Mr. H.!" squealed the boy, hobbling quickly to the principal, intent on a bear hug. Knees cracking, Steve lowered to his haunches. The move worked as a signal. Jay knew something important was coming. "I want you to be extra nice to your teacher, Mr. Redford. He's new to Greenside and he might need your help. Do you think you can do that?"

Jay nodded excitedly. "Sure Mr. H.," he drawled. "I'll be real good, all year, real good." The boy issued a silly grin. "I already help. I here early and help Tiny with the bag."

Steve smiled. The boy and Tiny were special friends to be sure, but Jay was easily confused, especially in the cacophony of opening day. Jay's perception of activities and description of facts were often at odds with actual events.

Jay's face suddenly sagged as a worried brow creased.

"What's the matter," asked Steve, concern rising rapidly.

The boy stared at his friend and principal. "Mr. H., why cats so mean to mice?"

Steve had no idea what the boy was talking about. It did remind him that Jay loved animals so he asked the boy if he looked like a penguin.

A puzzled Jay did not understand the question. Steve pulled out the penguin picture book he had retrieved from the library and pointed to the pictures. Jay exploded with laughter, nodding excitedly and guffawing an awkward-sounding, "Yeah, Mr. H. is a penguin!" Steve carried the penguin book around most of the morning, continually asking students if they thought his shirt made him look like a giant penguin. The primary children laughed and giggled and nodded. The eighth-grade students smiled wryly and scanned the attire, "Yeah Mr. H., you look really cool." They proceeded to tease him further. The penguin tuxedo was not much different than his usual garb. Mr. H. always wore dorky clothes. Steve responded with chuckles and reciprocated ribbing.

A tired but happy Steve was taking a break in his office at the end of the day. He had just peeled off his special shirt and put on his principal uniform of a collared shirt and khakis. The penguin tux had opened dialogue doors with students all day. It had done its job and had been worth every penny Steve had paid for it. The quiet through the building was eerie and provided a moment for Steve to ruminate on the first day.

The assembly had gone well. The piano was horribly out of tune and Joan Mackenzie was out of practice playing the anthem. Though the students did not notice, there were more than a few winces from the adults. The younger children had belted out the school song with gusto while the middle-school students stayed quiet, uncomfortable to be seen participating in the kiddie tune. Somehow, "Go, Go Greenside Gators" was not high on the thirteen-year-old hit list. Steve mouthed the words to keep up appearances—he had a singing voice that could clear a room in seconds.

At noon Steve had passed out the muffins from the third box he had purchased. He knew which students were in need of a lunch. He had brought a few apples, bananas, and granola bars to distribute as well.

Three student names were picked from the over one hundred entries in the jar that had correctly identified his new clothes as the penguin shirt. Only one student, Janet, an eighth-grader, had spotted the second piece of clothing, the Tiger Woods belt.

"Isn't he that creepy golfer guy who cheated on his wife, slept with a bunch of women, then lied about it?"

Steve struggled for an answer. "Well, yes, he has made some unfortunate choices," was all he could manage. "But he is a great golfer," he added lamely.

"Who cares Mr. H? The guy's a jerk. How come you're wearing a belt with his name on it?" She eyed her principal warily. "He's not your hero, is he?"

"No," Steve blurted quickly. "I don't support his behavior." Following a pause, hands raised in surrender. Complete capitulation was to follow. "Okay, okay, I should not have worn the belt."

"It looks new," commented a smiling Janet. "Can I have it?"

"Can you have what?"

"The belt, as my prize. I'm the only one who got the answer aren't I?"

"Ah, it's a little big for you Janet. I thought you didn't like Tiger."

"I don't, but my dad does. He's a pretty big guy, just like you Mr. H. It's his birthday coming up and I don't have much money to get him a good present. He'd like that goofy belt. Can I have it—please?"

Shrugging, Steve nodded and the girl had issued a high-pitched shriek. He had to give it to her after school since he was afraid his pants might fall down without it.

Three children had been hurt on the playground, though not seriously. Their parents were contacted to pick them up. Steve filled out a three-page Accident Incident Report required for each one. Two first-grade boys in Joan's class did not make it to the urinal in time, wetting their pants. Steve provided the boys with sweatpants the school kept on hand for such emergencies. The boys could develop rashes so Steve completed the two-page Health and Sanitation Incident form for each child.

At recess a football was thrown onto the roof. A soccer ball was kicked through an open classroom door that knocked over a bookcase in Emma Martinez's room. The distraught teacher contacted the office. Tiny was inexplicably off the grounds. Steve and four seventh-grade boys hauled the bookcase upright and packed the materials onto the shelves while Emma took her class outside for an unscheduled break.

Two crying first-grade students suffered separation anxiety and were picked up by their mothers, a foreshadowing of upcoming incidents when the Kindergarten children began attending the following week. This called for the completion of an Emotional Trauma Incident form signed by Steve and Anne Shaw.

Tiny hauled in two eighth-grade boys who had been hiding behind the old elementary school across the field puffing on cigarettes during recess break. Why Tiny was in that area during recess was a mystery to Steve who was too busy at the time, and too tired at the end of the day, to ask.

First day challenges were never limited to the students. The photocopier hummed steadily until noon. Overworked and underappreciated, it went on strike. Wisps of smoke slid through cracks in the metallic side. A comatose photocopier was guaranteed to fray teacher nerves since everyone used the service. Toner, cartridges, and paper gobbled a quarter of the school's budget. Fortunately, Steve had a good working relationship with the service technician and she arrived in the afternoon and catastrophe was avoided.

Two teachers forgot their playground supervision duty and Steve recruited Anne Shaw to cover for one while he watched the primary play area in place of the other adult.

The school board office sent a flurry of emails requesting accurate student enrolment numbers hour-by-hour, the apparent panic caused by unexpectedly low student enrolment district-wide. Fewer students meant fewer dollars. Too busy with student-related matters, Steve ignored the requests.

The Special Education department, no slouch when it came to generating emails, sent numerous reminders to ensure proper labeling of students with special circumstances. That too, meant money or lack thereof. Steve planned to respond by the end of the week.

Twenty minutes later, just as the lunch period was ending, a panicked Emma reported that River Coolwater was missing. He had gone to the bathroom and not returned. Steve found the boy helping Tiny and Jay Woznicki gather food scraps into plastic buckets. Ecstatic to have found River so quickly, he paid little attention to the janitorial tasks the boys were conducting. If Jay and River wanted to help Tiny clean up after lunch then so be it. Steve and Emma agreed to be flexible and encourage the connection between Tiny and the new student. River needed a friend.

After school Steve checked on Colin Redford. The man sat blank-faced and mute at his desk. "Are you okay?" he asked softly. He spotted eye movement and a hint of recognition. "You're alive!" he chirped cheerfully.

Colin's elfin face sagged as if an unknown entity was sitting on the floor and pulling his cheeks downward into hell. Looking up with expressionless eyes, he muttered, "Barely. Does that Jay Woznicki kid ever stop talking? He keeps going on and on about you and penguins!"

"Jay likes animals."

"No kidding."

Patting Colin on the shoulder, Steve had said, "I'll take your kids into the library for the first hour tomorrow. I can start a research skills unit like a treasure hunt. You can use the time to do some extra prep." He smiled watching a titch of color return to Colin's wan cheeks. "Joan Mackenzie said she would help you if Emma is unwilling. Joan is a fantastic teacher. I used to be a high school teacher too. I've learned a great deal about teaching elementary children from her, and you will too."

Tired eyes had looked appreciatively at the principal. "Thanks Steve, you know just what to say at the right time. I'm so bagged and I've got a ton of prep tonight. I don't want to appear like a total dolt who doesn't know how to teach. I appreciate Joan's offer. I want her to see me with the potential to be a solid elementary teacher, even without computers."

"You want Emma to see you that way too, don't you?"

Colin exhaled a weary, heavy sigh. "Yes," he agreed tiredly, "Especially Emma."

The last meeting of a long day was with Bridget. "Nice day?" he asked at the conclusion.

"Not bad," replied Bridget. "How about yours?"

Steve shrugged. "Same as yours I guess, not bad." He sat back and grinned, "Pretty quiet actually. I hope the rest of the year goes as smoothly."

11

By Thursday Steve was exhausted. The Ferrari pace of school was far different than the turtle speed of summer vacation. As he was readying to leave, a somber Tiny knocked on the door and without hesitation began blurting about a gnawing personal issue. A third evening tryst with Chelsea loomed. Movies were always good choices for initial dates. Tiny had chosen *Captain America* and followed that by taking Chelsea to *Thor*. He regarded these movies to be cool beyond words. Chelsea though, seemed less impressed. How anyone could be bored with such awesome action was beyond him. Tiny was looking for a new experience that would show that he understood girls and was not just another big, dumb oaf. Though he was pretty sure Chelsea liked him for who he was, adding a little class to a relationship was never a bad thing. He needed to ask his boss. Mr. H. was a smart and classy guy.

"I got a date with Chelsea tomorrow night, kinda celebrating the start of school." Tiny grinned. "That's where we met."

Steve nodded, remembering the two students trading barbs in his basic-level classes at Lakeview High. He did not want to discuss this issue at the end of the penultimate day of the week, but a glance at Tiny's hopeful eyes was too much to resist. Looking directly at the young man, he asked, "Where have you two gone before?" He fought to mask the grimace when Tiny told him.

"You could take her to a play like *West Side Story*," suggested Steve. "The summer theater program has been working on it for a month and it opens tonight. It's being performed at our old school, Lakeview High. You helped with the production of *Grease* when you were in high school, remember?"

"That was cool," Tiny mused, dredging up a distant memory. "Chelsea liked it too."

"Well, *West Side Story* has young tough guys in it, just like *Grease*." As Steve explained the story, Tiny became more interested; at least until the principal explained that the play was a modern version of a Shakespeare's *Romeo and Juliet*. Tiny frowned at the mention of the bard. Steve quickly added that the language was not Shakespearean and there were gang fights and more than a bit of romance between young people.

Tiny scrunched his face, a sure sign he was thinking. Chelsea might like the romance part. "The guys aren't dressed in those weird clothes like leotards and stuff?"

"No, *West Side Story* is a modern version with two gangs called the Jets and the Sharks. They wear T-shirts and jeans and fight each other with knives and chains."

"That sounds cool," Tiny admitted. "I'll give it a try Mr. H." He raised thick eyebrows. The eyes squinted and the face twisted. He was thinking again. "If Chelsea doesn't like it, can I say it was you who talked me into something dorky like that?

Steve laughed. "Sure, you can blame it on me."

Heading home, Steve abandoned any semblance of self-control and purchased a pepperoni pizza, one day earlier than household tradition dictated. Charles was pleasantly surprised and scarfed his large piece quickly lest the treat existed only as a transitory dream. The sound of the doorbell interrupted Steve's munch on a fifth slice of doughy, cheese-smothered pizza. Padding to the foyer, he opened the front door and found golf partner Terrel Lewis holding a hybrid-five golf club in his hand.

"You lent it to me on the last hole on Saturday," he explained.

Grateful for conversation that would not involve school, Steve invited his friend in for a beer.

Terrel readily accepted. He followed Steve to the backyard patio and snatched a slice of pizza before the last remnants disappeared into the ravenous stomachs of Steve and Charles.

It was common for those with youthful leftist ideals to fall victim to the lure of material satisfaction in later life. A time-worn phrase summarized the shift, often erroneously attributed to Winston Churchill, "If you're not a socialist at twenty, you have no heart; if you're still a socialist at thirty, you have no brains." Terrel Lewis was one of the few people moving in the opposite direction. He was a youthful-looking late thirties, with a full head of curly black hair he was growing into a 1970s-style afro. He wore John Lennon glasses that straddled a thin face of dark complexion. His wardrobe blended professional with bohemian, costing impressive wads of cash. He had completed an engineering degree before working on several global resource extraction projects. Pleased with the salary but unhappy with the travel, he became a stock broker at Darrington Investments. He specialized in commodity trading before being heartlessly dumped by manager Chuck Palmer. It was then that Steve and Terrel joined forces. Terrel eventually led the Namibian mining-college project initiated by Steve's fifth-grade class at Meadowvale Elementary. Steve often wondered whether that project had prompted the former superintendent to appoint him to a principalship. If it was, Steve did not know whether to thank or curse the guy.

Terrel's leftish politics made him controversial in the corporate world and therefore a must-read on the business pages. He provided a fresh counterpoint to the usually conservative editorials. Lately Steve had noticed a malicious streak surfacing in his friend, an all too common trait with journalists hungry to take a big bite from a power-broker's backside.

"Who were those guys Capelli and Chow were talking with on Saturday?" asked Terrel, his journalist nose sniffing for information. "The little guy looked smarmy."

"I don't know." Steve suddenly perked up. "What little guy?"

Terrel took a moment in thought. "You might have left by then. There was this little sleazy guy who came to their table. Everyone yakked for a few minutes, then he left. Unlike the dapper duo who had been there first, this guy was Mr. Walmart. He had a big bandage on his forehead." Terrel caught Steve's strange look. "Smarmy is a word, like a low-life weasel, sort of like Chuck Palmer at Darrington Investments a few years ago."

"That's not what I was thinking," said Steve. He did not know whether to tell Terrel about the mysterious Greenside duct-crawler or vent about Chuck Palmer. He chose the latter. Palmer had lied to Steve when the teacher had been planning a return to the financial industry. Steve refused to take the vacant position when Palmer had terminated Terrel's employment. Ironically, a few years later Chuck had been terminated from Darrington. His insistence on being heavily weighted to American banks did not sit well with his clients during the 2008 financial crisis.

"Chuck's a sales rep for A-1 Education," stated Terrel, "As if that asshole knew anything about education." Terrel finished his beer and plunked it on the patio table. He shook his head at the offer of a second. "Remember I'm not around Saturday so you have to find another guy for the foursome."

"Yeah, I remember," Steve said, though he didn't. "I'll get Perry. He plays sometimes."

"Not this weekend he won't, I already asked him. He's going to a fringe festival on Salt Spring Island in BC."

"Perry?"

"Yeah, I think he's met someone. He's got a lot more prance in his step."

Terrel left. Devoid of human company a mawkish Steve opened a pale ale and wondered who Perry was seeing. The beer and the ruminating expired simultaneously so Steve shifted mental gears and focused on school work. He tromped to the den to prep for another library treasure hunt he was conducting with Colin Redford's class.

The first week of school was nearing an end and everyone was settling into routines. For Tiny that meant covertly gathering the trapped mice before anyone else arrived, bundling them into a gunny sack, and taking them away. After lunch meant a quick sortie to complete another secret task, accompanied by Jay Woznicki. The new kid in school, River Coolwater, usually joined the pair.

On the first Friday of the year, Tiny was heading to his regular rendezvous with Jay. He spotted eighth-grader Kevin Johnson looking as if he was talking to the wall. Tiny strode closer. Facing Kevin, his back against the wall, was a much smaller boy, River Coolwater.

"What's going on?" Tiny asked, though the frightened look on River's face told the story better than words ever could.

"Nothing," claimed Kevin.

"Nothing," agreed River.

"You head back to class, River."

Kevin snickered until Tiny shot an icy glance.

River scooted away, relief flooding his face. "Not you," Tiny barked as Kevin tried to slip away. "Don't tell me you're picking on fourth-graders now?"

Kevin shrugged. He wondered how Tiny knew the new kid. "He was gonna give me some money."

"Give it to you, yeah right." Tiny set his broom against the wall. "I'm waiting for the day you tell the truth." He jabbed a finger at the scowling boy. "I'm waiting for the day you pick on somebody your own size."

"You can't touch me," spouted Kevin, fearful, not defiant.

Tiny edged closer to the boy, the huge frame dwarfing the lad. Gulping, Kevin tried to back up but he was already against the wall. "I'm not gonna hurt you," said Tiny, suddenly reaching into his pocket. Flinching, Kevin narrowed anxious eyes. "I'm gonna give you the same amount of money that you were gonna get from River. How much was that?"

Kevin gulped. "A dollar. I was going to get another dollar from somebody else."

"What for?"

"I wanted to buy chicken pie at lunch next week. The little kids get the free food first. By the time the older kids are allowed in, the sandwiches are gone. That's why Mr. H. gets the chicken pies for the older kids. But we have to pay."

"Make your own damn lunch." Tiny was angry and when he was, his choice of language was not the best. Kevin did not seem to notice. Droplets trickled down the boy's cheek. He quickly brushed them away. Remembering his own childhood Tiny softened his tone. "There's no food?" He waited, anticipating a lie. There was always some food in a household, at least most of the time.

Kevin did not provide the expected answer. "There's usually food, mostly bread and jam or peanut butter. Sometimes there's no meat or cheese. I could grab an apple or something like that when we've got some at home."

"Your mom can't give you a couple of bucks? The food here is real cheap."

"I don't wanna ask her. She gets mad. I don't want one of the free lunches either."

Tiny nodded with understanding. If Kevin was one of the few eighth-grade students to get a free lunch every day he would stand out for all the wrong reasons.

"I tell you what I'm gonna do," Tiny concluded firmly. "I'm gonna give you two bucks to buy a piece of chicken pie or whatever Mr. H. is selling any time you want it." Tiny held up a second finger for emphasis. "Two, I'm not gonna tell anybody about it, not even Mr. H. You're gonna keep your mouth shut about it too." Kevin nodded though Tiny held up a hand to stop the gesture. "I ain't finished yet. Three," another finger added. "You ain't never gonna bully another kid into giving you money ever again. If you do, I'm gonna kick your ass so hard you won't be able to sit for a week." He fixed a menacing glower at the subdued Kevin. "That's why you push kids around isn't it? It's a shakedown for money." Tiny waited as Kevin stood silent. "You can nod now."

Kevin did as he was told.

"Have we got a deal?" Tiny demanded.

"Deal," Kevin agreed, and the man-mountain backed away.

Tiny was a man of his word. When he slipped into Steve's office to provide the daily report, he did so without mentioning the mousetraps, his forays with Jay and River, or his deal with Kevin.

"At least there aren't mice scurrying around anymore." Steve said, concluding the meeting and turning to the computer monitor.

Tiny bowed his large round head. "No, not anymore," he whispered sadly. Switching thoughts, he forced his brain to move on from thinking about trapped rodents.

"Is there anything else?" Steve asked, looking up toward Tiny. He wanted to leave for the weekend but Tiny seemed as if he had more to say. When the janitor simply wished his boss a good weekend and left,

Steve cleared off more emails. It wasn't long before Joan Mackenzie stood at the doorway. Though she checked the office area to ensure there were no eavesdroppers she still dropped her voice. "Don't forget the philosophy meeting," she said, the covert fashion rivaling Cold War espionage.

"I never would, Joan. It's the highlight of the week. I'll be a bit late, but I'll be there."

Though they lived in Taylerston, Joan Mackenzie and Gladys Simmons were an institution in Greenside. They had started their careers at the now-shuttered elementary school in 1970, the year Steve was born. The last of an era when a person could qualify as an elementary teacher with only two years of training, they had been only nineteen-years-old when they began their careers. They finished their university degrees through summer coursework.

Joan lived close to Steve, so he parked the car in his garage, grabbed a bottle of wine and walked the fifteen-minute route to her house. It was four-thirty. Friday was the only day Joan and Gladys left early. The Merlot Maidens would be riding a smooth red surf by now.

Steve knocked on the front door before entering. As if the juxtaposition of two school marms guzzling wine from hefty tumblers wasn't enough, classic rock and roll blared from the speakers. The Who, Bob Seger, and Steppenwolf were popular choices. Today it was the Rolling Stones. Steve struggled to catch up to the grape intake as the elderly pair wailed in disjointed unison to "You Can't Always Get What You Want."

Steve had learned more about teaching elementary-age children in these sessions than any university course could ever match. While Joan and Gladys were quiet and reserved at school, they shared a burning passion for public education. It was as if a week of quiet rectitude exploded in a dazzling array of insight and perspective on Friday afternoon. Fueled by the adult grape juice, it was as if the two were transformed, becoming part-critic, part-advocate, and part-soothsayers on the trials, tribulations, and future of the public system.

"Why don't you two ever speak your mind at school?" Steve asked, swigging the Merlot like it was lager.

The two veterans giggled as if their principal had touched on a forbidden topic. "Don't be silly Steve," chastised Joan. "We can't expunge . . . oops, silly me, expound, like the young ones can. I just teach. I don't know what half that new edubabble means." She took another pull of fermented grape juice. "I don't even use computers. That nice young man on our staff, Mr. Redford, has a struggle to teach without them."

Gladys turned and pointed a wobbly finger. "Who's going to listen to two old prune-faces like us anyway?"

"I do."

"Oh Stevie, you are such a sweet, smart, and classy man! Isn't he sweet Joan?"

"Very sweet," agreed Joan, though she was concentrating on the Stone's "Brown Sugar." "My, that is a very sad song," she muttered. She adjusted the beige cardigan draped over stooped shoulders. The horn-rimmed glasses were slightly askew. Joan Mackenzie was the poster child for the kindly grandmother turned pleasant school marm.

Sighing, Gladys brightened as she worked up a memory. "Mick Jagger was very, very sexy, especially when he took his shirt off!" Her tongue flicked over dry lips, forcing Steve to look away.

Joan giggled, then shook her head. "I like my men to be nice boys," she stated flatly. "I'll take Paul McCartney any day. Now he's sexy!"

"You never see him with his shirt off, the dull boy," countered Gladys.

"Exactly," Joan concluded with a ring of satisfaction, having decided she had scored a verbal victory. "He's got class, like our principal!"

"Thank you, Joan, that's very kind. Steve wavered slightly before plunking his empty glass on the end table with exaggerated flourish. "I've got to go now ladies."

"Have you got a date with Summer?" Joan asked bluntly before giggling and placing hand to mouth.

"I don't have a romantic relationship with Summer," Steve replied. Some other plan niggled at the back of his wine-addled brain. He had succeeded in catching up to the alcohol intake of the two women in a very short span of time.

"Don't mind Joan," she said. "She's always been so nosy." Slugging back the remaining liquid in her tumbler, she stared at Steve. "I saw Summer leave the school this afternoon with that nice man from the school board office."

"There is no nice man at that office."

"Shush Joan, this one is; Percy or Perseus or something like that."

Steve corrected Gladys with a slur, trying to picture his friend with Summer Martin. "He was named after Perry Como."

"Mr. Como was pretty sexy," said Joan, "For an old guy." She paused, "With his shirt on."

With that, Steve rose unsteadily and thanked the ladies for their insight on the afternoon's topics, especially the relative sexiness, with or without shirt, of Mick Jagger, Paul McCartney, and Perry Como.

Joan raised her glass, smiled uneasily and glanced at Steve's vacuous eyes. "You should know not to get mixed up with us on a Friday afternoon Stevie if you can't hold your wine. Be careful walking home."

"Again, many thanks ladies," the principal announced. "It was a pleasure." The fresh air and warm evening sunshine failed to shake the cobwebs entangling his synapses. He strode along quietly, singing a Lionel Ritchie tune. Instead of pizza for a second night in a row, Steve stopped at the local Subway sandwich shop and opted to eat in, ordering a meatball sandwich and Lays potato chips. When finished, his feet followed his belly home. Not fully engaged, his brain ignored a previous nagging feeling that he was forgetting something important.

12

Opening the front door Steve was welcomed by Charles issuing an irritatingly insistent meow. Despite devouring more than a fair share of pizza the previous evening, the cat expected the usual Friday evening meal. Seeing Steve empty-handed and woolly-headed, Charles snorted and padded to his bowl for the normal boring chow. "You're getting too fat," mumbled Steve by way of explanation to the snarky feline. The intense ring of the phone broke the tension between cat and human. Steve hustled to the kitchen, the wine, meatballs, and chips sloshing about in his stomach. There was no answering machine or call recognition. "Hello," he mumbled into the receiver.

"Oh, I finally got a hold of you."

Shit, it's Monique. Steve suddenly had a very bad feeling. She did not sound angry. That would have been better. She sounded . . . tense.

"I've been waiting for you. We were supposed to grab a pizza and then head to the movie."

"Movie?"

"It's old movie night at the Ridge, it's *Casablanca*," a pause, then, "Have you been drinking?"

"I had a glass of wine at Joan's." He thought the mention of the respected veteran in the eyes of fellow primary teacher Monique would help him out of this mess. There was silence at the other end. That was always the worst. He was forced to speak. "I'm sorry Monique, I forgot about the movie." He perked up. "We can still go. I can get there in ten minutes and we can have popcorn for dinner!"

"Did you drive to Joan's?"

A moment of silence as Steve tried to get the hamster moving along his brain's treadmill. Where was this question leading? "No," he answered cautiously.

"Because you knew you would be drinking, right?"

The hamster was too tired. Mentally Steve resembled the fly being pulled in by the spider. "Yeah," he agreed warily.

"So, after drinking for a couple of hours, now you want to drive, with me in the car?"

Hmm. That did not sound too good. "That's not what I meant. Well, yes, I said I could drive over but I haven't had that much to drink and . . ." he rolled his eyes to heaven, searching for inspiration. He needed to say something intelligent. "What I meant was, you could come over here and drive us to the movie." A deafening silence came from the other end. "Or," he added with less assurance, "We could forget about the movie and grab a pizza, a nice bottle of wine and stay here." He brightened. "We could talk, or . . . you could talk and I'll listen." Try as he might, he could not get anything coherent to exit his mouth.

"Don't drink anymore," she said testily. "We're leaving early tomorrow."

Uh, oh.

"You forgot that too, didn't you? We were supposed to drive to Vancouver to do a little shopping. A little American cash goes a long way in Canada right now." An audible sigh sputtered through the phone line. "Did you cancel your golf game?"

Steve groaned inside, trying to shake the webs the alcohol spider was spinning over his tortured brain. This discussion could not get any worse. "I can cancel," he said without conviction.

Monique snorted. In his stupor Steve actually had to work to decipher the tone. The brain-hamster was asleep at the wheel. "You, Steve, are a forty-one-year-old adolescent." Her voice was eerily calm as she continued. "You can get enveloped in your work. When you were a stock broker you loved money. Now you're a principal and you love education. But you can't put the same commitment into a relationship."

Suddenly sober, Steve fought to regain some dignity. "Monique, I'm really sorry but maybe this is a topic that should be talked about later, face-to-face, not over the phone."

An audible sigh blew across the phone lines. "You're right Steve. If we ever talk about this it will be later—much later. Right now, I just need a little space, okay?" The sigh bounced back across the line as if an echo.

"Okay," said Steve. He was a smart and classy guy. He wanted to say something romantic but couldn't get the words out. Monique clicked off.

Looking for solace, Steve searched for Charles. The grumpy feline, still smarting from the lack of a pizza treat, was in hiding, sulking.

Steve grabbed a beer from the fridge. A real relationship needed to be cultivated. Instead, he had yanked a seedling from the ground, roots and all, before it could be nurtured and sustained. Could he repair the damage he had wrought? The irony was noteworthy. Tiny thought that he was a smart guy. If that were so, why did he find himself trying to traverse a romantic minefield in which he had laid the explosives? And why was he totally bereft of any ideas on how to extricate himself without getting blown to little pieces?

The weekend was one to forget. A hangover and the morose vibe over Monique led to a disastrous round of golf. NFL football held little interest. Charles continued to be aloof. Monique was not the only companion alienated by Steve's wine-sotted memory lapses.

Monday morning brought little respite. Tiny Little was belting out, "Tonight, tonight, won't be just any night," throughout the school.

"You created a monster," Bridget moaned. "I can't shut him up and he can't remember anything more than that one line. The bleating is worse than trying to work this damn A-1 software program we're supposed to use for student demographics. I wanted to assassinate the computer. Now I want to terminate Tiny instead." Pleading eyes stared at Steve. "You've got to help me."

"Kill the computer. We need Tiny more."

As if on cue, the singing janitor sidled into the office, warbling the one line off-key. He paused to thank Steve, gushing about how Mr. H. was a smooth character who knew all about what women wanted. Tiny watched

Mr. H's face turn to a reddish hue, probably from being praised so much. "Are there any more of these cool theater things to see?"

Steve sighed at Tiny's description—theater things! "There's a show called *Phantom of the Opera* that is making a tour stop in Seattle. "It will be in a big fancy theater and the tickets will cost a lot of money."

"That's no problem," said Tiny, with a hint of a boast. Nothing was too good for his Chelsea. "We can get a hotel room and Chelsea can shop for clothes. She likes that." Steve waited for an off-color adolescent line about a night in a hotel room with his girlfriend but none came. Instead, Tiny asked, "What's this other show about? Is there romance stuff in it like *West Side Story*?"

"It's based on another book," started Steve.

Tiny grunted with displeasure. Why was all the good stuff based on books?

"But not Shakespeare," Steve added quickly.

Tiny was disappointed. He had to admit the Shakespeare guy could weave a good story. *Macbeth* and *West Side Story* were exciting. It was too bad that the guy couldn't write well enough for anyone to understand him. Tiny figured that Shakespeare could have made a fortune thinking up stories if he could get some other dude to write them down.

"*Phantom* is set in the Paris Opera House."

Groaning loudly, Tiny looked as if he had been hit with a bullet. "I saw a fat guy on TV once, singing way too loud in a deep voice. I think he was an opera guy."

"That was probably Pavarotti," said Steve. "And yes, he is an opera," he paused trying to find the right word, "guy."

Tiny shrugged. "He thought he was pretty hot stuff, showing off how loud he could sing. I couldn't understand any of the words. Listening to him was like reading Shakespeare. Both those guys need better writers."

About to launch into an explanation in teacher mode, Steve changed his mind. "Forget about opera for a moment," he said, working hard to insert patience into the voice. "A phantom is like a ghost. This one has half a face." The intrigued Tiny gawked and Steve plowed on. "The phantom has a girl as a protégé." Steve caught the puzzled look, "A student, and he is jealous of the man who loves her. The phantom controls her mind and takes her to the subterranean—ah, the basement, which is filled with water."

"Cool," said an enthralled Tiny, though the story seemed more than a bit weird. Anyone with a flood like that would pump out the basement. "Would Chelsea like it?"

"The songs are great. The story is sad with a lot of romance. I think she'll love it."

Tiny, the theater-going aficionado, beamed, happy and satisfied. Girls were tough to understand. Luckily, he had a friend like Mr. H., an older man who knew a lot about what women liked.

"Mr. H. I know the cats are around but I never find any poo or piss that has to be cleaned up. I can't clean it up if I don't know where it is."

The randomness of Tiny's thought process was not that much different than Summer Martin. The methodical Steve often marveled at the erratic patterns and disjointed connections. "If you can't find where they defecate—crap and pee, then that's a good thing isn't it?"

Shrugging again, Tiny answered, "I guess. I think they might go outside but I don't know if they'll still do that when the weather gets cold." He brightened. "Hey, maybe they can use the toilets!"

Steve groaned. "I think having kitty litter boxes in the janitor storage rooms is more realistic." With luck the junk on the second floor would be gone in a month or two and the mice and cats would vacate the school. "Remember what I said before. Unless the feline activity is hurting the kids or disrupting the school, I'm really not concerned."

Tiny had learned that feline meant cat. "I got it Mr. H. No more talk of any animals unless it's messing up the school or the kids." He grinned goofily. "And thanks for the tips for date nights. Chelsea's real happy."

For a moment, Steve wondered about Tiny's comment before reasoning that the young man meant mice when he referred to generic animals. He watched the janitor shuffle away. Steve smiled inwardly. He was supposedly the one who knew about women, at least in Tiny's eyes. But it was the young man who knew what he wanted and who he was. Steve wore three hats, one-minute a serious principal, the next a system-fighting zealot, and then an alcohol-guzzling adolescent.

Determined to be the serious principal over the following weeks, Steve stayed away from the central office. He sent only polite emails to those higher up the organizational food chain. He reduced his alcohol intake. If Steve was serious about repairing the damage he had caused to his relationship with Monique, he was going to do so as a mature professional. Once he had donned the serious principal hat, he planned to keep it on his head.

One of the first tests was a challenging personnel matter. Such issues were never easy for a principal and this one was particularly tricky. It was rare for Steve to issue directives, but he had waited a month into the school year and little had changed. As a result, a glum Colin Redford was sitting in his office. The teacher snatched a corner seat. A few minutes later Emma Martinez stomped in and dropped into a chair in the opposite corner. The two boxers waited for the bell.

Steve stared at the young teachers. "I'll come right to the point as I know you appreciate the direct approach. School's been in session for over a month. Don't you think the smoochy love-bird routine followed by the incessant bickering is a little juvenile?"

"What do you mean?" asked Emma in a snarky tone.

"You hold hands in the hallways, cuddle in the staffroom, write love notes to each other. Do you want me to go on?"

"What love notes?" asked Colin warily.

Steve held up a scrunched piece of foolscap. "It's written in French. I can make out some of it like, *je suis amoureux* and *tu es belle*."

Colin's face went as rouge as a ripe tomato.

"Have you been getting Tiny to go through my garbage can? Is he spying on us?" snapped Emma.

Steve glared with a level of anger that was foreign for him. "Tiny would never do something like that and I would never ask him." Smoldering eyes flared at the young woman. "Do I make myself clear?"

Not one to cower easily, Emma was about to bark a response when Colin's elfin face paled and dropped in sadness. "You threw my note into the garbage can?"

Now flustered, Emma stayed quiet.

Steve explained that the note had been balled up and lay on the floor near a trash can. Tiny saw Emma's name written at the top. He thought it had been a note from a parent that had been scrunched up by a child before the teacher had seen it and then left on the floor. Written in French, Tiny thought it might be important so he brought it to the office.

"You threw my love note in the garbage?" repeated Colin.

"You were just trying to suck up after your screw-up on Saturday night. Do I really care if it was a big game between the Dodgers and the Giants? We were supposed to go to a romantic movie." She turned to Steve. "It was *Casablanca*. It's only showing on Friday nights and this was the last viewing." Back to glaring at Colin, she seethed, "But you'd rather get pissed with your buddies." Grim-faced, she added, "I hope you had a good time."

Steve shifted his butt. Colin's behavior was far too close to home. He stayed silent. What else could he do?

"I forgot about date night, okay?" replied a testy Colin. "And the night wasn't so great. The Dodgers aren't as good as they used to be. They lost."

Steve groaned silently from his audience chair. Could Colin have picked a worse thing to say?

With an exasperated sigh, Emma glared at the young man. "That's not the point Colin! God, how can you be so stupid? All you care about are sports," she paused, "and beer. It's all so juvenile. None of it supports what you and I are trying to do together."

"C'mon Emma. I like computers too. I used that computer program in Calculus last year and found it really useful. If we had some A-1 software here and a few decent computers, that would sure as hell help too."

Another silent groan emanated from Steve, only more intense. Colin was clueless.

Emma turned to her principal for support. "Colin is clueless. We're talking about romantic commitment. Mature men don't forget a date because they're too busy getting drunk."

Steve's face turned ashen. This cannot be happening. It was as if he had entered an episode of *The Twilight Zone*, or the Bill Murray movie, *Groundhog Day*.

Silence filled the room. The emotionally spent teachers were waited for their leader to provide sage advice and learned wisdom. They could tell that Steve was clearly disturbed by what he had heard.

Stirring from uncomfortable contemplation, Steve said, "It is not my business to delve into the details of your relationship. It is my business to expect professional behavior from you when you're at work. The school is not the place for the intense emotional roller coaster you two have been riding."

"Fine," said Emma, turning to Colin. "See, that's how mature men handle things. I'm tired of going out with a teenager."

Insensible again, Colin responded defiantly. "Christ, don't be so stupid. I'm twenty-six."

Steve winced and looked downward. Redford was beyond hope.

Emma rolled her eyes as if she was trying to communicate with a brainless dog. "See," she pointed at her principal, "Steve can't even look at you, and neither can I." She rose and stomped out of the room.

"I do not understand her," said a bewildered Colin. He stared at Steve. "A man like you must understand women. There's Summer, and Anne; and those are only the ones I know about. How the hell do you do it?"

Startled, Steve sat back. He was frequently surprised by the directness common with young teachers. "Summer is a friend. Anne and I have a close professional relationship, that's all." Rather than reveal the behavioral shortcomings he shared with Colin regarding memory loss, date nights, and alcohol, Steve quickly changing the topic. He lobbed an equally blunt question back. "Do you know Ms. Capelli?"

Colin shrugged, unaffected by the conversational shift. "She's the superintendent. She likes computers and data. She permitted Mr. Chow to purchase the A-1 Education software I used in my Calculus classes last year. I sent her a report saying the software was very helpful." He stared at Steve. "Why do you ask? Is there a problem?"

"No, it's nothing like that," replied Steve casually. "I was just wondering."

After watching Colin's pitiable performance, Steve had a much clearer understanding of how Monique must view him. Three phone calls after the Friday debacle the previous month had gone to voice mail with no return message. Emails were not answered. He considered visiting her house and eventually nixed that idea. Secretary Bridget had recently conveyed that Monique was in the embryonic stages of a relationship with a teacher at Lakeview High. Summer was at the same stage with Perry. Two trains bound for romance had left the station. Steve had been left standing on the platform on both occasions.

13

Hearing the news about Monique's new romantic interest devastated Steve. Seeing the cause of his loss mirrored in Colin's juvenile behavior left little doubt about who was to blame. Steve needed someone to bark at. At least rocking the boat made him feel as if he was the one taking action. Being assertive made him feel less of a self-inflicted victim.

Further complaints to Jennifer Capelli were out of the question. She had already stated that she would inform Phil Chow and that the storage issue was the domain of the business manager. Attempts to meet with the unnervingly erudite Chow to discuss the junk piles failed. He didn't return Steve's emails and was frequently absent due to business commitments. The maintenance supervisor and the health and safety officer made it abundantly clear that they would not take action until they received a directive from their boss.

There was a slim chance that Lou Tayler could be convinced to provide assistance. At least the elementary curriculum supervisor was easy to contact. He was always in his office, working the phone, ferreting out the scuttlebutt about the latest educational bandwagon on which to clamber onto or leap from. He was Steve's only viable option.

"That doesn't change the fact that the responsibility lies with the maintenance department," Lou snapped with surprising curtness after listening to Steve's tale of woe.

Perhaps the man had more spine than he usually demonstrated? Steve decided to drop the feral feline angle and focus on what really mattered to Lou, public relations and personal image. "I just want the stuff out of here. The boxes are filled with elementary books, some of them hardly used. Taxpayers would be unhappy about the waste if they knew what was up there gathering dust. If I was a do-gooder, I'd wonder why those books haven't been shipped to a needy place, Namibia for example." He smiled as he caught an audible gulp from Lou. "If all that becomes public the whole mess will blow up." He paused. He could almost feel the anxiety slither through the phone line. "Jennifer's not going to take the fall—guess who is?"

"Maybe I could meet with you," stammered Lou. "I'm free on Monday after school. You could come here."

"No, you need a visual reminder," Steve countered. "You come to Greenside next Monday at five o'clock so Donna can make it after work. I want the chair of the parent council at the meeting."

Though Steve heard a sputtering of sounds there were no coherent words until, "Okay, I'll be there, but I don't know why you're putting this on my shoulders. I've already got too much on my plate. This is a mainte-nance issue."

Steve rolled tired eyes. "Yeah, I heard that the first time Lou." He could feel the man straightening his bow tie and adjusting his black-rimmed glasses.

Several days later, Greenside Parent Council Chair Donna Medford was seated across from Steve in his cluttered office. It was late afternoon with the wan mid-October sun sinking behind the cluster of fir trees at the edge of the school property. They were spending a moment together waiting for Lou Tayler, exchanging rumors that always swirled throughout a school district.

"I keep hearing that A-1 Education executives have been meeting with Capelli and Chow," said Donna. "That's the company that developed the new office system we're using. I hope we don't buy any more office stuff from them. I hate that program."

"I don't know anything about that, except that Bridget feels the same way," said Steve nonchalantly. He flashed palms outward in the universal sign of ignorant bliss. He stared at Donna and smiled, recalling how much he enjoyed her company. When they began seeing each other romantically he realized how much he wanted a family that included more than Charles. The social issues and avocational interests between the two were too wide to breech. They managed to part as friends. Donna reconciled with her husband and the couple line-danced a storm at a country bar every Friday night. Her man had not been in a beer-induced brawl in three years. At thirty-four Donna was back to her life as it was in her twenties, a pale-skinned, short, chunky, dedicated mother wearing velour tops and Wrangler jeans.

Steve was still drifting, partially tethered by golf, reading, and watching TV sports—truly anchored only by work.

"Maybe you should try one of those computer dating services?" Donna asked suddenly, often able to suss what was bothering Steve without him vocalizing an issue.

Steve snorted derisively. "Don't tell me your new A-1 Education software can do that too?"

"Probably. The company says it has software that can do just about everything else."

"I like the human touch."

"I know. That's why it's too bad about Summer." She caught Steve's annoyed look. "I heard she and prancing Perry were connecting." She paused. "I guess opposites do attract."

"You and I were different and that didn't work out so well."

"Yeah, but you thought husband Hank was going to kick the shit out of you every time we went out. That kinda cramped your style."

Lou Tayler knocked on the door, ending the trip along memory lane. He entered and sat in the chair opposite Steve. He was wearing the usual polyester white shirt and dark-blue dress pants. The navy bow tie with white polka dots was askance. So too, were the horn-rimmed glasses. He spent a moment surveying the lumpy principal. As usual Hepting was inappropriately dressed in a polo shirt and khaki pants. The broadly-set round eyes, wide mouth, protruding belly, and short legs made for a striking resemblance to Yogi Bear. Finishing the appraisal, Lou turned and nodded to Donna. She returned the gesture and assured Lou that she did not want the storage challenge to darken the school's name.

"I'm only here to tell you that unless someone orders whatever is up there to be moved, I'll put the issue on the parent council agenda." Donna issued a long stare. "You know how Greenside parents can be." She noted Lou's mild shudder. "I don't care if queen bee herself, Ms. Capelli, carts the stuff out." A scowl swept across her face when the supervisor indicated that they leave the office for a tour of the second story. "I'm not going up there with you," she said flatly. "If I see that junk and don't say anything, I'll be siding with the district and not with the parents I represent. Just get rid of that shit, no big deal."

"There is no need to use profanity," muttered Lou. He sighed and reached into a pocket for a set of keys. He reluctantly led Steve to the stairway at one end of the school and unlocked the door. The two trudged up the stairs as the panting supervisor complained that the endeavor was a waste of time. He had put in a long hectic day and he should be home at five in the evening. Lou was the perfect education bureaucrat. He remained busy without accomplishing anything. His ability to steer clear of contentious issues was usually based on a combination of laziness and self-preservation. With Greenside issues, his reticence was based on fear of the future. He wished he was totally ignorant. Though his awareness of the plan was limited, it was still too much knowledge for his pay grade.

Lou opened the door to the Language Arts room and immediately noticed the footprints in the dust. He squinted, then sneezed, once again displaying an allergic reaction. This did not stop him from eyeing two missing boxes of old primary phonics books. "Where did the *Fun with Words* picture books go?" he asked, the timbre close to a moan.

Steve knew where they had gone—to Joan's classroom, courtesy of Tiny. He vacillated between worrying about Greenside "borrowing" the books and marveling at Lou's uncanny memory for useless information. "Those books probably went to a high school," he stated firmly. Catching Lou's perplexed look, he explained. "They have a Young Rotarian group at Lakeview. They probably shipped the books overseas as part of an international aid project."

Nodding thoughtfully, Lou liked what he heard. He was off the hook. Any missing books would be an issue for the adult sponsor at the high school. "I should have been consulted," he griped. "High school people never follow protocol." Tempted as he was, Lou had no interest in taking the issue to Superintendent Capelli. Even he realized that bothering her over two missing boxes of old phonics books would incur more than a tinge of wrath for wasting her time.

Before closing the door, Steve scanned the shadowy room for the feral felines. There were none. Where were the damn cats?

Lou opened the door to the Math storage room. "Somebody's been in here too," he blurted.

'What do you mean?" asked Steve, wondering whether his impressions of Lou as a bumbling buffoon were erroneous. The man might be more Columbo than Clousseau.

"There were three boxes of *Math Moves* there," he claimed. "Look, you can see that the floor is not as dusty." He was grumbling with conviction now. The elementary Math program he had championed based on *Math Moves* five years previously was in disrepute. There were dozens of boxes with almost-new books, but it was the missing ones that groused Lou.

"Maybe someone in maintenance took a box or two to a high school?" suggested Steve. "The school's Special Education department might need them."

Lou had not considered that. "Right, yeah, it must be the Special Education people." His nose twitched prior to another sneeze. He sensed another presence in the room, but his inflamed nostrils forced him to depart quickly, sniffling into a formerly clean hanky. He was not interested in the next room where Science debris was housed. It originated from middle and high schools. He was equally indifferent to the office equipment and furniture piled high in a fourth room.

Erupting into a violent sneezing fit, Lou croaked, "I have to get out of here, there is too much dust." The sneezing and coughing ceased when he reached the first floor. "I don't think I can help you," he concluded. "I talked to Phil Chow before coming here and he says this is the first he's heard of any of this."

"I sent Capelli an email and talked to her at the beginning of the year. She told me that she would speak to him."

"Yes, but you should have sent a copy of the email to Phil. Maintenance is his area." Lou leaned forward as if sharing state secrets. "Between you and me I think he might have been a bit more cooperative if you would have followed proper communication channels."

Steve sighed. He had hurt the business manager's feelings by going over his head to Capelli. She, being a hierarchical nut, probably did not inform Chow, trying to teach Steve a lesson. Disregarding procedure would only encourage principals to engage in end-runs and ignore proper protocol. "Maintenance could move the stuff to the old Greenside Elementary School," he said, still searching for a solution.

"Yes, but they'd have to do a deep-clean in that building first so they could work in a safe environment. That would take a lot of time."

Sensing the dialogue might get even less productive, Steve waved an arm in frustration. "It's just junk! Who cares if it gets dumped into some decrepit, moldy school?"

"That's the point. The maintenance and custodial people won't go in there until it's properly fumigated. That costs money. You have to be patient." Lou said this softly, as if calming an over-zealous teenager. "Phil wants you to send him an email about this issue and get back to proper reporting procedures." He shrugged thin shoulders.

Trying to conjure a way out of this bureaucratic nightmare was taking a toll on Steve's patience. He still could not decide if Lou was an idiot or cunningly clever. Struggling to maintain an even composure, he agreed to contact Phil Chow. As Lou was readying to leave Steve took a shot in the dark. "Just one more thing," he asked softly, forcing Lou to stop and turn. "Is the district going to close Greenside School?"

Lou's face turned from pale to alabaster. His attempt to mask distress failed. "What do you mean?" he muttered. The delaying tactic failed to elicit a response. A tense silence ensued. Steve's stern countenance bore into him. Normally unfazed by angry eyes, on this occasion Lou inexplicably crumbled. With robotic tone he declared, "There have been no decisions made and the building will continue to operate as a school."

"That sounds like a mantra, Lou."

"There have been no decisions made and the building will continue to operate as a school."

Steve leaned forward. "Yeah, I got that the first time." Lou was still standing by the door, seemingly paralyzed. Steve was getting nowhere with the automaton masquerading as a human. He shifted topics, hoping to throw off Lou's mantra. "What is A-1 Education Incorporated and what is their role with the school district?"

The question overloaded Lou's fuse box. "There have been no decisions made and the building will continue to operate as a school," he chanted as he scurried along the corridor toward the front door.

Steve slowly returned to his office. He phoned business journalist Terrel Lewis and asked him to dig for information about A-1 Education. Terrel readily agreed, always ready and willing to chase a story.

The response came only two days later. Very little was known about A-1 Education since it was not a publicly traded company. It provided software in the education field for instructional and administrative purposes. Steve knew that already. Since the company was not listed on the stock market it did not have to provide various levels of financial transparency. "There's more," said Terrel, clearly excited. "Chuck Palmer, that asshole from Darrington days, is a sales rep for the company. And those guys golfing with Capelli and Chow were A-1 Executives." Terrel paused to catch his breath. "I couldn't find out who the little smarmy guy with the bandaged forehead is though. I'll sniff around and get back to you."

Steve winced. He must have got Terrel on a slow week. The man sounded like a ravenous cougar that had just seen a rabbit stroll across its path. Maybe it was normal vexation over the re-emergence of Chuck Palmer into his life but lately Terrel seemed more a member of the paparazzi than a responsible journalist.

Favoring frank and open discussion to backroom deals and sniffing-dog journalism, Steve decided that the cards should be put on the table. There was the summer tour of the school and the blunt Capelli reaction to his question regarding its purpose. No maintenance requests for Greenside had been completed. Lou Tayler could only stick to a well-rehearsed mantra that explained nothing. Like Terrel, Steve saw machinations swirling in the darkness. It was time to flick a light-switch and illuminate the shadows. Jennifer Capelli should be invited to a Greenside Parent Council meeting to talk about the future of the school. He phoned Donna and suggested the idea.

"Capelli, coming to the Greenside Parent Council?" Donna huffed into the receiver. "What have you been smoking Steve?"

"We don't have a school board representative from Greenside right now and I have some questions about various activities around the school."

"I take it Lou was not much help in agreeing to move that junk from the second floor." Donna paused. "Okay, forget I said that. What else can you expect from Lou Tayler the Jell-O man?" Her tone became serious. "You said activities, Steve, as in more than one. What else is going on?"

"I don't know. There's all these little incidents and meetings and occurrences. They may be unconnected. It might be coincidence—or they might be part of a plan regarding the future of the school."

"You mean close it?" snapped Donna before issuing a level of invective aimed at Capelli and Chow that would make a sailor blush.

Twice Steve tried to interrupt and stop the tirade, both times unsuccessfully. He waited patiently as Donna's rant eventually dropped to mere grumbling. "Let's not get carried away, okay? Just put it on the upcoming parent meeting as a general discussion item without mentioning any specifics." He felt Donna's comfort level drop at the suggestion. "That's not being secretive or dishonest Donna," though he wasn't sure that was true. He worked to justify the lack of transparency to the other parents. "We really don't know anything at this point. You and I should keep it that way until we know more. We'd look stupid if we made an accusation that was way off the mark. It's just good to have the superintendent visit every once in a while, to give us a district perspective on our school."

"Okay," agreed Donna, with a titch of reluctance. "But I know what Capelli thinks of Greenside school and it sure as hell isn't good."

14

Steve had promised to oversee Joan's Kindergarten children for a half hour while she led her first-grade students on a field trip to inspect autumn's falling leaves.

The conversation with Donna went longer than expected and Steve was tardy. Mouthing an apology, he quietly entered the room. Joan was reading a story, her students engaged, the classroom busy. When Steve taught Basic English at high school there was a considerable amount of down-time. Students often started shutting down as early as fifteen minutes before the end of class. Steve frequently finished everything he wanted to accomplish with ten minutes to spare, too late to start something new. But a teacher could not say, "Sit quietly and wait for the bell," to primary students and expect nothing less than chaos. Students were to be kept occupied every minute. If the children were not working on the teacher-appointed task, they would soon find something else to color, poke, prod, throw, or screech at.

The twenty-one children sat cross-legged on the carpet staring wide-eyed as Joan read the huge font and pointed at the pictures. Like most primary teachers she could read from the side so the huge picture book could face the students. Steve had watched Joan Mackenzie reading to her class more than a dozen times and she never needed to intervene to settle the children. The scene emulated the oral traditions of humans, the wise elder regaling a group of young children sitting rapt with attention. Whether in a classroom at Greenside Community School in 2011 or a fire-warmed cave at the dawn of humankind, the aura was the same.

"Look, children, Mr. Hepting has come to join us."

At this, Steve smiled. He pulled the teacher's chair to the corner of the carpet and plunked down. "Hello boys and girls."

"Hello Mr. H.," the voices rang, high and squeaky.

"Sit on the carpet Mr. H.," said one girl. "Then we can help lift you up like last time."

The rest of the class snickered. Joan interrupted, quietening them. "I think Mr. Hepting wants to use my chair today." She gave Steve an impish look. "Isn't that right Mr. Hepting?"

"Yes please, Mrs. Mackenzie."

Joan took the first-grade students outside. More adept at wardrobe changes than their Kindergarten classmates, it only took ten minutes to put on their coats, hats, and outside shoes. Steve was left with nine tiny Kindergarten children who were evenly divided into three groups. She had provided written instructions that involved the use of poker chips. Steve struggled to shoo the image of Joan, Gladys and similar matrons hunched over a dully lit poker table with Mick Jagger's "Honky-Tonk Women" blaring in the background.

The students were to use the poker chips to develop patterning by color and shape. A pile of three black chips were to be followed by stacks of six white, two red, four green and ten blue.

The initial gusto for the task soon dissipated. Two boys in one group did not know the colors and argued between green and blue. One finally pushed the other, sending the victim into a fit of sobbing. Steve chastised the assailant until he started crying too.

In the second group a bossy girl did not want the stacked piles in a straight line. She preferred them arranged in a necklace shape. Steve told the group to vote, straight line or semi-circle. Unfortunately, the concept of democracy was lost on Kindergarten children. They sat silent for a moment. Figuring that the majority would opt for the semi-circle, Steve decided on that option. "I want Mrs. Mackenzie back," wailed one child who had favored the straight line.

Joan had only been absent for five minutes.

The third group made progress and were completing the final stack of ten blue chips. Demonstrating admirable cooperation, the children agreed that there were only nine chips. They searched the area, sweeping their little arms across the floor. With one ill-fated swoop, a girl knocked every pile into a disorganized scatter. Without recriminations, they were gathering the chips to try again, first insisting on counting each color to ensure that they had the correct number.

By the time Joan returned with the first graders, Steve was exhausted. Two of the three groups were experiencing teamwork issues. The most cooperative group was no further ahead, hampered by the accident and over-zealous caution in counting the chips over and over.

"Mrs. Mackenzie," the group hollered as she re-entered the room.

Joan directed the first-grade students to store their leaf drawings in folders at the rear of the room. Several of the Kindergarten children were hugging her legs as she surveyed the classroom carnage. "How did it go," she asked, a wry smile forming across her wide face.

"Not bad," replied Steve, "Better than I thought it would." As anarchic as it had been, the time spent in Joan Mackenzie's class was more positive than talking to Lou Tayler, refereeing between Colin Redford and Emma Martinez, or worrying about a school closure.

The rest of the day was spent responding to emails and phone calls. Steve's pining for a return to a teacher position intensified during an after-school meeting with a chagrined Tiny. As he listened to the tale, he silently asked himself why he had been so stupid to accept the principal position? Gobsmacked, he sat in his chair, unable to take his eyes off the sullen Tiny.

"There have been dead mice around the school and you were," Steve had to choose his words carefully, "disposing of them?"

A tearful Tiny nodded.

"And now there are none in any traps you've set, downstairs or upstairs?"

"Mr. H. I know you don't wanna hear about the animals unless it's bad for the kids but this is really weird." With the principal's stare raising his anxiety, Tiny explained that there had been far fewer mice in the traps. For a few weeks no mice had been caught downstairs. For the last three days none were in the traps at the end of the second-floor hallway. "I hated using the traps and lugging the dead little gomers away. Now I don't know what's happened to them." The young behemoth sniffled. "They're all gone."

Soothing the distraught Tiny with soft words, Steve explained that he was very happy and proud of the initiative the janitor had shown.

Tiny calmed and accepted the praise. Even though he did not know exactly what initiative meant, it sounded pretty good. Embarrassed, he wicked a tear that had escaped from his eye and produced another quick sniff.

Steve probed cautiously. Tiny had a heart as big as Bill Gates' wallet. The young man loved animals and had buckets of disposable cash. There was no way to discern what the next chapter in this tale would reveal. "When you took the mice away, what did you do with them?" Steve asked gently, though his muscles tensed and teeth clenched. He was not sure he was going to like the answer.

"I bought a box to put them in."

"A cardboard box?"

"No, Mr. H. I went to one of those places where they put dead people in boxes and got a big shiny one."

"A casket? They're pretty heavy."

Tiny shrugged. "I guess," he said. "I got my buddy to help. He's into vampires and stuff like that. He thought it was pretty cool."

Long ago Tiny had nabbed a key to the old elementary school building next door to the current school. With no windows, the gym was the perfect place to house the casket. Early each morning for several weeks Tiny gathered up the dead mice in a small gunny sack and walked to the abandoned school. He put the little rodent bodies in the expensive, virtually airtight casket and shut the lid.

Tiny looked for guidance. "There aren't any more dead mice around our school now. Do you think I should take the box to the dead guy's place and put it in the ground?"

"You bought a plot for the mice?"

Shrugging again, Tiny replied, "I guess." He could not fathom why Mr. H. seemed so surprised. Sometimes his smart principal was a little strange. Where else would you put a coffin?

"I suppose you could wait a day or two and then bury the mice." Steve could not believe the words emanating from his mouth. He needed to move to a less surreal topic. "We've still got cats though?"

Tiny nodded. "They sleep during the day in the boxes upstairs. They wander around at night when no one is in the school."

"Maybe they ate all the mice?" Steve was trying to be helpful.

Tiny's face soured at the thought. He did not think so. The cats had lots of left-over lunch scraps and didn't need to chow down on mice. He struggled to stay silent. Mr. H. only wanted to know about animals if they were bothering the kids.

Steve thought Tiny might be withholding information. The young man did not lie, though at times you had to ask the right questions to pry information from him. Steve was too mentally fatigued to probe. After hearing about dead mice being put in a coffin and buried in a cemetery, he was afraid of what might come next. Sometimes ignorance was bliss so he ended his queries.

Needing a break from executive matters such as deceased mice and feral cats, Steve agreed to visit Emma Martinez's class the next day to talk about energy conservation. Despite his less-than-stellar performance in Joan Mackenzie's class, he was confident of a more positive experience this time.

Along with Summer Martin, Emma Martinez was the green warrior on staff. Unlike Summer, who exuded a laissez-faire, individualistic, bohemian lifestyle, Emma was political. She was anti-authority, anti-development, anti-capitalist, anti-imperialist, and anti-globalist. Her teaching job did not allow time for her to be a professional protester, but she was particularly active in the local group trying to preserve the forested area near Oak Grove High.

Emma was more Greenpeace than Sierra Club. Though it was natural that Emma's views would surface in her teaching, she made a concerted effort to provide a balanced view in the classroom. She railed against the quasi-science and educational fluff that was popular with some of her colleagues who used their classrooms as pseudo-political pulpits.

The fourth-grade students were focused on energy and the environment and their work was far from fluff. They had analyzed their school's energy use. Since Steve was the boss, they wanted him to hear their conclusions. Confident of an easy session, Steve stood at the front of the room facing the crowd as would a politician in a media scrum. The first three-some, assigned water consumption, claimed the school could save gallons of water by converting to low flush toilets. Another group, researching the same issue, noted that the kitchen sink water was left running when the parents washed the vegetables for lunch. The veggies should be washed in a large container with the water shut off.

Three groups examined electricity use. The first declared that the fluorescent lights needed to be changed to LEDs. A second group added that too many teachers left the lights on when the room was empty and suggested Steve devise appropriate punishment for each offending instructor. They glumly noted that the principal was the worst culprit, often failing to turn off the lights in in his office. He also had left his computer on twelve out of the last fourteen nights. Secretary Mrs. McKenzie always turned her computer off. The students had a graph to illustrate the point. Bridget had ratted on Steve and now the principal was forced to confront his sorry performance, aptly displayed in a colorful visual.

The third electricity group took no pity on the battered principal. They had another damning chart showing the discrepancy between the "on" hours of the bank of computers in the library and the hours of actual student use. The result was far from favorable. The group noted in a serious tone that Mr. H. was the librarian and thus responsible for the computers.

Sweating as if he was in a witness box with a smooth lawyer tap dancing on his face, Steve was in need of hydration. He reached for his water bottle but saw the stern looks of the next group. "Oh no," he thought to himself, "Another pummeling."

As if on cue, the next group taped a poster on the board with more data and graphs. The topic was waste generated from plastic bottles. "All the kids and most of the teachers bring plastic water bottles," they said. The students had echoed one of Summer Martin's ideas of piling all the plastic bottles in the gym for a week.

"I don't use plastic water bottles," said Steve lamely, trying to hide the one in his hand behind Emma's desk. "I borrowed this one."

"But the chicken pies you buy are in giant plastic containers and four of those are thrown out every day. Each one has the same amount of plastic as eight plastic bottles and that means forty each week and . . ."

"Yeah, I get that," admitted a weary Steve, "You have to give me a break here. I'm only the principal. That's how the pies are sold."

"Ms. Martin said the eighth-grade classes could make the chicken pies. If we did that, we would save the environment about 1,600 plastic bottles," said the leader of the seventh group. We checked recipes and you can make the pies for less money."

Was there no end to this shellacking? Steve managed to blurt out, "That's a very good point you make. I'll have to talk to Ms. Martin about your idea."

Mercifully there was only one more group. River Coolwater was the spokesperson, an indication of how well the boy had settled into the school. With teacher and parent permission, River and Jay Woznicki often helped Tiny clean up after lunch. Reflecting his personality, River's topic was different. He began talking about a proper environment for all creatures, not just humans. Emma had mentioned the boy's love of animals. Steve sighed. Though his brain hurt he forced himself to concentrate. Where was River going with this?

"We need to give this animal a good home," said the boy. He walked to the cloakroom. Fiddling for a moment he finally pulled out a carrying case with a wire front. Inside was a sizable snake, curled lazily in the center. Directing his statement to Steve, River said, "We named him Sammy. Ms. Martinez says we can't have animals in class anymore. But if we make him go outside, he'll die. It's too cold outside for him now."

Steve stared at the snake, fortunately too wide to slip through the wire grating. "Where did you find him?"

"He was in the cloakroom, sleeping underneath the blanket on the shelf."

"Oh God," thought Steve. 'The snake must have been gorging on mice. When the rodents disappeared, it had slithered to the lower level in search of food, finding a warm spot in Emma's cloakroom. "Did he bite you?"

"No," said River. "He scared me at first. I picked him up by the tail and we put him in a drawer in Ms. Martinez desk until Tiny could get a cage."

Tiny! Steve fired a glance at Emma and mulled over the bollocking he was going to give the janitor. Why did everyone keep him in the dark all the time? He was the damn principal.

Feeling twenty-four pairs of expectant eyes on him Steve sighed. Capelli had not said anything about banning animals. Not yet anyway. "You can keep Sammy for now but we will have to find him a better place to live, okay?"

The children cheered. River thanked his principal and assured him that Sammy did too. A surprised Emma Martinez was impressed. Steve Hepting was not like any other principal she had known.

Steve escaped to his office and closed the door. Why did shit like this always happen close to a parent council meeting? First, Tiny had been carting dead mice away and placing them in a coffin. Feral cats were supposedly chowing down on the scraps from children's lunches. A snake had decimated the mice population and was now curled up in a teacher's desk.

There was no need to mention any of this at the parent meeting. There had been no staff or student reports about vicious felines. He doubted Tiny's tale about the cats devouring food scraps. With no mice, they would likely leave the school in search of an alternate food source. He would have to mention Sammy the snake though. Notorious blabbers that they are, the children would surely pass on the good news that Mr. H. was letting the class keep the reptile. He sighed. Parent meetings were frequently unpredictable. This one could be especially so. It was not every meeting that the principal had to talk about a snake named Sammy holed up in a classroom.

15

Parent meetings were held in the library, starting at 7:00 pm. Steve's report focused on good news. The automatic flush on the primary toilets had again been repaired by Tiny. Anne Shaw was able to assist more students in her counseling capacity since Summer had been taking some of the load in Learning Assistance. The lunch program was operating well. The parents responded by noting that the successes were accomplished by school-based people, reinforcing their view that the downtown Taylerston big shots did nothing for the Greenside school.

There was only one challenging mother, Irene, "the Lizard," Linzel, the vice-chair. She was frequently enamored with self-proclaimed authority. The unflattering nickname originated from her dry, scaly skin and the habit of flicking her tongue to the sides of her mouth when she was thinking. Though it was a well-known label, no one used it in her presence. She snapped like a crocodile and sank ferocious fangs into anyone who disagreed with her. She did not like Donna, considering the chairperson to be a school-system toady. She had challenged for the leadership position at the final meeting the year before, losing five votes to one. Presumably her self-selection was the sole supporting vote.

"Is there a snake in the school?" she blurted. Though Mrs. Linzel's son was in Colin Redford's sixth-grade class, she was well connected to the Greenside grapevine. "We're not supposed to have animals in schools." She glared at the evening's special presenter, Anne Shaw, as if she had been the infamous counselor who had set the iguana onto unsuspecting children the year before.

Steve butted papers together akin to old-time TV news anchors at the conclusion of a broadcast. Thank God he had decided to refrain from tales of dead mice and feral cats. The animal issue could easily have spun out of control. "The snake is in a cage and as yet there has been no directive from the district." He noted the bobbing heads from the other parents. They had no issue with Sammy as long as the snake was kept in a cage. "The superintendent is looking for two parent representatives for the animal-policy committee. Are you interested Mrs. Linzel?" He gulped. He had almost said Mrs. Lizard.

"No," snapped the parent. "I don't like that Capelli woman. She's always plotting against Greenside."

The rest of the council members voiced similar concerns about the leader's views on the future of Greenside school and voted unanimously to invite Superintendent Capelli to the November meeting. Voicing Greenside concerns was timely. The community's school board member had resigned her seat and moved to Seattle. The Taylerston School Board could legally continue with six members and Capelli had convinced them to do so. By-elections were expensive and the district would have to bear the cost. With only one small school, the Greenside community was, in her view, ridiculously over-represented. She argued that a one-year absence of a Greenside trustee balanced the over-representation of previous years. Community members were surprisingly silent, fearful that the Lizard would be the sole candidate to run in a by-election since Donna's employee status disqualified her. Though few in Greenside would want the reptile masquerading as a human as their school trustee, no one would dare run against her.

"It's a great idea, but Ms. Capelli will never come," a parent said.

"Let's send a letter anyway," proclaimed Mrs. Linzel, ever the rabble rouser. "Capelli's gonna have to respond to it. She'd look like shit, especially since we don't have a Greenside trustee to bring our views to the school board."

The determined parents nodded in agreement. If the superintendent gave them answers they didn't like, they were never going to turn away from a good scrap. What they didn't know was that Jennifer Capelli never did either.

Thanks to special funding from gaming revenue, the parent council had a considerable amount of money to throw around, much more than what was available to Steve. The council's account books, such as they were, only had to be audited once every four years. If the group had a constitution, no one knew where it was. A good crowd at a meeting was eight parents. Steve and Donna had worked together to ensure a well understood process for setting the agenda, the manner in which complaints were dealt, and the procedure for accessing the funds so it was not spent frivolously or as the result of one teacher's active lobbying.

Usually a teacher was asked to attend the council meeting and provide a brief explanation of relevant grade-level curriculum, specialty subject, or support-service area. Most faculty members did not mind the task. Teachers loved to talk about their teaching style or their program. On this occasion it was Anne Shaw, explaining her role as the school's counselor. She completed a stellar job—too stellar.

"We should have Ms. Shaw provide an effective parenting course," Mrs. Linzel gushed. "God knows there's lots of folks in Greenside who could use it," the speaker of course not being one of them. Anne glanced at Steve, seeking direction. This moment was always a difficult task for a principal. Loony ideas could usually be shut down. On occasion, a proposal was sound and often involved the council seemingly directing a teacher as if that group was the employer. When this occurred, extricating a staff member from yet another workplace burden became much more delicate.

"Ms. Shaw would be an excellent person for such a program," praised Steve.

The Lizard sat back and scowled. She could feel a "but", coming. To her surprise there wasn't one.

Steve continued. "Perhaps the council could survey parents to see if there is interest and if so, we could look at a program such as the one you suggest?" He caught Anne's glare from the corner of an eye. Steve hesitated. "However, we would need another person to teach the course." He stared at the Lizard, knowing she was wondering why. Proceeding with the answer, Steve said, "Ms. Shaw would be in a potentially difficult situation, perhaps even a conflict of interest. She would want to describe real cases to be used as examples. Even though she would never do so knowingly, some parents might believe she was using examples from her Greenside files. The appearance, though mistaken, could impair the great job she is doing for the kids at the school."

The parents nodded in solemn unison. "I was wondering about that," claimed Mrs. Linzel. She flicked her tongue to the side of her mouth, causing Steve to stifle a grimace. "That could be a big problem," she concluded. "Greenside is a small community and everyone gossips," she, of course, not being one of them. "Maybe we should think about it for a while." With that, she withdrew the motion and Steve felt Anne's tension drain away.

Mrs. Linzel was not finished. Donna was reluctant to exercise authority, especially against the Lizard. The end result is that meetings could be focused or scattered. Most council members made an attempt to see the school through a wider lens. But as parents, they naturally viewed education through their children's eyes. If a daughter liked soccer, the mother pushed to have the fields improved. If a son was struggling with reading, a concern was raised about the availability of learning assistance. If a child loved music, there was a call for better instruments.

At times, a parent used the forum to parrot their child's views about a teacher, a tactic Mrs. Linzel tried now. "What is Mr. Redford's background for teaching sixth-grade children?" she asked, subtle as a sledgehammer.

"We do not discuss personnel matters at these meetings Mrs. Linzel," Donna stated firmly. She had been well coached by Steve.

"Fine," huffed the Lizard, turning to the principal. She caught a tinge of anxiety behind his firm stare. "Do teachers receive reports on their performance?"

This was an appropriate question and well phrased. Steve was going to have to be careful in his response. The education system had relied on principals completing reports on teachers for decades. This harkened back to a distant era when the principal was considered the master teacher, chosen for pedagogical skill. This foundation for selection rarely occurred any longer. Principals were chosen for a variety of reasons, one of the lesser being pedagogical skill. The attributes that made for a successful principal were a combination of positive interpersonal acuity, public relations acumen, communication ability, organizational strength, and computer know-how. Occasionally, curricular expertise was thrown into the mix. A principal's background could not include being a poor teacher since classroom incompetence would stretch the selection envelope too far. A reputation as an excellent teacher was a plus, but average classroom performance would do, especially if the candidate possessed marked ability in other attributes.

"Principals do write reports on teachers," Steve answered. This was true. Occasionally a teacher wishing to switch districts would ask for an evaluation. In a few cases a struggling teacher would receive a report. Steve had never completed one or had one written about him.

"Is there a process?" asked the reptile-cum-woman.

Steve was not sure if she meant a process as in a regular schedule which existed in name only, or if there was a procedure to be followed in completing a report. He chose the latter and answered truthfully. "There is a process and it is very detailed." He did not mention that it was so numbingly bureaucratic that it actively discouraged principals from any action.

Steve waited, hoping against hope that the Lizard would not ask if reports were effective in removing incompetent teachers from the system. Perhaps she knew that very few teachers were ever terminated for ineffectual teaching. She might be aware of the dismal efficacy of the report-writing process for that purpose.

With a break in the discussion, Donna jumped in. "Thank you for the question Mrs. Linzel. And thanks to you Steve for an enlightening answer. Let's move on to the other items on the agenda."

The parent council members were unabashed Greenside School supporters. They liked Steve, they liked the school, and they had the usual Greenside distrust of any Taylerston-generated action. They passed motions to express concern about the playground big toy—too old, the emergency supplies—too few, and the parking lot—too small. This latter problem was common throughout the district as everyone drove their children to school even if the family lived two blocks from the entrance.

After the meeting Donna sat in Steve's office. They reviewed the evening's activities, praising Anne Shaw, grousing about Mrs. Linzel, and debating whether Capelli would attend the next meeting in November—and if so, what she would say.

Steve thought Greenside school was not foremost on Capelli's mind. She and Phil Chow were enamored with computer-assisted instruction. When they weren't scrapping with the labor unions, they turned to their love of computers. He postulated that the Capelli-Chow meetings with A-1 Education were likely about expanding the new administrative program for the district's operational needs such as budget, leaves of absence, internal communication, and student records. That would explain Business Manager Phil Chow's involvement and the agenda item on the late-October administrator's meeting.

"Damn," muttered Donna, "I think you're right. There's gonna be more office computer systems coming. We're gonna have to attend more of those horrible training sessions. It's torture sitting through them."

The tales of anxious teachers, bored maintenance workers, and frenzied office staff confined to a characterless room for a two-hour computer-training session were legendary. Steve had survived more than a few. Most people needed at least five times that to digest what was required. The instructor would be an expert and not a teacher, or at least not a good one. The expert talked in techno-gibberish which most of the audience did not understand. Given the condescending attitude displayed when answering, questions were clearly unwelcome. Most of the audience members simply shut down. One of these garbled sessions was enough to make anyone realize that teaching was indeed a skill. It was 2011. Steve thought that school districts should have learned to educate their employees more effectively by now. He huffed. "I remember one session when I didn't know whether to shoot myself or take a bottle of pills."

"Always use the bullets, they're quicker." Donna took a playful cuff at his shoulder. "That's all big talk with you anyway. I've heard about you at workshops. You just fall asleep."

Pretending to appear hurt, Steve avoided a verbal riposte as a new thought entered his head. "The government wants to centralize everything. They won't let a dinky district like Taylerston install its own administrative system."

"Maybe we're going to be the pilot? Capelli and Chow are real snakes in the grass. They're always slithering around to make themselves look good." Donna rose, smiled at the principal and said, "Gotta get home to husband Hank. He can only handle two kids for so long."

Steve watched her leave before tidying up a few papers. He spent the rest of the evening at home, moping. The funk stretched for several days. Perhaps it was the realization that he missed Donna? Maybe it was the seeming loss of an opportunity for reconciliation with Monique? His juvenile behavior still stuck in his craw. It may have been caused by uncomplicated jealousy as Summer developed a romantic connection with Perry. She and Anne were the two women Steve saw the most often. One day, he ate lunch in the staffroom, a rare occurrence to the point that it drew stares from the teachers. He sat with Anne. She was eating a salad. He was downing a microwaved Mac and Cheese.

Realization hit Steve while chatting with the counselor between slurps of mushy pasta. It was an emotional drag when work was the sole anchor in a life, A return to a workout regimen would be a good start. Anne encouraged the idea and suggested Dumbelles, a workout salon frequented by women. Steve had been a member several years previously. Physical exertion would clear mental cobwebs and realign a wonky perspective. The anxiety he felt about the future of his school was not matched by the facts at hand. He was an embryonic crisis-junkie. He glimpsed snippets of plots and counter-plots swirling in shadows that only he and an obsessive journalist like Terrel cared about.

Anne could see that Steve needed a change. A life beyond work and golf was the answer. It had just taken the principal longer to come to that realization.

One of his passions in the past had been playing guitar. He was not good, not even average. His fingers were too fat and slow for nimble fret work. Deciding to haul the old Ovation out he spent an hour each night strumming and singing show tunes and eighties pop hits in his head. Becoming more confident, he began to sing aloud, sending Charles scattering to the far reaches of the house.

After a quiet weekend bonding with Charles, a dreary, rainy Monday morning in late October was as good a time as any to display Steve's rediscovered musical acumen and launch a little payback. He visited the seventh and eighth-grade guitar class, instrument in-hand. He was a leading proponent of the so-called frills, especially music. Admittedly, the number of people making a living in the music industry was relatively small. Yet it had to at least equal that of those making a living from calculus or literature. Music was everywhere, an important avocation for those playing an instrument, singing in choirs, or listening to whatever latest electronic gadget contained their personal playlist.

The twenty-seven students were caressing hand-me-down guitars from Lakeview High and making attempts at tuning by plunking strings and twisting keys. No one could decipher correct notes in the nightmarish cacophony. Since it was nearing the end of the term, these students were about as proficient as they were going to get and were scheduled to play two songs at the end-of-term November assembly.

On the blackboard, which was green, were the chords for "O Siem", the 1995 Susan Aglukark hit. The choice was a good one. Ms. Aglukark was an Aboriginal Canadian, an Inuk from Nunavut and there were several Native American students in the class. The song was relatively easy to play and sing and had been altered to the much more common key of G. Counting the initial time, the students watched for their entry measure. Some succeeded, others did not. The teacher grimaced, debating whether to start over. She chose to gamely plow on. Some students displayed smooth chord changes. Others took so much time getting the fingering correct they barely succeeded before the next chord was needed.

Right hand strumming caused even more earaches. Some students had a sense of rhythm and kept proper pace. Others were clueless and attacked the strings in a disjointed, ad hoc motion. The teacher was singing in a heroic attempt to keep time. She stopped the group and said, straight-faced, "That was pretty good. We have to work on our timing and some of you need to loosen your wrists so you can strum down and then up to create rhythm. Mr. H. would you like to try?"

Steve shrugged and accepted the gesture to come to the front. "Does anyone want to join me?" he asked, knowing there would be no takers. Most of the students were eighth-graders. Nobody at that age volunteered to look foolish in front of their peers. When the predictable silence fell Steve said, "I guess I'll have to pick someone." He thought of Kevin. He had been surprisingly bully-free this year. Kevin was a relatively good guitarist, perhaps a bit too good. That might make the other students feel worse about their skill level. He turned to the girl that had hoodwinked him into giving her his new belt on the first day of school; "How about you Janet?"

"Oh man, do I have to?" the girl whined. "I'm useless." Despite the teen's theatrical grousing, she glumly grabbed her guitar and tromped to the front, muttering the entire way. She flashed her principal a, "this sucks" look upon meeting him at the front. They angled their bodies away from the class for a moment, as if discussing musical strategy. "This isn't fair," she whispered. "I know what you're doing. This is payback for the Tiger Woods belt isn't it?" She caught the principal's quick smile confirming her suspicion. "Man, that was almost two months ago!" Though outwardly frowning, she had a twinkle in her eye.

"Yep," replied Steve softly through a wide grin. "This is a good life-lesson for you Janet, my young friend. You should never trip up a boss like me. He just might land on top of you."

16

For principals the Monday afternoon meetings reversed the usual authority relationship. They were the subordinates. Steve had to be careful and follow the advice he had given Janet and not trip up or stab his boss. Capelli would be more than willing to use her stiletto heels to skewer his pudgy flesh.

Flying in wearing a witch's hat and carrying a broom, the only hint that Halloween was a few days away, Capelli quickly discarded the props and called the meeting to order.

Sitting beside Steve was Perry Watkins, HR Coordinator, a man making inroads into Summer Martin's affection. Steve fought the urge to ask a blunt question stemming from a simple ego-driven desire to pry.

Capelli was at the plate with Chow on deck. The superintendent began using a computer projection to display a series of charts and graphs on employee absenteeism. Though she did not want those who were ill to come to work and spread more germs, she was convinced that employees, particularly teachers, were taking advantage of their employer's good will. The practice was diverting thousands of scarce education dollars into sick-leave coverage. Steve knew there was some truth to the claim. A small number of healthy teachers took days off to complete report cards or to spend the day with their own sick children. The same sense of entitlement had been evident when he had worked in the financial industry.

Capelli's solution was predictable. Once up and running, the new absentee software from A-1 Education was able to track all employees by the hour. It had visual capability using cameras inside computer monitors.

Even Capelli had not decided whether to expand into spy capabilities. There would be inevitable concerns about employee privacy.

"The system isn't working yet," whispered Perry. "I think the thing is a piece of shit and more onerous than the paper chase system we use now." Perry was people-oriented and old-school.

"Until the new system is operational, I want you to pay particular attention to teacher absenteeism, particularly on Mondays and Fridays and before report cards. Data indicates these are heavy sick-leave days. If you become suspicious, contact HR. Are there any questions?"

Mercifully there were none. Most site administrators were not likely to increase their diligence. They knew most staff members did not work well when they thought the boss was monitoring their every move and questioning whether they were really sick.

Phil Chow strode to the plate and outlined the new business software system from A-1 Education. He added ten minutes of corporate praise to Capelli's previous fifteen. The A-1 software would achieve substantial savings through better purchasing and inventory management. This was the solution to the Greenside storage issue that had been presented to Steve during a previous short meeting in Chow's office. The soft-spoken business manager had opened by criticizing Steve for going over his head to Superintendent Capelli with complaints about the second-story storage. "That issue is clearly my purview. An effective organization depends upon proper communication channels. The district would be a mess if everyone went to Jen about everything."

Steve bit his tongue. "Sorry about that. I was getting a bit frustrated and it clouded my judgment." He issued a contrite façade, wondering how much more sop Chow wanted.

"Your passion can be your undoing Mr. Hepting. Decision-making must be a rational process, devoid of emotion. You should know that from your stockbroker days. Never fall in love with a stock."

Apparently more groveling was required. "You're right Phil. If anyone should know better, it's me." Steve squirmed to appear uncomfortable and augment the boot-licking.

"I am told by various people that the mice have disappeared."

"Informants more like," Steve grumbled in his head. More crow to eat. "I think so."

"Have you seen any feral cats of late?" Chow smiled as if he knew the answer.

Shit, do I have to swallow the damn crow too? "I haven't seen any since the beginning of the year," Steve admitted.

A satisfied Chow nodded sagely and provided a planned solution. Without the animals, the urgency had dissipated. When the A-1 Education Software was fully implemented, the inventory data for all that was stored in the upper level of Greenside school would commence. With better data on the material stored there, decisions could be made and action eventually taken.

"When will that happen?" Steve had asked.

Chow shrugged. "Soon, the system has a few glitches at the moment."

That wasn't the line Chow was casting to the fish a half-hour later at the principal's meeting. After he completed his praise to the A-1 God, he and Capelli asked for questions and comments. There were none. Chow asked how effective the recent training had been for the clerical staff and how the office workers in the schools were adjusting to the new program.

Heads nodded in support. A few mumbles of "fine" sprinkled the room.

"What a bunch of spineless turds," whispered Perry. "HR is flooded with complaints from principals. In front of Capelli and Chow they won't say a thing."

Steve smiled. He did not know Perry had that much backbone. He was about to offer his own sardonic comment when Capelli moved to the next subject—the decline in the number of teachers aspiring to administrative positions. The pay differential between teacher and principal was much less than that between worker and manager in private industry. An increasingly militant cadre of teacher-union leadership battered the principals. School leaders were also burdened by the demands of a few power-hungry parents securing control of parent councils. That, diminishing budgets, and endless, seemingly purposeless meetings drove many prospective administrators away.

Capelli had booked a booth at an upcoming administrators' conference in Seattle to promote the Taylerston District. She distributed a brochure to the assembled throng who were given a few minutes to peruse the information. The administrators dutifully issued the expected platitudes. The splashy pamphlets contained information on district compensation packages for administrators. Steve raised his eyebrows as he scanned the document. It was common for employees to neglect including benefits when describing their compensation. Capelli had included that information, a reasonable and common practice among employers. However, she had added a new wrinkle and thrown Professional Development allotments, travel subsidies, sick leave provision, and even snacks at meetings into one large compensation pot. Steve could not believe how big the salary vat was, at least according to Capelli's deft use of data.

There was more than words and graphs. Photos had special appeal. Capelli had ordered touch-ups so every school in the Taylerston District appeared new, complete with large grass playing fields. Even Greenside Community School looked good. The photo on the front of the brochure was the ultra-modern school board office with an insert of the photogenic Jennifer Capelli smiling broadly for the camera. The motto, "Taylerston Schools: The Future is Now" was in bold lettering. Steve read the welcome from the CEO to a, "Progressive child-centered lighthouse organization blazing new paths on the educational frontier."

"You've got to be kidding me," whispered Steve to Perry, his partner in cynicism. "HR is going to distribute these?"

Perry hiked thin shoulders. "I showed it to Summer last night and I've never seen her laugh so hard." He smiled wistfully. "Then I showed her the DVD. She was rolling around on the couch, gasping for air through the guffaws."

Steve raised his eyebrows again, this time from picturing Perry and Summer rollicking on a sofa. "There's a video?" he asked.

"Yeah," confirmed Perry. "It's coming next."

As if on cue, Capelli announced that the administrators would be the first to view the video. With the click of a tech device, images flashed on the computer projection screen.

Ten minutes later, the DVD over, Steve sat in stunned silence. A few administrative colleagues clapped nervously. On air, Jennifer Capelli had discussed education while a collage of misleading images of Taylerston school buildings popped up behind her. The smiles of happily engaged teachers, janitors, secretaries, and carpenters looked painted on. Perhaps they were. Scene after scene of the joyous proletariat happy at work reminded Steve of an old propaganda film he had seen from the Soviet bloc made in the 1960s.

One section featured Capelli being interviewed. The CEO discussed the need for, "New Models of Education," and of "Breaking the paradigm that has existed for a century." She never directly criticized the system but asserted that there was a, "Gap between the reality of contemporary society and the structure of the education system." The interviewer, always off camera, was Phil Chow, clearly mindful that he was interviewing an educational visionary. Capelli concluded with, "We require decisive dynamic leaders who look to the future, not the past. We seek initiative and an enterprising spirit. We wish to break the mold and reshape education."

"Holy shit," Steve whispered. "That's pretty bold."

Perry shrugged. "I'm just the salesman pitching the brave new world. Capelli uses that phrase sometimes."

"She must have borrowed it from the Aldous Huxley novel. It's set in the future, about six hundred years from now. A man fights to be freed from a dehumanized, overly ordered, and technical life."

"Hmm," said Perry, "how apropos; it sounds like a world Capelli would love to create."

As October slid into a damp November, Steve fell into the regular swing of the school year. When he was a stock broker, a volatile market meant spurts of frenetic energy. When the market was in a channel and trading volume was low, the activity level dropped markedly. Steve could take a two-hour lunch and troll the business sites on the Internet. On those quiet days, he might only take two or three calls and perhaps one face-to-face meeting.

The pace was different in education. Teaching was a steady hum of activity. Students were always needy, whether to be educated or entertained. Steve had good moments and a few poor ones, inspiring days and ones best forgotten. But it was nothing like the craziness that could surround a brokerage house during a volatile market, or the serene calm in that same office when the market was lolling sideways.

The first of three report cards were being distributed in late November. Several elementary schools had implemented the district's computerized reporting program developed by A-1 Education and supported by Capelli. This allowed a teacher to allocate a numeric score for each learning outcome. The process was slick and time-efficient. This satisfied Capelli's intent to reduce the number of teachers taking sick days to write what she called anecdotal fables. For parents the numbers were refreshingly clear.

Colin Redford and Emma Martinez thought the old-style verbiage cute though arcane. Steve nervously agreed that teachers who wanted to use the new software program could do so. He needed to avoid the usual pitfalls of computer training. A phone call to Lou Tayler went as expected. "I don't think I can conduct any computer report card session," said Lou. "That's not my responsibility. Perhaps that feisty one, what's her name, Emma Martinez, can do it?"

"She doesn't feel like she knows enough. I checked your job description. It says elementary school reporting. That's what this is about. That means it is your responsibility."

The logic did not faze the bureaucrat. Training issues fell under the HR umbrella.

Steve had to admire the man. Lou Tayler was good—too good to be cornered by a principal like him. He convinced Emma to conduct the workshop. All the teachers, except Joan and Gladys, attended. Summer's participation surprised everyone. She was much more computer savvy than people realized. Emma was reasonably competent. Computer whiz Colin needed little time in getting oriented and the pair made themselves available for emails and phone calls from nervous teachers. If the computer screen went blank, the information that had painstakingly been entered might shoot off into cyberspace, never to be seen again.

Waiting for Tiny to provide an afternoon briefing, Steve reflected on the first term. Halloween had gone well. All the students dressed in costume, even the eighth-graders. Steve had cautioned them about overly grotesque images such as knives through bloody hearts and daggers sticking into heads. They had largely complied, even Kevin. The boy was having a great year, in part due to a close bond with Tiny. Only a few primary students had ruined portions of their costumes, resulting in tears. Jay Woznicki came dressed as his principal, complete with a cushion tied to his belly. He wore a dark polo shirt with khakis. Jay had Steve's mannerisms down so well he was allowed to sit in the principal's chair. Bridget even buzzed Jay over the intercom a few times sending the boy into a giggling frenzy.

Sammy the snake had been well cared for by Emma's students, particularly River Coolwater. His mother had found an apartment, and this was the longest River had stayed in one school. She assumed her husband was in Seattle and was unaware of her whereabouts. She had chosen Greenside for its relatively remote location instead of another dingy abode in the big city. To this point in time, the decision had been a good one.

Eventually the time had come for Sammy to depart. One Saturday, Steve took River and Jay to Lynwood, north of Seattle, to deliver Sammy to a reptile shelter. The entire class dripped tears as they bid farewell to the placid snake. The veterinarian had been impressed by the special bond between River, Jay, and the animal. As a treat, Steve took the boys to a pizza parlor for lunch and they toasted Sammy by clinking their pop glasses together.

Bringing Steve out of his trip down first-term memory lane, Anne Shaw stood in the doorway. "I'm sorry," she said with a smile. "I had an appointment with the principal. You're much bigger than the guy I saw a week or so ago."

Staring at Anne, Steve wondered what the hell she was talking about before grasping the jest. Was his brain slowing with the onset of middle age? "Jay was pretty stoked about being the boss."

"I'll say," chuckled Anne. "He asked if I had an appointment when I stopped by." A momentary silence was followed by her question, "You wanted to see me?"

"Oh, right, yes. I wanted to thank you for our little talks, you know, about how I struggle forming adult relationships and focus too much on the job. I think I got a better handle on how I've always, well, you know, related to women, and how I need a better work-life balance."

"It helped?" Seeing Steve nod, the counselor added, "You can thank Tiny. He's the one that formed the basis for most of the advice. He's got a Forrest Gump quality about him. The world is there and he participates in it without analyzing it. He has a keen sense of how his participation affects others. Haven't you ever noticed that he almost never thinks of himself, yet always is himself? That's why he has such a good relationship with Chelsea. That's why the kids love him. He doesn't have any barriers."

"And I do, I mean, did?" Steve said, trying to sift through the counselor talk.

Anne shrugged. "Most adults who score higher than Tiny on an IQ test put up barriers. They know how to do it and find that it works for them, at least some of the time. That young man has none. What you see is what you get."

Steve shook his head and thanked the counselor who then departed for an appointment with River Coolwater and his mother. Tiny Little had always thought Steve was the smart teacher who knew about Shakespeare and books and stocks. Tiny was an affluent young man engaged in savvy investments while attending theatrical performances in Seattle playhouses. Tiny owned five *Phantom of the Opera* T-shirts. He could remember the chorus lines from three songs, so his baritone voice displayed at least some variety. Chelsea was proud of her sophisticated boyfriend. As crazy as it seemed, Steve could do much worse than emulating Tiny's approach to life and relationships. The world was full of amazing irony.

Tiny had an uncanny knack of arriving when his name was being bandied about, in words or thought. The janitor's big frame shrouded the doorway. "The chairs and the coffee urn are set up in the library for the parent meeting Mr. H. All you have to do is flip the switch before you leave." He issued his trademark goofy grin. "Who else but you could get Lady Macbeth to come to Greenside on a cold late-November night? It might even snow." He marveled at the principal's persuasive powers. "It's like you're that Phantom guy."

Steve chuckled. "Look what happened to him in the end."

"Yeah, but even I know that was just a make-believe show. You do that phantom stuff in real life." Tiny readied to leave. The young man shook his head and did not say anything more. Mr. H. never took credit for how smart or cool he was.

17

Just before he was leaving the school, Steve received a phone call from Jennifer Capelli. The CEO almost never used the telephone, it being far too low on the tech-tree. There were no initial pleasantries and her tone was a mix of tough and flustered. "I'm not coming to the meeting tonight. It's going to snow. You should cancel it. It would look bad if you showed up and I didn't since we both live in Taylerston."

"I have my dinner in Greenside on parent council nights," said Steve.

"You still have to drive back."

It was not Steve's meeting to cancel. Capelli was upset at his "jelly backbone" and told him to contact the chairperson. Donna had a modicum of sense. She would cancel. "The switchboard closes at four," snapped Capelli. "I never give out my private number." There was a pause. "Well, almost never. Email me instead."

Steve reached Donna at the maintenance department after the first ring. She cussed and swore when he told her that Capelli thought the meeting should be canceled due to impending snow. "She's bluffing. She just doesn't want to come."

Though Steve agreed with the assessment, he did not think the CEO bluffed. She expected the meeting to be canceled. If it wasn't, and it snowed, she had a reasonable reason not to venture to Greenside. Despite the name, the proximity to Mt. Baker meant the community received significantly more snow than coastal Taylerston.

"What about you?" quizzed Donna. "I know you eat at one of the local diners but you'll still have to drive back home."

"That's only one direction and my vehicle has four-wheel drive. Capelli will claim she would have to drive here in that fancy Lexus she has. She probably doesn't even put snow tires on."

Donna pecked away at a few computer keys and pulled up the weather forecast. Three inches of snow was forecast for Taylerston, six for Greenside. "What do you think?"

"I think you should go ahead with the meeting. Besides me, everybody lives in Greenside and they're used to snow. If Capelli doesn't come we can always re-schedule for January since we don't have a December meeting."

Donna agreed and Steve emailed Capelli the decision.

The terse reply bordered on seething. Capelli was furious at what she referred to as a ridiculous decision. She barked that Steve had, "Bowed to illogical parental pressure." She claimed that the chair of a parent council, "Is not expected to have the same level of judgment as a principal." Steve had, "Failed to exercise courageous leadership." More invective followed for good measure. The superintendent stated that she would not be in attendance. In a pique of frustration, Capelli copied the email to Donna Medford at the maintenance department. The stubby little woman and her good-for-nothing husband Hank were two more examples of poor hiring by past Taylerston administrators.

Moments later, Donna rang, more annoyed at Capelli's swipe at Steve than the superintendent's impending absenteeism. "What a bitch! Did you read that? She can't say that about you and send me a copy. You should complain to the principals' association."

Steve didn't care. He may have been upset if the Capelli missive had been sent to someone other than Donna. At least without Capelli in attendance the parent council meeting would be mercifully brief.

True to Steve's prediction, the agenda items zipped by, including any discussion about Capelli's no-show. Only Mrs. Linzel was especially frothy. "Is Capelli too much of a big shot to come out and talk to us? Is she afraid of a little snow?"

"She would have to drive from Taylerston to here and back," said Donna, taking the high road and publicly defending a leader she mistrusted and disliked.

"The rest of you may be wimps but I'm gonna drive to Taylerston tomorrow morning and plunk my ass in that fancy school board office. I'll show this Capelli woman what Greenside people are made of. I'm gonna find out if she's planning anything for our school."

The next morning, an angry Mrs. Linzel, dressed in a black polyester pantsuit at least one size too small, ignored the police warnings to stay off the Taylerston-Greenside road. She stomped into the reception area near Jennifer Capelli's office shaking the loose snow from her brown vinyl boots, staining the new carpeting. She demanded to see the superintendent.

The CEO was ensconced in her office, phone receiver in hand. A fuming face and shiny fingernails rapped against the desktop and hinted at truculence. Waiting for that useless secretary at Greenside to locate her equally incompetent principal was sending Capelli's blood pressure to unsafe levels. She ordered Bridget to have Hepting phone her immediately and slammed the receiver into its cradle.

Steve had returned from recess supervision wet and unkempt. He had broken up a facial snow-washing scrum as the seventh and eighth-grade boys launched a sneak attack on the girls. He had built two snowmen with the first and second-grade children and shaken white accumulations from several dangerously bending boughs. Snow tumbled onto his Seahawks toque and the shoulders of his black parka, much to the giggling delight of River Coolwater and pal, Jay Woznicki.

"I need to change my shirt and pants," he said when Bridget told him the superintendent was expecting a return call. "They're soaked." He always kept a change of clothes in his office during the winter. Sneaking out of the office five minutes later, guitar in hand, he went to Joan's room. He was scheduled to play "Frosty the Snowman."

When Steve returned to the office, Bridget flashed pleading eyes, the receiver was held high, covered by her hand. "It's Ms. Capelli on the line again. She's not happy."

Steve smiled and shook his head, receiving a bogus scowl from Bridget in return. "I promised I'd read to the second and third-grade class today," he whispered, leaving the Ovation guitar in the office and picking up a dog-eared copy of Charlotte's Web.

The children gave a quiet "Yay" when Steve entered. He called the students to the corner carpet and settled them into their spots. He reminded them of proper carpet behavior and asked who could remember what was happening in the story to this point. Though Steve had not read to the students in four days, hands shot up in eager enthusiasm. Step by step, Steve let each hand-raised student tell a portion of the tale before beginning to read. For twenty minutes Jennifer Capelli was so far away from his thoughts she might as well have been shuffling through a Bhutanese monastery.

Bridget was holding the phone receiver airborne again when Steve returned to the office. The pleading gestures had advanced to an undignified level. When Steve nodded, she almost pulled her hand away from blocking the receiver while yelping "Yes." Straightening her back, slapping on a professional tone, Steve heard her say, "Yes, Ms. Capelli, Mr. Hepting is available now. He just walked in." Bridget paused as she listened. "I think he was involved with a reading performance." She frowned and waited. "Yes, I think it had something to do with analyzing and charting the student reading data that was due at the end of last term but I'm really not sure." Uncomfortable now, Bridget said, "Yes, it is very important that he is directly involved in gathering meaningful statistics."

Steve waited in his office listening to Bridget's occasional acknowledgments to Capelli's lecture. "I'll just be a minute. Tiny needs to talk to me." It was more payback time. Bridget had baked Tiny a home-made Black Forest cake last week, a treat she had not presented to Steve since school start-up. Bridget's excuse that she was helping the principal lose weight just did not cut it in Steve's view. She would learn that he was no second-class employee, he was the principal. His ridiculous behavior in refusing to take Capelli's phone call had been petty, juvenile, and supremely satisfying. At least he had demonstrated some pity and ended Bridget's pain. Capelli was still on hold. Pleased at his successful retribution he settled in to listen to Tiny.

"Chelsea and I saw that movie you told me about, *Mamma Mia*."

Before Steve had an opportunity to respond, Tiny had launched into a critique. "There are these three guys and two of them love this woman; the other guy's gay. The two guys never even told her how they felt when they were young. What a couple of idiots eh? Now they're like major old and they still can't tell her. I mean how stupid are these geezers? Finally, one guy tells her near the end of the movie. He turns out to be the dad of the girl that's getting married. Shit, oops sorry about swearing Mr. H., but there was no surprise in that movie."

Steve wanted to tell the youth he had seen the movie and the play but he could not get a word in. Besides, Capelli was still on hold and he really should pick up the receiver.

Tiny was not finished. "The music Mr. H." he wailed. "It was horrible. The main guy couldn't sing and all the songs were mega old and they all sounded the same and . . ."

"Did Chelsea like it?"

"Oh yeah," said Tiny. "She loved it. The play is coming to Vancouver near Christmas time." A proud look shone toward his former teacher, "That's in Canada. I've never been to Canada before. I heard it's cold."

"Vancouver is about fifty miles from Taylerston, Tiny. The weather is almost exactly the same."

Never long on one topic, Tiny switched effortlessly from meteorological worries to theatrical prediction. "Chelsea heard it's even better onstage. I've already bought the tickets." A brainwave hit, "Maybe one of the guys will be an old Mountie in the stage play. That would be cool."

"I don't think so Tiny. Just because the play is being performed in Canada does not mean there will be Mounties in it." He glanced at the phone. A light indicated Capelli was still on hold.

"Too bad," sighed the young man before brightening with another thought. "Mounties might be the security guards at the door." He switched the topic again. "I want to go to a hockey game. Jay watches them on TV. He says there's always lots of bumping and pushing, even fighting." He paused. "I don't know if Chelsea will like it though."

It was Steve's turn to sigh. Leaving Capelli holding a silent phone for several minutes felt good as a kind of juvenile revenge, similar to what he had done to Bridget. Monique had been right. At times he really was an overgrown adolescent. The conversation with Tiny was going on too long. Capelli would be blowing a gasket on the other end of the telephone line.

Bridget slid into his office wearing an evil grin. She slipped a note on his desk with the scribbling, 'I hope Capelli claws you to an inch of your life. You made me listen to six phone calls from her just because you didn't get a damn cake? You are going to pay big time'! She pointed at the phone and made a slit across her throat. Then she jabbed a finger at Steve, flashed a sinister smile, and left to plot what she was sure would be sweet revenge.

Capelli snarled on the other end of the phone, "Hello, hello. God damn it Hepting, answer me." Steve's hello was greeted by a howl of curses. "I don't appreciate having to wait for the likes of you clowns at Greenside. You, Mr. Hepting, don't have the attitude, the fortitude, and the aptitude to be a principal. Your weak leadership rubs off on the rest of your staff, especially that Mackenzie woman who has been putting me off all morning." Steve was about to correct the nuanced error regarding Bridget's surname when Capelli continued her rant. "Never mind, I already sent an email to you and that useless secretary, word-for-word." Pausing to catch her breath, the CEO regrouped. "Where the hell have you been? Oh hell, never mind, I don't want to know. The explanation will just be bullshit." Damn, this Hepting asshole could get under her skin! The CEO flipped gears. "Tell me about Mrs. Linzel. She's been parked outside my office all morning grumbling and mumbling. Isn't she the one who got her knickers in a knot when we didn't have a by-election for a Greenside school trustee?"

"That's the one," said Steve.

"What's her beef?" Capelli asked. It was relatively common for citizens to run for a position on the school board on a single, sometimes frivolous, issue.

"She doesn't like the teachers' union."

"She'd have had my vote on that." It was the closest Capelli came to making a joke.

"She's more of a three-beef type person. She dislikes how snail-like the system is."

"Damn," remarked an impressed Capelli. "We should have let this woman run for office. What's the third beef?"

Steve smiled before answering, "She hates bureaucrats the most. You're not on her Christmas card list Jen."

Capelli went silent for a moment. For a moment the Linzel woman had been sounding like a soul mate. "What the hell does she want?" she asked curtly.

"She's upset because you didn't come to the parent council meeting last night. She just wants to talk about the future of the school. Donna didn't send her so she's not an official representative."

"So, it's got nothing to do with computers?" blurted Capelli, coarse sandpaper in the voice. She did not wait for an answer. In a huff, she terminated the call.

"Computers?" Steve wondered, receiver still in hand. Where the hell did that come from?

It did not take long for the Lizard to revel in her new stature. Just prior to noon the grinning Mrs. Linzel returned to Greenside and was parked in Steve's office, outlining her meeting with "Jen." Over two coffees and a slice of banana bread she and Capelli had a wide-ranging discussion. Ms. Capelli was clearly misunderstood. She was a dynamo, tough and visionary. She understood Greenside school and the importance it had in the community. She planned to keep the school operational.

Steve was surprised that Capelli had provided such information to Mrs. Linzel so easily. He never received quick, straightforward answers like that. Then again, he was only the principal.

Mrs. Linzel and Capelli had also exchanged common views on the reactionary role of the teachers' union. They agreed that the organization had morphed from a one-time progressive force to an ultra-conservative bureaucratic entity. It was only interested in maintaining a traditional delivery of education services. Mrs. Linzel was also pleased that Greenside was getting a major electrical upgrade and excited that new equipment and building improvements were being planned. She was going to run for the Greenside school trustee in the next election and be part of a bright future of education innovation.

Steve tried to appear nonchalant about this new information. "It's great about the upgrades and changes," he agreed casually.

"Jennifer was not able to say too much right now," claimed Mrs. Linzel. "I guess you know about as much as anybody." She granted a sickeningly sweet smile. Her tongue parted thick lips on the right side of her mouth before traveling to the left, flicking outward the entire way.

Steve struggled to avoid looking away in disgust. "Well, nothing's for sure yet," he replied softly. He provided visual relief by gazing downward at his loafers.

"I understand you cannot speak of the changes just yet," the Lizard said. Steve risked an upward peek. Mercifully the tongue had retreated into the mouth. "Jennifer assured me I would be the first parent leader to be informed when details have been arranged." With a flourish she rose and left.

Teeth clenched tightly as Steve watched her stomp off. The woman grated on him like a rasp. He needed to digest the puzzling information. For the moment he had more important matters, like discussing the progress of various students with counselor Anne Shaw.

Every second day after the post-lunch issues had been settled, Steve met with Anne Shaw. For Steve, it was often one of the best moments of the week. The two unwritten rules were that the counselor would be the first to start, and secondly, that her comment had to relay something positive. This morning the good news was about Jay Woznicki. The boy was making good academic progress in Learning Assistance. He and River Coolwater worked with Tiny for fifteen minutes every day after lunch. Anne hiked thick shoulders. "I have no idea what the three amigos are up to, but River and Jay are happy and that's the important thing."

Steve nodded. He often found the two boys in the library, engrossed in animal picture books. They were most interested in small mammals such as beavers, raccoons, and meerkats. River liked raccoons. Jay was particularly interested in skunks.

The second comment was also of the good news variety. A third-grade girl, previously a little hellion, had been extremely well behaved of late. Anne had no direct explanation.

Steve believed that the girl had to be separated from her sister, which had been done through class placements. Secondly, she needed a counseling program, and thirdly, firm, yet fair, disciplinary action. In Steve's mind, the girl was receiving all three. He suggested de-labeling the girl's behavior-challenged tag. Anne agreed.

Last year, at a special education meeting, Steve had asked for a form to de-label a girl whose behavior had improved to the extent that she no longer exhibited the symptoms of whatever special needs sticker had been plastered on her head. There had to be a form—there was one for every-thing. The specialists sat in wooden silence, nervously shuffling feet until the chairperson had cleared her throat and informed Steve that there was no such document.

"Why not?" Steve asked.

"We've never had a need for one," she admitted.

A new form was devised. Interventions to assist a student had to have worked occasionally to the point that the child could be considered broadly normal. This would not be possible with all students, but there should be a modicum of success with some behavioral issues. If there was never any positive change, what was the point of continuing to repeat the same interventions over and over again and expecting a different result?

Continuing the positive news, Anne explained that there had been no reports of Kevin bullying any children. She looked at Steve to see if he had had any contrary information and the principal shook his head. "Tiny's been giving him money," said Anne. "I saw it happen a few times."

"Payment to stop bullying?" stammered Steve incredulously.

"No, I think the money is for lunches. Kevin's bullying was a form of extortion for lunch money. Don't say anything to Tiny," she warned, cor-rectly reading Steve's thoughts. "If he wanted you to know, he would have said something. Speaking of Tiny, Janet has a crush on him."

Steve paled. "Kevin's girlfriend? Is it one of those pubescent here today, gone tomorrow puppy-love flings?"

"To us it might look like that. To Janet, it's the real deal. Tiny caught on and he's really worried. If Chelsea ever found out Janet was messing with her man, she would grind the girl up so badly she'd look like dog meat." The counselor looked at Steve, trying to gauge his reaction. Normally she could suss out his reaction before he spoke. On this occasion he was eerily difficult to read. "Those were Tiny's exact words," she concluded.

"Tiny's right. A relationship that incompatible has disaster written all over it." He looked sheepishly at Shaw and softened the tone that had grown edgy. "You've got to nip this one in the bud Annie."

Anne's cheeks pulled upward to wide-set eyes, wondering what had prompted the unexpectedly lively response. "I'm on it Steve, don't worry." Attempting to mollify Steve, she shifted gears. "Speaking of lovebirds, Emma and Colin are on much better terms and both said I could relay that to you. He's not going to see the other woman anymore. Emma's going to lay off the green warrior routine."

"Good. Isn't your guy a tree hugger?" The sudden probe surprised Steve as much as it did Anne.

"No, he's got a green lantern streak for sure, but he's more of a ski and surf dude. I'm not into that stuff much but I'm trying." She chuckled. "He does his stuff, I do mine. It works, at least for the time being."

Before she left, a hesitant Anne stood at the doorway. The matter sounded silly but Steve had to know in case the mythical became reality. "River Coolwater has a feeling that his father is nearby. His mother believes her son's premonitions. He's had them twice before and each time the father showed up soon afterward. River seems to have a sixth sense."

Steve nodded before slipping into thought. That might explain River's other-worldly connection with animals. It was a bond the boy shared with Jay Woznicki and Tiny Little. He wondered if there was more going on with that trio of oddball buddies than simply a shared interest in animals of all shapes and sizes.

18

There's a giant cake in your office," Anne noted. "Is it a present for your birthday?" She and Steve had finished a stroll around the school. A peek through the doorway of the principal's office revealed the gourmet treat.

"My birthday's months away." Steve replied absently, busy putting yet another new form back on the absent Bridget's desk. He caught Anne fighting to suppress a wry smile. "What does it look like?" he queried, suddenly suspicious.

A bemused Anne stood silent for a moment. "I don't know, it's a Black Forest cake, bigger than any I've ever seen. It looks yummy so make sure I get a piece." The bouncy steps to the staffroom indicated a happy counselor persona filled with eager anticipation.

Yummy? Anne never used words like that. Skipping like a schoolgirl? She never did that either. Steve walked into his office, working hard to appear casual. The impressively decorated cake sat on the desktop, a gastronomic treat made by Bridget. Steve scanned the outer office, then the adjacent corridor—no sign of Tiny. This cake was intended solely for the boss. He examined it. He poked it with a finger. He smelled it. He lifted it to determine the weight. Bridget was clever and could have included ingredients that did not smell or weigh much. Unsure, he carried the cake to the staffroom. He was the head honcho. Just as in medieval times, the king was not going to be the food taster. He left it on a table and returned to his office. "Nice try," he said to Bridget who had returned from whatever task she had to complete. "Let's see if you can sit here and let the innocent people in the staffroom dive into that tainted cake."

Pleased with snuffing out Bridget's poor attempt at revenge, Steve picked up the phone receiver. Unlike Capelli, he liked the device. Emails were impersonal. Despite being efficient at transmitting information, they were abysmal as a communication tool. Phones weren't great communication devices either, but they were a hell of a lot better than emails. A person could hear variation in vocal tone, laughter, snorts of derision, even sighs. Silence as a response could be an important signal. Even these minor nuances were impossible through email. For a few years Steve received emails using capitals or bold face to indicate intent. Now emojis were being used. Even then, misinterpretation and resulting bad feelings were frequent.

Steve connected with the Special Education department. He requested a de-labeling form and then asked about the slowdown in the screening of Kindergarten and primary age students. Anne Shaw had been right about the testing backlog due to staffing shortfalls. Seven of the students on the eight-member list were boys. To Steve, the elementary system was overly feminized. It was not simply that the teachers were almost exclusively female. It was that the entire aura of the organization worked against boys. Students sat at desks—boys wanted to move about. Students were to take proper care of materials—boys liked to pull things apart. Students were to keep hands off each other—boys preferred to push and grab. Students were taught to use words—boys leaned toward action. More and more it was the girls who were being successful in school and the boys lagged behind, sometimes markedly so.

It was near the end of a week. It had been filled with the Bridget revenge cake that contained God knows what, the Capelli and Linzel machinations, and the River Coolwater premonition. An exhausted Steve needed a real break. He chomped on a sandwich in his office before the noon break. Culinary correctness had not entered his realm. Steve often ate surreptitiously at his desk, gulping processed food from plastic containers and then, forsaking recycling, chucking them into the office garbage can. If Summer or Emma ever found out he would suffer mightily. Fortunately, Tiny would never squeal on him. School lunches were usually of the pre-packaged variety, a tasteless commercially-made pasta dish with a few packets of Cheese Whiz and crackers. Individual containers holding strawberry yogurt was the most common dessert. On occasion Steve remembered to throw in a pear or apple if he found one hiding in the kitchen.

A calm respite to eat rarely happened. Usually the phone rang, or a teacher, paraprofessional, parent, or child entered without knocking, issue-at-hand. Today it was quiet except for the staff members gushing appreciation for the wonderful cake Bridget had brought for him. No one had suffered ill effects. The teachers believed that their thoughtful principal had forsaken the treat and donated it to them for a noon-time treat. The uber-considerate Steve had not even taken a slice. It was a shame since the cake tasted heavenly, probably the best Bridget had ever made.

Noon break for Steve meant distributing food from the lunch program, walking the hallways, and supervising the playgrounds. He tried to snatch ten minutes of quiet time prior to each noon bell, sometimes to eat, at others simply to decompress. Today it was the latter and he was ruminating on the passing of Apple founder Steve Jobs who had died earlier in the month. He admired the contrarian rebel who had left Apple in 1985, only to return and bring the company back from near bankruptcy in 1998. Steve had the left the world of finance. Unlike Mr. Jobs, he never returned to his former position. At times he regretted the decision, especially when Tiny or Terrel Lewis told him about hot stocks. Even with stock splits in 1987, 2000 and 2005, Apple was trading north of $370.00 a share. Steve recalled the stock had been hovering around $14.00 when he was a broker. If he had bought a stack of Apple shares and held them, there would be enough wealth for him to buy and operate his own school. As pleasant as a quick sojourn into a fantasy world was, reality was much different.

Perhaps there were current opportunities for financial windfalls staring him in the face? There was always the next tech company vying to become the next Amazon, Microsoft, or Cisco. Could it be A-1 Education? That morning, Terrel Lewis had emailed Steve an A-1 press release announcing an Initial Public Offering (IPO) for publicly traded shares. Steve had read hundreds of such statements during his stock broker days. Since his career shift to education, he had paid scant notice to the usual company claptrap. This time his interest was high. This time it was almost personal.

Mimicking the standard publicity drivel, the A-1 executives claimed the company was a leader in education software. They were excited about the IPO. They looked forward to participating as a listed company on a stock exchange. They welcomed the increased regulatory scrutiny involved in the move from a private equity firm to a publicly traded company. Unstated though clear, A-1 Education believed the benefits of raising more capital through the purchasing of shares outweighed the unfortunate requirement to adhere to regulators.

In preparation for the IPO, the A-1 press release stated the company was, "Diligently assembling the required financial data." After reading most of the page filled with the usual business babble, Steve had learned nothing new. It was the short closing paragraph that grabbed his attention. "A-1 Education Incorporated will be launching exciting new initiatives that will consolidate its presence as the leading provider of educational software from Kindergarten to post-graduate university study. In conjunction with its partners, A-1 Education Inc. plans to expand its footprint by initiating bold educational operations as a trial basis in selected jurisdictions." The press release concluded with, "For more information see your registered financial institution."

Steve stared at the screen. What the hell does, "Bold educational initiatives," mean? Whatever it was, it would likely mean more conflict, as if there wasn't enough in education already. All the stakeholders—government, school boards, teachers' associations, parent groups, administrators, and public-service unions, grappled in a never-ending tussle to snatch more control from the competitors. Steve left the office in the late afternoon in a sullen mood. An unusually attentive, affectionate Charles did not improve the vibe, nor did slowly sipping on a bottle of quality pale ale.

At these low times Steve wished he were near retirement like Joan and Gladys, two old-fashioned teachers using supposedly outdated methods. But he was not of that generation. Similarly, he had little in common with young green-warriors like Emma Martinez, with their environmental consciousness that bordered on eco-bullying. The twenty-something

Colin Redfords with their heads buried in tech-toys seemed distant. Forty to forty-five years of age was mid-career for most educators and often posed a professional mid-life hurdle. Too much classroom mileage had dulled the enthusiasm of the early years. Too many years ahead made retirement shrouded in distant haze. For many teachers there was a niggling disquiet that was difficult to identify. Some returned to university for upgrading. That experience often pumped energy into their work. Others shifted grades or subjects. Some moved in or out of specialist positions such as counseling. Some changed schools. A few, like Steve, moved into administrative positions.

This was only his second year as a principal. Already the fascination and excitement of the new job was wearing thin, like sandpaper stripping the veneer from a table top. He knew the underlying wood and the table legs were strong. Unlike an earlier career hurdle about whether to return to the financial world, Steve knew he loved education. Yet a shiny coating to cover the imperfections of the crazy system would need to be re-applied every few years lest cynicism take hold.

In a bid to break from his work travails and stagnant social life, Steve invited Perry and Summer to dinner one Saturday evening in early December. The two had become more than friends and, according to Perry, extremely creative lovers. To ensure the conversation did not center solely on educator work, Steve asked Terrel Lewis to join the group. The man accepted with hesitation. He was wary of an evening with a trio of educators who would launch into teacher-talk at the slightest provocation.

Steve spent the day vacuuming and dusting Charles' hair from every nook and cranny of the bungalow. He was not much of a chef but decided to go full out with a cooked meal rather than most of the food being purchased ready-made at the local grocery store.

When Perry and Summer arrived, Steve was busy in the kitchen. Summer clucked about Charles' chubby frame. "I thought you stopped feeding this poor cat junk food? I think he's more obese than a few months ago."

"He's big-boned," explained Steve. "And you should not talk in front of him like that. He's sensitive."

Summer turned her attention to Steve's music holdings, a collection she had pooh-poohed previously. It largely comprised 1980s pop—Wham, Lionel Ritchie, Whitney Houston, and Elton John, who by then was moving into his elevator-music stage. All the Andrew Lloyd Webber musicals were represented. So were theater albums from an ancient era such as, *My Fair Lady*, *The Sound of Music*, and *Oklahoma*. "Hey Perry," she said gleefully, "Here's an album just for you, *Perry Como Sings Broadway!*"

"My God," said the recently arrived Terrel, "Does Mr. Hepting actually own that?"

"I was going to give it to my good friend Perry," Steve claimed defensively. "He appreciates good music."

Summer chuckled. "I've already convinced him that Celine Dion is not the only singer out there." She flipped through the vinyl albums, noting Paul Simon's *Graceland*. "At least there's one decent guy among this sorry collection." Though fifteen years younger than Joan and Gladys, Summer shared a love of music from the late sixties and early seventies. Unlike the rocking grannies, she preferred Donovan's flower-power and the folk-pop of Dylan and James Taylor. The bands favored by the Merlot Maidens—the Who, Stones, and Led Zeppelin were of little interest to her.

Steve's hard work in the kitchen paid off handsomely with a superb meal. Incessant Taylerston winter rain lashed the roof and windows, providing background percussion to the lively conversation. Charles cruised the floor searching for errant pieces of chicken. The humans talked of the new iPad that Apple had launched with much fanfare the previous year.

"It is a brilliant tool," claimed Perry, the technology expert. "Where can you get an instrument that small that can do so much without a keyboard. Once you get the hang of it the swiping motion, it's great."

Techno-phobes Steve and Summer tried their best to repudiate the efficacy of the devices, difficult to do since they did not own one. Steve's only knowledge stemmed from watching a completely engrossed Colin Redford swiping at a screen and blocking out all other stimuli, including sometime-girlfriend Emma Martinez. Summer possessed at least rudimentary iPad knowledge, having borrowed Perry's to check out the graphic apps.

"Imagine the possibilities for schools," enthused Perry. "The potential is enormous. Each kid could have an iPad once the price inevitably comes down. It would be a virtual library at the touch of a fingertip. The software packages to assist instruction these days are of very high quality. I've seen some of the material A-1 Education has produced. The graphics and the linkages are damn good."

Steve groaned. He was tired of hearing about A-1 Education. Terrel Lewis had uncovered nothing nefarious. The Taylerston District was acquiring a new library software program, not yet installed at Greenside. A fitness program that monitored physical activity and changes in blood pressure, heart rates, and caloric reduction had been purchased for high school Physical Education departments. The only controversy was the partnership with some tech heavyweights to acquire land from the school district. The real estate, adjoining Oak Grove High, was to be used for a proposed data-center. Local environmental groups were trying to block the sale and save the Garry Oaks on the property, Emma Martinez being one of their ardent supporters.

Terrel had been sniffing around the IPO that was due to hit the markets on February 1, 2012. From the documents that had been made public, A-1 Education was a California firm with a strong management team who were seen as innovative and progressive. "Chuck Palmer is one of their sales reps. The company can't be that good," he grumbled. When Summer flashed a questioning look, Terrel took a healthy gulp of wine and provided a passionate, biased, but mercifully brief background about Palmer. The man had been the manager at the brokerage house where Steve and Terrel worked. "The guy is an A-1 asshole," declared Terrel. He chuckled at what he regarded as a witty quip and gulped more Shiraz.

The extra wine helped him recall further research that had a personal twist. "Did you know Palmer applied for the business manager position that went to Phil Chow?" Terrel huffed. "Not even a school district would hire that guy." He poured more wine into a half-filled glass. It was the only sound in the sudden awkward silence shrouding the dining table. With a rapidly reddening face, Terrel quickly muttered apologies to the assembled trio of public-school employees. "Sorry about the school district hiring comment. I didn't mean the way it came out."

Steve accepted the fib. Many private sector workers, especially those like Terrel who were self-employed, were envious of public sector job security and hefty pensions. The lengthy vacations in the education field added to the invidious comparisons. "No problem," Steve offered. "After all, the district hired Capelli for the top job. She's Chuck Palmer on steroids." He smiled as the ensuing laughter broke the tension.

Terrel continued, explaining that Chuck had separated from his wife and moved to Everett. The man had convinced A-1 Education that he was knowledgeable about education since he had worked with Terrel, an adult instructor in Namibia, and Steve, a public-school teacher, now a principal. "The bastard sold himself as the one who actively encouraged us to go into education."

"Unbelievable," muttered Steve, stunned at the man's brazen twisting of the truth.

"No shit," Terrel muttered. "I'm still digging. I'll keep you informed."

With the ice-cream dessert sitting comfortably in his satiated stomach, and an after-dinner brandy nearby, Perry began pecking on his iPhone.

"Honestly," scolded Summer gently, shaking her head. "Put that contraption away." Even though Summer was more computer literate than she let on, she disliked the epidemic of inattention sweeping society. Cellphones beeped, iPhones were checked, and iPads were scrutinized when attention should be paid to another person. It was disconcerting to see how the continual presence of a piece of technological hardware was turning the human into the appendage, not the other way around.

"Apple was up on Friday," Perry chirped, examining the screen. "Keep buying those iPads." He smiled at Steve. "Didn't that big janitor of yours," he searched for the name, "Tiny, make a fortune on Apple already? You could still get in on the action. It's going to go through the roof."

"Yeah," agreed Steve. "Tiny tells me that all the time."

"There's always the chance to get in on the ground floor of the next Apple," noted Terrel, draining the Shiraz in his goblet. He hiked thin shoulders. "Maybe it's right under our noses, A-1 Education!" He poured and quaffed more wine. "Wouldn't that be a hoot?"

Stock market vagaries were not a usual topic of conversation among educators despite their pension plans being significant investment machines. The topics turned to movies, books, and plans for the Christmas holidays as the evening wound to a close.

The lingering effect of an enjoyable evening with friends was not the only reason for Steve's relaxed mood as he washed and cleaned up. With the school's winter concert over, he predicted that the upcoming week would be relatively quiet.

Steve was correct, at least until the school doors closed the following Friday afternoon. Then his work-related challenges began in earnest.

19

The Friday night phone call was unexpected to say the least. That it was from an agitated Emma Martinez made it truly mystifying. "Can you come and pick me up?" she asked, mixing angry defiance with tones resembling a schoolgirl plea.

"Emma? Where are you? Are you okay?"

"I'm fine. I'm in—jail, on Grand Avenue."

Jail? Realizing that this was not the time for a cavalcade of questions, Steve answered as calmly as possible, "I know where it is. I'll be there in ten minutes."

When Steve entered the Whatcom County Courthouse, muffled complaints and curses could be heard wafting through the heavy door that separated the foyer from the cells. A nervous Steve received a long stare from the clerk, preceded by a blunt assessment of his mentorship skills. "You should tell your daughter to be careful who she hangs around with. Some of these eco-nuts are bad news." He passed the register to Steve.

"I'm not her father. I'm a," he searched for a credible phrase, "family friend."

"Well, your friend is lucky tonight. We got a tip-off that a demonstration was being organized. We arrived just before these idiots started to chain themselves to the Garry Oak trees. We hauled all of them here on charges of disturbing the peace. Only the two biggest mouthpieces are being held overnight. Your friend's not one of them." He glanced at the big man. "You sign for her release, she's your responsibility."

Steve nodded. A form emerged, as long and convoluted as one Capelli would devise. He filled in the numerous blank spaces scribbling in teacher as his occupation.

Emma was led through a doorway by a female police officer and entered the reception area. "Thanks for coming," she muttered. "Let's get out of here."

As Steve drove to a coffee shop, at least one of his many questions was answered. "Thanks again Steve. Colin and I have split and I swear to God it's the last time I want to be near that bastard. He actually wants the data-center built." She snorted in derision and turned away to stare out the passenger window. Steve caught a glimpse of tears forming in reddened eyes.

It was not difficult to find a purveyor of coffee in downtown Taylerston. Every corner had a least two. Steve pulled into a Starbucks, expecting a comment from Emma who did not like the corporate giant and the coffee they peddled. Instead she stayed glumly silent until they were huddled in a corner cradling their Americanos.

"I guess you're wondering what I was doing there?" Emma caught the slight nod. "We were saving the trees from being bulldozed tonight. They were going to clear the land before any formal approval. That would have handed the city a *fait accompli* with little choice but to approve the data-center. They were waiting until the winter holiday when there would be virtually no traffic in and around the high school. A perimeter of trees was going to be left standing and the center section cleared. Our lawyers just filed an injunction. It's unclear who controls the land so the injunction is in place. The school district owns it but there is some kind of lease arrangement with a real estate developer. Some zoning issues have not been resolved either."

"Who are the 'they' you're talking about?" asked Steve.

Emma shrugged. "Big tech companies are behind it but I think the front group is A-1 Education. The school district is probably involved too."

"How did your group know they were going to clear the land tonight?"

"We've got a guy on the inside. Well, he's not really one of ours. He's an urban mercenary."

Puzzled, Steve took a sip of java. What the hell was an urban mercenary?

As if reading his thoughts, Emma explained that the guy was, as she described, "A professional shit-disturber." He could be hired by anyone with an ax to grind from any political stripe. "He'll organize protests, spy on corporate competitors, pay off county officials, whatever. He bragged to me once that he did a job for the school district." Emma took a pull of coffee and winced. "Tonight, he was ratting on it."

A sudden realization hit Steve. Surely this shit-disturber could not be the same guy? "Is he a smarmy-looking little guy?"

"He's a creep, and yeah, he's tiny, like a jockey."

"Did he have a bruise on his forehead earlier this year?"

Emma chuckled. "Yeah, he told me he bashed his head crawling around the duct work in a few schools."

"What the hell was he doing?"

"Most of what he does is either illegal or ethically shadowy, so its hard to know for sure. That's why organizations hire the guy in the first place. I don't know exactly what the job was, but it was something about testing the width of the vents for air circulation. He said the school vents were old and the original drawings were either lost or incomplete. There was some question whether the location and size of the ducts was accurate. The district needed someone small enough to crawl around and verify the drawings they had. Otherwise they would have up-to-date ones made." She shrugged. "That little bugger will do anything." She stared at her boss. "You think one of the schools was Greenside?"

"Tiny saw him but couldn't catch him." A piqued Steve took a sip of coffee. "Why didn't you tell me?"

"I didn't know it was Greenside. Even if I did, I didn't know you at the time. It was before school started, remember?"

"What's this guy's name?"

Emma let out another chuckle. "He goes by a lot of them—weasel, shithead, worm, scumbag—hell, Steve, I don't know. You're not going to find him listed in the phone book." She tried soft reasoning. "C'mon Steve, sometimes you care too much about your precious school. The little asshole didn't take anything. He didn't bust anything. Tiny probably stopped him in the middle of what he was doing. He hasn't been seen around the school since, has he?" She shrugged, "So who really gives a shit?"

There was not much more to say. Emma did not want to talk about her involvement in the protest. Steve really did not want to know any more than he did. When he arrived at Emma's apartment, she thanked him again and planted a chaste kiss on his cheek. She said that for an old guy he had a funky vibe.

"I don't even know what that means, let alone having it."

"You're funky enough for Anne." She gawked at Steve's nonchalant reaction. Did she have to hit this guy over the head with a hammer? "You knew Anne broke up with her boyfriend this week?" She did not wait for a reply. "He was going to bugger off with a guy pal and go back-country skiing. Then he told Anne that he was heading to Australia in February." Emma stared at Steve, trying to gauge his reaction. Whatever the man was feeling he was hiding it well. She groaned inside. Maybe her supposedly mature boss was as oblivious as Colin.

"Anne is too young for me," Steve said suddenly. "I mean, if I was interested; which I'm not." He raised an arm toward his head, as if to shake away the cobwebs around his brain. "Not that I'm clueless. You're right, Anne is a great woman. It's just that . . ."

Emma chuckled. "Forget it Steve. Don't say anything more. I liked it better when I thought you were mature and sophisticated." She opened the car door and headed for the apartment door.

Steve had to face reality. He really was clueless. What was worse, he was aging. Being a tongue-tied teenager when talking to girls was one thing. Being the same at middle-age was quite another. He could feel his age when at work too. Was the mindless education bureaucracy altering his personality just as money had done to him a decade before? Steve had noticed an increasingly cynical Terrel Lewis. The journalist was drinking too much and becoming more interested in uncovering the scandals of unscrupulous officials rather than probing the essence of a salient social issue. For several years Perry had been drowning in the dark abyss that was Human Resources work. Was there ever a more thankless position? It was Summer Martin that had pulled his soul from the brink. At the moment there was no one to grab Steve's hand and prevent him from heading along the train tracks into the tunnel of negativity. One faint light beckoned at the far end. To reach it Steve was going to have to clamber onto another romance train and make sure he had a chance of hanging on.

Throwing jail visits and duct-crawling scoundrels into the memory banks, Steve spent part of the Christmas break in Tacoma visiting family. A beer session with Peter was always in the cards though Steve talked more than he drank. It was good to have a listening post.

"I can't figure out why this puny dirtbag was crawling around in the vents or why the district didn't do any maintenance work in the school. I don't know much about education so I don't know what that Capelli boss of yours is talking about when she yaks about bold new futures." Peter took a hefty swig of pilsner. "Hell, your school is supposed to be a quiet spot in a small community. It sounds like a lunatic asylum, populated by an evil little duct-crawler and reptile-woman."

"The Lizard."

"Whatever. That word-salad, visionary bullshit Capelli is spouting is just regular bafflegab from a CEO trying to sound important." Peter sank the remaining third of the bottle. "I just don't see how closing Greenside school and A-1 Education are linked."

Steve methodically picked at the label on his bottle in an effort to conjure inspiration. He replied sullenly, "I don't know. It's just a bad feeling I have. I talked to Terrel and he checked into A-1 Education." Steve tugged on his ale. At least his brother appeared interested so he plowed on. "The IPO," he caught a questioning look, "Initial Public Offering, is set at $3.00. Terrel thinks that is very cheap."

"Are you going to buy any?" Peter asked, eyeing his brother while twisting the cap on another bottle. Making money trading stocks had been like a narcotic to his brother. Once an addiction was beaten no one wanted to see it return. He smiled when Steve shook his head. "It doesn't sound like a cheap stock offering is that big a deal to you," Peter concluded. "I'd be more worried about them closing the school."

"Yeah," agreed Steve. "I think you're right. But Capelli told the Lizard that the school was staying open."

"Can you trust the big boss?" asked Peter. "You always said she was a master manipulator."

"No, I don't trust her," replied Steve bluntly, tiring of thinking about work and Jennifer Capelli. He shifted conversational gears. "What do you think is the maximum appropriate age gap for a romantic relationship between a man and a woman? For real people," he quickly clarified, "Not old-man celebrities picking up trophy wives."

'You have an interest?"

"I don't know. Maybe." He signaled Peter for another beer. With a fresh bottle in hand he attended to Peter's take on age and romance. He listened carefully. Deciding to dip a toe into the roiling waters of romance was a difficult decision when you were a notoriously poor swimmer.

Returning to Taylerston after Boxing Day, Steve had time on his hands. That meant time well wasted reading mysteries, watching football, and bonding with Charles. The cat had been upset at being left alone and Steve provided pizza and ice cream to repair strained relations. Slowly the big, humble human was being treated with less disdain by the controlling feline. Steve continued to attend Dumbelles fitness salon, having done so since November. Still, even the elderly Merlot Maidens would place him a distant second in a hunk contest with Elton John. He needed to drop more than a few pounds and firm up the stubborn flab that was leftover.

For the remaining few days of the holiday Steve padded about the house in a morose daze. He stopped attending Dumbelles. Not even football held much interest. The Seahawks had a mediocre season at best. The New England Patriots dominated the NFL. Some things never changed. He spent New Years' Eve listening to Paul Simon and watching one of his favorite movies, *Raiders of the Lost Ark*, for the sixth time. On New Year's Day he read a book on establishing positive vibes. Summer had lent it to him. The adjective funky was actually included, described as casual bohemian attire and décor. Steve worked hard to avoid scoffing at the intellectual fluff.

Human Steve and feline Charles were happiest when one predictable event followed another. Unlike the cat at home, Steve could not control the pace of change at work. Of course, Charles did not have a stifling bureaucracy, petty politics, and malicious bosses to contend with. The organizational chart in the bungalow was set and was not likely to change any time soon. Charles was the head of the pack. As far as bosses went, the cat was pretty good. Charles was better than Chuck Palmer in the Darrington investment days, or Jennifer Capelli now.

Blustery winter weather accompanied the January return to school. Steve's SUV was excellent for plowing through the snow-filled highway that linked Taylerston and Greenside. The normal thirty-minute drive had taken an hour on the first day of school. Steve stopped twice to help push stuck cars back onto the road. Unlike several nearby school districts, Taylerston rarely closed due to snowfall. But on the first scheduled day of return even Jennifer Capelli was forced to issue a shutdown. The CEO was labeled "Tahiti Capelli" for her insistence that blizzard-like conditions were really not that bad. She lived in a harbor-side waterfront condo, a fifteen-minute walk to her palace masquerading as an office. She reasoned that if she could make it to work, everyone could.

Employees huddled at home, listening to the radio in anticipation of school being canceled due to snow. Some chose the district web site for information in order to spare themselves the inevitable supplementary blabbering by the CEO. A snowy morning meant a prime audience and Jennifer Capelli was not going to miss an opportunity to boast about the Taylerston District, "Moving boldly forward," like the Star Trek tag. She never elaborated on the departure point or intended destination. Perhaps neither existed. Steve always assumed that if there were no departure and arrival points it would be difficult to know whether an organization was moving in any direction. Education administration was full of meaningless drivel dressed up to sound officious.

Steve realized that he was becoming too cynical. Not normally one for New Years' resolutions, he made a promise to himself to curb the tussles with the system. His previous rebellious efforts had not changed anything. The bureaucracy would always lumber along. The current professional bandwagon was as faddish as all the others before it. There were good people working in a hobbled system. Positive change was possible. Not all innovation was old ideas dressed in new clothes. Not all those outside the bubble of school life were clueless. In 2012 Steve was going to embrace reasonable change and move boldly forward, destination unknown. Jennifer Capelli would be proud. So would Anne Shaw.

A favorite Capelli airwave mantra was, "Tackling the future, head on." She was fond of using sports metaphors since they spoke of action and determination. Another Capelli favorite was adding a warrior tinge to her proclamations, especially when she assumed a Churchillian tone. She thought it invoked a rallying cry to defeat the enemy. This was becoming a popular technique to describe social policy initiatives in the United States. There was a war on poverty, a war on drugs, or a war on illiteracy. Capelli often used the phrase, war on complacency. In announcing a rare school cancelation, Capelli had managed to insert several of her pet phrases into the discussion with the ever-patient radio host. Capelli never met a microphone she didn't like.

Feeling obligated to make an attempt to arrive at work, Steve carefully negotiated the winding road. There could be parents who had not heard the closure news. Others may have heard but dropped their child at the school anyway. Schools provided cheap babysitting. Some teachers may arrive. There was always catch-up work he could do during a quiet day. After listening to Capelli on the radio Steve was even more determined to, as Summer Martin once described it, "Paddle on the river of change." Sometimes Steve had felt that he wasn't even in the same canoe as everyone else. It would be so much easier for him to clamber in and paddle in sync rather than struggling upstream through class-six white water. A warm glow enveloped him despite the frigid conditions. Could it be that the work-life road he had traveled was about to become a hell of a lot smoother? Steve Hepting smiled at the possibility that tranquil waters lay ahead.

20

The first school day of the new calendar year had been blissfully quiet. Tiny was the only staff member to arrive and he spent the early part of the morning washing already-clean hallways. Steve tackled a backlog of emails and skimmed a leadership monograph that had been gathering dust on an office shelf. In the late morning he challenged Tiny to a one-on-one basketball match. The two lumbering, wheezing men were evenly matched in ineptitude and lethargy.

Tiny claimed victory, made possible by some dubious physicality that stretched beyond the rules. Mr. H. might be a tough guy when fighting for his school, but he was a marshmallow when physical contact was required. No wonder the boss liked golf. He probably liked bowling too.

Jay Woznicki entered the school in the late morning and for a time he and Tiny disappeared. Later the boy arrived at Steve's office seeking the jelly bean game. "No jelly beans," lamented Jay, noticing the absent jar. The boy had become so proficient he wasn't learning any new patterning or sequencing. He had seriously depleted Steve's poster collection. Steve was surprised the boy had any vacant space left on his bedroom walls.

Anne had given the principal a new idea, focussing on Jay's love of animals. Steve agreed to switch the procedure. With the snow muffling outside noise and the school empty except for Tiny, the day seemed like a good opportunity to pilot the new game.

Steve gathered a number of animal picture books from the library. Jay would have to name a selected creature. If correct, the boy would have to make a sound or devise an action that represented the animal.

Initially dubious, Jay immediately said "lion" when Steve showed the boy a picture of a pride on the African veld. Jay gave a growl and showed menacing teeth before grinning goofily and holding out an expectant hand. Frowning, he stared warily at his principal. Where were the jelly beans?

"Are you okay?" asked Steve, noticing the boy's reticence. Like many students with special needs, Jay liked routine. This new game was unfamiliar territory.

"I'm good," muttered Jay though the tone did not match the positive response.

Steve showed a picture of a skunk.

Jay scowled and burst out, "Need food."

A confused Steve corrected the boy. People did not eat skunks.

Jay held his nose and chanted, "Smell bad, smell bad!"

Steve eyed the strange reaction. At least the boy got that part right.

"River food," Jay shouted excitedly, pointing to a picture of raccoons.

"Raccoons," Steve corrected.

"River food," Jay insisted.

"Yes, they are washing their paws in streams," agreed Steve, deciding to go with a fluid teaching flow ala Summer Martin.

"Sammy, Sammy family", shrieked Jay when Steve showed a picture of a snake.

"There's only one snake Jay," said Steve, holding up a finger.

Shaking a troubled head, the boy suddenly blurted, "I talk to Tiny." He rose, grabbed his lunch kit and scooted from the library.

Ten minutes later the janitor was at the door. Steve agreed that they should close the school and go home. A curiously subdued Tiny promised he would lock up and walk Jay home.

Steve exited the front door and trudged through the snow that covered the parking lot. As he clambered into his suv, he gazed back at the school, trying to link Jay's bizarre answers and Tiny's quiet demeanor. He shrugged. Neither one of those two were truly normal. Tiny probably wanted to teach the boy how to play one-on-one basketball. A match against Jay would mean another victory.

Despite additional snowfall in the evening, Tahiti Capelli was not going to shutter schools two days in a row. She was jabbering on the radio the next morning, proudly proclaiming that schools were open. Then she spent the next five minutes on a monologue of favorite mantras. The taped recording meant she was on-air every twenty minutes. After hearing the spiel for the second time, Steve turned the car radio off and focused on controlling the slipping and sliding SUV the remainder of the way to Greenside.

The parking lot was not plowed, though Tiny had cleared the snow from the front walkway and sprinkled gravel to increase traction. Students would be arriving soon, more excited to be back at school after the long holiday than bubbling about the snow. Students went crazy on the first Greenside snowfall of the year. They raced around like banshees, screaming and yelling. They made snow forts, snow men, and snow angels. They fired snow balls at each other. It was if they had never seen the white stuff before, even though Greenside received a foot every year, occasionally more. By January, the novelty of snow had long since dissipated. The white flakes were white noise—just there, like bleached dust.

Steve slowly exited his seat and closed the vehicle door. A snowball banged into the front windshield. He glared at the culprit, locating the grinning janitor near the front entrance.

"I've always wanted to do that," Tiny yelled proudly. "I could have hit you Mr. H., but I thought you might get mad."

"You couldn't hit the broad side of a barn," Steve shouted back. "You're pretty brave standing in front of the windows so I can't fire one back."

"Not brave Mr. H., just smart." He reached down to pack together another ball. Satisfied with size and shape, he fired it at his principal. This time Steve had to duck and the snowball whizzed over his head.

"You missed again," Steve yelled, pondering how he could coax the janitor away from the windows. As he came to a full upright position a snowball fired from a different direction crashed into his back.

"But I didn't," came a boast, followed by a cackle. It was Colin Redford.

Steve wheeled about to face the new assailant. Placing his briefcase in the snow, he grabbed for icy ammunition. Before he could pull to full height and face Colin, a snowball beaned him in the back of the head, the splat cushioned by his Seahawks toque. Tiny's aim had been good.

Facing a two-front war, Steve resorted to whining. "Hey, this is two against one, that isn't fair." When that provoked no response, he tried sounding officious. "Don't you guys have anything better to do, like maybe working?"

"No," Tiny and Colin hollered in unison and sent snowballs flying from each direction. "This is a lot more fun."

Deciding on a frontal assault, Steve grabbed the briefcase. Using it as a shield, he charged across the parking lot. Two snowballs met their mark, smacking into his parka. The briefcase blocked two more. Suddenly Tiny shrieked as a snowball was fired from the corner of the building. "What the hell . . ."

"I'm with you boss," came a proud cry as Anne Shaw's shot beaned Tiny. The young man scurried away from the windows, chased by the scrambling Anne who managed to move quickly in a thick ski jacket and winter boots.

Joan Mackenzie ended the show. She climbed out of her Toyota Corolla and surveyed the bedlam—four yelping, laughing adults engaging in a snowball fight that school rules forbid. She slammed the car door, the sudden noise bringing a brief halt to the mayhem.

"Uh oh," thought Steve as he and teammate Anne tried to slide into the school.

"Just a moment," barked Joan, halting their retreat. "While I am sure you overgrown children are having a wonderful time breaking school rules, the students will be arriving soon. Don't you think this silliness should cease? Frank," she declared, always referring to Tiny by his proper name, "I need help with the boxes from my trunk. Then please check my computer mail." Joan did not use the computer at work. Each week Tiny went through her emails and cleared them off. He had neglected the duty and had not done so since mid-November.

"Yes ma'am."

She turned to Steve. "Mr. Hepting," to Joan he was always Mr. Hepting at work, "You should be ashamed of yourself. I expect much better from you. You are the leader are you not?"

Sheepishly, Steve nodded.

"Boss man's in trouble," chanted Colin in a childish voice. He was grinning like an idiot.

A stern stare was followed by, "Really Mr. Redford, when I am talking to Mr. Hepting you are to remain silent. Do I make myself clear?"

Colin nodded before staring downward at soaked boots. "Sorry Joan." He absently kicked at some snow. "Can I go now?"

"Yes," she said.

Happy to be freed with a minimum of scolding, Colin quickly grabbed a pack from his car and skittered into the school.

Joan turned to the others, waving an officious arm, "Now scoot. End this silliness."

Anne slipped into the school. Tiny rummaged in Joan's trunk and began hauling several full boxes into the school. Steve searched for his dropped briefcase. As he picked up the wet baggage, a snowball banged into his buttocks. He did not turn around. He knew who the assailant was by Tiny's effusive praise, "Nice shot Mrs. Mack."

Joan's classroom was at the far end of the school. Though the boxes were numerous and heavy they posed little difficulties for Tiny. Joan indicated an empty corner to store them while she straightened an already orderly room. The reading lesson to start the first day back had been written on the board in December. She pulled potted plants from the boxes and placed them on the counter that ran along the windowed wall. She asked Tiny to haul a crate, covered with a blanket. In it was a gerbil.

"Cool," yelped Tiny, staring at the animal. "What's his name?"

"Jimmy," replied Joan, "Jimmy the gerbil."

"Like Sammy the snake," gushed Tiny, "He was in Ms. Martinez' classroom. He was in her desk before I got him a cage and he was there because there weren't any mice for him to eat anymore and River Coolwater convinced Mr. H. to keep Sammy until we found him a good home and . . ."

Joan flashed a patient smile—one that was so common among primary teachers since they were often forced to listen to the disjointed long-winded tales of children. "Yes, thank you Frank. Perhaps you could look at my computer?"

"Sure thing Mrs. Mackenzie," Tiny said, clicking the machine on. "Aren't you afraid the cats will scare Jimmy?"

"I just brought Jimmy for today since we won't be able to have animals in the school anymore. What a silly rule that is." She shrugged. What could you expect from education big shots who paid more attention to lawyers and insurance people than teachers?

"It won't be the same without animals." said Tiny sadly as he coaxed life into the computer. "We haven't done this since November," he remarked, scrolling through pages of emails, readying to delete. "Do you want me to start with the oldest one?"

Joan sighed. "I suppose, but don't spend much time on each one." Tiny was a slow reader.

The janitor only occasionally studied the title and did not need much time to delete each one. One of the oldest emails had a striking header. He opened it and slowly read the contents. There were a lot of long words and he read it twice for better comprehension. He thought he had the gist, but the message was so strange he remained unsure. He always had trouble understanding what he had read. "Mrs. Mackenzie, I think you should read this."

Joan walked slowly over to the machine and put on her reading glasses. She squinted at the unfamiliar material. "Oh my, this is very personal," she said as a deep frown shrouded her face. "What happens when you take this off the machine?"

"It goes into cyberspace."

"Well, wherever that is, I don't want that message on my computer. We'll keep a paper copy, one for you and one for me. We'll decide what to do later."

Tiny reached into a back pocket and pulled out a crinkled sheet of paper. He unfolded it and gave it to Joan. "This is another note just like the one on your computer."

As Joan read, her frown deepened. "Where did you get this?"

"I found it in Ms. Martinez's room. It was scrunched up in a ball. It was the only piece of paper in the garbage so I picked it up so the can would be clean when school started. I didn't mean to open the paper ball but I saw Mr. H.'s name on a little part that was sticking out. I don't think the note on your computer is very nice. I don't think this one is either."

"What should I do?" asked a worried Tiny, receiving the wrinkled paper from Joan. "I'm kinda mad. These are bad things to say."

"I know Frank. We must think for a while before deciding what to do."

While Tiny and Joan were discussing nefarious notes, a distraught Colin Redford was in Steve's office. The meeting had started with jibes about the earlier snowball fight before sharing pleasantries about holiday activities. Colin fired a verbal salvo about the last-place Cubs. Originally from Los Angeles, he had moved to the Silicon Valley to go to university. He had grown up an ardent supporter of the Dodgers, a franchise significantly more successful than Steve's favorite team.

"I'm forever positive about the Cubs," said Steve, "Even the Phoenix rose from the grave."

"Zombies do too, but they're uncoordinated and ugly," Colin replied before the male banter turned to stony silence.

Steve stared at the young teacher. Somber to the point of morose, Colin clearly had not come to the office engage in raillery about sports. Steve gently probed for an explanation and the young man wicked a tear from sad eyes. The angst the young man was about to saddle onto Steve was being caused by a woman who was far more problematic than Emma Martinez.

The emails sent to Colin had been frequent and bordered on vitriolic. The parent claimed that excessive boredom was causing her son's poor behavior in class. The boy was intellectually curious and needed challenging assignments—there were none. He was bright and required enrichment activities—they too were lacking. It was the teacher's lack of ability and skill that was causing the boy's poor behavior.

While the lad was a hard worker with good study habits, Steve did not believe he was gifted. Neither did Colin, though with little elementary-level experience he was cautious about voicing opinions. For once, Steve had seen some value in standardized testing. He had used the information with the parent in an earlier conversation about her son's alleged gifted-ness. "His achievement score does not reveal any special ability," Steve concluded. "He is a solid student, though not necessarily gifted."

Mrs. Linzel was eerily astute on occasion and could hit a nail on the head. Steve always assumed it was simply dumb luck. Since the Lizard snapped her tongue on boundless occasions, she would eventually catch at least one fly. "You are helping me make my point Mr. Hepting," she said. "You are showing me my son's achievement results which, as you say, are solid. The point is, with his superior cognitive ability his achievement level should be much higher. Jennifer informs me that the district is moving to personalized learning plans. I wish my son to have an educational plan directly linked to his needs. You are aware that since I met with her in November, Jennifer and I are in close contact. She is an educational vision-ary who is being held back by an unresponsive system."

Steve cursed silently. The Lizard was an annoying bully. "We are not yet in a position to implement personalized learning plans. Mr. Redford has twenty-seven students in his class and has to cover all subject areas. What you are asking for is very difficult, if not impossible."

Steve wished that district officials, and even a few gung-ho principal colleagues, would be honest with the public. The total state education budget was in the billions of dollars and seemed staggering. Yet the 2011 allocation per student was about $7,500. This funded about two hundred days of instruction, each with approximately five hours of class time for a total of one thousand hours. Expressed in this manner, formal teaching in the education system cost about $7.50 per hour, the rough equivalent of a babysitting service. The coaching of sports teams, sponsorship of clubs, and any extra help after school was provided with labor exceeding the hourly instructional rate. Only the truly insane would say that the evening babysitter provided the equivalent service. The system operated on a group model with twenty to thirty students at one time. Providing individual-ized service would cost twenty to thirty times more, a financial burden no politician would dare ask taxpayers to support.

"Ms. Capelli assures me that competent teachers can accomplish this."

Steve gritted his teeth. Jennifer Capelli had not taught in a classroom in more than fifteen years. Whatever she once knew about teaching had long been buried under an avalanche of school board politics, bureaucratic forms, labor grievances, and marketing ploys. Colin Redford was a reasonably competent teacher doing his best in an unfamiliar, and in many ways, unfair assignment. Often the vagaries of a collective agreement worked well for the union members with seniority at the expense of their less-seasoned colleagues. Steve assumed Colin's low rank on the seniority pole had caused his transfer.

Colin had not responded to the Lizard's holiday emails, which served to increase the rate and vitriol of the missives. In several notes, the parent boasted about her relationship with CEO Jennifer Capelli. She stated that she acted as the spokesperson for the Greenside Parent Council. She hinted at upcoming school board elections and that she would be running for the Greenside position, likely unopposed.

"What should I do?" asked a grim-faced Colin.

"For now, just keep doing what you're doing," answered Steve after skimming through the pages. "Send Bridget a copy of all the emails the woman has sent you. If the parent bothers you at work see me immediately. Don't worry, I'll find a way to deal with Mrs. Linzel."

"Thanks Steve,' said a relieved Colin. "I could have sent Emma after her but we broke up, this time for good. Emma's tough and she fights dirty. She's taken a round out of me a few times."

Steve scanned the thin body, elfin face, and wire-framed glasses. With his new goatee Colin looked like a Kropotkin-inspired Russian anarchist from the 1880s. Steve had no doubt that feisty Emma could pound her ex-boyfriend into submission. She would be a match for the bulky Mrs. Linzel too. "That would be quite a scrap," admitted Steve. "But leave Emma out of this tango, okay Colin? I can be tough too."

21

Tiny poked his head into Steve's office before the principal had a chance to consider how to approach the Lizard. "There were a lot of vans at the school over the Christmas holiday. A company was working on ventilation and electrical stuff. Some guys were measuring rooms too."

"Taylerston guys?" asked Steve, "in Taylerston vans?" He was referring to the district vehicles with "Taylerston Schools: The Future is Now" plastered on the side panel.

"No."

Steve offered a thin smile. The work seemed similar to what the Lizard had predicted. Tiny seemed anxious for an explanation. "The only thing I can think of is that the electrical and ventilation is pretty old so maybe it's a safety issue or a Fire Marshall order. That would explain the need to get the work done over the holiday."

"Okay," muttered Tiny, fidgeting as if a match was burning in the back pocket of his jeans. The contorted face meant he was thinking. After apparent inner turmoil, he stated, "I think Ms. Martinez wants to see you." He paused, then hurried away.

Classes had not yet started and the crazy day was already chipping at Steve's resolution to wear a happy face when dealing with school district activity and nutty parents.

"Did you see the email?" snapped Emma, standing in the doorway.

"No, I haven't read any since we broke for the Christmas holiday. I needed a break."

"Check your machine. Capelli found out about my time in jail and sent me a scathing email. She mentioned that if I had been arrested, I could have been suspended or even fired."

"How did she find out?"

"Probably from that loser mercenary toad I told you about. He can work three sides of a two-sided coin."

"But you weren't arrested, so nothing is going to happen, right?"

"Not to me, but she sure ripped you apart in the same message. I guess she discovered it was you who had picked me up at the jail. Basically, she said your weak leadership and unbridled negativity toward the district encouraged sedition and treachery among your staff."

Seething inside, Steve pasted on a nonchalant countenance. "Hmm, sounds like I've been a bad boy." He didn't know if this is what a man with a cool, funky vibe would say but it was the best he could do. He listened as if only half-interested as Emma told him that such an attack from his boss should be taken seriously, especially when it was sent to another employee. "Don't worry about me. Just stay out of this and keep your head down. You may want to lay off the eco-warrior bit for a while too. With the injunction nothing is going to happen to that property until the lawyers start sucking all the cash from the money trough. He caught Emma's questioning orbs. "I promise I will take some action with Ms. Capelli." Steve watched Emma trundle away in a semi-huff. Capelli may have been into the wine the night Emma had been detained. After all, it was the start of the winter break. As he knew all too well, too much wine was not an excuse for unacceptable behavior.

There is a pattern to work in schools, just as there is a pattern of activity in other organizations. Work life is often a repetition of tasks with enough variance to produce a modicum of interest. On occasion there is a single event that shakes the staid pattern. It consumes thought and action. It rocks the orderliness of the workplace. A particularly distinctive statistical anomaly would be two significant events occurring within a twenty-four-hour span. In the future, Steve would often point to the events of January 4 and January 5, 2012 as the turning points in his career. Though riled up about Capelli's email, that message, as significant as it was, would be moved to the back burner.

After cleaning the lunchroom kitchen with two eighth-grade students, Steve walked along the hallway toward his office. Like birds on a wire, miscreant students would be lined up on office chairs awaiting some form of reprimand or discipline. Greenside did not utilize the new glitzy acronyms for managing student behavior such as HOOP (Hands Off Other People), or the popular WADE (Walk Away Don't Erupt). WAITT stood for "We Are All in This Together," which had a soft communal ring appealing to Kumbaya-type teachers like Summer Martin. Steve preferred his private acronym, KISS (Keep It Simple Stupid). Most minor behavioral infractions were the result of simple playground misunderstandings. It was the adults that made the issue complicated by probing, analyzing, labeling, intervening, and ultimately monitoring as if whirling helicopter blades.

There were four students of varying ages waiting for him. After dispensing Solomon-like justice, Steve chose to ignore the long list of emails, each one screaming for an answer. Instead he decided to take a walk to clear the corridors of stragglers. Instead, he found Mrs. Linzel and Colin Redford in a hallway stare-down. "What seems to be the issue?" he asked, comparing the parent's sourly stern expression with the teacher's exasperated visage.

"Mrs. Linzel wants to be a volunteer in my class, all day, every day."

"Your school wants parent volunteers, does it not Mr. Hepting? That's what all the school newsletters say. I am simply answering the call."

Greenside did need parent volunteers; Steve had indeed asked for them. It was usually for specific purposes such as driving on a field trip or phoning the homes of absent children as part of the attendance-monitoring program. Occasionally parents helped with a special project in the classroom for a defined time. The district had issued protocols about parent volunteers. It was doubtful whether a volunteer had legal authority to assist, support, or chastise other children—all of which was bound to occur if the person was in a specific classroom every day for any length of time. There were labor relations issues as well. If an extra adult was required for a considerable length of time, a reasonable argument could be made that a formal paraprofessional position was required. As such, the person must be selected via the hiring process as outlined in the collective agreement and become a member of the appropriate union. The teachers' association could become involved too, crying foul about the Lizard's bluster. The employer had a responsibility to provide a harassment-free workplace.

Mrs. Linzel was a proficient bully who could be surprisingly clever. District rules could be flung in her face. She would retreat under the flurry, only to return waving her own selected set of regulations. Bureaucracies were rarely consistent. In one document parent volunteers were encouraged. In another the role was curtailed to barely minimal utility. Clauses in the collective agreement outlined teacher autonomy regarding methods and resources. Then, through Lou Tayler, the district imposed a Math program few teachers wanted. Steve had no intention of hiding behind a bureaucratic smokescreen. In his world, the only way to meet a bully was to do so head on. He was going to be tough and, if necessary, an asshole.

He commenced by ordering Colin. "Go and teach your class Mr. Redford."

The young man sensed the authority oozing from the principal's pores. He took a quick peek at the scowling Mrs. Linzel, gulped, and opened the door to the classroom. He made sure to close it after he entered.

The Lizard tried to follow.

Steve stepped in front of her and blocked the path. His big frame obscured most of the door.

"Are you denying me entry to be a volunteer in my son's classroom?" snapped the parent.

"That is an accurate gauge of my intention. You will only cause disruption to the students in Mr. Redford's classroom."

"You're trying to protect your teacher."

"Yes, that's true," said Steve, "The kids, the classroom tone, and the teacher." The blunt answer surprised the parent. She had expected him to say, "It was all about the kids," like educators always did.

Mrs. Linzel was over five-and-a-half feet tall with a mesomorph physicality. Though much smaller than the principal, she was not easily cowed. "You're trying to intimidate me and it won't work. I know men use their size to advantage like you're doing now. I know your tricks." She leaned forward narrowing the distance between them. "I've got some tricks of my own Mr. Hepting. I could easily say you touched me inappropriately." Her body was almost touching his. Up against the door, Steve shifted strategy and leaned forward so his chest stopped inches from her breasts. She bounced back, aghast. "How dare you!"

"We should have a reasonable discussion in my office, not out here in the middle of the corridor."

"After what you just did to me?" the parent hissed. "I'm not going into your office alone."

"Well, we are not continuing this disagreement out here. You'll have to leave the building now. Don't return until you are ready to have a private and rational discussion." He spoke calmly, though he was bubbling with anger internally. "If you wish, you can have another parent with you."

"Oh, like our Council Chairperson Donna, your ex-girlfriend," Mrs. Linzel spat. The odor of her lunchtime devilled egg sandwich spilled into the air.

Steve stood mute as wood. With narrowed eyes he cocked his head toward the front door.

Mrs. Linzel studied the darkened face, gauging her opponent's resolve. She had to think fast. Her last ploy of leaning forward had been met with an unexpected counter. "You're throwing me out? What are you gonna do Mr. Hepting, call the cops?"

"I am ordering you to leave the building now. If I phone the police to have you removed your son will be the laughing stock of the student body. That is not fair to him. You are to leave now. I don't ever issue a directive three times."

A seething Mrs. Linzel wheeled about. "Fine, but your boss is gonna hear about this. Jennifer told me what she thinks of you and it isn't good. She thinks you're wimpy pain-in-the-ass dinosaur."

"Mr. H.'s no wimp. Lady Macbeth doesn't like him because he stands up to her." It was Tiny, five steps away. The janitor could move with surprising stealth. He had found the skill useful in occasional nighttime sorties for tires and hubcaps during his teen years.

Distracted, the parent turned her mottled face to the janitor. What the hell is the fat-head juvenile delinquent saying? "Who is Lady Macbeth?" she sniped.

Tiny moved forward, stopping only when Steve issued a warning glare. "It's a woman the Shakespeare dude made up and wrote about. She was real bad. Don't you know nothing you stupid . . ."

"That's enough Tiny, this is not your issue." Complying with Steve's order, the young man backed away, reluctantly.

The cussing reptile-woman stomped off. "This isn't over, Hepting. I'm going to see Jennifer."

Tiny watched her leave before turning to his boss and mentor. "That was pretty cool Mr. H. You're one tough guy when you wanna be. Don't worry. I got your back, and when Tiny Little's in your corner you got a real good chance of coming out on top."

Steve thanked the janitor, issued a hefty exhale, and tromped back to his office.

"I caught most of the tail end of that circus," said Anne Shaw as they settled in for a meeting in Steve's office. "Are you okay?"

A slightly shaken Steve explained that Jennifer Capelli apparently thought he is a wimpy dinosaur who doubled as a pain in the ass. He was furious that the CEO had provided a personal view, and a negative one at that, about him to a parent. Personnel issues were between employer and employee. That was one of Capelli's favorite axioms.

Studying her principal carefully, Anne struggled to find the right words and the correct tone. Steve Hepting was anything but a wimp. She had rarely met a principal more willing to stand up for the students and teachers, often at risk to his own career. God knows he had reasons to be cynical. The school system was far from perfect. The man needed an outlet—a purpose beyond work that was more emotionally rewarding than golf. She patted him gently on the knee. "You're not a wimp Steve. Don't let Capelli toss you into the toxicity pit."

Steve fired a strange look that set her back for a moment. "Thanks Annie. Don't think you don't influence me to be better." He thought of sharing further thoughts with the counselor. He gazed at Anne for a moment, then, for some unknown reason, chose to keep it to himself. "I guess my best is still not good enough for Capelli." He let out an audible sigh. "It's like that woman inhabits another planet."

"She does, in a way. You're kid-friendly and school-oriented. Capelli's . . . well, I don't really know what she is." Anne jabbed a thick finger toward the principal. "You have to focus on the positives at Greenside school, not dwell on the negatives in the system. To hell with the system, screw Capelli."

"I'd rather not," muttered Steve.

"Not literally, you silly man," chirped Anne, restoring casual rapport. "I thought you were an English major who had more than two hundred words in his vocabulary. Isn't using big words how you charm the ladies?"

"Seriously, many thanks Anne. What you said means a lot to me." Shifting to a jocular tone, he continued. "I have the vocabulary to charm the women, but the words come out like foot-in-the-mouth disease. Tiny does better than me on that front. He wouldn't top out at much more than three hundred words, most of them monosyllabic."

Anne decided to let the comment pass. "Speaking of Tiny, I had a long talk with lovesick Janet this morning. She's not salivating over him anymore. She said her link with Tiny is ancient history. She's back to really liking Kevin now.' The counselor laughed. "Then it will be Joe, and then Manuel by the end of the month." She shook her head. "Janet is looking for a bad boy. Some girls like those guys. There's an air of excitement to them, like forbidden fruit."

Steve sighed. An image of the Merlot Maidens drooling over Mick Jagger slipped into his head. He fought to shake the visual off.

"You need to decompress," Anne said. 'Let's do our meeting another time. Don't worry about Jennifer Capelli."

"Who?" Steve joked.

A sure way to forget Jennifer Capelli was to work with Jay Woznicki. Steve geared up for their regular meeting. Capelli could go to hell.

"Hey, hey Jay, whady'a say?" Steve blurted when Jay entered near the end of the day. "I'm with my pal and we're gonna play."

"I have a new game for us today," explained Steve, deciding to forsake the animal routine which had caused the boy such consternation. Before Jay could scrunch his face, the principal added, "It's about sports!"

The boy shrieked with glee. He liked sports almost as much as he liked animals.

Steve grabbed a cardboard box, the type that the reams of school paper arrived in. He pointed to Jay to pull over a plastic bin. Initially frowning, the boy grinned when he saw sports equipment. There was a toy hockey stick, a nerf soccer ball, a pee-wee football, a mini-basketball, a plastic baseball and bat, and a miniature lacrosse stick in the bin.

The game was relatively simple and put more responsibility on Jay. Steve held up the logo of a professional sports team. Jay had to name the team and pull out the appropriate equipment. This was to be followed by a demonstration of the sport. Steve hoped the activity would work within the confines of his office. If not, they could always move to the lunch room.

Steve pulled out the first logo from the box and set the container aside.

"Chicago Cubs," squealed Jay with such astonishing delight that Steve could not stop grinning. The boy pulled out the little baseball bat and searched for the plastic ball. With both in hand he swung mightily. Surprisingly, he connected. The ball zipped past Steve's ear and smacked into a bulletin board, knocking several posted papers to the ground.

"Jay be Pujols, hit home run," the boy squealed with delight, making an unsuccessful grab at the ball lying near Steve's feet. "St. Louis Cardinals good, Chicago Cubs bad," he spouted, trying to pry the ball from under Steve's big shoe. Surrendering with humor, the boy followed the teasing with a riotous laugh. He knew Mr. H.'s baseball preferences. Jay favored the Cardinals, a team that was more often winners than losers. They had won the World Series in the early part of the school year. In comparison, the Cubs last matched that accomplishment in 1908. Jay's favorite player was the Cardinal's slugger, Albert Pujols. Steve was unsure whether the boy was aware that the star player was moving to another team for the 2012 season. He did not want to be the one to the tell the boy.

"Be careful with that bat," Steve admonished. He decided to select a hockey team, convinced the lesser-known sport would confuse Jay. The last thing he wanted was another home run ricocheting through his office. He slid his chair closer to the boy and parted his big feet in a v shape indicating the goal. Like Jay, Steve was learning and adapting as the game went on.

"Vancouver Canucks," said the excited Jay, grabbing a plastic hockey stick and puck. Concentrating with astonishing focus, Jay fired the puck into the goal. He raised his arm in celebration, duplicating the NHL pros he must have seen on a Canadian sports network.

Not believing Jay to be knowledgeable about basketball, Steve selected what he believed to be the most difficult team. The Toronto Raptors was the only non-American squad. The logo was an animal and Jay got the Raptors answer easily. "I like animals," he explained excitedly, responding to Steve's surprise. "I like dinosaurs best, skunks too."

A laughing Steve sat back in his chair and held out his arms. He linked fingers to make a wide basket. Jay fired the ball hard and low as if he were a baseball pitcher aiming for the strike zone. Before Steve could react, the ball landed with a direct thud in Steve's groin, rattling his private parts. The uncomfortable feeling known to males the world over fluttered through his core.

Steve groaned and leaned forward in masculine discomfort. He tried desperately to avoid grimacing. He vowed to make a mental note to keep his hands ready for errant shots when Jay was shooting hoops.

Jay chortled. Like most boys he had been hit in the soft area at some time in the past.

Steve leaned forward and began slowly rocking, no longer attempting to hide the anguish.

'I like this game," gushed the boy as Bridget knocked on the door and opened it.

"It's a long story," groaned Steve, looking up at her while still rocking gently.

"Mr. H. got hit in the . . ."

"That's fine Jay, the last bell has gone," interrupted a bemused Bridget. "I think I know what's wrong with Mr. H. I'm looking forward to his story." She hesitated. "When he's able to tell it." A wry smile split her lips.

"Mr. Redford said you wanted to see him." She looked at a memo slip she held, avoiding Steve's eyes. "And Ms. Capelli's office phoned. You're supposed to return the call as soon as possible."

"Not good timing," grumbled Steve. He resumed rocking back and forth. The angst over what was to follow was worse than any remnants of unease from his still-throbbing private parts.

22

Almost fully recovered from masculine trauma, Steve balked when he saw that Emma was intent on attending the meeting. Colin's issues were personal. If the young man wanted to share the information with her at a later time, so be it, that was his choice. When the young man insisted Emma be present, Steve finally agreed. The two must be in a reconciliation stage. Earlier they had split up "forever." Now they were close-knit and willing to share personal information. They were like eighth-graders who went through a love-hate-love relationship in a single day.

Steve relayed much of the story about the hallway confrontation he had with Mrs. Linzel. He chose to disregard the likelihood of her formal complaint to the CEO. That was going to be Steve's problem, not Colin's.

"What a bitch," muttered Colin, shaking his head. "She's just an old-fashioned bully. I should go to the union president." He looked to Emma to confirm that was the correct course of action. She remained surprisingly silent.

Steve groaned in his head; the union guy was almost as much of a bully as the Lizard. "I'm sure the situation is under control for the moment," he said softly. "Just keep doing what you're doing and let me know if Mrs. Linzel tries to contact you or attempts to enter your class again. Okay?"

Happy that his principal had the situation well in hand, Colin left, followed by Emma, who turned and whispered her first words, "Thanks for supporting Colin."

Seconds after, Bridget was buzzing on the intercom. "I hate to bring you more bad news but I'm reminding you of Ms. Capelli's call. And if you haven't had time to notice, it's snowing like crazy out there."

Steve grimaced. Mrs. Linzel must have already whined to Capelli about the hallway dispute. This was not likely to be a friendly conversation with the boss. Knowing the Lizard, the allegation could be as serious as sexual assault. He needed to be prepared. Capelli would not stop at a single phone call. Emails would flood tsunami-like into his inbox. The phone line would be tied-up, full-time. "I'll call her back later," declared Steve. "I better get outside to the parking lot. It will be a more of a zoo than usual."

"Okay," Bridget noted softly while glancing at the phone. "It's your hide."

It seemed that every child was driven to school. At the end of each day the parking lot was barely organized chaos. Today the slush-filled space was true anarchy. Tires spun snow and ice into the air. Cars slid hither and yon. Back bumpers fishtailed before traction could be attained. Children ducked in and out of parked and departing vehicles. A few older boys hitched a bumper ride as a pick-up truck slid away. One horn blew, then another. A cascade followed. Alone to control the mess, Steve played traffic cop; few paid him any attention.

When he returned to the office, tired, shivering, and soaked, Steve faced the prospect of phoning Capelli's office. He was in no condition to engage in a potentially career-altering discussion. Who knew what lies reptile-woman had spouted? Who knew what the CEO would think? Surprisingly, Capelli had not called again. A check of the inbox revealed no email. It was strangely advantageous. It was not as if he was looking for a reason to call the central office. His toque, coat, and boots were already on. Departing work was the sensible course of action. He decided to go home and let the shit hit the fan tomorrow.

Steve spent the evening with Charles on his lap and an Ian Rankin novel in his hand. The crusading Inspector Rebus was a particular favorite of his. A sound night of sleep led to the following day starting well. The expected early morning phone call from Capelli never materialized. The morning staffroom chatter revolved around Steve's gutsy stand against crazy Mrs. Linzel. Word had spread. Tiny had told Summer. She told the music teacher who had had similar issues in the past with the parent. Joan Mackenzie shook her head in disbelief at the parental behavior. Someone had to stand up for teachers and Steve had done so in fine fashion. She huddled with Tiny in the hallway. She did the talking. The young man nodded intently.

Emma and Anne were particularly impressed. Steve was unlike any other principal they had worked with. Emma was considering an administrative career, though she had kept such thoughts private. If she ever found herself a captain of a school ship she would endeavor to be just like Steve Hepting.

Normally low-key, Steve was enjoying the sudden limelight. The support of the Greenside staff buoyed his spirits to the point where he felt confident about his chances in the inevitable clash with Capelli. Gulping more to gather fortitude than express unease, Steve phoned her office. The executive assistant confirmed that Mrs. Linzel had been waiting for the CEO yesterday afternoon but Ms. Capelli had been in conference with state officials. Since that meeting was continuing this morning, Mrs. Linzel had been told to return this afternoon. The parent had an appointment with Ms. Capelli at 2:00 pm. Equally frustrated by the delay as relieved at the respite, Steve could at least concentrate on what he hoped would be a more normal day.

In the afternoon it was clear that those hopes would be dashed.

After lunch, a distraught Emma Martinez sat in Steve's office, flanked by a worried Colin and a stoic Anne Shaw. Panting, eyes wide in near-panic, she said, "River's missing. I usually let him work with Tiny for a few minutes after the lunch break. Colin saw him with a man in the near playfield."

"He feeds the raccoons," blurted Colin.

Emma rolled her eyes at Colin before turning toward Steve. "That's just Colin listening to River's silly stories. There aren't any real raccoons. River just likes to hang out with Tiny and Jay, or he needs a break from class, or—oh Christ, who gives a shit right now Colin? You said you saw River with a strange man."

Steve was out of his chair in an instant, motioning Colin to follow. Emma and Anne scrambled behind. He pointed to a photo plastered on the staffroom bulletin board, partially covered with an advertisement for a yoga class at the Greenside Recreation Center. "Is that the guy, River Coolwater's father?"

Colin stared. "I'm pretty sure that's him. He was here yesterday too. I caught a glimpse of him as he left the edge of the playground."

"River was absent yesterday," said Emma. "The asshole's back looking for him today."

"I should have recognized him," groaned Colin.

"It's okay Colin. Now you've got to listen to me. Bridget's on her break and in town. I want you to phone the police and then stay in the office. Emma, you take your class, and Colin's, to the gym. If there is a group already in there, they will have to stay in the gym as well. Anne, see if you can find Tiny and tell him to scan the rear entrances, but he is not to go outside." He checked for understanding. "I'll be around the front parking lot. Make sure all of you stay in the school. I'll get Clara in the library to man the office. That will free up Colin." He alternated looks between the calm Anne and the intense Colin. "You two then check the kids' restrooms and escort each kid you find back to their classroom. Have you got that?"

Gulping, Anne nodded, followed by Emma and Colin.

Heading down the hallway and into the office, Steve grabbed the microphone linked to the public address system. "Teachers, please excuse this interruption. Elvis has left the building. There is no mistake about this event, Elvis has left the building. Once again, there is no mistake, Elvis has truly left."

The Elvis lockdown warning was much less discernible to children than what would be an easily recognized code-red. By reiterating that there was no mistake, Steve had conveyed that the exercise was not a drill. Teachers were to keep all students in the classroom and move them away from any windows in as subtle a manner as possible so as not to raise alarm. That schools had to practice such procedures in addition was as sad a comment on the state of modern society as could be found.

Striding along the hallway to Colin's classroom, Steve ducked into the nearby library. He sent the worried library clerk to the office. "Once Colin is off the phone with the police, I want you to get a hold of Bridget and tell her to not return to the school. Try Leo's Cafe first. I think she was meeting a friend there for lunch. If not there, then try Armando's. Have you got that?"

"Leo's then Armando's, don't come back to the school," she stammered. "I think I got it."

"Good. Use my office. I don't want you out in the main reception area."

Steve watched the determined woman leave. He scanned the outside through a wall of windows that formed one side of the library. Out of the corner of his eye he saw a tall, stocky man dragging River Coolwater by the scruff of the neck. The boy was making a half-hearted effort to free himself. He seemed to realize that it was wasted energy.

The duo was heading for the parking lot that straddled the front and side of the school.

Steve whipped through the corridors and nearly bowled over Terrel Lewis who was entering the building. "What the hell are you doing here?"

"I got a call to pick up some . . ."

"Never mind," snapped Steve. "I've got no time to talk, get inside the school and stay there. We're in lockdown. The police are coming. He pointed to the man hauling River through the snow. "Use one of your tech gadgets to get a photo of that guy dragging the boy through the snow."

Steve ran off, heading along the hallway to the front door.

"Christ, Steve, what the hell is going on?" There was no answer. His friend had left the building and was slipping and sliding along through the still unplowed parking lot. He wore no coat, gloves, or boots, clad only a light sweater and casual suede shoes.

Sliding around the corner of the building, Steve came face-to-face with the abductor. "Let the boy go, Mr. Golbeck."

Surprised at hearing his name, the man recovered quickly. His low-life ex-wife must have told this lump of lard his real name. "Who the fuck are you?" he groused. Then he remembered. "Get out my way Yogi."

It was Steve's turn to be thrown off-kilter, hearing a familiar nickname. He recovered quickly. "I'm the principal and I'm telling you to let River go. On school grounds that is a lawful order. Steve had no idea if that was true but it sounded good. He was confident he could talk this man down.

"Oh, fuck off," barked Golbeck, the stench of cheap alcohol shrouding his breath.

As the man moved by, Steve grasped a grimy coat collar. A fist from nowhere smacked into his jaw. He tumbled backward into the snow. Golbeck trudged past.

"Mr. H., are you okay?" A desperate River, glanced back at the fallen heap of humanity. Steve heard only a muffled undecipherable array of sounds rumbling about in an addled brain.

"Shut up," barked Golbeck, pulling the boy along. He caught a glimpse of a man with a cellphone, filming the incident through the library window. 'Shit," he muttered, picking up the pace. Approaching his battered Chevy Nova, he fished for pocketed keys. River began struggling with more energy and almost broke free. Golbeck managed to open the door and threw the boy into the passenger seat. Doors were locked. Keys were jammed into the ignition. The car pulled away, gaining a semblance of traction in the snow.

"Jesus Christ!" Golbeck cried out as a disheveled, crazed face suddenly appeared on the front driver-side window. A soaked, shivering Steve was striding alongside the car, pounding on the window and holding the door handle. "This guy's fucking crazy," Golbeck blurted as he gunned the car. The rear tires spun uselessly for an instant, kicking up snow and ice. Then the car shot forward, causing Steve to lose his grip and meet the snow face-down for the second time in the last minute.

Golbeck accelerated too fast and the car lost traction, slid, and rammed into Emma Martinez's Toyota hybrid. He backed up and spun forward. There was little purchase along the gap between the cars. The bald tires spun uselessly. Slush and ice splashed onto the sides and hoods of dormant vehicles.

Pulling himself from the snow, Steve stumbled to the parking lot entrance, hoping to close the metal swinging gate before Golbeck's vehicle arrived. Fingers fumbled in deep pockets, trying to grasp cold keys. The frigid digits had little dexterity. By the time he extricated the key chain, it was too late. Golbeck was heading for the opening that marked the end of the school parking lot and the beginning of the public street.

Without thinking, Steve leaped in front of the slow-moving car.

In hindsight Golbeck wished that he had run the crazy principal down and kept going. His quick reaction was based more on instinct than analysis. He swerved to avoid a crash. The Nova rammed into the cement pillar on which the swinging gate was attached. The hood's metal crumpled. The car twisted sideways. He tried to reverse but a portion of the squashed front was lodged against the gate. A cursing Golbeck grabbed River and the pair tumbled out. Steve was on the ground again, covered in snow and ice. Though Golbeck had a head start, River's wiggling and squirming was hampering his progress. He let the boy go and ran onto the street, a risen Steve only a few yards behind.

Steve's quick glance confirmed that River was unhurt. With adrenaline pumping at a feverish pitch, Steve continued the pursuit. He was shivering with intense cold. His adversary was a better brawler. The man may even have a weapon. But Steve's primordial instinct had kicked in. He was the hunter. His prey would not escape without a fight.

Turning into a front yard, Golbeck took a running leap at a tall fence. He reached for the top, first with desperate digits, then hands, and finally forearms. He was near the fulcrum point when two vice-like grips locked onto his ankles. Steve's downward yank pulled Golbeck off the fence and the men tumbled into a heap amidst snow-covered bushes. Golbeck was on his knees first, fist clenched for another blow to the principal's head. He grunted as a high-velocity ice-ball smacked into his face just below the right eye. Stunned, he shook off the impact. He looked for the source just before another slammed into his nose, breaking it and sending his hands flying to the pained proboscis. Wheezing helplessly in the snow, Steve grimaced as he heard cartilage break.

Golbeck slowly rose to his feet. Dripping red blotches dotted the snow like polka-dots. A tremendous flying force pummeled his chest, knocking the air from tired lungs and sending his body crashing, face down, into the snow. A scarlet rivulet seeped along the white ground as Golbeck lay semi-conscious. Then an object, harder than the ice balls, struck his head and everything went black.

"Are you okay Mr. H?" Tiny helped Steve struggle to his feet.

"Yeah, I'm cold as hell though."

"I'll watch over this asshole, oops, sorry Mr. H."

"I don't give a shit if you swear right now," panted Steve. "Nice tackle," he wheezed.

"I never heard you talk dirty before Mr. H. It's kinda different." Tiny too, was gasping, his thick chest heaving.

"Well, I'm allowed to today." Steve was still sucking in air. "It's not a normal day for a principal. I'm kinda pissed off."

"I hope I didn't hit him too hard," said a concerned Tiny, staring at Golbeck's prone body. The face oozed blood. "The cops will be here soon. I heard the sirens."

Steve slapped the janitor on the shoulder. "I was wrong about your aim," he said through a heavy breath. "You really can hit the broad side of a barn."

"Oh, I didn't wanna hit you when we were having that snowball fight in the parking lot," said Tiny. He looked at the stricken Golbeck, now slowly writhing in the snow and holding his nose. "I guess Mrs. Mackenzie was right. You really can get hurt by snowballs."

Twenty minutes later Steve was in his office, glad for the change of clothes he always kept handy. The shivering had stopped. Anne had made him a cup of hot chicken soup. A bruise was developing on his jaw. His body hurt from the numerous tumbles to the ground. The police had hauled Golbeck away. They commandeered Terrel Lewis's cellphone, much to the chagrin of the reporter. He had followed behind Tiny and taken a visual of the entire episode. The police were going to view the evidence and interview Steve, Tiny, and Terrel the next day. The lockdown was lifted. River's mother had been contacted and she accompanied the boy to the police station so River could provide a statement.

In all the commotion, Steve had neglected to contact the central office. The police officers had not either, believing that the school had done so.

They were more interested in maintaining safety and catching perpetrators than spending valuable time on bureaucratic niceties. Terrel Lewis insisted that he listen to Steve's upcoming conversation with Capelli. Tiny was strangely insistent that the journalist be allowed to do so. Bone-weary and with little fight left, Steve acquiesced. Who cared if Terrel heard the discussion? Steve punched the numbers. He pushed the speaker phone button when he connected with the executive office. With exhausted body and nervous mind, Steve waited for Jennifer Capelli's voice on the other end of the line.

23

"Ms. Capelli is not here at present. She is out for a coffee with a parent. She is not expected to return to the office today."

Steve stared at the receiver, unsure of what to do next. Capelli must be meeting with Mrs. Linzel. He had almost forgotten yesterday's incident when he had thrown the Lizard out of the school. It seemed so long ago.

Capelli's executive assistant confirmed that the superintendent had phoned Steve late yesterday afternoon. The parent, Mrs. Linzel, had been extremely upset. With Ms. Capelli in important meetings Mrs. Linzel was forced to return the following day. She arrived still agitated, so Ms. Capelli decided to take her out for coffee. The assistant did not know where they had gone.

"I need to talk to someone about an attempted abduction."

"Oh my, there is a form that must filled in when an incident like that occurs."

"I get that, but right now I need someone to talk to so I can explain what happened. It's going to be all over the Internet soon. The crisis intervention team needs to be contacted." Steve rolled weary eyes as the assistant thought out loud. The issue was an operational one, not political, thus eliminating the need to directly involve the chairperson of the school board. The Health and Safety Coordinator was on a lengthy leave after falling off a ladder. The Special Education Director was across the border at a conference in Vancouver. Phil Chow was in Seattle, meeting with A-1 Education representatives.

"I'll put you through to Lou Tayler."

"God no," screamed Steve inside his head. Before he could verbalize the thought the line went quiet. "Christ," he whispered to Terrel, "I'm being put through to the world's greatest flunky." When Terrel went blank, Steve explained, "Mr. Bureaucrat never makes a decision. Getting him to commit is like nailing Jell-O to a wall."

Soon Lou was on the line. He was always in his office.

Steve kept the man on speaker phone and told him that crisis intervention counselors would be required at Greenside the following day—the normal practice after an abduction attempt and lockdown. Lou provided the expected response. "I'd like to help Steve, but that's Jennifer's call. She's the one that organizes the Intervention Team. Did you try Maggie in the Special Education Department? No, sorry I forgot, she's out of the district. So is Phil. You might try the health and safety supervisor." He paused. "Oh, I forgot about the stepladder incident. It doesn't matter, I doubt whether she has the authority to assemble the team. Jennifer likes to keep control of that process herself."

"She's out of the office having coffee," Steve said, his voice pavement-slab heavy.

"Well I'm sorry I can't be of any help." The line went silent for a moment. "You don't sound too well Steve."

"God damn it Lou! I've been punched and nearly run over twice. I ended up in a wrestling match with the abductor in the snow. I need you to help me. You are the senior leader over there right now, aren't you?"

"If you have been the recipient of physical force you must fill out the appropriate accident reports. Jennifer will insist on that. And yes, I'm the senior person here right now. But I'm only responsible for elementary curriculum."

'I don't give a shit about forms right now. I just need some help out here tomorrow and this is an elementary school." He jumped in and said what he knew to be Lou's next comment, "Except for the middle-school-age kids." The fatigue was nearing overwhelming levels. "Aren't you even the least bit concerned about what happened to the kid?"

"I'm glad you acknowledge that the older students are middle-schoolers. Not everyone out there understands that, especially Summer with her elective program."

Terrel stopped gawking at the futility. A pained head was buried in his hands in abject pity for his beleaguered friend.

"Of course, I care about the child," declared Lou. "But injuries and abductions are hardly curricular matters. Jennifer insists that every incident is dealt with by the appropriate personnel. I'm sorry I can't help you."

With surprising calm, Steve clicked off.

A grinning Terrel was holding up a tech gadget. Though the police had confiscated his cellphone, a well-prepared reporter always had more than one tech toy. He had recorded the entire conversation.

"You're taping a private call?" Steve asked wearily. "Oh Christ, never mind," he sighed, surrendering with a wave of a lethargic arm. "That shit with Lou Tayler goes on all the time." He appreciated Terrel's obvious sympathy. "What were you doing here anyway?"

"I live near Greenside, remember? Tiny phoned me this morning and asked me to drop by. He wanted my opinion about some printed emails he had." Terrel held up a sealed envelope. "With all the excitement I haven't had time to read them."

"Knowing Tiny it's probably a list of some hot stock picks."

"Most likely," agreed Terrel. He pointed to the phone. "If that's the kind of shit you have to deal with, I'd start following Tiny's stock advice. Make some money. Get a new career."

Steve nodded. "That bureaucratic crap does drive me nuts. The kids are great though. I deal with them and the teachers far more than the form-addicted people like Jell-O Man."

Terrel shrugged. "Go home, drink a bottle of wine. Better yet, drop into Summer's place, pick up a little herbal medicine, smoke it—then drink a bottle of wine." He flashed a wry smile at Steve. "It works wonders."

There was no crisis intervention team at Greenside the next morning. Steve met with the teachers before school to explain the events of the previous day. Joan sat quietly, her mouth agape. Colin Redford was in mild shock. A distressed Emma buried her head in jittery hands. She blamed herself for the near-tragedy. Tiny was shuffling large runner-clad feet, nervous at the notoriety. For most of his life, any teacher, principal, or police officer aiming attention his way meant that trouble was on the horizon.

Leading the rumbling and grousing about the almost unbelievable levels of ineptitude was the usually mute Joan Mackenzie. "Lou Tayler and Lady Macbeth have really pissed me off this time." The collective eyes of the stunned colleagues flitted nervously. Joan Mackenzie had used profanity!

"That's a great nickname for Capelli," muttered Emma. "Who thought of it?"

Normally Steve would have intervened. If employees wanted to be ultra-critical of their bosses they could do so at the pub—or, like Joan and Gladys, in their homes. Today he was too tired and too fed up to care. "Tiny thought of the name,' he said. "It's a very long story."

All eyes turned to the rotund janitor and his dancing feet became more active. Last night Chelsea had been effusive in her praise. She likened her man Tiny to the dashing, misconstrued scoundrels she read about in Harlequin romance stories. Chelsea was always reading books. Tiny did not know what a dashing misconstrued scoundrel was but given the sex with Chelsea into the wee hours of the night, it was something damn good.

Steve had received a phone call the previous evening from the president of the principals' association. She had been subjected to an email from a crazy parent named Mrs. Linzel. The parent had demanded action about alleged harassment by Steve Hepting. The rude Mrs. Linzel chastised Hepting's supposedly professional principal colleagues. She claimed they would ignore the event and skulk behind privacy excuses like they always did.

The principal colleague had not heard about the attempted abduction at Greenside. Apparently, Lou had kept the information to himself. Stunned, she listened to the story. Who would have thought that the meek and mild Steve Hepting was a closet street brawler? It was as if her colleague had an alter ego like Clark Kent and Superman. "Damn it Steve, you could have been hurt."

"I am hurt," he complained. "I just don't want to fill out the damn forms."

"Good luck with that," came the reply. You'll need a few days off just to do the paperwork."

Needing to plan the morning on the fly, Steve had met briefly with parent council members who were clamoring for information. Fortunately, the Lizard was not present. Next, Steve visited all the classes, keeping the message short and age-appropriate. Gradually the ugly rumors of River Coolwater being packed in a gunny sack, Steve being crushed by a pick-up truck, and Tiny being knifed, were put to rest.

Anne talked with River. The boy seemed pleased with the notoriety. He had transferred schools too many times to risk developing close bonds with classmates only to sever the connection on the next move. The one exception was Jay Woznicki. The two boys shared a love of animals. When they weren't helping Tiny with what they claimed were secret tasks, they were in the library gazing over picture books of mammals and reptiles. On this morning, River was a boy of renown. Eighth-grader and former tough guy Kevin Johnson was always pleasant to River. But today the smaller boy was his special amigo. He stuck close by River's side, either to provide an assumed need of protection or to bask in vicarious glory.

With morning classes underway, Steve was sitting in his office with the door closed taking a short break. He had not talked with Jennifer Capelli. She had sent a message through Bridget that Steve was not to speak to any members of the media. She was the one and only spokesperson for the Taylerston School District.

As Steve was decompressing in his office, a senior-level meeting was taking place in the school board office. Jennifer Capelli had received a phone call from the president of the principals' association, another pain-in-the-ass so-called professional who was acting more like a trade-union leader every day. Upon hearing about the astounding events at Greenside, Capelli huddled with Phil Chow. He had recently returned from Seattle. The always-available supervisor, Lou Tayler, was also in attendance.

"Maybe we should call in the publicity specialists," suggested Chow.

"I think Phil is right," chimed in Lou. Capelli almost mouthed the next words she knew was coming from the wormy supervisor, "Media relations is their job."

Capelli rolled frustrated eyes. It was difficult staying calm when working with buffoons like Tayler. "You guys don't get it. This is a great opportunity," she argued. "We have an attempted abduction and our courageous principal stops the perpetrator in his tracks." She took a sip of coffee. "We can point out that it's not just our supervisors that are steadfast. Even the damn janitors are brave. Hell, I remember that Frank Little kid when he was a student at Lakeview. Everyone called him Tiny. All the dumb lug could do was play football." She raised her hands as if a healing preacher. "But look what a steady job working for a great organization like the Taylerston District has done for that once-hopeless case." She paused, "God, the spin is brilliant." She cradled her cup, lost in dreamy thought.

Chow chose not to initiate conversation while the boss was thinking. Lou never did.

A sly smile spread across the CEO's lips. "Jesus, I always thought a loose cannon self-appointed rebel like Hepting should never have been appointed as a principal. He really is crazier than a shit-house rat. I mean it's good for us and all that, but what the hell was he thinking?"

Lou piped in. "He wasn't thinking Jen. If he was, he would have known that an attempted abduction is a job for the police and that an incident report must be completed."

Chow joined Capelli in staring numbly at the supervisor. The CEO sighed. "Lou, just tell us what you said to Hepting yesterday afternoon. Then you can go."

The comment pleased Lou. This meeting had a disturbing vibe, as if he had not followed proper procedure. "I followed your protocol to the tee Jen. You weren't here, neither was Phil, there was a Special Education conference and . . ."

"Yeah, I got all that," Capelli interrupted, her patience wearing thin. "So, you took the initiative?"

"Absolutely," replied the confident Lou. "I told Hepting only you could assemble the crisis intervention team."

"I guess he didn't want one," concluded the CEO. "That would be just like Hepting, wanting to fly solo in his Tiger Moth."

Chow emitted a throaty chuckle. "He'll get his wings clipped pretty soon."

Lou stared at his bosses, puzzled. "No, Mr. Hepting wanted the crisis team. I told him he had to follow proper protocol."

"Did you tell him to give me a call in the evening?" She glared at Lou. "I know, I know, it's not in the protocol." Staring at the blank face, she exhaled a heavy sigh. "So, we have no crisis response team at Greenside right now?"

"No," replied Lou, wondering why it had taken the normally astute Capelli so long to ascertain that fact. She had not ordered such action.

"Oh shit," muttered Capelli, glaring at Tayler. Why hadn't she fired this waste of skin? "Lou, just get your sorry ass out of here." She turned to Chow. "Phil, you stay. We've got a problem, a big problem."

The uber-organized Capelli moved quickly. As part of the investigation, the police were interviewing the appropriate school personnel that morning. They were to brief her at noon. A press conference was scheduled for one o'clock. That was enough time for the print reporters to file a story for the late-edition Seattle newspapers. The story could be the lead on the evening news. Perhaps it was big enough to cross the border and interest the Vancouver media? Capelli could spin the absence of a crisis response team at the school on her confidence that Hepting had the situation well in hand. The small school operated in a tight-knit community. Anne Shaw was a top-notch counselor.

Anxiously waiting for the police report, Capelli had little time for Mrs. Linzel who was camped outside her office yet again.

The coffee-klatch meeting with Capelli the previous afternoon had not mollified Mrs. Linzel. The superintendent had been vague about the disciplinary action she would take on the sexually aggressive bully, Steve Hepting.

Capelli needed to get rid of the annoyance. She called the scowling parent into her office. In less than two hours she was going to be giving a press conference and praise the courageous efforts of her principal in saving a student from a horrific abduction. This was hardly the time to focus on a harassment issue, one she was convinced was bogus. Hepting was about as far from a male alpha wolf on the hunt for female victims as a heterosexual guy could get. Mrs. Linzel hardly exuded victim typology. "You can see that this is not the best time for me to be launching action against Mr. Hepting?" Capelli explained patiently.

"Just because he's stupid enough to get punched in the face, almost run over, and wrestle about in the snow like a little kid? He put that River child in real harm." Shaking with disbelief, Mrs. Linzel added, "What kind of kid's name is River anyway? I mean really, how stupid?"

Capelli mulled the possible patter that the principal had put the child in danger. That spin would have been golden if the rescue had been thwarted and the boy held captive—or, heaven forbid, injured. But Hepting had pulled off a dramatic rescue with the help of his burly lap-dog Frank Little, aka Tiny. She would have to stick with the Hepting-as-hero angle and muzzle attack-dog Linzel on the harassment issue.

"From what you've told me, I don't think we would be able to substantiate your allegation." She raised a hand to halt the anticipated protest. "I am not going to lie to you. Mr. Hepting's recent heroism is the main reason." She saw Mrs. Linzel scowl. The tongue-flicking commenced. Capelli fought to hide her disgust. Though potentially handy, this nut-case woman really was a piece of work. "There were no witnesses to the alleged bullying. A very reliable employee heard you threaten Mr. Hepting, using my name, and blurting out statements from our private conversations." She held up an annoyed hand, again to the same effect. "It was not the Tiny Little character. The witness has much more credibility than him. For the moment I cannot tell you who, but I do have a statement in writing." Capelli was referring to Anne Shaw who had emailed the superintendent about the incident almost immediately after the event. The counselor had recited Mrs. Linzel's claim that Capelli had referred to Steve as a wimpy pain-in-the-ass dinosaur. Capelli fixed ebony eyes on the parent. "Those public comments about our private conversations did not demonstrate the best judgment. Mr. Hepting could accuse you of intimidation and harassment." Capelli jabbed a narrow finger at the parent. "He might have a case."

Mrs. Linzel had not considered this. Seeing the issue from the opposite edge of the canyon, the view did not look so rosy. "Do you think he will pursue the matter?"

"I don't think so, especially if you leave it in my hands. We both share the need for bold action and systemic change, don't we? It would be a shame if all that is planned would be lost in a relatively minor personal grudge match." She saw a flash of anger in the parent's eyes. The woman did not see her altercation with Hepting as minor. "I know you can see the big picture," soothed Capelli. "Let me handle it."

Sighing audibly, Mrs. Linzel knew that without Capelli's support there would be no headway made in the claim against Hepting. The Lizard scaled back. Even she realized that on occasion you lost a battle but won a war. "Okay," she said. She stood, shook the superintendent's hand and tromped out of the office with a huff, an action conveying at least a degree of displeasure.

"Shit, go back to your swamp," grumbled Capelli as she returned to preparing her speech. Steve Hepting's lunatic behavior had handed her a golden opportunity. She was going to make him the poster child for the courageous employees of the Taylerston School District, a lighthouse organization led by the visionary educator, Jennifer Capelli.

24

Dozens of media personnel stared when Capelli walked into the board-room at one o'clock. Most of the print reporters sat with iPads. A few of their elderly colleagues clutched pens and notepads. TV cameras were positioned. The accompanying blazing lights made the room uncomfortably warm. Black cables slithered snake-like across the floor. A female TV reporter stepped forward to pad powder on Capelli, eliminating any sheen on the CEO's face.

Dressed in a smart navy suit with white blouse, the superintendent looked out over the room. She nodded to the familiar Taylerston media crowd. They were competent, earnest reporters working for solid community-oriented newspapers, strangers now in their own house. They were dwarfed in numbers by the swarm from Seattle who had driven to Taylerston over slush-covered roads. The metropolitan reporters sent non-verbal signals that this press conference in small-city Taylerston better be worth their time.

Capelli smiled and struggled to dredge up the name of a local African-American reporter who was sitting at the end of a row, midway to the rear. He had been involved with a major school project, though she could not remember which one. She thought he might be a member of one of the three Taylerston Rotary Clubs. She was in another. She vaguely recollected that he was a freelancer who focussed on business stories—Terry, Tensig, something like that. She had to get his name and make positive contact. Given what was to be implemented in the district in the near future, he could be a valuable conduit to disseminate information. Messaging was a critical part of the plan.

She welcomed the members of the media throng. She reminded those gathered that additional copies of the police press release on the attempted abduction at Greenside Community School and subsequent arrest of a suspect were available on the table at the rear of the room. Those with copies glanced at the details of the dry report. They were more interested in the human element of emotional fortitude, courage, and the conflict between good and evil. The public did not want a litany of dull facts. They wanted a good story: Jennifer Capelli was about to deliver.

Even the cynical Seattle media veterans admitted that the CEO of the Taylerston School District appeared impressive. She was articulate. She was photogenic. She had chosen an outfit that was perfect for TV.

Capelli began to drift away from the incident to more than passing mention of her leadership in the innovative Taylerston organization. She hired the best and the brightest who were, "Not afraid to take bold action, as so ably demonstrated by Mr. Hepting yesterday." She encouraged initiative and creativity in finding solutions to complex problems. She insisted that employees at all levels of the organization display a hefty measure of loyalty and enthusiasm for their tasks, whether they be acting in routine or exceptional circumstances. She caught the eye of the public relations specialist held on retainer. He had been annoyed that Capelli had not vetted the speech or rehearsed responses to anticipated questions. With eyes narrowing slightly, he was gently pulling a hand across his mouth. It was time for the CEO to stop talking. The police report and Capelli's speech had covered the angles. She had provided solid quotes that media members could use. They would add statements from a few shocked Greenside citizens for color. Tidbits from any so-called expert on child abuse and neglect would be gathered to add needed *gravitas*. With that, the story was in the hopper, ready to go.

Terrel Lewis stood. He introduced himself and shocked the crowd by announcing that he had video-taped the entire abduction attempt. The TV people, in love with visuals, went berserk, clamoring for a copy. The second shock came when he told the gathering that the video was not for sale.

Terrel still believed in right and wrong. The police and prosecutors needed to proceed without an online sensation clouding the skies of justice. His immediate goal had been met. He had everyone's attention.

Laser eyes shot toward Capelli. She did not gulp, though a lump stuck in her throat. This scene had a feeling of doom all over it. She just could not picture what this hack could have in his possession.

"It was interesting that you stated you were so proud of the courageous actions of Mr. Hepting."

Capelli struggled to remain silent. A dagger was lurking in the shadows. She simply nodded.

"You also stated that," Terrel checked his notes for added drama, "Mr. Hepting epitomized the strong leadership that permeates your district."

Narrowing her eyes, Capelli nodded again. Where the hell was this going?

"Well, Ms. Capelli, I have a written statement from you, less than two months ago, that Mr. Hepting," Terrel read the communique, "Lacked the attitude, fortitude, and aptitude to be a principal. That's a lot of 'tudes' that he supposedly lacked. Did Mr. Hepting have a workplace epiphany in the last month?"

Paying rapt attention now, the audience chuckled. The story was taking on a new angle, a complementary one that might become juicier than the original.

Though Terrel had not arrived with malicious intent, Capelli's self-congratulatory platitudes had driven him to a quick decision to expose her hypocrisy. The revelations and the limelight that came with it was like a narcotic. Terrel was quoting the scathing email Capelli had sent when secretary Bridget McKenzie and Steve Hepting had apparently colluded to ignore her phone call. She had waited a long time for Hepting to respond while Mrs. Linzel was fuming in the outer office. The angry and frustrated Capelli had erroneously sent the missive to Joan Mackenzie, teacher, instead of Bridget McKenzie, secretary. The email had eventually been opened by Tiny Little when clearing Joan's inbox.

Enjoying the momentum, Terrel pulled out a crumpled paper. It was the email Capelli had sent Emma after hearing about the young teacher's incarceration. Reading directly from the note, Terrel quoted Capelli. "I cannot blame you solely. Your principal, Steve Hepting, lacks courage and displays weak leadership. He hides his cowardice behind flippancy and juvenile rebellion. Clearly his lack of leadership is having a deleterious influence on you and no doubt the rest of the employees at Greenside by encouraging sedition and treachery." Terrel looked up. "There are a number of spelling errors in the note. Though it was sent at 10:00 pm on the Friday night at the start of the winter break, I will not speculate on the reasons."

Capelli resisted the urge to hop off the stage, grab the paper, and strangle this asshole. She remembered the wine-inspired email to Emma Martinez, written shortly after the teacher's stint in jail. The eco-nuts had caused a court injunction, forbidding further action on the property. That had been a minor setback to the grand plan. The data-center would be built eventually.

Though it was reasonable for Capelli to believe that Emma or Steve had supplied the copy to the journalist, she was in error. Emma had printed the email while at the school during the holidays. Furious, she balled the paper and pitched it into the garbage can rather than using the recycling bin. It was gone on the first day back from the holiday. She had wondered about its disappearance but had followed Steve's advice to lay low. For his part, Steve had been too busy tussling with the Lizard and brawling with Mr. Golbeck to discuss the missive with Capelli. Tiny Little, encouraged by Joan Mackenzie, had given the note to Terrel. The janitor was a financial backer of the Namibian College project and knew Terrel from that joint effort. Tiny considered Terrel the second smartest man he knew, besides Mr. H. of course.

"Hmm, hiding his cowardice, lacking courage—I don't know about you but saving a child by chasing a perpetrator through the snow, trying to halt an escape vehicle bare-handed, and grappling with a known street thug sounds like pretty courageous behavior to me."

The audience chortled. Capelli scowled. She resisted the urge to bark that Hepting had not followed procedure; that his actions were so fool-hardy they had put him and the child at risk. "There are many ways to demonstrate courage," she replied tersely. "Clearly Mr. Hepting did so during the attempted abduction."

Terrel closed scorpion pincers around the CEO's neck. "It was interesting that you also chose to praise the custodian, Mr. Little." He was back to checking his notes. "Yet, didn't your email also state that Mr. Hepting's lack of leadership was having a negative impact on the staff?"

Capelli fumed behind a soft smile. "That's the second time you've paraphrased that note. I take it that you're finished?"

"Not quite." Terrel summarized the phone conversation between an exhausted Steve Hepting and Lou Tayler, noting that Steve had given permission for it to be taped. No one, except Capelli, seemed to care that Lou Tayler had not granted the same approval. There was little she could say at the moment without appearing petty.

The summary sounded bad, really bad. Capelli had been out of her castle for coffee with a parent. Her assistant did not know where she was and did not contact her via email. She had left at 2:00 pm and was not going to return for the remainder of the work day. She was the only one who could assemble the crisis team to support students. Rules were rules, according to the supervisor who had taken Mr. Hepting's call.

"Was a crisis response team in place to support the students and staff at Greenside this morning?" Terrel asked.

"No," said Capelli firmly. "I can promise you I will take a serious look into that situation," silently cursing the imbecilic Lou Tayler. "I cannot comment further since personnel matters are solely between the employer and employee. I don't make comments about one employee to another."

Terrel scanned his notes, giving the impression that he had more. "Did you voice to a parent that Mr. Hepting was a 'wimpy pain-in-the-ass dinosaur'?" Anne Shaw had told him about Mrs. Linzel reiterating Capelli's description of the principal. While Anne was credible and the recitation accurate, the veracity had not been checked and appeared as little more than hallway gossip. That Terrel had not asked for Anne or Mrs. Linzel's permission to make the comment made the journalistic error more serious. A line of integrity had been crossed.

Capelli sensed an opening to recover at least a semblance of control. "That seems to be your style, gossip and rumors over fact—more tabloid than truth. I would hardly label your work as responsible journalism." She stood confident in the spotlight. Jennifer Capelli was no wimp. She stared into the lights, forcing herself to refrain from squinting. Narrowed eyes conveyed a tough, no nonsense vibe.

Hands shot up. Fingers reengaged iPads. The TV cameras were rolling again. Everyone waited to see how, or if, the superintendent would continue her response.

Capelli followed the standard public relations response to disasters and scandals. The leader had to be out front. In one commonly used strategy, the leader was at the heart of the mess. With a well-rehearsed blend of humility and angst, full responsibility would be assumed and a heartfelt apology issued. This would be followed by a promise that the transgression would never occur again.

While this strategy could not save extreme miscreants, it worked for many others, just as it did this day for Jennifer Capelli. Even Terrel Lewis grudgingly admitted Capelli's performance was slick.

After watching the evening news clip, Joan Mackenzie, Anne Shaw, and Emma Martinez thought it disgraceful. Conversely Colin Redford thought the reporter had been rude and disrespectful, typical of the media jackals. Tiny simply labeled it, "A bunch of bullshit," and went about his work the next day, dancing and singing with his broom.

While the staff chatter was focused on the previous day's news conference, Tiny's brain was occupied with other matters. Standing in the outer office, he informed Steve about an upcoming weekend trip with Chelsea to see a touring production of *Cats* at a Seattle theater. He claimed the animal-loving River Coolwater and Jay Woznicki wanted to go with him but Chelsea was having no such nonsense.

"I'll just keep watching movies with the kids after my shift. We always watch animal movies like *Madagascar* and *Ice Age*. We like the *Madagascar* ones the best. The animals aren't the same as the ones here at Greenside like cats, and snakes, and raccoons, and skunks. In the movie they've got .. ." Tiny could not recall the four main animals in the movie and went silent.

A confused Steve stared blankly. "I know we had mice and a few cats on the second floor for a while but . . ."

"Penguins!" gushed Tiny, interrupting Steve. Tiny suddenly remembered that the penguins in *Madagascar* were really funny. He giggled, recalling the penguin shirt Steve had worn on the first day of school.

Steve marveled at the inconsistent operation of Tiny's brain: one minute creating silly hyperbole about Greenside animals, then remembering an article of clothing worn on only one day, more than four months previously.

As if to demonstrate more scattered thinking, Tiny shifted off penguins and blurted, "You've got a cat, don't you?" His boss nodded. "I think they're pretty cool. I might get one too. I like dogs better but Chelsea likes cats. After we see the show, I'm going to get one." Sucking in air for a moment the excited youth rambled on, "I bet your cat's name is Shakespeare."

"Charles, he's named after Charles Dickens." This drew a blank from the janitor. "The Christmas story about Scrooge was written by Mr. Dickens. There's even a character called Tiny in it."

This resulted in a vague recollection. "Cool," Tiny concluded, prior to wandering off. He had messed up big-time! His blabbing had spewed out the big secret. He had tried to cover the mistake by launching into rapid-fire talk about penguins and cat names to confuse Mr. H. Maybe it had worked. Maybe Mr. H. had not noticed what he had said.

Steve smiled at the departing Tiny, so able to glom onto a subject and jabber nonsensically for a minute or two. He made a mental note to keep his door closed most of next week unless he wanted to hear renditions of songs such as "Memory" and "Magical Mr. Mistoffelees" until his ears fell off. Bridget was in for a week of despair. She could only hope that the young man's repertoire would extend beyond three lines of a few songs.

The central office response to the Greenside incident was never going to fall solely on Jennifer Capelli's shoulders. She adroitly launched into the second textbook tactic used by CEO's after a crisis. Even if the scandal or disaster had been caused by others, the solemn leader would still take full responsibility. The heartfelt apology would be followed by a promise to, "Investigate the issue to determine responsibility and take appropriate action." This latter comment was a well-understood euphemism for,

"Someone is going to take the fall and it sure as hell isn't going to be me." This strategy had an exceptionally high success rate.

Jennifer Capelli's ill-fated press conference was an example of reacting to a scandal using both strategies simultaneously. The poised and articulate Capelli took responsibility and appeared earnest, honest, and trustworthy. She was strong, yet humble. The chairperson of the school board issued a statement that the members were, "Impressed by the courage Ms. Capelli demonstrated in accepting responsibility for her unfortunate choice of words and her quick action to initiate difficult personnel decisions."

Lou Tayler's demotion had been the stickiest point during an in-camera meeting of the school board. Two of the powerful Tayler clan were members, but even they could not derail the inevitable. Two weeks after the fateful press conference, Lou Tayler found himself back in the role of Elementary Library Consultant, a full two pay grades lower. A new position was created with the vague title of Special Projects Coordinator though there were not any projects large enough to command the sole attention of a district official. The hiring was put on hold until the spring.

Though the white polyester shirt and navy bow tie still adorned Lou Tayler's slim frame, a deeper look revealed a different man. Having completed an inspection of the Greenside library, he was parked on top of a table discussing the situation with Steve. "I think I have a good handle on what is needed here," he commented with satisfaction. He scanned a long sheet. Frustration had given way to determination as he clucked and grumbled about the state of the holdings. "I never realized the collection was in such sorry condition. I never knew the budget Phil Chow was providing was so low. It's almost as if they want the library to close." Lou bore no ill will toward Steve. "I can get some library material to you." He grinned conspiratorially. "I have a pretty good handle on the location of some unused stuff lying around the district."

"Thanks Lou, and I'm really sorry it worked out the way it did. I never thought that Terrel would use that tape of our phone call the way he did. He said he made the decision to use the information at the press conference. He just could not stomach the way Capelli was babbling on."

Lou shrugged. "My demise would have happened eventually. I'm not her kind of guy." He leaned in for a stage-whisper, "She's not exactly my cup of tea either. She's really pissed that I get to keep my supervisor salary for two years."

"Good for you."

"And good for you too Steve. You got a public apology from her." He shook a slender head in disbelief. "Only Jen could pull out of that fiasco and come away with more power than she had before. God knows what's going to happen now."

25

Just as a week can be a long time in politics, a month is an eternity in a school year. Busy teachers can become enveloped in an issue. Then the tyranny of the moment strikes. Ever-ebullient Summer talked about the positive energy the school community drew from Steve and Tiny's early-January action. Even she admitted it waned.

Steve morphed into a short-lived media hero. The invitations for him to speak at various events were politely refused. Requests for interviews were dealt with in the same quiet manner. With the attention span of the media little better than children, the attempted abduction rapidly moved from talking heads jabbering on TV panels to ancient history. Steve was able to return to his standard leadership style at the school, quiet and supportive. Capelli's behavior had left scars on him though. His resolve to eschew cynicism toward bumbling bureaucrats and the malicious machinations of leaders had disappeared. That new year's resolution had been dumped in the trash can. Steve the system-fighter had returned, Phoenix-like.

One employee never lingering long on the negativity platform was Tiny. He too had avoided the limelight. He did lead a boozy session with his old football buddies. They were proud that their underused gridiron skills, handy only in the occasional barroom brawl, had been useful in apprehending a low-life criminal. More than her boyfriend, Chelsea swooned in the attention. The school district had provided three days off and the youthful pair took a first-time ferry trip to Victoria BC. Steve had been offered the same three-day peace offering. His first instinct was to climb aboard the horse called pride and refuse. Anne talked him into accepting and he visited his family in Tacoma.

Despite the overwhelming evidence in Terrel's cellphone visuals, Mr. Golbeck clung stubbornly to a ludicrous yarn about taking his son for a midday pizza. That the boy clearly did not wish to leave the school did not register with the man. That he had a restraining order to avoid contact with his ex-wife and son was lost on him. That he already had two convictions for assault was, to him, a similar *non sequitur*. He intended to sue Steve for pulling him off the fence. Litigation was promised against Tiny for assaulting him with ice balls and tackling him in the snow, using his great bulk to unfair advantage. It was as if Golbeck's brain resided in a dimension undisturbed by factual reality. Eventually the man was sent for psychiatric assessment.

One claim irked Steve. Golbeck's friend was a cook who had been flipping dough in a Lynwood pizza outlet. He thought he had spied Luke, River's birth name, sitting with a weird kid and a big, tubby man who looked like Yogi Bear. The trio had been talking excitedly about a pet snake in a school, not usual conversation in a pizza parlor. The cook told Golbeck, who was trying to track his son's whereabouts.

Golbeck scanned hundreds of school websites until he spied an old photo of the distinctive Yogi look-a-like, posing with a group of children from Meadowvale Elementary in Taylerston. The students were providing assistance to an African country with an unpronounceable name. Arriving in Taylerston, Golbeck picked up the school district's annual report lying in a heap of papers in a grungy coffee shop. There was a photo of Yogi on the back page, adjoining an article about the African project. The camera-hog's name was Mr. Hepting, the current principal of Greenside Community School.

Initially, Steve had been furious at Terrel's press conference attack. The use of Capelli's emails sent erroneously to Joan Mackenzie was off the mark, though far less so than using the tape of Steve's conversation with Lou Tayler. Worse yet was his quoting Mrs. Linzel about Steve being a wimpy pain-in-the-ass dinosaur. Terrel had not heard the comment, only receiving the information second-hand. He had not bothered to check the Lizard's side of the story.

The latter point was the only one in which Terrel agreed he had crossed a professional line. As to the rest of Steve's concerns, he simply shrugged them off. Investigative journalism was not for the faint of heart. He was never going to morph into a jaded tabloid-tommy, chasing ambulances for sensational stories. He issued a muted apology. The affirmation of partial wrong-doing calmed Steve to the point that the two remained friends.

Terrel still had issues he wished clarified and he requested a meeting with Jennifer Capelli. To his surprise, she agreed. Fully recovered from the public relations fiasco, she needed to continue to demonstrate her soft leadership skills. It was not as though she lacked them, she just never used them much.

For his part, Terrel needed to convey that neither Emma Martinez nor Steve Hepting had provided him with the emails. He expected Capelli to push for a name. Surprisingly, she stayed silent. Terrel was most interested in probing the relationship between the school district and A-1 Education. The company's Initial Public Offering (IPO), had recently opened trading at a surprisingly low $3.00 per share.

Terrel asked about speculation circulating about a personal connection between the company and Jennifer Capelli. She responded with a derisive snort.

The journalist asked about another rumor linking Phil Chow to the company. The superintendent paused, as if contemplating voicing an opinion. She seemingly made her choice and told Terrel that she had no comment. If he had any other questions on that topic, he should ask Chow directly. Capelli also refused to comment about the relationship between the company and Greenside school. She took pleasure in watching the journalist crave more information, akin to a junkie hankering for a fix. A barely perceptible curled lip and satisfied smirk crossed her face. Though she loathed the man, she believed that Lewis was perceptive, perhaps even bright. He would have caught the delicately subtle hint she had issued. Lewis was a proverbial dog to a bone who would continue digging and digging until he was halfway to China. Capelli smiled as the journalist left her office. A bold tale in a new book would soon open. She was the one who would choose the time and place to crack the spine.

Terrel left the meeting more perplexed than when he entered. Capelli was playing him, he just didn't know the tune. A week later, one February Friday after work, he found himself in Steve's living room watching snowflakes flutter to the ground. Steve was in the recliner, a feline lump of fur on his lap.

Perry Watkins sat at the other end of the couch, a beer bottle in hand. "I thought you'd be slurping vino with your Miss Marple buddies this afternoon," he said to Steve.

"I went last week. Gladys, she's the really wild one, started gyrating to Steppenwolf and belting out "Born to be Wild.""

"I see," said Perry, though he was trying hard to do the opposite.

The juxtaposition of the matronly Merlot Mermaid and hard-rocking Steppenwolf caused awkward silence. It took a moment to withdraw the visual from the memory banks. The friends shifted conversation to the stock market—getting better, the continuing mediocrity of the Seahawks—getting boring, and political scandals—getting more commonplace. It was not long before thoughts of impropriety were followed by animated discussion linked to Machiavellian leadership. Prompted by Terrel, this eventually connected to Jennifer Capelli. It was a neat, direct association.

As a business journalist, Terrel had seen CEO shenanigans many times over; he was alternately impressed and repulsed by Capelli's style. He was convinced that there was a story behind A-1 Education and the Taylerston School District that had enough leg-power for a few laps around the track. He just could not put his finger on the heart of the matter. Since going public at $3.00 a share the week before, A-1 Education had shot up to $3.80. Now it was sinking back and threatening to dip under the initial price.

Steve rose, sending Charles scurrying. "That's not unusual for an IPO in the first week or two," he called from the kitchen.

"Let's face it," Terrel said bluntly. "Something smells. Capelli took A-1 Executives on a tour of the school last summer. Company big shots were golfing with Capelli and Chow. Chow used to be a director for the company in its early days, and a major initiative is in the works. Chuck Palmer confirmed those last points. It was a good idea to interview him, even though it was under false pretenses."

He and Steve had debated the ethics of interviewing Palmer. What particularly rankled Steve was the phony excuse. Terrel was supposedly conducting research for an article on managers changing careers in mid-life. Neither man liked the idea of lying, but their dislike of Palmer trumped the dubious ethics. Years previously, Steve had refused to return to the investment industry after uncovering Palmer's lies. Terrel had been fired from the brokerage house where Palmer was the manager. Given the past acrimony, Terrel decided to hold his nose and conduct the phony interview. That he was concerned enough to grapple with the ethical issues pleased Steve. Some of his friend's former standards were reappearing.

Swallowing considerable buckets of pride, Terrel traveled to Everett to interview his former boss. Initially cautious, Palmer relaxed when Terrel did not appear to hold a grudge. The journalist seemed honestly interested in Palmer's new position at A-1 Education. He commiserated with Palmer about losing the business-manager competition to Phil Chow. Terrel appeared impressed when Palmer expressed pride that he had landed on his feet after a major disappointment. "I made a big mistake complaining that the school district had only hired Chow because he was a visible minority."

Terrel gulped. Where was this going? "Your mistake was?"

Palmer was matter-of-fact. "I wasn't wrong about the minority thing; I just should have kept my mouth shut."

Terrel groaned inside. Palmer was as big an asshole as he had been before. The journalist struggled to maintain a neutral visage.

"Capelli became the superintendent. She and Chow got real tight." Palmer saw the reporter's eyebrows raise. "Not in that way." He thought for a moment. "At least I don't think so."

Palmer had told Terrel about his new job, flogging the merits of A-1 Education and its world-class software programs. He also hinted that there was going to be a major initiative in partnership with a school district. Palmer's area, the north Cascades, had been selected for a pilot project, specifically the Taylerston area. Despite a combination of subtle and overt probing, Terrel had not been able to solicit details.

"Chuck Palmer is an A-1 bullshitter, no pun intended," Steve remarked, after hearing Terrel's claim of nefarious dealings yet again. He switched the George Michel CD for *Evita*. "The supposed big deal is probably nothing more than a contract to buy a bunch of Math software."

"I don't think so," said Terrel. "Palmer hinted that it was much more than that." He stared at his half-full bottle of ale. It's so hard to get information about the days when A-1 Education was a private company. Palmer said that Chow was a computer geek at one time and helped develop software in the early days of the company. We know he's not a director at the company now. A-1 had to declare all that information when it went public."

"He could still have some shares in the company though?" asked Perry.

Terrel nodded, for the moment engrossed in his feet. "What?" he asked, snapping back to the conversation. "Yes, Chow could be a shareholder in the company."

Principals and school district personnel in a position to purchase material frequently had shares in the companies acting as vendors; whether it was owning Apple stock when buying computers, Xerox when purchasing photocopiers, or John Deere when buying tractors and mowers for grounds maintenance. Teachers too could be involved. A Sewing teacher could own shares in Janome. A Science teacher could have shares in VWR which owned Boreal Science, a major supplier of Science equipment to schools. Most of this activity was at a sufficiently low level that almost no one thought about it. But a business manager with significant holdings in a relatively small company, in public start-up mode, in a field where one or two initiatives could move a stock price? That might be an entirely different matter.

Despite Herculean effort, a frustrated Terrel was unable to uncover any further information about the relationship between the school district and A-1 Education. The various officials met from time to time. They golfed together on occasion. The school district was purchasing company products. There was nothing untoward. The only possibility was a weak historical link between Chow and A-1 Education that might have some promise if parlayed into a story with a conflict of interest angle.

While Terrel spent February and early March on a fruitless search of an exciting scoop, Steve settled in to the mid-year pattern of a school. Capelli was strangely low key. The district's anti-animal policy was now set. There was precious little idiocy emanating from the central office on which Steve could pounce. As Anne Shaw had advised, his sole focus was on Greenside school.

There was a dichotomy to most schools during the mid-year span and Greenside was no exception. An inexplicable aura prevailed, a blend of organizational inertia and animated activity. Each was dominant for a day or two before submitting to the opposite ambience. Eighth-grade, boy-crazy Janet still pined for the opposite gender. Anne and Steve worked closely on a number of school-related issues. She won two more wagers about special education designations. Steve tried to convince her that the cheap Bulgarian she received as her prize was equivalent quality to expensive French selections. That claim ended when she invited him to drink it one Friday afternoon after work.

The Mermaids kept rocking along Merlot lane on Friday afternoons. The Emma Martinez and Colin Redford battles were reduced to skirmishes. Summer and Perry were a couple. Either love or herbal remedies were causing a happy vibe to emanate from both, normal for Summer and pleasantly different for Perry. The Lizard still griped, her tongue slipping out between thick lips. Tiny continued to bring videos of animated movies starring animals for River Coolwater and Jay Woznicki to watch after school. As for Steve, he continued to do what he loved, work with the students and support the teachers. He waited anxiously for the start of golf season as he always did. At home, the guitar was back in the case. Charles continued to scarf pizza and put on weight.

The relatively harmonious routine of the school's mid-year term was about to be shattered.

Like many corporations, A-1 Education announced that it was about to make an announcement. This ridiculous fluffing of information had an advantage of grabbing two newswire flashes instead of one. The company was small with a market capitalization of two hundred million dollars compared to firms such as Apple Computers which was in the several tens of billion-dollar range. The sheen on the company's February IPO had worn off. The stock had opened at $3.00 per share on the first of the month, moved upward during the initial glow of optimism and the expectation of a major announcement. With no news forthcoming, enthusiasm waned, and the share price had slipped to the current mid-March level of $2.70.

The early weekday mid-March date for the major announcement had been carefully selected. For investors who followed stock markets, the start of a new week always brought a sense of anticipation focused on the opening trend for the week. Hence the timing of A-1's initial announcement. Tuesday was usually a slow news day and grabbing a headline was much easier, thus the timing for the second notice. That it would be another few weeks before first-quarter earnings would be dominating the business headlines was another consideration.

The upcoming school spring break was key timing as well. The powerful public-sector unions in the education system would be blindsided. The Tuesday announcement meant that the leaders would have only three days to react before their members would be on holiday and separated from work connections. Their initial attacks would be uncoordinated and little more than loud posturing. Combatting this seismic shift in public education would require their unified and aggressive response. But the unions were giant bureaucracies themselves. Time would be required for them to analyze information, reach consensus among their internal factions, and then launch a coordinated, well-structured counter beyond simply yelling foul. The three signatories, The Taylerston School District, the State Department of Education, and A-1 Education, hoped their organized-labor opponents would overreact and take radical action. Nothing would galvanize public opinion more than a sudden strike. Such action would only serve to add proof to the validity of the bold new approach.

The A-1 publicity specialists and the leaders in the education partnership would have the media almost to themselves during the week of spring break. The world of public education was an emotional one. The company had worked diligently to develop a reputation as a caring, considerate employer, free of scandal. It had an eye on the twin pillars of the betterment of human lives and the bottom line of a ledger sheet. By the end of March, the market would have spoken and the price of company stock would be soaring.

The partners had scheduled a joint media conference for 10:00 am. Anticipating a large crowd, Jennifer Capelli had booked the conference room in Taylerston's largest hotel, the Lake Vista Inn, an unsightly concrete structure clinging precariously to former glory. At five stories it dwarfed adjacent buildings. From the top floor, one could catch a glimpse of Tayler Lake on a sunny day.

The invitation to the media outlets promised, "A significant announcement that will alter the future of public education." Easily recalling the superintendent's tendency toward hyperbole, even the talented publicists at A-1 Education had difficulties convincing the Seattle media outlets to make the trip to Taylerston. A round of deftly dropped hints by sales representative Chuck Palmer helped. He suggested that high-ranking state officials would be in attendance, including the State Superintendent of Schools. The Governor may even be present. The metropolitan media crowd took the bait and were out in full force, half hoping the photogenic local superintendent would be caught in another gaffe in front of the cameras. More than a few reporters reviewed the stories of the previous repartee between Capelli and Terrel Lewis. That event had been two months ago. The dynamic exchange and subsequent controversy had been a treasure trove for conflict-hungry journalists. Hints had been dropped that the upcoming announcement would dwarf that episode. Capelli had delivered before. The media hoped she would do so again.

26

"I have no idea what's going on," Steve answered to Anne Shaw. He checked his gold-embossed invitation for the fifth time. "Terrel only knows that there's a major announcement about a partnership." He glanced at Summer, looking for an answer. She shrugged. Apparently, Perry was not in the loop either.

"Donna or Hank Medford might know something," Anne offered. "Donna's the chair of the parent council and Hank is on the union executive."

"I checked," replied Steve. "Both received invitations and neither has any idea what's going on."

Clearly Greenside was the focal point since the chair of the parent council and the principal had received invitations. They were the only school-based invitees. The Greenside mayor was the sole civic leader on the list.

"They can't be closing the school," declared Steve pensively. "Two public meetings are required and there hasn't been any. The state-level big shots wouldn't attend a meeting about the closing of a dinky little school like ours. Schools are closing all over the interior of the state."

"I don't get the A-1 angle," Summer said. "I know the district buys their software but it's not that much different than other educational material on the market." The step-by-step, almost rote progression of most software programs was in direct contrast to her self-described teaching style of free-form fluidity. She admitted that the A-1 programs Perry had shown her could be useful for particular students at certain times.

"I heard Mrs. Linzel has been invited," huffed Anne, her positive coun-seling aura having vanished temporarily. She stared angrily into her coffee. "How did she warrant getting an invite?"

Steve tried to shake the image of the woman with the reptilian smile and flicking tongue from his mind. He had not heard a word about the Lizard's alleged harassment complaint. Either Capelli had ignored it or the parent had dropped the matter. "Mrs. Linzel is now the chair of the Taylerston District Parent Council," Steve informed the group. "It's a new group created by Capelli. Our boss hates bureaucracy except when she controls it and the members are behind her one hundred percent. There's only three parents on the new committee."

"Perry says the other two are just like Mrs. Linzel," remarked Summer. "They're a couple of neo-conservative nut-bars who want to bring Tea Party lunacy to local education issues. Emma nodded with gusto, clearly sharing Summer's view of the uber-conservative splinter group. Steve had only a vague knowledge of the Tea Party cohort and chose to remain silent.

No further along the road to understanding, the group dispersed. Steve promised to inform them of any significant information. He was sure about one issue. Any partnership that involved Jennifer Capelli, Mrs. Linzel, and Chuck Palmer was unlikely to produce anything positive. That their guns were trained on Greenside Community School made the pos-sibilities all the worse. It was with heavy trepidation that he settled into his suv and drove to downtown Taylerston, for once not bothering to listen to music along the way.

The Lake Vista Inn had rarely looked better in the last decade. The carpets had been vacuumed. The faded brass railings had been polished. White linen covered the tables. Coffee was brewing in large old-style percolators, not sitting in a plastic bag covered by a cardboard shell from Starbucks. A hotel employee had poured cream from a carton into a ceramic jug embossed with the hotel logo. The sugar cubes were no longer in a cardboard box. They had been placed in small bowls with metal tongs for the appropriate delicate handling of the sweetener.

"Nice spread," noted Perry, eyeing the croissants and fruit as he and Steve entered the reception area. They grabbed a coffee, filling the ceramic cups. Steve used his fingers to grab two sugar cubes. So did Perry. "I heard the State Superintendent and the Governor backed out at the last minute—too bad for Capelli."

"She'll get more face time on stage and more air time with the mike," noted Steve absently, scanning the room. "She wants this twisted glory, whatever it is, to be as much about her as she can."

Steve spied Terrel Lewis sitting across the room with assorted media members. They had agreed to sit apart in case Terrel was going to lambaste the CEO again. He had said he had information on Phil Chow but had kept whatever it was under wraps. "Don't worry," he said to Steve over the phone. "The information is in the public interest and not my personal vendetta." When Steve pressed him, he turned silent, before adding a mysterious, "You'll see," and hung up.

While not a parent, Steve reasoned that this is how a person must feel when sitting in a hospital waiting area for news about a seriously ill child. It was taking a massive amount of energy to remain calm and tame twitching nerves. His muscles, weak as they were, wanted pulsating action. He wanted to pace, even jog. He craved caffeine, fighting to sip the java rather than downing it in one gulp and refilling for another shot. His emotional link, Greenside school, was about to undergo some kind of risky operation. Steve had not even realized it had been deathly ill.

Perry pointed to two seats near the rear of the room. Steve smiled a greeting to Hank and Donna Medford who were angling their way to the area occupied by the public-service union leaders. The teachers' executive members were seated nearby, their feet shuffling and eyes darting, silently wondering what caper Capelli was about to pull.

Steve perused the front page of a provided brochure. Such pamphlets always contained fluffy drivel as opposed to any real information. The publicity specialists did not disappoint. The logos of the three entities, the Taylerston District, the State Department of Education, and A-1 Education were enclosed by a bold-lined circle with "Partnering for the Future" written along the edge. One page of the brochure's two inside sheets was dedicated to a description of the dynamic Taylerston School District with a photo of Capelli. School board members and Phil Chow were included in a list of names. The adjoining page comprised a bland, almost cautious, portrayal of A-1 Education. It too had a photo of the CEO, a listing of the Board of Directors, as well as the name of representative, Chuck Palmer. Whatever had transpired had helped earn the manipulative Chuck a promotion.

The pamphlet's back page contained Department of Education information complete with a photo of the State Superintendent and meaningless political candy floss about her commitment to public education. Steve revisited the A-1 page and scanned the write-up, internally grumbling about how Chuck Palmer had popped back into his life. A familiar tug on his shoulder brought tangible evidence to that fact. Chuck had landed with a thud.

"Hey, Steve, I see you still got the teacher clothes." Palmer eyed the long-sleeved navy-colored polo shirt with gray corduroys. "Don't you get more dough when you become a principal?" He let out his trademark snort.

Steve groaned. Not even the expensive suit, white shirt with red patterned tie, and black wing-tip shoes could hide the boorish persona that was Chuck Palmer. Steve could not believe he and Chuck had once been in the same golfing foursome. Palmer had added ten pounds and there were a few more wrinkles lining his tanned face, particularly around the eyes. Yet the wide, plastic grin, the arm around the shoulder, and the never-ending patter was still the same.

"I guess Terrel interviewed you too?" He caught Steve's perplexed look. "The article he was working on, about career changes. You had a career shift too old buddy, remember?"

Steve remembered, and he was not Chuck's old buddy. He forced a thin smile.

In the past Chuck never waited for an answer before he moved on to what he wished to say. "Remember I gave you that heads up about A-1 Education in the fall, just to show there were no hard feelings." Steve did not recall any such conversation. Palmer looked at Steve expectantly, though the pause was just to catch his breath. "Well now it's happening, old buddy. I hope you bought some shares." He leaned in conspiratorially, another mannerism that had not altered. "I have changed. I know you find that tough to believe. These A-1 Education guys are ultra-sensitive about their image. One hint of scandal or impropriety and you're toast. I'm on the straight and narrow."

"I'm sure you are," said Steve, the sarcasm missed by the grinning Chuck.

"Hey, here's my card," the salesman said, shifting to a serious timbre. "I'm going to be in Taylerston a lot over the next few months. Give me a call. We can go out for a few beers and talk about old times—Darrington days, our former mutual love interest, Charlotte, shit like that. I know you were pissed off at me way back and for good reason. I was an asshole and I owe you for the wrongs I did." He stared at Steve. "I've been through the God-damn wringer and come out the other side. I'm a hell of a lot better guy than I used to be."

Slipping the card into his wallet Steve smiled and nodded. While Chuck was a first-class liar there was a hint of sincerity in the man. He decided to accept the statement as honest. There really was no point in holding a grudge. Chuck Palmer was no longer an important part of his life. If he wanted to have a few beers one evening, what harm could it do?

Precisely at 10:00 am Jennifer Capelli took the mike. Steve had to admit she always looked professional. In front of an adult crowd she displayed a subtle tinge of sexiness that men and women noted, though with differing reactions. Tall enough already, she was wearing unnecessarily-high three-inch heels, a bold red suit, and a white silk blouse. She thanked the assembled group and launched into a tedious spiel about the Taylerston School District. It was only when she started a critique about the lack of innovation, the mounting costs of public education, and the need for bold action, that the union and principal representatives perked up. The media was still sleepy. They had heard the blather before about the need for systemic change in education. Lots of people talked about it and no one really did anything. Reform was always more hot air than anything substantive.

Capelli bore into the audience. "The Taylerston School District, in conjunction with A-1 Education Incorporated and the State Department of Education, has devised a vision and a courageous plan to make that vision a reality. The successful implementation will be a blueprint for the future of public education."

Steve wiggled in his chair. Oh Christ, get on with it.

"The Taylerston School District is pleased to be in partnership with senior government and a progressive company such as A-1 Education. It is through education that we can make the world a better place."

A glance at Donna Medford and Steve rolled his eyes. C'mon Capelli, just tell us about this supposedly earth-shattering deal of yours.

"It is only through cooperation that we can achieve our lofty goals and triumph over the forces that work tirelessly to keep twenty-first century education stuck with twentieth, even nineteenth century methods."

Steve grimaced. Oooh, that was a shot. The unions will be more than a little pissed off with that.

The media reps remained unimpressed to the point of boredom. The education groups were always firing venomous bullets at each other, each one claiming that they were speaking, "For the kids." If this was another one of those tedious turf wars this whole exercise was a waste of time.

Fed up with the maundering, Steve needed another coffee. He set his lifeless eyes on Capelli, begging her to stop the mindless prattle and spit out this remarkable plan that will alter western civilization.

Capelli paused. She knew the audience was slipping away. It was the perfect time for a jolt of the educational equivalent of crack-cocaine. She leaned forward, about to press a point. The opening credits were over and it was time for the show to begin. It was as if she could read Steve Hepting's mind.

Upon later reflection, a somber Steve wished that Jennifer Capelli had continued to spout drivel and had never launched into an explanation of the audacious plan.

But she did.

Speaking with unchained hubris, Capelli appeared to add several inches to her statuesque, high-heeled frame. "As a step toward the goal of public education excellence, Greenside Community School will be leased to A-1 Education for five years commencing in the 2012-2013 school year." The CEO paused for unneeded effect. Even the media cynics were paying attention now. "A-1 Education will operate the school and provide software for children in Kindergarten to the fifth grade. The sixth, seventh, and eighth-grade students will move to Taylerston Middle School. Any elementary-age children with special needs will be transferred to other schools until such time as appropriate software has been field-tested for this small cohort of students. The software programs at Greenside will cover all curricular areas and be the basis for a personalized education plan for each child."

Steve almost choked. Had Capelli actually said the company would operate the school? She must be in the middle of some kind of minor epileptic fit.

On a roll, Capelli headed down the track like a locomotive powering a freight train. "The approximately one-hundred-fifty students will be divided into two relatively equal-sized groups, one primary and one intermediate. Every student will be issued an iPad. The students will be housed in current classrooms of about twenty-five per room. There will be one teacher for each of the two groups."

An audible gasp shook the room. The teachers' union leadership sat in stunned silence. Jaws dropped and seething scowls shrouded venomous faces. Did Capelli say one teacher for seventy-five students?

The superintendent raised a hand to quieten the agitated crowd. "I know that you are thinking about safety provisions and adequate supervision in each room." This was far from what the union leaders were contemplating. They were thinking about jobs. Capelli ignored their viper eyes and explained the removal of walls to make adequate space. "A parent associate, a new position hired by A-1 Education, will be responsible for supervision in each room. That person will take educational direction from the classroom teacher." She stole a quick glance at the beaming Mrs. Linzel.

It was the support-staff union leaders' turn to seethe. "You can't do this Capelli," barked the president of the local. "We have a closed shop. This is blatant union busting."

"Bang on," shouted the president of the teachers' association. "Teaching jobs in this district are union. You must be insane if you think you can get away with this."

The media were really paying attention now.

Capelli smiled as if a spider welcoming a fly into its web. "Both contracts call for union positions in schools operated by the Taylerston School District. That will not be the case at Greenside. The school will be operated solely by A-1 Education. What they do with their employees is their business." She stood back from the microphone and let the buzz rumble through the room. It took several minutes before the grousing to settle to an angry mutter. Media microphones were out. TV cameras were rolling. Photo-snapping iPhones flew upward like sunflowers greeting a brilliant morning sun.

"Phil will explain some of the financial implications," said Capelli as she moved to the side of the stage, clearly reluctant to relinquish the spotlight.

Phil Chow stood and surveyed the room. Slow moving, tall, slender, with olive-toned skin and unruly dark hair, his spectacles and rumpled jacket made him appear professorial. He explained that, for the first two years of the agreement, the State Department of Education would provide funding to the school as usual. With a non-union custodian and office worker, no special education paraprofessional, a reduction from eight teachers to two and the elimination of the principal position, the annual personnel savings would be approximately three quarters of a million dollars. This included factoring in the cost of two parent supervisors. He emphasized that this was an annual savings and that Greenside was small. "If applied to even moderately larger schools in the future, the savings would be substantial."

He admitted to charges associated with altering the facility, including the removal of walls to accommodate larger-sized student cohorts. More expensive upgrades to the Greenside building, specifically electrical and ventilation refits, would be costly. Chow said, "We have already analyzed the level of required upgrades."

Steve tensed, scowled, and stared. Yeah, with the help of your little toady, the smarmy guy you hired to crawl around the ductwork.

Chow paused as he caught the glare from the Greenside principal.

"You said that in the first two years the government would continue to provide the same level of funding," noted a Seattle-based reporter. The statement was directed to the state representative. "That means a pretty healthy profit for A-1 Education, especially if this is duplicated in a number of other jurisdictions. I don't see any break for the taxpayers."

"We have not yet opened the floor for questions," said Capelli, her voice a low growl.

"That's fine Ms. Capelli." The representative rose and moved to the stage mike, edging Chow aside. She apologized for the absence of the State Superintendent. Flitting eyes and several mild coughs were followed by, "Firstly, I am from the Department of Finance. We expected a number of questions regarding reductions in fiscal outlay." She peered directly at the reporter. "You are correct," she stated bluntly. "There will be no savings for the government in the first two years. However, in year three we will reduce our funding level by ten percent with an equivalent ten percent diminution in each of the subsequent two years of the five-year agreement. We are confident that when this model is successfully implemented in other schools there will be significant financial benefits to the taxpayer."

Hands shot skyward, questions shouted, grumbling echoed in the hall.

"Each one of you has a ticket with a number," said Capelli, edging the woman aside and stepping to the microphone. Her presence established a semblance of calm. She watched as the assembled crowd hunted in pockets and purses for a ticket. Some held one up triumphantly, others narrowed frustrated eyes. "I will pull a number from this jar. If your numeral matches, you can approach the microphone. I realize you have many questions about this unprecedented initiative, but we need to maintain an orderly flow of communication."

The first number drawn was held by an Everett reporter with a soft question that had been suggested by Chuck Palmer. Capelli threw the answer to an executive of A-1 Education. The next three questions dealt with details about the financial implications. Phil Chow answered them precisely and in plain English. Two more questions were about the quality of the software programs. The A-1 executive turned to Chuck Palmer who had prepared a visual of one such program, choosing fifth-grade Mathematics. Palmer joked, to mild mirth from the media types, that he had struggled to solve some of the problems.

Another facile question was lobbed. "Do you think computers can be as effective as humans in teaching curriculum?" Most of the audience expected Capelli to answer with a yes. Steve however, did not. She was much too clever and erudite to fall into that trap.

"There will still be trained teachers," she reminded the group. "The most effective method will be the computer software programs as the basis of instruction, with support and guidance provided by a trained teacher."

"Shouldn't it be the other way around?" mumbled Steve to Perry. He paused as the next number belonged to Terrel Lewis. He had significant information. Now he was going to unload it, likely right on top of Capelli, and maybe Chow. He looked confident as he strode to the audience mike. Steve caught a barely perceptible wince from Capelli. She looked wary, though she fought hard to mask it.

The audience recognized Terrel. He had been Capelli's public nemesis in a previous showdown. Murmurs filled the room. An eerie silence fell when the self-assured journalist arrived at the mike.

27

Part showman, Terrel paused and perused his notes. A slow lean forward was followed by, "Is there a conflict of interest policy in the Taylerston School District?"

Capelli frowned, then answered with a confident yes.

"Do you have any financial ties to A-1 Education, Ms. Capelli?"

A hush went over the room. The air between the reporter and Capelli was thick with animosity. "No," she answered warily.

Terrel smiled. It was the answer he had been expecting.

"Was Mr. Chow once a Director of A-1 Education?"

Capelli shot a glare to Chow who nodded. Silence hung heavily in the room. This was an unusual tack. She glowered at Terrel. That was for the audience. Inside, she was smiling. The fish had taken the bait she had dangled at their earlier meeting. Soon he would be flopping about on the boat deck waiting to be speared.

"Were you once a manager at A-1 Education Mr. Chow?"

A rumble of anticipation echoed through the room. The slender man stood. "Yes, I was. We were a small company then. I was in charge of developing administrative software."

Terrel nodded. It was the answer he had been expecting. "Were you a significant shareholder of A-1 Education stock prior to the agreement?"

"Yes, I was a shareholder, though I don't know the level to which you would call significant."

A confident Terrel continued. "Did you report that information to the school board members as part of the Conflict of Interest policy prior to this agreement?" Terrel had checked the minutes of every school board meeting since Chow had been hired.

Phil Chow looked straight through Terrel. He smiled and said, "Prior to the agreement, of course. I informed the school board members in writing and offered to bow out of any involvement with the process. I also provided this information, along with my background with the company to the State Department of Education. I always assumed I would be asked that question by a person of your journalistic integrity Mr. Lewis."

Terrel winced. This exchange had taken an unexpected turn. "Did you divest your shares at the time the agreement was reached?"

"Yes, though I was not required to. I had already followed proper legal and ethical procedures."

Trying not to appear chagrined, Terrel went temporarily silent. There had been no reference in the minutes. "You say that the information you provided was in writing?"

Chow nodded.

"Was it recorded in the minutes?"

Another nod, followed by a brief explanation. "In the in-camera portion of course. It was deemed to be a personal matter. You are free to request the information through the appropriate state privacy statures and their relevant regulations."

Terrel fumed inside. Senior corporate executives were required to list the shares they owned in the company. Not so with public entities since they were not regulated in the same manner. In his zeal to unmask a scandal, Terrel had sprinted before he could walk. He could acquire the necessary information but that would take time. The damage had been done. The moment was now, in front of the large audience. The opportunity had fizzled. The cool, funky intellectual vibe Terrel had cultivated had been replaced by a languorous brow of a middle-aged man.

Capelli warmed inside—one less asshole to deal with.

"Holy shit," muttered Steve, watching Terrel slink back to his seat. His brain became numb as the meeting continued. Question after question focused on the cost savings or the response from the unions. Precious little was asked about the students.

Over the next three days leading up to the spring break, Steve tried to comprehend the impact of what was to transpire at his school. He was out of a job, again. And the work that was his passion was riding a tsunami of change that he could not see working well for students. In the glare of the spotlights and the questions about saving money, the real issue had seemingly been lost. Seventy-five students would be hunched over screens that resembled modern day versions of chalk tablets. They would be supervised by a parent prowling the aisles. It all seemed more nineteenth than twenty-first century.

The mainstream media, rarely interested in education details, was never going to be able to pick this calamity apart. The unions would scream and yell and appear solely self-interested. Their cause would be lost, as it often was, in their bluster. Someone, or something, was going to have to be crazy enough stop this locomotive. Try as he did, Steve was at a loss as to what that might be.

The media described the plan as the, "Taylerston Teaching Tango," when referring to the "dance" between the school district, A-1 Education, and the government. The stunning arrangement split public opinion, largely along political party lines. Interestingly, both groups chose mythological entities as a symbolic reaction. The educators and most parents saw a despicable dragon readying to render to cinders a peaceful community, using computers as a modern-day inferno. The business and tax-aversion groups regarded the innovation as a Phoenix-like bird arising from the ashes of its predecessor. Serviceable public education would be retained at a reduced cost.

Since statistics were almost always manipulated, no one seemed to have an accurate handle on the exact compensation provided to an average teacher in salary and benefits. This was especially so when additional contractual perks were thrown into the mix such as preparation time, professional days, allocations for training, and attendance at conferences. Some members of the more creative conservative media called the teaching day six hours of work and threw in every benefit they could, including holiday time. Their statistic for the hourly compensation figure for teachers was astoundingly high. As with Steve's reaction to the distorted principal compensation in Capelli's cleverly designed recruiting brochure, most teachers read the document, looked at their pay stubs, and shook an angry head at the distortion.

Supported by the tax-eschewing reaction of many stock market investors, the A-1 Education share price jumped to $3.80 two days after the announcement. It hit the $4.90 mark during spring break. Two days after school had re-opened, it was approaching $6.00 a share.

Capelli was correct in her interpretation of the contract. Even the teachers' association lawyers believed the collective agreement only referred to those schools being operated by the Taylerston District. Steve had long believed that the never-ending hyperbolic disaster scenarios portrayed by union leaders contributed to the supposedly constant low morale among its members. It was almost as if the leaders wanted the system to be dark and gloomy. They could then be a beacon of light cutting through the murky shadows. This time, however, the vitriol was justified. Like the fabled character who cried wolf once too often, the overall effect was muted.

"The Russian Army could march through the instructional holes in this plan," groaned Steve one spring break night, sipping wine with Summer and Perry. Anne was present as well, long past the relationship with the ski and surf bum. She held dual American-Canadian citizenship and was contemplating a return to what she regarded as the more subdued Canadian culture. The hermit-like Terrel had remained at home, still licking professional wounds.

"The programs I saw have too many gaps," echoed Summer. "I don't think recording and graphing how far you walk each day is really physical education, even if you check your heart rate. Being able to identify the sounds of fifty instruments is not the same as playing one."

"They've got canned music and synthesizers on the music programs," said Perry, trying to bring balance to the conversation.

"It doesn't even sound real. It sounds like disco music." Anne taunted him, anticipating for a return volley.

"It sounds more musical than Steve's guitar strumming," joked Perry, though the verbal jab lacked the usual jaunty spirit.

Steve took a good-natured swipe at his friend and warned of hoisting his long-stored guitar and belt out a tune. It was a serious threat. His singing voice could clear a room in seconds. "The special needs kids are being forced to move. It's a return to ability-based segregation, cleverly wrapped in a blanket of bullshit called a personalized education plan. He raised his glass of Shiraz before plunking it back onto the table. He stared glumly at the untouched wine. Despite his best efforts, his 2012 resolution to be less sardonic had vanished.

The group agreed that the "Taylerston Treachery," as the teachers' association had dubbed it, had a simplistic appeal and the lead in public opinion. Perry pointed out that the general populace was not interested in long explanations about the intricacies of teaching methodology. "Arguments about the efficacy of software don't sway many people," he declared. "You either really like computers, or you believe they have significant limitations. It's like taxation. You are either willing to pay a certain level of taxes for public services, or you believe any taxes are, by nature, too high. We should see this as a potential opportunity to adapt, not as a battle to the finish."

"I don't get what you're saying," said Steve. Summer and Anne nodded, similarly confused.

Spurred on, Perry continued, claiming that the atmosphere for reform had been created by Capelli. Everybody was talking about the plan but only in simplistic terms. A person is either for the specific arrangement or not. Educators did not agree with the plan because they believed it was harmful to the education of children who need a trained, guiding adult as before. But was there a chance to seize the aura of change and have a real discourse about the future of public education without the usual rancor?

"As if that will ever happen," scoffed Steve.

Anne however, nodded agreement toward Perry as she reached a better understanding of the point he had made. There had not been much of a positive track record when it came to education groups working together. The so-called stakeholders in the system had been scrapping with each other for a long time. And where had it got them except where they were now, teetering on the edge of the precipice? It appeared as if the stakeholders would tumble off the cliff together and take a face-planting splat at the bottom.

"I get what you're saying about opportunity knocking," said Steve. Staring at the untouched Shiraz in his glass had put him into a thoughtful state. Suddenly he snapped out of it with a burst of insight. "I can think of a few needed changes right off the top of my head. Let's start with retooling the ridiculous bureaucracy. Then we can move on to the education professors at university."

Summer jumped in. "You can't prejudge it, Steve" she gently admonished. "That would not be true discourse. We need to get past this initial furor about the Capelli caper. She's sold it by oversimplifying a complex issue. That's what is giving it traction. A counter-thrust will need a simple message that grabs the media's attention. We'll find one," she declared with conviction. "It will probably be something that has been hovering over us, too obvious to see."

Capelli's announcement rocked the Greenside community. Only a few parents, led by the Lizard, supported the system-shattering agreement. On the other end of the spectrum, Jay Woznicki's mother wanted to launch a lawsuit against the district but lacked the finances to do so. Joan and Gladys were considering retirement. They had enough seniority to obtain positions elsewhere in the district, but neither could envision teaching in another school. A-1 Education recruiters offered Colin Redford the Intermediate teaching position. He was also rumored to be in line for the newly created school district role of Special Projects Coordinator. The job was a euphemism for close liaison with A-1 Education. Capelli had used the Lou Tayler demotion to slide the new position onto the payroll. Colin's clear interest in both jobs caused the vexatious Emma Martinez to sever their relationship, vowing that this time it was permanent. She was not going to share sleeping arrangements with a right-wing nut-bar. Colin started seeing his old flame, claiming that life was far less complicated without pit-bull Emma continually chomping off chunks of his skinny hide.

The beauty of childhood meant that the primary students were not even aware of any potential change in their lives. They were preoccupied with play days, recess, and what was in their lunch bag that day. Some of the older students had strong opinions about the announcement. Kevin, Janet, and others hated the idea. Both were glad they were out of Greenside, heading for the ninth grade at Taylerston High.

Like Colin Redford, Tiny was approached by A-1 Education recruiters. The hours allocated for janitorial work was less, as was the wage offered. Tiny did not really need the money. He liked working in Greenside but would miss River and Jay who had to move to another school. He was worried about Mr. H. too. Who would be the principal? He shook off those thoughts. He had good news to tell Mr. H.—news he was sure would make the boss happier.

"We know why we don't find any cat piss and shit," Tiny blurted one afternoon. "We know how they go to the bathroom." He stared at the gloomy principal. Mr. H. must be in a down mood. He didn't even bother to correct him for using bad language. "I'm trying to cheer you up Mr. H. This is good. It's been bugging us the whole year. We figured out how the cats go to the bathroom."

"Tiny, I have told you on several occasions that the location of cat waste is not a big deal. Right now, it doesn't even make the top one hundred issues I'm concerned about. In fact, it never has." He quickly noted the distressed look on the husky janitor's face and silently cursed his churlish tongue. "Look, I'm sorry," he muttered, issuing a tired exhale. "Tell me how you found out." He paused, stirred by a tinge of curiosity, "What do you mean, we?"

Not expecting the latter question, Tiny quickly became furtive. Mr. H. had a whole bunch of problems already. "Well, ah, River and Jay and I have been trying to figure it out for a long time. We're kinda like this team you know, like the Ghostbusters. There are more than cats upstairs—there's a family of skunks, a bunch of raccoons, and more snakes. They're in different rooms than the cats." Tiny giggled. His jowls jiggled, the eyes sparkled, and the face reddened to a soft rose. "The skunks and raccoons have had babies," he tittered.

Steve groaned as his meaty hands met a bowed forehead. As if there could be more shit flying around Greenside school. This crazy trio of Tiny,

River Coolwater, and Jay Woznicki had discovered a mini-zoo on the second floor of his school. If true, it was a God-damn Noah's Ark. That's all he needed; wild animals discovered by a slow-thinking janitor and two special education kids, none of whom who should have been upstairs in the first place. Steve bit a lip and chose to refrain from a reprimand. He had already been too snippy with the well-meaning Tiny. "You make it sound as if it's an animal hotel up there," he asked warily while raising his head, hoping against hope that the tale was a Tiny fabrication.

The janitor smiled, "Yeah, Mr. H., that's what it is, an animal hotel. Anyway, River, Jay and me have been kinda feeding them most days with the scraps from lunch. We gather the left-over grub. Then we go up there real quiet-like after school and leave food in each of the rooms. We've been doing it most of the year. Jay's the only one who'll visit the skunks." He stopped and gauged Mr. H.'s reaction.

"Shit," thought Steve, repeating the head burial-in-hands routine. "What a fucking mess."

Tiny stared at his boss. Mr. H. did not seem upset, just lost in thought. He did that a lot. Mr. H. was a smart guy.

Sighing heavily with the weight of unresolved issues, Steve pulled up and asked glumly, "Did you tell River and Jay to keep this a secret?"

Tiny shuffled big feet as eyes locked to the floor like a miscreant schoolboy. "Yeah," he whispered sheepishly. "When the time was right, I should be the one to tell you. I was the one breaking the big rules."

About to chastise the janitor for being so secretive, Steve carefully asked, "What big rules?"

"We're not supposed to have animals in the school. Ms. Martinez told me. So did Mrs. Mackenzie. I thought if I told you about the snakes and skunks and raccoons, we would have to get rid of them. The chagrin softened as Tiny slowly raised his massive head. "You knew about the mice and they're not around anymore. You knew about the cats too. You didn't seem to mind them as long as they didn't bother the kids. They didn't, and neither did the other animals." The talk of cats shifted Tiny's brain back to defecation. "I didn't even have to clean up cat shit and pee." The countenance brightened. "I told you. I know where they go to the bathroom now."

Steve held up a hand. Who gave a shit where the damn cats went to the bathroom? He was bone-weary and fed up with Capelli and Chow machinations, insane government regulations, and Tiny blabbering about non-paying guests at the Greenside animal hotel. Steve's engine was out of fuel and there was no gas station on the horizon.

"I knew if I told you about the other animals you would have to talk to Lady Macbeth and Mr. Chow," claimed a sullen Tiny. "They'd take them from their homes and kill them or somethin'. No adults know." Tiny paused with sudden recall. "Except Mr. R.—I brought him upstairs one day so he could look at the old books. I took him to the wrong room. He saw two of the snakes in the boxes. It was so funny, he screamed and . . ."

"Tiny," Steve warned, trying to bring the babbling janitor back on track. "I take it Mr. R. is Mr. Redford."

A nod was followed by, "Mr. R. wanted the numbers books. The cats live in those boxes in the room next to the snakes. One almost scratched Mr. R. He asked if there were any more animals. I thought since he had seen the snakes and cats, he could take a look at the raccoons and take a peek at the skunks." The young man repeated the head-drop, not easy to do when a person has virtually no neck. "Don't be mad at Mr. R. It was my fault. I made him promise to not tell you."

Mr. H. needed to hear better news. The first batch had not worked so well. The poor principal was slumped sullenly in his office chair, elbow propped on the desk, holding up a sorry face, "I gave some money to . . ." Tiny looked skyward, searching for the letters, "the SPCA. They're gonna take all the animals out of the building and find new homes for them before Lady Macbeth and Mr. Chow do something mean to them. The young man beamed. "I got the extra money from trading A-1 Education shares."

Tiny had purchased boatloads of A-1 Education stock at the Initial Public offering in February at the surprisingly low $3.00 per share. He sold the shares two months later at the end of March when the tripartite agreement caused the value to soar to $6.00. "Terrel told me he thought there was something funny going on with the shares. It's not a big company. I think others sold a bunch of stock at the same time I did. The price dropped to under $5.00 two days afterward. I was real lucky."

Noting a more receptive Mr. H., Tiny was happy to continue. "The SPCA is gonna talk real nice to Ms. Capelli and Mr. Chow and offer to take the animals away, so the school won't have to spend any money. The A-1 Education guys are gonna want the place cleaned up before they take over. If people found out about all the animals and bad chemicals on the second floor nobody would want to buy shares in the company." Tiny shrugged. "The stock is gonna tank when people find out." He smiled. "Nobody likes a company tied in with bad news."

Steve had never been a fan of overworked clichés in literature, believing an author to be too lazy to devise a more lucid explanation. The bolts of inspiration that populated novels rarely electrified him in real life. This time though, the volts and amps were sparking as if he had jammed his finger into an electrical socket. Was it as Summer had predicted? A simple counter-thrust had been in front of his eyes the entire time? Steve bolted from his chair and scanned the outer office. Bridget was on a break. Colin Redford sauntered by. Steve shot out a beefy arm, twisting the slender man's body sideways. "I need you," he said gruffly. "I need you right now!"

28

The manhandled Colin looked nervously at Tiny who issued a blank stare in return. He was dumped into the principal's faux leather chair and listened as his uber-excited boss jabbered instructions. Rather than query, Colin obeyed and began pecking at the keyboard.

Turning attention to Tiny, Steve asked about the snakes, raccoons, and skunks. Was Tiny sure they were living on the second floor?

Unnerved by Mr. H.'s wide-eyed excitement, Tiny nodded warily. More custodial concern followed when Mr. H. clapped his hands, grinning stupidly. "Excellent," he muttered. The strange smile stayed plastered across his face. "Tell me where the cats go to the bathroom."

Tiny was happy that Mr. H. was smiling, weird as it looked. He had not been secretive about the cats so would not be in as much trouble. "I got an idea from the *Cats* show Chelsea and I saw in Seattle. It's from this book about all kinds of cats and . . ."

Steve struggled to remain patient. "Yes, I know. The poet was T.S. Elliot. The collection was written in the 1930s."

Tiny doubted this but didn't say anything. The show did not look that old. "There's this cool cat called Mr. Mistoffelees who's super smart. There's even a song about him being magical." He started to sing a few bars.

Steve grimaced. "I know the song Tiny. How do the cats go to the bathroom?"

"They use the toilets in the primary wing, the ones that flush without pulling the handle. They're smart and almost magical like . . ."

"I know, Mr. Mistoffelees," Steve said before Tiny could launch into the first note. Cautiously, he asked the next question. He was not so sure he wanted to hear the answer. "How do you know the cats use the toilets?"

"We filmed them," Tiny said proudly, "Me, River, and Jay. We came in here during spring break and hooked up a camera onto the emergency light. River's really good at that electrical stuff. Jay is too. Anyway, the cats come in at night. They don't bother the kids during school time. He warmed to the story when Mr. H. nodded agreement. "Anyway, the cats jump up onto the toilet seat one at a time and piss and shit." Again, Mr. H. did not say anything about using bad words. Happy to be continuing without reprimand, Tiny said, "One cat jumps off. Then the toilet flushes. Then the next one jumps on. They don't budge in line or nothin'."

"You have this on video?"

"Oh yeah," boasted Tiny. "It's mega-funny. Do you wanna see it?'

The printer started whirring and Colin rose to babysit the finicky contraption. "I found what you were looking for," he said to Steve. "The copies are on the printer tray. There are six in total and no responses on record."

Almost manic with energy and purpose, Steve fought to establish focus. The next phase of his hastily devised plan needed to be rolled out. After thanking Colin and shooing him from the office, he asked Tiny to retrieve the video. Then he dialed a familiar phone number. Fortunately, the person picked up on the third ring. He listened intently as Steve relayed the information. Happy with the response, Steve put the receiver down. Calming tense muscles and loosening a clenched jaw, he pondered the wisdom of his next move before snatching a card from his wallet and making a second call.

A flurry of activity followed Terrel Lewis's afternoon arrival at the school. He interviewed Tiny. He obtained parental permission and had extensive conversations with River Coolwater and Jay Woznicki. Terrel needed an airtight story. At the recent press conference, he had let emotion override integrity. The result had been a very public failure to corner Phil Chow regarding a conflict of interest. Some colleagues were beginning to regard

Terrel as just another sleazy media hack. His reputation damaged, he did not want to become like many of his jaded, sardonic compatriots.

There were immediate concerns. Though honest, Tiny was a young man prone to exaggeration. The younger boy of the two, River, was learning disabled and had a checkered school record, academically and socially. The older lad, Jay, was mentally handicapped with significant language impairment. All three loved animals and it was possible the tale was, at the very least, exaggerated. At worst it could be a fabricated fantasy contrived by two needy boys and a kind-hearted, though slow-witted, janitor.

Terrel needed real evidence, not the yabbering yarns of three young misfits. "Can I see the rooms?"

The request sent Tiny to thinking. Only he, Jay, River and one other person had seen the animals. If Terrel wrote a story, everyone would know about them. He decided that the SPCA could remove the animals safely before something bad happened. He finally shrugged. "Sure, let's go after school."

Tiny tromped up the stairs, followed by River and Jay. Steve and Terrel were in the rear. He unlocked the door at the top of the stairs and flicked a hallway switch. The wattage was woefully inadequate to cut through the shadows. Using another key, he opened the door to the first room and peered inside. Jay remained in the hallway, seemingly uninterested. Terrel and Steve followed River and peered into the room. It was difficult to see clearly. The weak late-afternoon sunlight struggled to penetrate the grime crusted on the windows. In the shadows there were dozens of stacked boxes marked Language Arts.

"This used to be the mice room, but the snakes live here now," explained River. "For a while Sammy was the only snake I saw. He was pretty small." The boy looked at Terrel. "He's at the reptile home now. Capelli is a much bigger snake than him. She's curled on the top of that big box."

Terrel's narrowed eyes descried a shadowy outline of the reptile. "Sammy?" he whispered, glancing back at Steve. He caught a return look that said an explanation could wait. "Capelli?" he mouthed and caught Steve's clueless shrug. "Where are the mice now?" Terrel asked, turning to Tiny.

The janitor was busy staring at River. He had never heard the boy name any of the snakes except Sammy. He liked the name Capelli and wondered why River had chosen it. But Tiny's brain could not handle too many questions at one time. Terrel's query about the mice threw him in a different direction and his attention back to the journalist. In a sad tone he mentioned the cemetery, proud that he had remembered the term for the dead people's place.

A perplexed Terrel turned to Steve. The principal nodded, indicating he had heard this sub-plot to the storyline. Returning to the hallway, he motioned for Tiny to tell a shortened version of the coffined-mice tale while River shut and locked the door. Tiny kept the explanation mercifully brief. Sad stories should be short, he reasoned.

At the conclusion, a slack-jawed Terrel remained silent before shaking the shock away. "So, you bought a casket, put it in the old school gym and placed the deceased rodents in it?" He caught Tiny's slight head bob. "Then there weren't any more mice so you had the casket buried at Greenside cemetery?"

Puzzled, Tiny answered, "If deceased rodents mean dead mice then that's what I did. I didn't want to kill them in the traps; I didn't know what else to do at first. I felt real bad so I had to do something nice for them. Then they weren't in the school anymore."

"I think the big snakes like Capelli ate them," offered River.

Terrel ignored the comment and stayed on the mice-in-a-secret-coffin angle. "I believe you Tiny, but my boss will want to make sure. Is it okay if I check that you bought the casket and the plot in the cemetery?"

Shrugging, Tiny answered. "Sure."

The group moved to the Math room, similarly packed with dusty boxes. The hallway bulb and diminishing outside light provided scant illumination. Terrel could barely see the shining eyes of at least a half-dozen cats. "They sleep in the boxes in the afternoon," explained Tiny. "It's pretty cool how they go to the bathroom," he said excitedly, recovering quickly from the sad mouse story.

"It certainly is," replied Terrel, not really believing that cats were using the auto-flush toilets. "We'll get to that later."

Upon arrival at the science storage area, home of the skunks, Jay slowly opened the door while hushing the group. "Skunks scared, big smell. Jay go in." In this room blinds had been pulled down to cover the windows and the room was eerily dark. With their excellent smell and hearing, the skunks had become accustomed to Jay's odor and his soft whispers of, "Jay with food." He coaxed one of the creatures to come out from under the piles of science tables and stools for a bite to eat. It was a striped skunk, the most common, and one that is occasionally domesticated. It calmly grabbed the food scraps from Jay's hand. Returning to the gathered humans at the doorway, the boy grinned. "Skunks like Jay," he boasted.

"What's in those jars and pails?" asked Terrel.

"I think the jars have science powders with mega-long names," answered Tiny. "The pails have old cleaning stuff for the floors.". Being a janitor, he could answer that question with more certainty.

Terrel asked if he could take a photo of the skunks and the canisters.

A determined head shake and whispered "No," came from River. "We did that during the Christmas holidays. We snuck in here on a Friday afternoon when the men were working on the big tubes that carry air. I had the camera and Jay was feeding Chow, that's the big skunk's name. The flash scared him and Chow let out a spray. Jay got it dead-on and I was hit a bit. It smells real bad. The workers must have smelled it too because they went home early that Friday."

Terrel glanced at Steve. "Chow?" he mouthed softly and watched the baffled Steve shrug again. "Could I borrow the photo?" he asked, beaming when Jay nodded his head. This bizarre story just kept getting better and better.

"We only took one picture of the skunks," explained River. "You can see one or two of the pails with the smelly stuff. Maybe that's why the skunks like it in here. There's always a bad smell."

"Smell not bad from skunks, bad from water in pails," countered Jay, ready to defend the small, striped mammals.

River nodded, unwilling to trigger an ongoing debate. He brightened when talking about his favorite animals, the raccoons, holed up in the next room. "We've got lots of photos of the raccoons. Babies came last week. It was so cool! The mama and papa raccoons are real proud of the cute little ones. They like getting their pictures taken with them."

"Skunks have had babies too, they just not show off for camera like raccoons," piped in Jay.

Terrel stared at Steve. This entire afternoon had to be a dream. He knew Summer's homegrown weed was potent but his last toke had been the previous night. Maybe she was adding a titch of hallucinogens for added pizzazz? "The raccoons like to have a family photo?" he asked, hardly believing he was mouthing the question. He issued a timorous chuckle. Unlike Alice, he did not want to follow the White Rabbit and tumble into the rabbit hole. If he did, all the animals on the second floor might start talking to him. Then what would he do, answer them? Terrel shook his head. He gawked at River, then at Jay, and finally Tiny. These kids had to be joking or gobbling happy pills for lunch.

Steve was wondering whether raccoons posing for family photos and skunk babies holed up in science and janitorial waste was a boon or bust to his plan. At least Tiny's tale of the mice casket added a touching element to the entire affair. He knew that account was true. Tiny may exaggerate on occasion but the young man could never string that long a story together with so many details. He also knew that Jay and River would never joke about a tender story of proud raccoon parents wanting family photos, or skunks having babies in discarded boxes of textbooks housed in a school. Maybe the raccoon parents even put their babies in a frame for display on top of a dusty photocopier? Could the skunks want family photos too but were afraid to ask? He stopped, realizing the loony quality of the questions. He really did not want to know the answers.

Tiny grinned goofily as he leaned toward Steve and whispered, "Babies, that's so cool isn't it Mr. H?" He giggled. He always did when copulation, the act or the result, was discussed.

The final stop on the zoo tour was the office storage room, filled with furniture and old copy machines. River was the human contact for the raccoon families. He walked into the room, dropped some food on the floor and said hello to the three animals which slipped out from inside the dead photocopiers.

"Have you named any of these guys yet," asked Steve.

River admitted that he had not. He had not been able to think of a good name for any animal until Jay had provided one a few days ago. Jay added that he could not decide on any names either, until River had given him an idea. The boys were like a comedy-writing duo, each feeding off the other. Creativity can germinate from strange seeds, in this case, the boy's mothers. Each woman had recently the received the bad news that their special needs sons were being forced to leave Greenside in the next school year. They kept the information from the boys. Why cause them distress at this point in time? Jay heard his mother claim that someone named Capelli was a, "Snake in the grass." A few other words had been thrown in—words that Jay had been warned never to say. River overheard his mom say that someone named Phil Chow showed behavior that, "Smelled like a skunk." She too, added a few colorful descriptors. When the boys met, they relayed the stories. Henceforth the biggest snake was named Capelli and the heftiest skunk, Chow. The boys planned to tell Tiny so he could help with more names but had not done so yet.

When the group returned to the office, a stunned Terrel watched the video of the cats using the toilets. That the cats segregated themselves by gender was almost too good to be true. With the video and photographs in hand, story in place, and copies of Steve's emails in his satchel, Terrel left. He needed to go home and ruminate on this fantasy-turned-real. To do so he would need a heaping quantity of Summer's special herbs—the extra-strength variety.

The following day, a slowly recovering Terrel phoned Steve to confirm the reality of the previous day's events. Steve was a strait-laced guy, even boring. He did not ingest Summer-grown herbs. His tastes ran to beer and wine, lately imbibing only in moderate amounts. He would have needed a keg of each before being looped enough to have dreamed up yesterday's freakish escapade. Confirmation was provided. Relieved that he had not had a bizarre dream, Terrel checked with the cemetery about Tiny's purchase of a casket and plot. That too, was confirmed. He read the Department of Education orders regarding animals in school. Then he crafted the first of several articles. After they hit the print media, he planned to release the video that was bound to turn Greenside Community School into a social-media sensation.

The highest hurdle to overcome was convincing the news editor at the *Seattle Gazette*. Terrel needed an air-tight proposal. The public collapse of Terrel's ill-fated conflict-of-interest probe against Phil Chow had poked a considerable hole in his credibility. Burying paparazzi zeal and maintaining a professional comportment, Terrel explained that he had checked the background stories. He had received permission from the parents to interview the boys and to mention the educational challenges each one faced. Terrel showed the editor the photos with dozens of apparently proud raccoons atop decrepit photocopiers. There was an image of a skunk perched on a pail containing what Terrel had discovered was inappropriately stored chemicals. He provided emails the principal had sent to school district leaders. He had copies of the state-wide directive about animals in schools. Finally, he showed the video of the toilet-trained cats. The veteran editor, rarely stunned, was on this occasion. She had a story with longer legs than a runway supermodel.

The first article was published on a Thursday and focused on the "Animal Hotel" operating on the second floor of Greenside Community School. Each of the snakes, cats, skunks, and raccoons had checked into separate rooms in an astonishing display of cooperation. The article noted that the Department of Education had issued a directive to school districts to develop a no-animal policy. While the Taylerston School District had complied, inexplicably their leaders, Jennifer Capelli and Phil Chow, had failed to follow their own regulations. This was despite the principal's pleas via phone, face-to-face meetings, and emails. This was the same principal who had risked life and limb when thwarting an attempted abduction in January. He had apprehended a child-battering perpetrator who was now removed from contact with youngsters and residing in a home for the criminally insane.

The most touching aspect to the initial story was that the boys who uncovered the existence of the animals were two special-needs students. The youthful janitor, a former special education student himself, acted as their mentor and had assumed responsibility for not informing the principal. He was aware that rules were being broken and afraid that the animals would be removed and likely harmed if Superintendent Jennifer Capelli and Business Manager Phil Chow knew of their existence. Terrel did not mention Tiny's windfall donation to the SPCA. He did note that the big-hearted custodian need not have been worried. Capelli and Chow were aware of animals in the school and yet did nothing. Terrel concluded with another dig. "It is ironic that the two boys, along with other special-needs students, will themselves be removed from the school in September once A-1 Education Incorporated assumes operational control of the building."

Terrel used a quote from Tiny to summarize the affair. "I would have told Mr. H. (the principal) right away if the animals were going to bother the kids at the school, but they weren't bugging nobody. I broke the rule, so I should be punished. I guess the bosses broke the rules too because Mr. H. asked them real nice to help move the cats and mice out a long time ago. They didn't follow the rules. They should be punished too."

29

Huddled in the inner sanctum on Friday morning, Jennifer Capelli slammed the previous evening's *Seattle Gazette* on the coffee table. This Lewis hyena was really beginning to piss her off. So was Phil Chow. "Shit, Phil—snakes, raccoons, skunks, why the hell didn't you get those fucking animals out of there."

"Hepting only complained about mice and cats. That's what I checked. The mice had disappeared. The cats didn't bother anybody. That big goof custodian couldn't find any cat urine or feces around the school."

"Damn football lunkhead," muttered Capelli under her breath. "That Tiny Little has shit for brains, no pun intended."

Ignoring the muttering, Chow caught Capelli's severe look. "Don't look at me Jen. I don't know where the mice went. Neither does my source."

Capelli shot fire through molten eyes. "They were probably eaten by the God-damn snakes or chased away by skunk stench. Maybe they were booted out to make room for the bloody baby raccoons?"

Chow winced. He reiterated that no one in authority, including Steve Hepting, knew about the snakes, raccoons, and skunks. The principal had warned the district officials about the more common pests like mice and feral cats. Hepting certainly would have whined and sniveled about the presence of snakes and skunks. He watched Capelli scowl at the logic. She was clearly wary about Hepting's motives. The woman really disliked the man. Chow agreed that Steve Hepting was annoying when he wore his white-knight cloak, but Capelli was becoming obsessive about the guy. "Don't worry Jen. I can prove that we were taking action to clear the junk out of there. I have a contract with a third-party organization." He grinned. "We're not even paying for it." He explained that an anonymous donation had been sent to the SPCA.

"Better late than never," Capelli snorted. "At least the price is right." She took a gulp of coffee, the privacy of her office permitting less-than-polite slurping. "When will the animals be hauled out of there?"

"In about a week, two at the most."

The news had been welcomed by the A-1 Education CEO whose dis-satisfaction with the breaking news story had been palpable during a morning phone call. Though he and Chow were friends from the early days of the tech start-up, no CEO liked the company to be linked with the kind of news in the *Seattle Gazette*. The plummeting share price, $3.50 at the Friday opening, was bound to climb back to the five to six-dollar range when news of the no-cost solution to animal removal by the SPCA was announced. A satisfied Chow smiled and asked to be excused from Capelli's office. He had work to do and an important phone call to make.

The second article was published in Friday's late afternoon edition of the Seattle newspaper. This time, Terrel's focus was the massive, special needs adult and former football hero, Tiny Little. The kind-hearted young man felt so badly about the deceased mice he had purchased a casket and cemetery plot so the rodents could have a proper burial. Terrel painted a masterful picture of a heart-wrenching hunk of humanity.

The funeral director was quoted at length. The big lad, close to tears, had revealed his plan when he had initially purchased the casket. The director thought the story a fictitious yarn from an intellectually challenged cus-tomer. But some weeks later, the janitor returned with the casket. When the funeral director checked the contents, it was clear there were more than three dozen mice displaying a surprising lack of decomposition. His explanation, quoted by Terrel, was the casket's high quality. The mice were stored in an airtight compartment of low humidity with insects kept at bay. It had been late autumn and the cold temperature of the oncoming winter had also helped. Interestingly, the young man had wrapped the mice in linen, copying the mummification process he had seen in pictures in various library books at his school. It was, according to the embalmer, a well-meaning, though ultimately unnecessary gesture.

Adding fuel to an already uncontrollable wildfire, Terrel also emphasized that the janitor was a former local Taylerston District football all-star who, only ten weeks ago, had assisted the courageous principal in the apprehension of the deranged child-molesting thug. The janitor, Frank "Tiny" Little had beaned the abductor with an ice ball and then knocked the man senseless with a football tackle that replicated the crushing collisions he had once routinely launched on hapless quarterbacks.

Again, there was no mention of Tiny's SPCA donation.

On Friday evening Steve and Charles planned to enjoy a quiet night at home. Charles had taken a shine to Guinness stout. He regarded it as catnip on steroids. There was little the cat liked more than a juicy slice of pepperoni pizza and a hit of the dark, heavy Irish brew. While the culinary part of the evening's plan was successfully implemented, the quiet aspect was not. Steve ignored the first three phone calls, eventually acquiescing on the fourth. When he picked up, a snippy Jennifer Capelli was on the other end of the line.

"That Tiny Little moron was putting mice in a casket, storing it in the old elementary school gym and then bought a plot in the cemetery? Damn it Hepting, tell me this is bullshit."

"Well," Steve paused, enjoying the moment, "I think Terrel Lewis's article about the mice casket is true." He pulled his ear from the receiver as Capelli hurled a series of invectives across the wires. Lewis is a muckraking asshole. Tiny is not only stupid but certifiably crazy. As for Steve, Capelli chose incorrigible, intolerable, inept, and incompetent as appropriate descriptors. "I told you about the mice and the cats Jen," Steve claimed, struggling for air time against the tsunami of censure. "I swear I didn't know about the snakes, skunks, and raccoons."

"I rest my case," she snapped, "Inept and incompetent. You don't know what the hell is happening in your own God-damn school. The place is a bloody loony-bin."

Ignoring the broadside, Steve kept his enjoyment level high, fueled by the pilsners he had quaffed. "You have to admit Jen, the raccoon babies being born in our school is pretty cool."

"Oh, shut up Hepting. It's useless talking to you." Capelli slammed the receiver down with such gusto Steve checked on the condition of his at the other end of the line. He grinned and looked at Charles, slurping Guinness from its dish. "Well, my friend, that went well."

Jennifer Capelli spent Friday night drinking single-malt scotch. She needed a weekend war, revolution, or natural disaster to knock her school district off the front of the media freight train.

Phil Chow spent the same evening at home, numb with consternation. He had already made the critical connection on Friday morning, long before the second Gazette article appeared in the evening. There was little he could do until Monday morning.

Tiny's rodent funeral arrangements kicked the story from a regional to state-wide level. A large-bodied, special needs janitor, big-hearted enough to buy a casket and plot for dead mice was instant news. For many media types, anxious to display their literary background, it was as if Lenny from *Of Mice and Men* had morphed from fictional character to real-life person. He had jumped off Steinbeck's pages after missing a few generations and was currently pushing a broom at Greenside Community School.

Early Saturday, the angry A-1 Education CEO took action. Unlike leaders in public enterprise who could resort to delay by forming committees, private sector companies had an obligation to shareholders. When a stock went into free-fall, money was lost. Nobody liked that. To bolster confidence in the company prior to the opening of the stock market on Monday, A-1 Education Inc. issued a statement reiterating their expectation that the Greenside facility be in first-class condition before the company assumed operating control of the building.

Terrel Lewis and the *Seattle Gazette* were not finished. A damning article in the Saturday edition created a firestorm of powerful reactions. The A-1 Education CEO was outraged. Jennifer Capelli was in a fit of epileptic rage. Phil Chow sat numbly on his living-room couch, frozen with fear.

This time Lewis focused on the failure of the Taylerston District to adhere to basic health and safety standards when storing potentially toxic science chemicals and hazardous janitorial detergents. Terrel had needed more than one photo of the pails, jars, and canisters scattered about the storage room. The planned length of the article would require three or four photos to break up the text and highlight points made via the written word.

Jay Woznicki's mother had agreed to allow her son to undertake a dangerous mission, so angry was she at the school district officials for literally throwing her son out of the school the following year. Jay had been skunk-sprayed before and was willing to take the chance of being doused again, reasoning the only significant downside would be the necessity to take numerous baths.

Quietly entering the upstairs science storage area, Jay clutched Mr. Lewis's special camera in one hand and calmly provided the skunk named Chow with tasty treats. Chow-the-skunk was usually much more agreeable when he was munching his favorite treat of oily chicken.

Noting skunk-Chow's satisfied demeanor, Jay nervously raised the special camera and pointed it toward the pails. With one last check at the striped mammal, he clenched his teeth and took three photos. The flash lit the room and scattered lesser skunks to the far reaches of the dark room. The glory-seeking skunk named Chow froze, then scampered to the containers and scrambled to the top of a large metallic pail with a rusted lid. It stared at Jay, apparently in a pique that it had not been in the first shots. Jay obliged with additional flashes and quickly left the room.

When Terrel scanned the five photos and could not believe the good fortune. Jay had captured a variety of images of liquid-filled pails, jars, and containers. More importantly, there was a photo of a wide-eyed skunk sitting on top of a pail with paws outstretched as if proudly displaying the noxious booty. Even better, the skunk was named after the business manager.

Toxic waste made for excellent copy. When it could be linked to vulnerable children it was sensational. Talking heads immediately popped up on the Sunday morning TV news shows to lambaste the school district's serious dereliction of duty. Pedantic health and safety experts, with monotone vocals and multi-syllabic words, were poor choices for TV. Fortunately, their tedious lectures on proper storage procedures were punctuated with captivating photos of a tipped container oozing liquid. Another picture, this one of a particularly brazen skunk seen posing on top of a rusting pail filled with vile liquid, was visual dynamite.

The media-savvy animal-rights advocates were much better in front of a TV camera. They displayed passion and used everyday language. The beguiling topics, namely mistreated animals and fornication leading to babies, helped keep viewer interest high. The rights advocates postulated that the health of the skunks was at risk, given that they were living near toxic chemicals. The raccoon babies in the room next door could be affected as well. An animal cruelty lawsuit against the school district was being considered. No animal should be forced to live in close proximity to toxic chemicals and cleaners.

All the talking heads agreed that it was unconscionable that a company as apparently ethically pristine as A-1 Education, and a government that frequently boasted about its clean environmental record, would partner with such a spectacularly inept organization as the Taylerston School District.

When the stock market opened on Monday, A-1 Education's share price took an express elevator to the basement, bottoming at $1.00 per share within the first half hour. Thereafter, trading was halted.

"Jesus Christ Phil, how stupid can you be?" barked Capelli during their Monday morning meeting. "We're getting the shit kicked out of us in the press."

"The damn media is treating those common chemicals and cleaning fluids as if it's leaked radiation from a nuclear plant. The stuff may not be stored correctly, but last year the health and safety people said there was no significant risk. There has never been a poisoned kid or teacher. I forgot most of that material was there. Like you say Jen, no harm no foul. I can't stay on top of everything."

Ever the one for organizational protocol, Capelli shot back, "Storage is a maintenance responsibility and the business manager is in charge of the non-educational side of the district. It was your job Phil. She glared at the distraught man. "Stop looking at your damn iPhone. What the hell could be more important than this mess?" Capelli leaned back in the jet-black leather office chair. Chow was working the iPhone again, his slender digits tapping madly at the tiny keys. She rolled angry eyes but stayed silent. Someone had prompted that Lewis shithead to write these stories, as if that sewer rat needed prompting to dive headlong into the journalistic cesspool. She stared at Chow, the fidgeting feet and sheen of perspiration on his face spoke volumes. The man was a wreck. She resumed the deep thought. The organizational leak had to be from that asshole Hepting. Most importantly, she knew how to confirm it. Then, through Lewis, she would broaden the audience and deflect the blame to where it really resided—with Steve Hepting. It was his school. He was the principal. Lewis had had the gall to ask for a meeting that afternoon. Capelli's smile lacked any semblance of mirth. She was going to take him up on that offer and then the son-of-a-bitch was going to be in for a surprise.

Phil Chow went home at mid-morning, sick. Even Capelli, who had no time for malingerers and shirkers, could see the man was ill. The usually olive-toned skin was almost gray.

The morning edged along too slowly as Capelli engaged in important research. Ready now, she almost willed the clock to move faster so she could start the meeting with Terrel Lewis. Finally, the lunch period was over and the conflab would soon begin. She drummed long fingers and retraced her spiel. It would be verbal blitzkrieg, quick and irrefutable. She checked her fact sheet. She had the miserable Hepting dead to rights.

The intercom buzzed. Terrel Lewis had arrived with Steve Hepting in tow. Capelli quickly adapted to the unexpected arrival. She was proud of her ability to think on her feet and smiled as the two men entered. Struggling to hide a grimace as she stared at Hepting, she turned her attention to the slender Lewis, wearing John Lennon glasses and decked out in a jean shirt, khakis, and suede desert boots, all designer-made. She regarded Hepting's attendance as fortuitous. She might as well open and close the show in one act.

Capelli offered coffee. Both men refused. They traded pleasantries for less than a minute. Steve Hepting appeared nervous. Capelli stated that she would start the meeting since she had important information for Lewis. The men glanced at each other. Terrel Lewis had asked for the audience and assumed he would open. Steve did too. Rather than commence with a disagreement with Capelli, the men nodded. Hepting appeared timorous and particularly vulnerable to Capelli's claws.

The superintendent praised Terrel's journalistic integrity. She admitted that the animals should have been moved much earlier in the year. When Steve was about to speak, her raised hand quieted him. She explained that the principal had only complained about some mice and a few cats. Again, Steve was about to speak and was met by the same gesture, resulting in further inaction on his part. Capelli continued, claiming that Hepting at the very least knew about the snakes. He had hidden that information from the senior staff. She smiled at the surprise across Lewis's face and Hepting's fidgeting discomfort.

Mrs. Linzel had informed Capelli of Hepting's decision to allow a snake called Sammy to be kept in a classroom. Not one to automatically believe parental yarns, Capelli recalled that conversation and then rechecked the now-incarcerated Mr. Golbeck's testimony. His cook friend had reported that a large fleshy man who looked like Yogi Bear and two odd boys were having lunch in a Lynwood pizzeria. They had been swapping stories about a snake named Sammy living in a school. The cook recognized one of the boys as Golbeck's son, River.

A satisfied Capelli leaned back. "Some say you look a lot like Yogi Bear, right Steve? Wasn't that your nickname back at Lakeview High?" She turned to Terrel Lewis. "I trust that your next article will clarify this fact. Neither I or Mr. Chow can be held responsible for inaction about something we knew nothing about." She leaned forward, waving a long-fingered hand for emphasis. "Given that the snakes are next door to the skunks, who are living with supposedly toxic chemicals, and who are next door to the raccoons—well, I guess you see my point, Terrel." Capelli smiled, revealing a set of well-formed white teeth. "May I call you Terrel?" She did not wait for an answer. "I agree we should have moved more quickly ridding the school of the cats and mice. We would have been lightning fast if the principal had informed me about other animals such as snakes, raccoons, and skunks. He should have told Phil Chow about the old science chemicals and janitorial cleansers. That's how the chain of command works. If Principal Hepting had followed it, most of this unfortunate mess at his school would never have occurred." She paused, requiring a moment to catch her breath. "In the interests of an impartial and objective press I take it that you will write another article which will include this new information." An imperious Capelli sat back and waited for a response from the two silent males. "That was easy," she thought. "What a pair of spineless twerps."

30

Though Capelli's claim was based on truth, it was somewhat distorted. Initially withering from the verbal blast, Steve gathered energy from a supportive glance at Terrel. He admitted that he had shown poor judgment. Sammy the snake should have been removed from the school immediately. He reiterated that he did not know about the other snakes, the skunks, or the raccoons. He knew there was science and janitorial material stored on the second floor but believed it would be removed after he had talked to Phil Chow earlier in the year. As Capelli was about to speak, Steve raised his hand in a gesture for her to remain silent.

Perturbed by what she considered insubordinate behavior, Capelli saw the determination in Hepting's eyes. Surprising herself, she complied and stayed quiet through the long and complex story. Her initial impatience morphed to interest. It finally ended with transfixed, slack-jawed incredulity. She sat quietly for a time, tapping scarlet-polished fingernails on the desktop.

Just as the silence was becoming excruciatingly awkward, Capelli looked at Steve and Terrel and used a surprisingly soft tone. "Thank you for the information. I can assure you I regard it as extremely serious. Your thoughtfulness in providing me enough time to take appropriate action is greatly appreciated." She turned to her least favorite principal. "Steve, I am stunned. I just don't know what to say." Not normally one to search for words, Capelli went silent again. "Son-of-a-bitch," was all she could muster, speaking more to herself than to the two males sliding quietly out of her office.

It was at the end of that work week when the news broke. In the morning, Jennifer Capelli issued a statement that the Taylerston School Board had terminated the contract of Business Manager Phil Chow. She had acted quickly after the Monday meeting with Steve and Terrel. She surreptitiously obtained facts without Phil Chow being aware, which was a difficult task. She had to gather the school board members together to discuss the matter without Chow's knowledge— equally challenging. Chow had almost as many ears and eyes throughout the organization as she did. The trustees were taking political head shots and body blows akin to the physical punishment a Muhammad Ali opponent endured during the boxer's prime. School board work was so much more enjoyable when nobody knew who the trustees were or what they did. When CEO Capelli revealed the sordid details of what she had uncovered at an in-camera meeting, it was not difficult for the school board members to decide that firing Phil Chow was the only possible course of action. Capelli made the announcement before Terrel Lewis's article was printed in the *Gazette* on the following Friday evening.

Capelli's quick action added to her image as a tough, honest, though occasionally over-zealous, leader. She admitted that her trust in her business-manager subordinate had been misplaced. She promised that the chemicals and janitorial fluids would be removed immediately. She announced that the SPCA would find the most humane way of removing the animals. The costs were to be borne by a sizable donation from an anonymous source.

In a lengthy article, Terrel detailed an elaborate insider trading scheme perpetrated by Phil Chow. The business manager had readily admitted he owned shares in A-1 Education prior to the announcement of the partnership agreement between the company, the school district, and government. He had dutifully reported this to the school trustees. He had not revealed any information beforehand when contracts had been signed with the company regarding instructional, office, library, and administrative software. Chow believed these to be sufficiently small in scope and size to warrant a perception of conflict of interest. Like Tiny, Chow had purchased a sizable number of A-1 Education stock at the Initial Public

Offering of three dollars per share. He sold it shortly thereafter on the initial IPO bump. Thus, as he had informed Terrel at the press conference, prior to the formal signing of the tripartite agreement, Chow had indeed divested his shares and reported that action to the school board members.

What he did not reveal was the repurchase of shares in the intervening few days between the signing and the press conference. Only when the agreement was announced publicly did the A-1 stock surge. He sold the shares when the stock doubled to six dollars after the profit potential, as discussed at the press conference, had been digested by investors.

But Phil Chow was not content to simply double his investment once. He planned to repurchase A-1 stock when the share value crashed, as he knew it would. Chow was aware of the animal hotel on the second floor of the school. He was even aware that Terrel was writing an article exposing it. Chow knew that when the story hit the press, the A-1 share price would drop—and it did, to near the original three-dollar-a-share value. Chow repurchased his original one hundred thousand shares at half the price he had sold them, pocketing three hundred thousand dollars.

While Chow knew a great deal about what would happen, he could not control all that had occurred. Eventually, that was his downfall.

A celebratory Saturday evening soiree was held at Steve's bungalow. Perry and Summer came as did Terrel and Emma. The young teacher was clearly enamored with the older crusading journalist with a demeanor that blended bohemian with professional. Anne Shaw was present as well, ready for a night of frivolity.

Well into the wine before the pizza arrived, Perry asked, "How did Chow know the skunks and snakes were there?" He paused as a second thought wound through his brain. "How could he be so sure the story would hit the press?"

Emma winced before launching the explanation. "I can answer the first question. My ex-boyfriend, tech geek Colin, told him about the animals. Colin had talked Tiny into a foray to grab some old Math books. That's when he saw the critters. Colin blabbed to Chow at one of the monthly district computer meetings. Before the year even started, Colin had been promised a position with any new arrangement with A-1 Education."

"So that's why Capelli and Chow wanted him transferred to Greenside," blurted Perry, connecting the dots.

"Yes, and that's not all," said Emma before taking a sip of wine and flashing a smile at Terrel. "I have recently discovered that Colin had done some slippery backroom dealing in his Silicon Valley days. He left there under a cloud. That's why he ended up teaching school in Taylerston and making a pittance compared to what he once earned." She shrugged and presented a who-the-hell-cares visage. "I heard he's going to look for a job in an international school."

"Hmm, young Redford; a high flyer in a money-making factory reduced to working in public education." Terrel looked at Steve. "Does that sound familiar, big guy?"

"Almost as much as a rich stock analyst-turned-reporter," answered Steve with a smile. "I certainly read Colin Redford wrong," he added. "I always think it's my bosses who are the weasels." He decanted his first Merlot with the delicacy of a sommelier before pouring more into Terrel's half-filled glass. "You get to answer the second question. How did Chow know the animal story would be reported in the media?"

"I was used," stated Terrel. He caught Emma's surprised look and quickly added, "But I knew there was an evil plan underfoot when I received a phone call from a crazy woman."

"It was Mrs. Linzel," interrupted Steve to groans from the three Greenside teachers.

Terrel continued. "Reptile-woman told me about the animals on the second floor. She was working at Chow's behest with a promise of a job as one of the parent supervisors in the A-1 school. Then Steve phoned me. Tiny had finally told him about the animals so I knew the woman's story had legs." He took a solid pull of Merlot. "Chow wanted the animal hotel story to be printed so the A-1 Education stock would take a dive. He could buy his shares back at a much lower price. He never considered my follow-up stories about Tiny's mice casket or the real kicker, the toxic science chemicals and janitorial cleaners."

Steve noted that the share price was now hovering around one dollar. He explained that the unemployed Chow was facing criminal fraud charges. His bank account had been frozen and any profit he had made on the first buy-and-sell round had been placed under control of the court. For Steve, the real kicker was not the Lizard's phone call to Terrel. It was how the information about Chow's nefarious stock dealings came to light. In contrast to Colin Redford's turncoat behavior, Chuck Palmer's action was a pleasant surprise.

Tiny's explanation of potentially profiting from A-1 Education stock fluctuations due to the scandal of snakes, skunks, and raccoons provided Steve with an idea. He knew the information grapevine about Chow and A-1 Education was limited to swirling rumors. Despite his investigative skills, Terrel did not know who to turn to for solid answers.

Steve did. It was Chuck Palmer.

Following up on Chuck's casual offer to catch up on old times, Steve contacted his ex-golfing buddy and former boss. The two spent a night quaffing beer in a Taylerston bar. Palmer had never been able to accept that he had lost to Phil Chow in the competition for the business manager position in the Taylerston district. Palmer still retained contacts in the financial services industry. After considerable soul searching and drinking five pints of beer to Steve's two, he outlined what Chow had done. While newly found ethics may have been a factor, Palmer's enmity toward the business manager would not allow him to silently stand idle while Chow made a pile of money through nefarious means.

"These are words I never thought I would say," claimed a smiling Steve. "Here's to Chuck Palmer."

The assembled group raised their glasses. "Here's to Tiny," gushed Emma. "Without his cat-pissing video we'd only have regional fame. It's gone viral and we're a world-wide sensation, at least for a few days until another loony stunt will take the prime slot."

Terrel had waited until all the serious issues were made public in the *Gazette* before launching what he considered to be the fluff that gave the entire affair a humorous twist. Astonishing to him were the hundreds of thousands of people that were so fascinated by watching cats peacefully lining up to use toilets that they would play the scene on their computer screens, over and over.

The amicable cooperation displayed by the defecating felines did not stretch to the politicians. With the calamity seemingly unending, the Governor stepped into the fray and announced that the arrangement between the Department, the Taylerston School District, and A-1 Education was null and void.

As Summer had predicted earlier, it had taken a simple solution to derail the blockbuster plan. The public cared more about ribald animals, curious boys, vulnerable children, noxious chemicals, and crazy cat behavior than pedants rambling on about instructional pedagogy. Though the average citizen may not understand the details of insider trading, they were well aware that the stench of money could often trump honesty and ethical behavior.

The state's finance people took a swipe at their education counterparts. The State Treasurer only agreed that the Taylerston District had been a poor choice for the initial arrangement. He refused to allow what he believed to be a promising arrangement die. "The plan was sound. The locale was poor. The Education budget is too onerous and the taxpayer simply cannot afford to fund public education in the manner demanded by those in the system. We must search for more creative ways so we can deliver the best value for the dollars spent."

It was more of the same. The very existence of the system had been challenged by a bold, if educationally indefensible plan. In the future more political proclamations were sure to come. Meanwhile the education bureaucrats would lumber along with eyes closed. The stakeholder groups—parents, unions, administrators, and school boards would squabble over smaller slices of a dwindling pie.

Steve knew that good people, like the ones enjoying Merlot in his living room, could eventually find cooperative, mutually beneficial solutions to the complex issues that required attention. As with many males, he self-defined by his work and he was ready to give it his all. He grinned goofily as he surveyed the chattering, raucous group of happy faces. Anne Shaw flashed a special smile. A flash of promise swept across his mind. For now, he was content. As it was for many educators, work was a calling, like the siren song of a Merlot Mermaid. His occupation may not be lucrative. His body may not be sexy. His style may not be funky. But he, and those around him, had slain a dragon intent on burning their enterprise into unrecognizable cinders. The beast would return, breathing more fire. Steve Hepting knew that he and his friends would be there, shields in hand.

CPSIA information can be obtained
at www.ICGtesting.com
Printed in the USA
BVHW082319250920
589682BV00001B/2